RESURRECTED

More Books by Suzan Harden

(Each series is in suggested reading order)

Bloodlines

Blood Magick

Zombie Love

Zombie Confidential

Zombie Wedding

Amish, Vamps & Thieves

Blood Sacrifice

Love, War & a Bulldog

Zombie Goddess

Ravaged

Sacrificed

Reality Bites

Ghouls in the Grocery Store

Resurrected

Bloodlines Shorts Anthology

Bloodlines: The First Boxed Set

Seasons of Magick

Spring

Summer

Autumn

Winter

The Seasons of Magick Anthology

Tales of the Twelve

*The Trickster Priestess
and the Demon*

Justice

*Sword and Sorceress 28
("Justice")*

*Sword and Sorceress 30
("Diplomacy in the Dark")*

Justice: The Beginning

A Question of Balance

A Modicum of Truth

A Matter of Death

A Touch of Mother

A Twist of Love

A Virtue of Child

A Hand of Father

A Measure of Knowledge

A Hint of Thief

A Cup of Conflict

A Barrel of Vintner

A Sprout of Wild

A Glimmer of Light

The Justice Thalia Stories

Snowfall

Murder Most Fowl

The Sweetest Poison

A Granddaughter of Mine

Too Many Fish in the Sea

Crossover Worlds

Invasion!

888-555-HERO

Hero De Facto
Hero Ad Hoc
Hero De Novo
A Very Hero Christmas
Hero De Jure
Hero In Camera
Hero Amicus Curiae
A Very Hero Wedding
A Very Hero New Year
Hero Ad Litem
Queer Eye for the Super Guy

Solar System Services, Inc.

Alone Is Not Lonely
Halloween Harvest
("A Place at the Table")
A Place at the Table

Millersburg Magick Mysteries

Spells and Sleuths
Fae and Felonies
Magick and Murder
Feline Navidad

Soccer Moms of the Apocalypse

Pestilence in Pumpkin Spice
Famine in French Vanilla
War in White Chocolate
Death in Double Mocha
Demons Run at Halloween

The Enchanted Bakery

Chefs, Shrooms, and Sherry
Cakes, Cookies, and Conjuring

Miscellaneous

Sword and Sorceress 31
("Pig-Headed")
Sword and Sorceress 32
("Unexpected")
Practical Witches
Revenge Served Hot
The Yule Switch
Chocolate for Dinner
Silver Shoes and Pigs' Ears
Snipe Hunt

For updates, news, and giveaways, join Suzan's mailing list at suzanharden.blogspot.com/p/contact-me.html, or visit her website at www.suzanharden.com. You can also check her out on Facebook @SuzanHardenWriter.

BLOODLINES #9

Resurrected

SUZAN HARDEN

RESURRECTED
Bloodlines #9

This is a work of fiction. All characters, organizations and events in this novel are products of the author's imagination and are not to be construed as real. Any resemblance to persons, living or dead, is entirely coincidental.

The names and descriptions of the fictionalized versions of Angela Penrose, Libbie Hawker, and Jim Penrose are used with permission.

ISBN-13 - 978-1-938745-51-5

Published by Angry Sheep Publishing LLC
Findlay, Ohio

Cover Design by For the Muse Design
Interior Design by JW Manus

To Dee, who's been reading from the beginning

AUTHOR'S NOTE: This story takes place six months after the events in *Ghouls in the Grocery Store*.

Prologue

Tiffany

A century ago, my great-great-grandmother was sent to a concentration camp. Oh, the American government called them "relocation camps," but that didn't alter their true purpose. It didn't matter that Great-Great-Grandma's own great-grandparents had followed their uncle Kensai Osaka to California long before it had become part of the United States. It didn't matter that she was loyal to the red, white and blue. It didn't matter that she was an honest, hard-working, tax-paying citizen.

Maybe not that honest. She had secretly married my great-great-grandfather. At the time, it was illegal for someone of Asian descent to marry a Caucasian. So when she was taken by the authorities, my great-great-grandfather couldn't do a damn thing. Not without being arrested and imprisoned. Which would have left Great-Grandpa Montgomery and Great-Aunt Tilda in an orphanage since his family were the ones who betrayed my great-great-grandmother to the government.

But then, betrayal has always run in our circles.

My first love, Ptolemy, betrayed his older brother Caesar, only to be murdered by their sister Selene when he had regrets over his deeds.

My fellow ambassador, Duke Millanthropas of the Seelie, betrayed his queen and placed his puppet on the throne to keep our peoples from slaughtering each other.

My sister-in-law Sam betrayed me when my husband Max was critically injured trying to save our daughter. Sam may be a goddess, but Max was human. He died because she refused to lift a finger to help him. Her own damn brother, for the love of Murphy!

In every case, each betrayer would proclaim they were trying to prevent a war, but they were all wrong.

The war was already here.

Chapter 1

Angela

Angela Penrose fingered her tarot cards. Last night's nightmare had been unsettling at best. She would have blamed it on the latest Godzilla movie if it hadn't been three months since she and her husband had watched it on Netflix. It also didn't explain the recent spate of other weird dreams she'd experienced. Or the odd behavior of the animals at his job.

"Honey, I'm heading out to the aquarium!" her husband called. "FYI, Priscilla is hiding under the bed again. Did we have another tremor?"

"Just a minor one! Not even a two-point!" Angela smiled to herself. At least Jim hadn't tried to coax the cat out. Their bedroom reeked of tuna for a week after the last time he was determined to save Priscilla.

"You need anything from the store on the way home?"

"No, thanks! Love you!"

"Love you, too!"

The front door slammed shut. Now why didn't she want him to see the spread when she hadn't even shuffled the cards yet? She'd told him she was a witch on their third date, and that had been three decades ago.

She quickly rifled the cards, cut the deck, and laid out five cards. The same five cards she'd drawn for the last three days no matter which deck she used or how many times she shuffled the decks.

The Wheel of Fortune reversed. The Seven of Swords. Judgment. The Tower. Death.

Bad times. Betrayal. Incorrect decision. Destruction. The end of something, or someone.

The nightmares and repeated tarot readings said the same thing. Something awful was about to happen. Something big. And she'd give just about anything if the impending disaster didn't happen in her own backyard.

Angela glanced out her office window. It was an unusually bright morning for the Seattle rainy season. The icy top of Mount Rainier gleamed under the sun's rays. She examined the cards again.

Only one suit card. The Seven of Swords could be the seventh week of autumn or seven days from now. She checked and double-checked her calendar. Either way of calculation placed the event three days after Samhain. Halloween. A shiver ran through her.

Too soon . . .

Chapter 2

Ptolemy

The moaning of the damned never stopped on the shores of the Styx. If Ptolemy Antonius had one regret about the afterlife, it was the lack of his digital music player. That and a pair of earbuds could do so much to bring joy back to his life.

Or actually his death.

But then, the lack of comfort was the entire point of damnation, wasn't it?

He perched on a boulder and watched the shades drift back and forth along the gravel-strewn banks. Some had been there so long they were nothing more than amorphous gray blobs. Most had gone insane millennia ago. Only a handful of souls had come to the dock since Hermes had deposited him here . . .

It could have been hours. Years. Centuries ago.

There wasn't any way to know in the unrelenting grayness. No sun. No moon. No sleep. No waking. No eating.

Nothing to mark the time.

And no way out. Not without a coin for Charon.

At first, he had been thankful Hermes collected his soul. If it had been Anubis, he would have been brought before Osiris and the forty judges, instead of being stranded on the shores of the Styx.

He would have been condemned for betraying his brother. His soul consumed by Ammut. His existence erased from reality for his sins. Even Hermes had stated he wasn't sure which underworld was the worse punishment when he left Ptolemy here.

"Ptolemy, darling, why aren't you hunting with Jubba, Alexander and the others?" Selene drifted closer. This time, his sister wore an ephemeral version of a Roman matron's stolla and spoke Latin, which explained her question. Selene was reliving the past again.

"Too busy debating the merits of the *Ars Amoratia*." He smiled.

She settled next to him on the boulder and clucked her tongue. "Which girl is it this time?"

"A Ptolemy doesn't kiss and tell." They had the very same conversation over two thousand years ago, and twice since Hermes brought her to the edge of the realm of Hades.

She'd been insane with fury when she arrived. What little he'd been able to glean from her was that her spawn, Duncan St. James, had tried to kill her lover before killing Selene herself and that two years had passed between Ptolemy's death and his sister's.

He was a little surprised Caesar managed to hold St. James back for those two years. Or maybe he should be more surprised she evaded the Briton's vengeance for that long. He'd told her more than once when they were both still alive that killing St. James's Normal kin was unwise, but she took any rejection so personally.

Over time, Selene's initial outrage sank into ancient memories as the mind-numbing drift along the Styx ate what little was left of her sanity.

"Come on. You can tell me." Selene nudged his shoulder with hers. Or tried to. She didn't seem to notice what passed for their bodies merged and parted, wisps of mist in the constant chill of the Underworld.

Grief as cold and gray as their surroundings filled him. Maybe her madness was a blessing. How long would it be before he followed her? Before they both became as incoherent as the older shades drifting along the shore.

"Phillippa," he lied.

Selene leaned back to examine him. "You can't—"

He held up his hand to stop her usual lecture regarding the Amazon. "Like I could touch her even if I wanted her. She wields thunderbolts with the precision of Lord Zeus himself. The discussion was purely intellectual." No one outside him and his siblings had known the truth about Phillippa at the time.

His sister's ectoplasm morphed into something more recent. The suit she wore was from the middle of the twentieth century, her hair matching the style. "We need to kill her," she whispered in English.

"How do you propose we do that?"

"We drink her blood while she sleeps." Somehow, Selene's dull ectoplasm managed to convey a maniacal gleam in her eyes. "If we don't, she'll burn us all."

He would have sighed if he still could. This was a new take on Selene's paranoia.

Before he could think of an answer that wouldn't set off her temper, her ectoplasm shifted again. This time, she wore jeans and a turtleneck sweater. "You're in love with St. James's brat!"

"What?" If he still had blood, it would have chilled in his veins. Had she guessed the truth, or was this part of her paranoid ramblings?

"You're as bad as Alexander! Both of you let your dicks do all your thinking!"

"Selene—"

"I'll kill you for betraying me!" The edges of her ectoplasm blurred as her rage escalated. Her mouth opened, far wider and with far more teeth than her physical form had. She lunged for his throat only to pass through him. The rough gray blob, all that was left of his sister in her mad fit, charged along the shore, shrieking incoherently.

"Well, that was an interesting performance."

Ptolemy turned to find Lord Hermes floating a sword-length above the gravel. The wings of his sandals lowered him gently to the ground. He took the seat Selene had vacated.

"So, how's it going?" The Olympian looked distinctly uncomfortable.

A ripple of unease fluttered through Ptolemy. The gods were never uncomfortable around mortals, regardless of whether the mortal in question was Normal or supernatural. The dead were even less of a threat to them.

"May I help you, my Lord?" Hermes's nearness made him acutely aware of his sister's furious screeching along the banks of the Styx. Maybe there were worse things than going mad.

"I'm here to ask a favor." The god twirled his caduceus in his hands. His two snakes hung onto the wooden staff literally for their dear lives. One glared at Hermes through slitted eyes, but she didn't dare utter a word.

"While I am pleased and honored to assist you, my Lord, my skills are quite limited at the moment." Ptolemy held up his gray misty hands.

The god stopped playing with his staff. His snakes looked relieved, or at least Ptolemy thought they did. Hermes stared at him with an intense expression. "How would you like a second chance at life?"

The unease turned to full-blown panic. There was a reason the Mafia dons were referred to as "godfathers." Like the Olympians, one simply didn't say no. Not without severe repercussions. And saying yes often meant an even worse fate.

"What service must I perform in return for this . . . favor?"

Hermes's face split into a wide grin. "I love a clever man."

Ptolemy waited. Patience had been something he sorely lacked when he'd been alive.

And a hard-earned lesson on the shores of the Styx.

"You will need to acquire an object."

Ptolemy waited and let idle thoughts drift through his mind. Was it summer or winter? On this side of the river, one never knew if the Queen of Hades was in residence.

"It's a magickal object."

Ptolemy waited. Another year could be passing on Earth. Had Tiffany gone to college and met a boy there? Maybe it was a good thing he had died. She was safe from his attraction to her. She had been coming into her own womanhood, oh, so beautiful, when Selene had shot him in the heart.

Finally, Hermes said, "You will deliver it to someone you know. Alexander Stanton."

"Stanton?" He hated the enforcer with a passion. Stanton was blond, blue-eyed, and handsome with charm oozing from his every pore. He could attract any woman with a smile and a wink.

And worst of all, Tiffany adored him. They shared a passion for the idiotic sport of surfing. If one could call balancing on a wooden board among the ocean waves a sport.

"And how am I supposed to acquire this object of yours?" Ptolemy punched the boulder on which he perched. His fist passed into the rock. He yanked and gray ectoplasm rushed from the stone and reformed into his hand.

Hermes's nostrils flared before he said, "You'll have a body to use.

The catch you're looking for in our offer is that you'll be living another man's life."

"Normal or supernatural?"

"Does it matter?"

Ptolemy waited some more.

Hermes sighed. "Normal, but he's a part-time day enforcer with your old coven if that helps."

The god's lack of specificity worried Ptolemy even more. "Augustine Coven?"

"Um, it's, um, no longer Augustine's." Hermes kicked at the gravel beneath his sandals.

"My brother's dead?"

Hermes started twirling his staff again. "No. He's very much alive."

Ptolemy narrowed his eyes. "Then why isn't he the coven master?"

The god finally met his gaze. "Because his wife found the cure to the V-virus."

"Bebe found a cure?" If he had still been alive and actually had a body, he was sure it would have gone into shock. "How many years has it been since—"

"You died?" Hermes stopped spinning his staff. The snake who had been giving the god dirty looks stretched out and bit his thumb. "Ow! Stop that!"

"Then quit spinning us," the snake hissed. Her partner nodded.

Hermes ignored the irritated reptiles, but he laid his staff aside. "It's been almost nine years since your sister shot you."

"But I'll be living another man's life?"

"Yes."

"Why?"

Hermes exhaled heavily. "Because the only way to return you to the land of the living is to put you in a vacated body."

"A ghost can't possess a body for long."

"We would give you help to last long enough to accomplish your task."

"Another vampire's?"

"No," Hermes said. "The man is what you would call a Normal."

Ptolemy had to admit the idea was tempting. A short time to breathe again. Walk. Feel the sun on his face. Ghosts couldn't last a week in a body. The gods wouldn't break the rules of life and death. They may bend them, which meant he might have a few extra days before he died again.

Would it truly be worth it? Oh, Hades, he already knew his decision, but he needed more information.

Ptolemy snorted. "What's the other catch?" He held up his left hand when Hermes opened his mouth. "Let me guess. I can't tell my brother I'm back."

Hermes waved his right hand nonchalantly. "Go right ahead. You may need his help."

"With acquiring this object of yours?"

The smile Hermes gave Ptolemy renewed the chill of his ectoplasm. "No. With capturing a goddess."

Chapter 3

Tiffany

I braced myself before I opened my own front door, regretting once again I had allowed Uncle Duncan talk me into letting *her* babysit my daughter. "Ellie! I'm home!"

"We're in the kitchen, Mommy!" my baby's sweet voice answered. She claimed she was a big girl now she was in first grade. I told her she'd always be my tiny, red, squirmy worm who peed all over the doctors and nurses the night she was born.

I dropped my bag and books in the new mauve armchair in the living room. Hardwood covered the floor now. I couldn't handle keeping the carpet that had been soaked with my dead husband's blood. That had been the first thing to go. Once Jake and I decided to live together, the rest of the old furniture had to go, too.

I could have simply sold the house. It wasn't like I couldn't afford something better, but the Tarzana ranch-style place was the closest I ever felt to "home" my entire life. This is where I started my own family.

From the kitchen came Ellie's voice, then *hers*, then someone I didn't recognize. Rage burned my blood. Of course, *she* would flaunt my rules about no visitors while sitting for my child after school. *She* didn't think rules applied to *her* anymore.

The bitch needed to die, but how can you kill someone who's already dead? Even worse, how do you kill Death personified?

I eased my gun out of my waist holster anyway. The silver-and-garlic-laced steel bullets were specially designed by my boss to handle just about anything in the supernatural range. No one outside of me and a couple of other St. James Coven enforcers knew the real special ingredient was Maltese dog fur.

And if anyone had ever told me years ago, Alex Stanton would have a tiny fluff-mop for a pet, I would have laughed my ass off. In fact, most vampires didn't have pets. Something about competing predator instinct.

But no, my manly man boss had a girly dog. I kind of wished she was here now.

I eased around the wall between the living room and the extra-large kitchen, gun raised. Five strangers sat with Ellie and *her* at my table.

"Mommy, put your gun down. That's rude." My daughter's expression was the same cross one she had when someone farted in her presence. Who would have thought I'd be raising a princess? "Aunt Sam and I are teaching her friends how to play poker."

Okay, maybe a princess who can wipe the floor of any casino in Vegas.

I lowered my weapon only because Ellie was sitting between *her* and Morrigan. And I'd dealt enough with the sidhe over the years that I actually respected the Celtic goddess.

Nor did it take a rocket scientist to figure out who the rest of the players were considering the predominance of black, red and white clothing. Ellie's pink princess dress and tiara stood out among the assembly.

I blinked and looked again. That wasn't the toy tiara Jake had bought for her. The way it sparkled under the sunlight coming through the huge picture window overlooking the backyard, my daughter wore a fortune in diamonds on her head.

Shit. I didn't need three guesses to know who the tiara came from.

I holstered my gun. It wouldn't do a damn thing against this group. "That's nice, babycakes, but please, go to your room. The grown-ups need to talk."

Blue eyes wide, Ellie climbed down from her chair and scampered up the hall, pink taffeta fluttering behind her. She'd learned not to talk back when Mommy used her growly voice.

I was definitely growling when I whirled toward Sam. "What the fuck makes you think you can flaunt my rules? No guests while babysitting!" My hand slashed in the direction of the other goddesses. "I don't care who they are."

My sister-in-law had the grace to look embarrassed. "You're home early," she muttered.

"And that makes it okay?" My voice rose to a shriek.

"Our deepest apologies, Ms. Stephens." The woman in the black kimono rose and bowed. The red and white flowers on the fabric shivered if I looked at them too closely and became maggots wiggling through droplets of blood. "We didn't know our presence was banned by you. We would not have come if we were aware of the restriction."

I reined in my fury at my sister-in-law. It wouldn't be healthy to offend her guests no matter how pissed I was.

I bowed in return, an equal tilt of my body. Grandpa Kensai had taught me enough Japanese culture to understand the significance of a bow. "Your presence in and of itself is not the problem, Lady Izanami. Nor do I fault you in this matter." I glared at Sam. "The issue is Lady Samantha agreeing to my terms in return for visiting my daughter without supervision, and then breaking her word."

Three of the seated goddesses turned to Sam with a collective, "Ooooooooo!"

The fourth rose to her feet as well. She wore a black t-shirt with blood red leather pants, her hair braided and tied on top of her head with a thong that matched her lower half. The arc of her nose and darker skin said Native American. Her ear plugs and nose ring indicated south of the U.S. border. Her piercing black eyes arrowed on Sam. "Is this true?"

Pink flushed Sam's cheeks. "I thought Ellie should get to know you guys, Miki."

Miki. Mictecacihuatl. My stupid ex-sister-in-law brought the Aztec goddess of death into my home. From the pounding in my ears, my blood pressure had to be well over anything remotely in the healthy range.

"You definitely scrooched the pooch, baby girl." Kali shook her head. Maybe if Sam didn't listen to me, she'd listen to the Hindu goddess's disapproving mom voice. "Folks like us can't go back on our word. It can break things." She leaned closer and fake-whispered, "Like the universe."

"All right." Morrigan slapped the table with her palms and stood. "Ladies, we're outta here while somebody—" She also glared at Sam. "—kisses some ass if she ever wants to see her niece again." She turned back to me. "Again, we're sorry, Tiffany."

The other goddesses followed Morrigan to the front door.

The blonde with the pale skin and ice blue eyes, who hadn't said a word, was the last. She inclined her head in my direction. "*God middag,* Ms. Stephens."

Something moved under her black broomstick-style skirt. Something I didn't want to see, much less let my daughter see it. I forced myself to face her and inclined my head as well. "Good afternoon, Lady Hela."

She glided out of the kitchen. Only when I heard the front door close did I whirl to face *her*.

"How could you, you fucking bitch?" Part of me was thankful I wasn't screaming hysterically. "I didn't ask a lot, except for you to obey the same rules as all the other babysitters."

She raised her hands in a defensive gesture. "Kali asked what I was doing, and I texted her a picture of Ellie in her princess dress. Next thing I know, they're all in the living room."

"Oh my god, Sam! This isn't a kegger!" So much for keeping my voice down. "You let five goddesses of DEATH play with my DAUGHTER!"

She stared at the chips in front of her. "I didn't want to be alone in case Jake got here before you," she mumbled.

My brain took a couple of seconds to translate her mumbles. "What?"

"I didn't want to be alone with Jake, okay?" She looked up at me. "Things have been going pretty good with Duncan, and I . . ."

I pulled out one of the vacated chairs and sat down. "Is this about your marriage, or is this about my relationship with your ex-fiancé?"

She sucked in a deep breath. "Both."

"Are you that pissed Jake moved in with me?"

"No." She reached for a napkin next to the nearly empty box of Oreos and dabbed her eyes.

I would have to address the sweets issue, but one crisis at a time.

"I think you two are good for each other, and he adores Ellie," she continued. "It's . . ."

"It's what?" I was trying very hard not to lose what little patience I'd regained.

"You guys are the family I couldn't give him."

Old rage boiled to the surface of my thoughts. "So, are you going to take him from me, too?"

"What?" She tried to look surprised, but I didn't buy it.

"You heard me."

"I don't want to argue about Max. Not today." She covered her face with her hands.

"Then you shouldn't have used the past as an excuse to break my rules," I snapped. I pushed away from the table, jumped up, and charged for the fridge. I needed to do something, anything, before I started blowing holes in my sister-in-law.

Not that it would do any good.

I grabbed one of Jake's orange-flavored beers and twisted off the cap. It was petty of me, but I didn't offer *her* one. After two years, I still couldn't forgive her for letting my husband, her own damn brother, die.

Even Grandpa Ares was on her side. Telling me she didn't have a choice. That she had to obey the rules.

Was that the real reason I agreed to Jake moving in with Ellie and me? A little perverted payback since he was her ex-fiancé?

No, I told myself firmly. Jake was funny and sweet, and he could deal with the insanity of my family. Honestly, he was the first Normal guy I'd ever dated. Max and I . . .

I took a swig from the bottle. My husband and I never really dated. We went straight from sex to pregnancy to marriage. Hell, it was a wonder we lasted as a couple as long as we did.

Sam stood. "If you don't want me around, I understand." And I finally realized she wasn't wearing her normal t-shirt and jeans. Instead, she was cloaked in a high-collared black coat straight out of the Matrix with matching slacks and boots.

Either the garb truly reflected her new duties, or Uncle Duncan's lack of fashion sense was rubbing off on her.

I slammed the fridge door shut and tossed the cap in the trash. "That's not the point." I jabbed a finger in the general direction of my front door. "Everyone else who was here apologized, except the one person who should have. You."

She stiffened. "I—"

The ringing of my cell phone cut her off. I held up an index finger to tell her to shut it. I expected Jake to call. Things on the set had been running behind for the last week and a half.

I pulled the phone from my jeans pocket, but it wasn't his ID on my display. It was his mother's.

"Hey, Audra. What's up?"

"T-t-tiffany, there's been an accident." She was crying. Audra Wong was not a crier.

My entire body went numb. "What hospital?"

"Cedar Sinai."

"I'll be there in twenty." I thumbed off the phone. *Please let him be okay. I can't go through this again. Not for the third time.*

"Mommy?" Ellie peered wide-eyed around the corner of the hall.

I forced a smile. At least, I think I did. I couldn't feel anything. "Babycakes, I need you to go pack a bag real quick. You're going to stay with Grandma Phil tonight." My thumb was already punching the number.

Except the phone and the beer bottle were sliding from my hands.

Sam caught them both. "Go do as your mom asked Ellie." She set the bottle on the table and guided me to the chair. A voice came through the speaker, and she raised it to her ear.

"No, Phil. It's Sam. Can Ellie stay with you tonight?"

I made a half-hearted grab for my phone, but Sam danced out of reach.

"There was an accident at the movie set. Jake's been taken to Cedars." Pause. "No, we don't know how bad it is yet." Pause. "I'm taking her."

That statement reminded me I was still pissed at Sam. "No, you're not."

She glared at me. "You're in no shape to drive." Her attention returned to the phone conversation. "We'll be at your door in five minutes." She thumbed off the call.

"I hate teleporting," I grumbled.

"You were right about what I did," she said.

"Well, halle-fucking-lujah," I muttered.

"I'm sorry for disobeying your rules. Let me make this up to you and help."

I glared at her. "If you let him die, I will fucking stab you through the heart, bitch."

She nodded. "Understood. Get your bag, and I'll make sure Ellie has her toothbrush." For the first time in years, she sounded like the old Sam.

And that scared me more than anything.

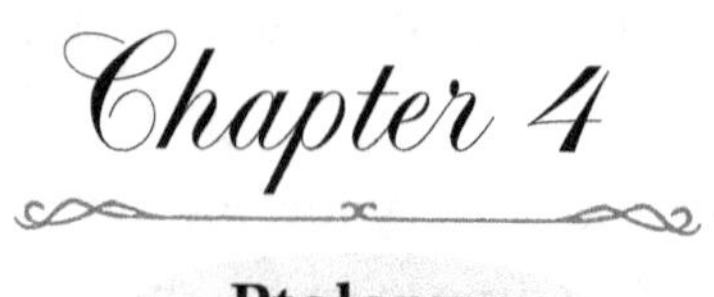

Chapter 4

Ptolemy

For the first time since arriving on the shores of the Styx, Ptolemy was glad of his ectoplasmic state. He'd be exhausted by now even with his old vampiric stamina.

He had followed Hermes along the shore until they were well away from the other shades. When the river dumped into a dark, bottomless chasm, they turned to the right, and toward what Ptolemy thought was the land of the living.

Even the god's snakes appeared bored. They had slithered from Hermes's caduceus and draped themselves over his shoulders, hissing softly to each other.

The path widened until only the occasional boulder marked the way. Ptolemy couldn't see the stone ceiling anymore. The gravel beneath their feet turned to sand. The grains felt odd under his soles.

He halted. *I'm feeling again.* The sand was warm, yet there was no sun. He kicked at a small mound. Bits flew into the air.

Hermes glanced over his shoulder. "Keep up. If I lose you here, I'll never find you again."

Ptolemy didn't question the statement. "Is there a reason we cannot fly?" he asked as he hurried to match the god's strides.

"Other than advertising your presence here and attracting every nearby predator, no," the god replied sourly.

Ptolemy extinguished a flicker of amusement. The Olympian didn't relish walking like a Normal. But the last thing Ptolemy wanted to do was irritate Hermes. He'd end up back on the shores of the River Styx.

Or worse.

"What is this place?" he asked. He kept his voice as quiet as the snakes'. Only the gods knew what prowled this place, and he really didn't want to find out first hand.

"The common mortal name these days is Otherwhere. It is the space between realms."

A shudder racked Ptolemy. The edges of his ectoplasmic body blurred and shredded. He heard enough from the witches over the millennia to know living things rarely survived long in this place. Even the fae trod lightly through Otherwhere. But the dead . . .

The dead were mere snacks for the things that roamed here.

Something far behind them howled. He automatically reached for his waist, but none of the weapons he wore when he was alive hung there. He looked wildly around and spotted a figure crouched on a boulder to their right. Gold eyes stared at him. Then they blinked.

"Lord Hermes?"

The Olympian said nothing, but he quickened his pace toward the boulder. Ptolemy had no choice but to keep up. The dark form leapt to the sand. As they drew closer, the figure's head resolved into that of a jackal. The rest of his body was human-shaped, but blacker than their surroundings.

"Hermes." The god inclined his long snout.

The Olympian gave a curt nod. "Anpu," he said using the ancient Egyptian name of Anubis. "Any trouble?"

"Nothing out of the ordinary." The Egyptian god twirled the long staff he carried. "Don't worry, youngling. I won't let the monsters eat you." His lower jaw hung open and his tongue lolled out in a canine grin.

Ptolemy definitely got the impression Anubis found Hermes wanting. From the tight press of the Olympian's lips, he knew it as well. Nor did he appreciate the comment.

"May I ask where we are going?" Ptolemy said.

Anubis cocked his head and stared at his counterpart. "You haven't told him?"

Hermes waved a hand. "I gave him the gist."

Another howl sounded from the direction they had walked. The Egyptian god snorted. "Too much risk staying here. I'll explain as we go." He set off at a brisk pace.

They had walked quite a distance, and Ptolemy wondered if he would have to ask again when Anubis spoke.

"There's a waiting area for the dead. A place for them to reside un-molested when there are . . . questions concerning their final disposition." The god's golden eyes flicked in Ptolemy's direction before resuming their watchful examination of the terrain ahead. "You almost ended up there."

There was no need to ask why. Remembering his many sins while he waited on the shores of the Styx had been a more appropriate punishment than anything Hades or the Furies could devise in Tartarus.

"Why are you taking me there? Lord Hermes said I was to live another man's life," Ptolemy asked.

Behind him, the Olympian muttered, "Dumbass. I explained it was a second chance."

Anubis glanced at Ptolemy again. "You know what happens when a shade possesses a living body for too long."

Another shudder rippled through his ectoplasm. He knew all too well. A possession gone wrong was the reason Caesar refused to hire any eclectic witch since the late 1600s. "So I only have a few days to accomplish this mission of yours."

"No. We're unsure of how long you may need or what difficulties you will encounter. That's why we're meeting others at the waiting area. There is a way to extend your time on the mortal plane."

"Why do I have the feeling I'm not going to like this?" Ptolemy muttered.

"You won't." Anubis stopped and stared at him. "However, you do have a choice in the matter. You can fulfill the task we give you and possibly redeem yourself, or Hermes can take you back to the shores of the Styx where you will eventually go mad like your sister."

Ptolemy crossed his arms, or tried to emulate the gesture. "Lord Hermes said the catch was I had to trap a goddess. Why? And what goddess?"

Anubis was silent for a moment, as if searching for the correct words. "Why? To save the universe. As for the goddess, well, she is quite young. The first of what will be a new pantheon. An infant really."

"Are you asking me to harm a baby?"

"Not harm. Restrain. So she doesn't starts eating mortals before her transformation is complete."

"What is she the patroness of that she would consume people?"

Anubis's tongue hung out of his snout again, definitely the canine equivalent of a grin. "Death always comes first. And she is always hungry."

Chapter 5

Alex

Alex Stanton heard their expected guests in the hallway before they rang the doorbell to his and Phil's condo. He yanked the door open before the sound died. "How's my favorite granddaughter?" He swept Ellie into his arms and twirled her around. His Maltese Kiki danced around his bare feet and barked at the excitement.

Ellie giggled. "Grandpa Alex, you're being silly. I'm your only granddaughter."

"And if you make her puke, you're cleaning up the mess," Phil yelled from the kitchen.

Ellie leaned close to his ear. "Mommy's upset. Uncle Jake's in the hospital."

"I know," he whispered back. "Grandma Phil's making cookies. Why don't you give her a hand?"

"Yay!" Ellie shed her jacket and dropped it on the floor before she ran for the kitchen. Kiki yipped and raced after her.

"El—" Tiffany started.

"Let it go this once," Alex murmured as he retrieved the bright pink garment with Hello Kitty embroidered on the pockets. "What happened?"

"W-we don't know much yet. His mom just said there was an accident." She looked on the verge of tears herself.

"I'm taking her to Cedars now," Sam said, as if daring him to say something.

Things hadn't been great between the women since Max died two years ago. He hadn't agreed with Duncan about getting in the middle of the mess between Sam and Tiffany, but maybe Duncan had been right to do so after all.

"Go. I'll meet you two there."

"You don't have to—" Tiffany started, but he held up a hand. The kid's relief at having someone else there was obvious, even to Sam from the way her lips pinched together.

"He's my employee, too. And I'm gonna make damn sure whatever happened was really an accident." Things had been quiet for the last year, other than the misunderstanding with the ghouls six months ago. But the peace Tiffany brokered with them had been invaluable in taking down the Vampire Liberation Front, and the threat of rebellion for withholding the cure from her own coven had gotten Virginia Dare to back off her planned invasion of St. James Coven's territory.

However, there had been no signs of Marcus Giovanni, the Sunshine Believers, or any dino demon since the ghoul incident.

Alex's gut said this was merely the proverbial lull before the storm. And it would be just like those assholes to target a Normal member of the coven. He glanced in the direction of the kitchen to make sure Ellie was still back there.

Give me a little credit, Phil's voice whispered in his mind. Of course, she'd been listening to the conversation through him.

Tiffany's eyes widened. "You don't think—"

"Don't worry about it right now. Get to the hospital. I'll be there in a bit."

"Thanks." Tiffany's voice trembled, but her back was ramrod straight. She and Sam winked out of sight.

He padded to the kitchen where his wife and Ellie were enthusiastically licking chocolate chip cookie dough off the beaters. Poor Kiki looked mournfully up at them.

"That looks delicious," he said brightly as he retrieved a doggie treat. He crouched down, and Kiki licked his fingers before she gingerly took the nugget from his hand.

Ellie paused. "Did you eat chocolate chip cookies before you got sick?"

"Nope. I don't think they had been invented yet." He winked, and she giggled. "I need to go run an errand." He rose and grabbed his keys and wallet from the counter.

Ellie's eyes narrowed. "You're going to the hospital, too, aren't you?"

He and Phil exchanged looks. *Don't lie to her*, his wife said in his mind.

Alex looked back down at Ellie again. "Yeah, sweetie, I am."

"Why can't I go?" Ellie asked matter-of-factly.

He knelt beside her. "Because the doctors want Jake to rest so he can get better. They won't let little girls into his room yet."

"Would they let me in to see him if Jake and Mommy got married?" she asked. "He said he was hoping to be my daddy real soon."

Alex swallowed his discomfort. Jake had mentioned he asked Ellie's permission when he dragged Alex along to shop for an engagement ring last week.

He wrapped an arm around Ellie. "I know he wants to be your daddy, sweetie. But even if he were already, the doctors still wouldn't let you in yet. You would need to stay with us, or Grandma and Grandpa Howell, or Uncle Duncan."

"That's not fair." Ellie stuck out her bottom lip. "I'm better behaved than Grandma Howell."

Alex couldn't look at Phil because he was having trouble keeping his own laughter in check. "If it makes you feel better, the doctors wouldn't let Grandma Howell see Jake right now either."

"Okay." That answer seemed to mollify Ellie. "I suppose you can go without me."

He smiled. "Thank you."

She threw her arms around his neck. "It's okay if you have to bite him to make him better, too."

He forced himself not to react. Concern rolled along Phil's thoughts as well.

Maybe Bebe had been right all those years ago. When they had first met the doctor, Tiffany had been in high school. Bebe had gone ballistic about Tiffany being raised by vampires. But not even as a teenager had Tiffany taken the V-virus this lightly.

Or maybe Ellie wasn't taking things lightly. Maybe she understood more than Sam and Tiffany had been willing to admit to themselves.

"Well, let's see what Jake's doctors says before we do anything."

"Okay." Ellie released him. "Can I watch some television, Grandma Phil?"

"Yes, you may, but—" Phil turned and pulled a clean bowl from the dish rack. "Take this to put your beater in."

Ellie accepted the bowl and took off for the living room. Kiki glanced at Alex before she trotted after Ellie. A few seconds later the overly sweet lyrics of a popular children's show echoed through the condo.

Alex rose and kissed Phil briefly on the lips. "I'll call you once I know something." He turned to leave, but she grabbed his arm.

"Wait."

"What's wrong?"

She laughed and forced him to pivot away from her. "Hold still. You have a blob of cookie dough in your hair."

Water ran in the sink behind him before the fresh scent of his wife mixed with the sweet smell of raw dough. He held still while she gently wiped the dough off the back of his head.

"There you go," she said. "But you might want to wash your hair when you get home."

He turned and pulled her close. "I will." She tasted like semi-sweet chocolate and brown sugar when he gave her a much deeper kiss this time.

Phil pulled away and swatted him on the ass. "You'd better get going. If Jake's all right, the hospital's going to need you to referee the girls."

Alex hoped she was wrong about Sam and Tiffany. But he still said a silent little prayer for Jake while he pulled on his boots. His goodbye didn't even register with Ellie who was engrossed in her program, but Kiki looked at him briefly before she curled up against Ellie on the couch.

Sometimes, it felt as if that dog understood far more than any normal canine. According to Phil, the Maltese breed were descended from pets created by a Phoenician god. Hell, for all he knew, Kiki might be a were-Maltese. It wouldn't be the first time he'd run into such a creature.

Five minutes later, he guided his pick-up through early evening Los Angeles traffic.

Or tried to. Rush hour was in full swing. Wilshire was already a mess. Santa Monica Boulevard wouldn't be much better. Time to take the back streets. He turned right toward Olympic.

"Buenos tardas, viejo amigo." The voice came an instant before the smell.

"Shit!"

His truck swerved. Horns blared. Alex yanked the wheel back, somehow missing any of the vehicles around him.

He shot an ugly look at the Uku Pacha monkey demon now sitting in the pick-up's passenger seat. "What the fuck, Francisco? Are you trying to get me killed?"

"Boss wouldn't be too happy with me if I did," the demon replied in English. The former vampire, now minion of Supay the Incan god of Death, still had the same charming voice he'd had while alive. However, his current resemblance to a desiccated monkey corpse with glowing orange eyes and wickedly sharp claws left something to be desired.

Alex guided his truck into the left turn lane for Olympic Boulevard and braked behind a minivan with a stick figure family in the rear window. Another glance at his visitor showed rotten teeth in Francisco's broad smile. "You couldn't have popped into my truck five minutes earlier when I wasn't driving in heavy traffic? Better yet, knock on my door like a civilized person?"

The demon shook his head. The motions sent dead skin and disintegrating hair flying through the cab of the truck. "Not with the little senorita visiting you. I did not wish to frighten her."

"What are you doing in the States? Shouldn't you be back in Peru, kissing your new boss's ass?" The light changed, and Alex pressed the accelerator.

"Aren't we in a piss-poor mood today?" The chittering sound Francisco made was the demon equivalent of laughter. "Did the lovely Phillippa kick you out of her bed for acting like an idiot?"

Alex's grip tightened on the steering wheel. Francisco was right. He was taking his worry about Jake out on the demon. "Sorry, my friend. I'm on the way to the hospital. One of my enforcers was in an accident. He's a Normal, and I don't know how bad his condition is yet."

Francisco grunted. "A Normal injured is never a good thing. They are so . . . fragile." Of course, he understood. He had been the chief enforcer for the Lima vampire coven before he died. For some reason, Lord Supay had taken a shine to Francisco and offered him a place in his court at Uku Pacha after the dino demons and their followers had killed Francisco for helping Alex and Phil track the bastards down.

"You still haven't told me why you're here?" Alex murmured.

"My Master wishes to collect on the remainder of your debt."

A chill ran through Alex. Owing a god, especially the Incan god of death, was not a healthy position for anyone, much less a vampire. "I got him his tumi back. You delivered it to him, didn't you?"

"Of course I did!" Francisco huffed. "Do you truly believe I'd be that stupid and not return it?"

"Then our debt is done," Alex declared. From the corner of his eye, he could see Francisco shaking his head sadly.

"In addition to His tumi, you promised to deliver those who took it."

"All three of the Old Ones' minions are dead. You helped Phil and me kill the two in Peru, and we took out the third one twice here in the States." Even though the third dinosaur demon had managed to breed a couple hundred demon babies, surely Supay couldn't count them as part of the debt.

"My Master had us hunt down the Normals and vampires who worked for the Old Ones' minions at the time his tumi was stolen, but we were never able to catch one," Francisco replied.

"Marcus Giovanni," Alex growled as he braked at the next red light. Olympic was just as bad as Wilshire traffic-wise.

"Yes."

The bastard had been Selene's lieutenant when she made her repeated bids to kill Caesar and take over the Augustine, now St. James, Vampire Coven. After their third failure and Selene's death, Giovanni had allied himself with the dinosaur demons and the human worshippers of their ancient gods.

Alex tapped the steering wheel with his thumbs as he waited for the light to change. It had been wishful thinking on his part that sad excuse for a vampire might have died when he'd been dragged to Otherwhere. It wasn't like Sam hadn't been hunting the bastard for the last two years in that alien dimension after he tried to Turn Ellie when she was still in preschool.

"So he's still alive. Do you know where he is?" Alex asked.

"He was last seen near the U.S. western coast. In the Cascade Range outside of Portland, moving north with two Normals."

The light flipped to green, and Alex pressed the accelerator as he considered the situation. Now, why would Marcus come back to the U.S., much less hang out in the Oregon back country? Unless he didn't consider Duncan a threat as the new coven master.

But Giovanni being back in the States and Jake's accident were too much of a coincidence. And why the hell would the rogue vampire be traveling with Normals?

"Is your source reliable?"

Francisco chittered again. "As reliable as Coyote has ever been." He sobered. "But he has no wish for the Old Ones' return either. My Lord considers the information valid."

"And Coyote is absolutely sure the pair with Giovanni were Normal?" Not that Alex questioned any deity given that his father-in-law was Ares of Olympus, but the Native American Coyote had a reputation as a trickster.

More skin flaked from Francisco's forehead at his frown. "You believe them to be demon spawn?"

"It's possible." When Francisco remained quiet, Alex continued. "Portland, huh? Could he be heading back to Seattle? The last dino demon had a nest there a few years ago."

"A possibility," Francisco admitted. "I have been making the rounds on our end to alert other deities and their entourages in this area."

"All right." Alex pulled into the parking garage closest to the ER. "I'll send out word to our enforcers." He guided the truck into the first available parking spot he found. "Is there anything else?"

The demon sighed. "Unfortunately, there is." Silvery white light filled the truck's cab. "My Master needs something delivered."

The little carved figure he held resembled something out of a Lovecraft story. It was made of the same space-age ceramic, titanium, and unknown metal as Supay's tumi.

Francisco's orange eyes held a terrible sadness. "I beg your forgiveness, my friend."

Vampiric speed meant nothing. The demon slapped his right hand over Alex's heart. The light from the strange object blinded him.

Alex couldn't scream if he wanted to. Something else owned his vocal cords.

Chapter 6

Ptolemy

Surprise jolted Ptolemy when Anubis stopped before a white door. He hadn't noticed them approaching the odd structure in their monotonous slog across Otherwhere. The door and its matching frame stood by itself in the black sand. Upright. It could have been any twenty-first century prefabricated door meant for a prefabricated twenty-first century office building.

A further oddity was the nineteenth century cut-glass door knob.

Anubis twisted the knob and swung the door open.

Ptolemy half-expected more midnight starless sky and black sand when he followed the god through the doorway. Instead, the opening revealed a room. A sterile white room lit by overhead fluorescent lights. It could have been a waiting room anywhere on Earth in the same century as the door.

White couches lined two of the walls. A white desk guarded the third wall to his right. The only colors in the room were the entity sitting behind the desk, the newspaper he held, and the coffee pot next to him. He looked human, and he wore the blue uniform of a LAPD desk sergeant. The silver name tag pinned to his shirt read "F. Ngyuen."

"*Hola*, gentlemen." The officer grinned. "Can I get you an exceedingly crappy cup of coffee?"

Anubis inclined his head. "No, thank you. Have the other parties arrived?"

The officer scowled. "Does it look like they have, Captain Obvious?"

Ptolemy looked down at the newspaper. It was a copy of the *Los Angeles Times*, dated twelve years before he died. The week of the South Central riots. The feeling of someone watching made him raise his head.

F. Ngyuen regarded him as he folded the paper and pushed it to Ptolemy. "You can read it if you want."

"I can't." Ptolemy reached for the paper to prove his point.

And jumped back. His fingers had touched the newsprint. Felt the rough edges. Pushed it a little across the desk.

"Welcome to Purgatory." The officer grimaced and rubbed his hand over his buzz cut. "The place where rules are merely guidelines. You'll be fairly solid while you're in residence." His gaze swept the room. "Guess we should be thankful they leave the gravity at Earth-normal in here."

"You're a shade."

The officer grinned. "Just like you. I'm not up for parole though."

Ptolemy glanced behind him. Anubis stood silently against the wall beside a couch, looking exactly like one of his statues at Thebes. Hermes splayed out on another couch lining the opposing wall from the officer's desk. His snakes were curled on his belly. All three were snoring softly. Ptolemy turned back to Ngyuen. "Is there anyone else here?"

The officer shrugged. "Don't know. I can't leave this room, and you're the first folks I've seen since I was dumped here. Hell, I'm not even sure how long I've been here. It's like Vegas." He waved at the walls. "No clocks."

Ptolemy told him the date of his own death. "Lord Hermes said it's been almost nine years since then."

Ngyuen smiled. "Thanks. I died a little over two years after you. You mind if I ask how?"

A bitter laugh erupted from Ptolemy. "My sister shot me after she stabbed me. You?"

"Road pizza." Ngyuen slammed his right fist into his left palm with a loud *smack.* "It was a hit made to look like an accident."

"A hit?" Ptolemy frowned. "Like the Mob?"

Ngyuen's mouth tilted at one corner. "You could say it was a particular Family. I was pimping out my hacking skills to some people performing illegal medical experiments. They thought I was blabbing on them."

"Were you?"

"No." Ngyuen shrugged again. "But when you're doing shitty things, you automatically assume everyone else does shitty things, too."

Ptolemy tapped the newspaper. "At least they give you some reading material."

"Only this issue." The officer flipped the paper over to the front page and pointed to an article on the right. "One of the worst days of my life."

Ptolemy read the headline and the first couple of paragraphs. "You shot a kid during the riots?"

Ngyuen grimaced. "The *Times* oh-so-kindly left out the part where the 'kid' was a gang member armed with an automatic weapon, and he was threatening to shoot another unarmed kid." He shook his head. "A white girl dumb enough to go down there in the middle of a riot probably deserved to get shot, but no, I had to play the hero." Sarcasm dripped from the officer's voice.

Ptolemy gestured at the story. "I can't believe you lost your job over this."

"I didn't." Ngyuen stared at his official portrait next to the article. "The nightmares and flashbacks put me on desk duty for the rest of my life. I gained a ton of weight." He shook his head, as if clearing the memory, then grinned. "Honestly though, I was pretty fucked up before that."

He leaned over the left arm of his chair, and Ptolemy turned to see what had attracted the officer's attention.

The white door swung silently open, and two more figures entered the waiting room. The woman wore an intricate dress of silk in a variety of browns, greens, and blues. Jade and bronze pins held up her blue-black hair in a design as intricate as her dress.

The man with her wore something similar to the linen kilts favored by the men of Egypt back when Ptolemy had been a child, but his chest was bare. The wide, white wings sprouting from his back were probably why he had forgone the shirt. His hair was as light as the woman's was dark, his eyes blue compared to her hazel. So pale blue in fact they almost appeared white.

Anubis shook himself and stepped away from the wall. "Has he agreed, Kuan Yin?"

Kuan Yin. The Chinese goddess of compassion.

The woman inclined her head. "Once he understood the danger to those he loved, yes."

Concern bubbled inside of Ptolemy. "Who agreed to what?"

"The mortal whose body you will be using," the winged man said. Or sang. That's what it sounded like anyway.

Ptolemy slashed a hand through the air. "Hold on. I've done my share of idiotic things, but I'm not going to put innocents in danger. If his family's in trouble, I need to know what I'm getting into here."

Hermes joined them, his snakes twined around each of his biceps. "His family is in the same danger as yours, Ptolemy Philadelphus Antonius. If you do not succeed in the task we give you, the humans will die either when the Old One breaks through the mortal plane, or when the infant god loses control."

The same sensation of falling when he died swept over him. "What is an Old One?"

Anubis sighed. "They were the ones who came before SHE-WHO-BRINGS-LIFE-AND-DEATH."

Ptolemy wanted to shout in frustration at their doling of unhelpful information, but that wouldn't get him anywhere. Not with this group. "Do you mean the entities here before Gaia and Neit?"

"Yes," the winged man sang.

"And this infant god?" Ptolemy asked.

"You have not met her, but the man whose body you will be using knew her," Kuan Yin said.

Ptolemy's patience snapped. "I need more information."

"We're giving it—" Hermes started.

"No! You're sending me into a situation blind!" Whatever semblance of ennui Ptolemy developed on the shores of the Styx dissolved. He threw his hands in the air. "Who is this man I'm replacing? Is it one of my nephews? And are you even going to tell me what god I'm supposed restrain?"

"First of all, pull your head out of your ass," Anubis said. "This isn't about your precious ego."

Kuan Yin laid her hand on Ptolemy's upper shoulder. "The recipe calls for a dead man who's alive. That is you in the borrowed body."

"A living man who is death," the winged person sang. "One of our compatriots will handle that, and the man will identify himself to you."

"A bridge," Hermes added. "Someone with the skills and tools to help you both. Again, another of our colleagues will handle that detail."

"And an icon of the new god's power," Anubis finished. "It must be a symbol and possession of hers. That, unfortunately, you must discover for yourself. We can't tell you because we do not know."

Ptolemy examined each of their faces. Worry was never an emotion he would have assigned to deities, but there was slight creasing in the skin on their immortal visages.

Except for Anubis. His worry lay solely in his golden eyes.

Ptolemy inhaled, or maybe it was a memory of breathing. "With all due respect, you still haven't told me who I'm replacing."

"His name is Jacob Jin Wong," F. Nyguen said.

Ptolemy turned to face the police officer who continued to speak. "His friends and family call him Jake. He splits his time between doing stunt work for action star/producer Johnny Chin and acting as an enforcer for your old coven. What Gabriel here—" He waved at the winged man. "—is trying not to tell you is that Jake died of massive head injuries a couple of hours ago from an accident on a movie set. My guess is Gabe's brother Raphael is fixing the physical damage so you can inhabit Jake's body."

Ptolemy nodded as the names triggered old memories. He turned back to the winged man. "You're an angel. You're here representing the Abrahamic deities."

"Yes," Gabriel sang.

"I know who all of you are, but how am I supposed to recognize the new god?"

Kuan Yin smiled. "She will come to you."

F. Ngyuen coughed not so discreetly. "Her name's Samantha Marie Ridgeway. I can say her name, but they can't. For reasons." He shook his head and rolled his eyes. "How are you four idiots planning to keep her from killing Ptolemy here?"

The four entities looked at each other. Never would Ptolemy have thought to see confusion on their faces.

"She's a goddess, and she's a telepath," the police officer continued.

"She's going to know he's not Jake. She's not going to take kindly to a stranger possessing her ex-fiancé's body."

Silence. The quartet looked at each other and fidgeted.

"He's going to need credentials," the police officer stated. "Something that tells Sam he's one of the good guys."

Hermes's frown deepened. "We had assumed once his vampire brethren confirmed Ptolemy's identity, it would be sufficient for her."

F. Ngyuen shook his head and smiled at Ptolemy. "With these rocket scientists, you're lucky I'm here. Tell Sam she needs to return my vintage Winne-the-Pooh watch to my sister Tranh. If she knows I'm vouching for you, she won't rip your head off."

"You know this Sam?" Ptolemy asked.

F. Nyguen leaned back in his chair, clasped his hands behind his head, and propped his feet on the desk. "You want to know the real reason I was sentenced to Purgatory?"

Ptolemy glanced at the gods and the angel, then nodded.

"She's the kid whose life I saved during the riots. I'm also the asshole who made Sam a god."

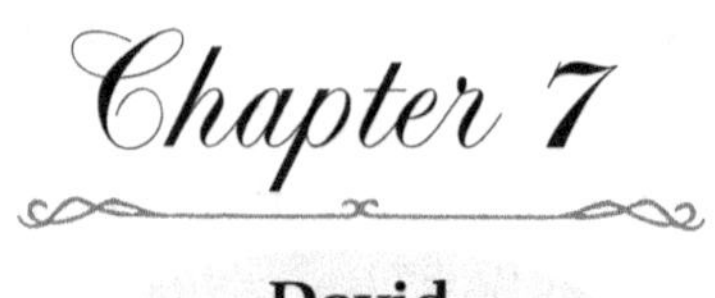

Chapter 7

David

The basketball bounced off the rim bolted to the clapboards above the garage door. David Head jumped and grabbed the ball. He dribbled across the driveway, switching hands as he zigged and zagged, avoiding imaginary opponents. Pivot and launch. This time the ball swished through the net.

Clapping came from behind him. Green and black magickal energy sparked at his fingertips as David whirled in the direction of the sound. No one had entered his little prison.

Not since the day Sam Ridgeway locked him in his own mind.

Baron Samedi sat on the porch swing of the farmhouse Mama and Papa had rented back in Nebraska. Or the representation of their old house. It had been built of the same wooden clapboards and painted white just like the two-car garage, except the house had a red brick chimney on the north side. They'd lived here back when Yvonne and he were little and neither of them had an idea what a necromancer was, much less that he was one. Back when Mama and Papa were both alive. Both happy.

The loa wore a white suit accompanied by matching shoes, gloves, and a top hat. He tapped his black cane, with its knob carved from bone to resemble a human skull, against the porch floorboards. "Come, David Jebediah Head. We have much to discuss. Oh, and your ball is rolling into the road. You might want to retrieve it before the storm comes."

David squeezed his eyes shut and shook his head. "I'm imagining things."

Except he hadn't really imagined much since he'd been condemned to the farthest recesses of his own mind. He tried to walk to town on the county road that ran in front of the old house a couple of times, but he always ended up back at the house. The one time he'd gone in the opposite direction toward the house of their landlady, old Mrs. Frederickson who lived a mile away in a farmhouse that mirrored theirs, same thing had happened. The ultimate in solitary confinement.

"Come now, David," Baron Samedi said. He patted the seat next to him on the swing. "We do not have much time before you awake."

David slowly walked toward the county road, considering the situation. Samedi was the baron of the crossroads. The guardian of the gate between life and death. David bit his lip. Had he been wrong all this time? Had Ridgeway killed him and sent him to hell for daring to want her lover?

Bright orange peeked from the weeds in the ditch on the opposite side of the road. He stepped onto the asphalt made hot by the afternoon sun. A deep horn blared, and he jumped back.

A brilliant red hotrod with white pinstriping roared by him. He blinked. It looked like the Charger the Haggerty brothers had restored and painted in the colors of their parents' alma mater. Mama had been terrified he or Yvonne would be hit at the speed the Haggertys traveled, but he'd thought their car was the shit when he was seven.

It was only the second sign of life he'd seen since Sam Ridgeway left him here.

David checked both ways this time before he jogged across the pavement to retrieve his basketball. He did the same on the return trip, but no vehicles were on the road.

A flash of light to the west caught the corner of his eye. He stopped and counted silently to fifteen-Mississippi before a low rumble followed.

He crossed the yard and climbed the steps to the porch. Watching the loa, he settled on the porch swing. They rocked in unison. The chains groaned and squeaked with the slow rhythm. For all of the loa's admonishments to hurry and join him, the baron remained silent and watched him in return.

"Why are you here?" David finally asked.

"You are needed for a task of some delicacy."

The skin around David's eyes tightened. "What kind of delicate task? And why me?"

Baron Samedi chuckled. "We need you because you are a necromancer. As for the task, we need you to restrain an infant god."

"Ridgeway." Her name hissed between David's teeth. A jagged streak of lightning split the dark clouds in the distance. More thunder followed, closer this time.

He should have known she was more than a zombie when he couldn't control her, but his obsession with Duncan St. James had clouded his vision. He hadn't figured out what Ridgeway was until she invaded his mind. "Why can't I just kill her?"

Even as he said the words, he knew it was impossible. Even someone with his powers would need more juice than he had. And since she blocked his powers . . .

"As much as she has embarrassed me and vexed you, you cannot destroy her, David." The loa tapped his cane against the porch floorboards for emphasis. "Your job is to keep her contained and alive until we need her."

"What on earth could you possibly need that bitch for?" David grumbled.

Baron Samedi glared at him. "Do you care so little for your sister that you would condemn her to non-existence?"

Icy rage filled David at the loa's blackmail. "You'll destroy Yvonne if I don't obey?"

The baron sighed. "No. She will die along with everything else you consider reality if you don't help us."

Wind gusted across the cornfields on the other side of the road, carrying to acrid scent of ozone. It tumbled the leaves and bent the branches of the apple tree in the front yard.

"Who are 'us'?"

"Not just the Loa, but the Neteru, the Olympians, the Pachas. All the hosts of all creation." Baron Samedi stamped his cane again for emphasis. "Everything will be lost to the Old Ones. My counterpart of the Pachas will come to you. He will help you obtain the tools you need."

Lightning speared the little copse of trees over by the Haggertys' fish pond beyond the cornfield across the road. Thunder boomed a second later. David watched as the clouds rolling in bubbled along their bottoms. "Baby tornadoes," Mama would have said before she hustled him and Yvonne into their basement. Destruction waiting to be born.

Wondering if he should suggest the same, David glanced at Baron Samedi. For the first time in his life, David felt fear from one of the Gheddes. The loa family of Death feared nothing. And in turn, the frisson of unease he'd felt at Baron Samedi's appearance transformed into full-fledged dread. The long ago counsel of Maman Brigitte to grow strong whispered through his mind. Had the loa planned to use him all along for this scheme, whatever the hell it was?

David frowned. It didn't feel like Baron Samedi was trying to trick him, but he wasn't getting the full story either. "What am I supposed to do? Feed Ridgeway to these Old Ones to appease them?"

The baron smiled. "Just the opposite. Keep her from eating the mortals until she can feast on the Old One."

Chapter 8

Tiffany

Nausea swam through my stomach as Sam popped us into a dark place filled with chemical smells and a thin strip of light near the floor.

"Seriously? A supply closet?" I muttered.

"Shush," she said. "It was the closest I could get to Jake's room without being seen. And don't move. There's a mop and a bucket full of dirty water right by your feet." She eased open the closet door and poked out her head. "Coast is clear."

"I'm surprised you didn't 'port me into the bucket of filth." I pushed past her into the corridor.

"Why would I do that when you're already pissed at me?" Except her words had none of her usual snarky tone behind them.

"When has me being pissed at you ever stopped you from doing something stupid?" I snapped before I charged down the hallway.

Jake's parents and several family friends were sitting or pacing in the ICU waiting room. When I entered, Audra Wong grabbed me and yanked me close. She was as petite as me and just as strong. I hugged her back.

Angry words of Mandarin interrupted us. Jake had taught me a little bit, especially the obscenities, and someone was definitely using the Chinese version of "fuck."

Audra broke her embrace, and we both looked at the source. Famed actor/director/producer Johnny Chin continued to scream some pretty awful things at Sam. He wasn't exactly Sam's biggest fan after some article she wrote about him. I think only my distant cousin Brent hated her more.

Except I beat both of them in the hate department the day she let my husband, her own damn brother, die.

I blinked and stared again. My sister-in-law was no longer wearing the Matrix-style coat and pants. Instead, she was clad in jeans and a plain black t-shirt.

And she calmly replied to Johnny. In Mandarin.

Whatever she said stopped the actor in mid-stream.

Jake's dad Eddie hugged me first, then Sam. "Thank you for bringing Tiffany here. The doctors said to call the family together."

I knew all too well what that meant. Been through it too many times. I took a shaky breath. "What happened?"

"Something that should not have!" Johnny slashed a hand through the air. Even though he spoke English this time, his accent was so thick I could barely understand him.

"Now's not the time," Eddie said. The two men had been friends since they were boys back in Hong Kong. Eddie had been Johnny's stunt coordinator forever. I knew both of them, as well as Jake, would have checked any set-up before filming started.

They all would have checked a million times.

"They were doing the high-rise stunt today," Audra said softly. "Jake's harness cable snapped." Her breath hitched. "The back-up, the b-back-up—" She dissolved in a round of sobbing.

My eyes burned with unshed tears. I wasn't sure who was guiding who to the couch. Eddie sat on the other side of his wife and wrapped his arm around her shoulders.

"Go see him," Eddie whispered. "The doctors have already talked to us about organ donation." He gave me the room number.

I rose and headed down another hallway. Suddenly, I was in the past, walking toward the death of someone else I loved. The wave of dizziness was worse than Sam's teleportation.

She caught me before I hit the floor. "You don't have to do this right now."

"Yes, I do." I pulled myself straighter and resumed my course, but everything inside me felt numb.

I entered the hospital room and stared. The figure in the bed didn't look like the man who'd kissed me awake this morning. If I could convince myself this wasn't Jake, then everything would be okay.

The logical part of my mind analyzed the injuries as I approached the bed. This man had a broken right arm. A light half-cast kept it stable. From the stitches, either he suffered a compound fracture, or the surgeons had inserted screws to keep the bones together.

The EKG machine beeped a steady rhythm, and the oxygen line hissed and sighed. His heart and lungs were still working on their own. Those alone were hopeful signs.

The dressings on the right side of his head and the flat line of the EEG machine bothered me most. His right eye was swollen shut. A shunt to drain the fluid poked out of a shaved portion of his head, the doctors' desperate attempt to keep the brain from crushing itself against the skull as the organ swelled.

"Why does it always have to be the face?" I murmured.

Sam didn't answer. She guided me to the visitor chair and sat me in it. "I'll leave you two alone."

She turned to go, but I grabbed her wrist.

"Is he—" I choked on the rest of the words.

She frowned. "Tiffany, don't do this—"

Her patronizing attitude galvanized me. "Is he still here?" I ground out.

Her eyes unfocused slightly as she examined the man lying there. "If you're asking whether there's a soul attached to the body, then yes."

I released her wrist and reached for an unbruised section of Jake's left arm. His skin was warm, alive, beneath my fingers. "Fix him."

"Dammit, Tiffany." Frustration filled her voice. "I can't heal someone. That's not my—"

"Then be useful," I snapped. "Go get Bebe or Ben Epstein or-or—"

Sam wasn't paying any attention to me. She stepped closer to the bed and frowned at the patient. "There's something odd—"

The EEG machine started beeping, a jerky, discordant rhythm compared to the heart monitor. The left eyelid of the man in the bed fluttered.

"Jake?" I said. I couldn't stop the hope blooming in my heart.

The eyelid opened and focused on me. I shrunk back. Whoever was looking at me wasn't Jake.

"Tiffany?" His voice croaked. It was Jake's voice, but not. The cadence and accent scared me the most. It was the same as someone else's. Someone I hadn't heard in nearly nine years. Not since the night he left us at a safe house when I pretended to be Bebe to get some assassins off the witch's ass.

Left me. He'd died that same night. Selene had murdered him just like she'd murdered everyone else I had cared about.

"Ptolemy?" I covered my mouth with my hands. This wasn't happening. I had to be hallucinating. Yeah, that was it. I'd passed out in the hall after all, and I was dreaming.

A dream broken when Sam seized the man's throat. "Who are you? What have you done with Jake Wong?"

He reached for me with his good arm. "Tiffany, tell her. You know me."

I'd seen a ton of bizarre shit in my twenty-six years, but I couldn't handle any more. I jumped out of the chair and shot out of the hospital room.

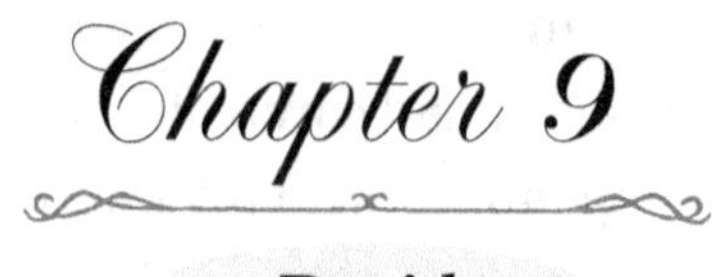

Chapter 9

David

David struggled to open his eyes. Grit stung and burned. There wasn't enough moisture, and sandpaper would have hurt less than his eyelids rubbing against the orbs.

A shadow stood by the window. The glass framed a twilight sky. Sundown or sunrise? Baron Samedi never said where his body was. Would his sister still have taken care of him after everything he'd done?

After he'd foolishly tried to kill her for betraying him to the Augustine Coven?

"Yvonne?" The sound coming out of his throat didn't even resemble a real word, but the figure turned anyway. It stepped closer and tapped a control panel.

A muted halogen blinked on above David. The figure was definitely not his older sister.

"Brandon?" David croaked.

His ex-boyfriend covered his mouth with both hands. A muffled "Oh, my god" slipped between his fingers. Silver threaded his dark hair, and lines David didn't remember fanned from Brandon's eyes and mouth. How long had it been?

Brandon's hands dropped, and he leaned close. "David, did you say my name?"

"Yes." The effort to get out the third word left him exhausted.

"Oh, my god," Brandon repeated. Tears welled in his eyes, but he grinned like a fool. "I need to get the doctor. And call Yvonne. Stay awake for me, baby. Can you do that for me? Stay awake."

David nodded, or he thought he had. Whatever he did sent Brandon racing from the hospital room and screaming for someone to get their ass to David's bedside now.

An hour later, the overwhelming exhaustion hadn't claimed David, but it crept closer. He wanted to sleep, but part of him was afraid to. The medical staff spent the entire time checking skin sensitivity (excellent), reflexes (piss poor), muscle tone (atrocious) and memory (damn fucking perfect).

The only bad part was when the doctor asked him about the accident. "Accident?"

Brandon squeezed David's hand and leaned close. "Don't you remember? You were going to sell the Malibu house and decided to have one last party at the place. Yvonne and I were there. Duke Miller came, but he left early."

His ex hinted at whatever cover story the supernaturals had concocted, but David didn't trust any of his talents at the moment. His telepathic control had never been the best before the shit that went down with Augustine. All he could do was play along.

"I remember the party. You weren't real happy finding a naked guy in my bed, even though nothing happened between him and me. We had a fight, you drove away, and I grabbed a bottle of liquor. Started drinking." David looked at the doctor. "Sorry. I don't remember anything else after that."

The doctor shot Brandon a suspicious look.

"Hey, I already went through all that with the detectives in Malibu seven years ago." He held up his hands. "Other party witnesses verified I was nowhere near David when he fell into the pool."

Seven years? Baron Samedi hadn't bothered to tell him that much time had passed. No wonder Brandon looked older. What the hell else had happened while he'd been comatose?

Once the doctor was satisfied with Brandon's answers and David's initial responses, he left to order more tests.

"Where's my sister?" David watched his ex, looking for some sign of deception.

"She's on her way back to St. Elmo's." Brandon smiled. "She was just pulling through the gates at the Key Biscayne estate when I called her."

"Key Biscayne? She's living with that goddamn vampire?"

"Calm down." Brandon pulled the visitor's chair closer to the bed and sat. "There's no sense giving yourself a stroke after you just woke up. A lot of things have changed in the world since . . ."

David tried to extend and curl his fingers once again and could barely move them against the blanket. Yvonne had warned him for years his temper would get the best of him. The doctor's examination left him so fucking tired, but he wanted to see his big sister, even if she spent the entire time telling him, "I told you so."

He looked at Brandon. "Why are you here, man?"

Since his ex sat on the non-IV side, he took David's hand in his. "Because I still love you, and for once in our lives, you needed me."

"I always needed you," David whispered. "You're the one that bailed on us."

"I know." Brandon's gaze dipped for a moment. "And if I hadn't, maybe you wouldn't be in this mess."

"Maybe." David looked at Brandon. Really looked. "But probably not. You deserved better than me. Someone who gave more of a shit about your feelings."

Brandon squeezed his hand. "There's never been anyone else."

At those words, wetness trickled down David's cheeks. "How-how long have you been here?"

"Yvonne and I take turns, but otherwise, the whole time."

What the fuck could he say? Seven years of devotion from a man who didn't owe him a goddamn thing. Tears and snot poured out of him thick and fast as all the old regrets came spilling out.

Ridgeway was right. He was as fucked up as Mama's second husband. How could he have done what he did to Brandon?

"I-I'm sorry," he choked out. "So, so sorry. You shouldn't have let guilt keep you here. I don't deserve you after what I tried to do—"

"It's okay, baby." Brandon murmured the words over and over again in his ear as he held him. "The nightmare's over."

Except it wasn't. Not by a longshot.

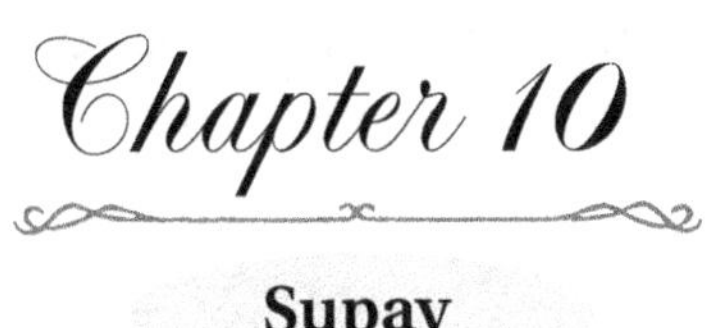

Chapter 10

Supay

Clenched fingers slowly released the steering wheel. The ache in my temporary body delighted and appalled me. It had been millennia since I felt something so simple and so complex as pain.

"Master?" Francisco stared at me. "Are you all right?"

I straightened and took a deep breath. Other than Alexander Socrates Stanton screaming impotent insults in the back of my mind, the possession was complete. "Yes."

"The Olympians will not be happy about this," my demon warned.

"The vampire's oath to me precedes his oath to his bride."

Francisco sighed. "While I understand, Master, the Amazon and her father may have a different interpretation."

I glared at the demon. A faint blue sheen affected my vision.

Francisco had the audacity to grin. "The good news is you'll pass for a vampire."

I held my hand out for the icon, and the demon dropped it into my waiting palm. Without my essence in the vessel, the blood inside would degrade within a day. I needed to deliver it before the sun sat again. Luckily, no one would question a vampire's need for the elixir of life. I tucked the icon in my/Alexander's shirt pocket.

"Good luck, Master." Francisco popped out of the cab and back to Uku Pacha. He was the only one of my demons to master teleportation. I often wondered if it was due to him being a vampire when he was alive.

Perhaps I should make a deal with the vampire coven at Lima in order to gather more demons with this ability. It would make certain of my tasks far more convenient.

I put the idea aside and reached for Alexander's phone. A sliver of amusement ran through me as I pressed the icon for the infant's device. Because she had turned my marriage proposal down, I didn't feel quite so guilty at deceiving her.

"Alex? Where the hell are you?"

"Change of plans, Sam." I was rather pleased at my mimicry of Alexander's drawl. "I got a lead on Jake's accident. I've got reason to believe Giovanni was behind it."

"Shit," she muttered. "I knew it. We've got a bigger problem here though. There's someone else in Jake's body." Her breath whistled sharply through the speaker. "He claims he's Caesar's baby brother."

I issued a stream of curses. Well, I repeated Alexander's words. He could be quite colorful with his language when the spirit moved him. At this point in our plan, I could not admit I knew about the ghost in Jacob Jin Wong's body.

"What do I do?" she asked. "Jake's family knows the guy's awake. The doctors are checking him right now. I can't keep his parents out for too much longer."

The mortals could very well do something drastic, like lock Ptolemy in a psychiatric ward, which would make it difficult to retrieve him later without attracting too much attention. I sorted through Alexander's mind. Despite being a vampire, he could be a brilliant tactician when the situation called for it.

"Tell the imposter to play at being Jake for the time being. You can coach him if necessary. Call Caesar and get him over there. He'll know for sure whether the entity inside Jake is really his brother."

"Caesar can't read minds," she hissed. "He's Normal now, remember?"

"I remember." I couldn't continue this conversation much longer without revealing myself. "There are things only he'd know about his family though. If the imposter protests about seeing Caesar, we'll know we've got someone dangerous on our hands."

"Alex, I think we've already got confirmation that he is Ptolemy," she said softly. "Tiffany totally freaked when he spoke. She ran out of his hospital room. I need to find her first."

I closed my eyes in frustration. I had been so worried about the dead prince doing something to cause a problem I had slipped again. Of course, Alexander would be more concerned about his daughter by marriage. He mocked me for my second mistake in the back of my mind.

"Shit," I said. "This is getting messy fast. Do what you can until Caesar gets there, Sam. I need to get moving before I lose Giovanni's trail. We can't let him get away. Not this time."

I ended the call and thumbed another number, again using Alexander's analysis of his enforcers.

"Whatcha need, boss man?"

According to Alexander, Miko Osaka would ask fewer questions than any of the other Los Angeles personnel.

"Wheels up in a half hour. I'll meet you at the airport." I hesitated for a moment. Normally, Alexander would call his coven master directly about a potential threat. But the new master of the Western United States Coven was Duncan St. James.

Alexander's maker and Samantha's mate.

I'd already slipped with Samantha twice.

"Do me a favor, and let Duncan know what's going on while I call Phil."

Miko laughed. "Oooo! Don't want to piss off the wife, do we?"

"More like the father-in-law," I grumbled. My words drew more laughter from the mortal woman.

"No problem, boss man! See you in thirty."

Except I didn't call Alexander's wife. The last thing I needed was the Olympians interfering with my mission.

I started the pickup and backed out of the parking space. A horn sounded behind me. Taking the rude motorist's soul would have been preferable. Instead, I returned the other driver's one-fingered salute before I pulled away.

The slowness of the trip irritated me. The arrogant attitude of the mortals toward each other on the roadways exacerbated my aggravation. It had been millennia since I had done the little things that humans do. Five minutes as one of them, and I was ready to return home to Uku Pacha.

Except the fates of the mortals and the gods were intertwined. So, I hammered on the vehicle's horn to express my frustration same as the humans around me as I made my way to the place where the mortals kept their flying machines.

Chapter 11

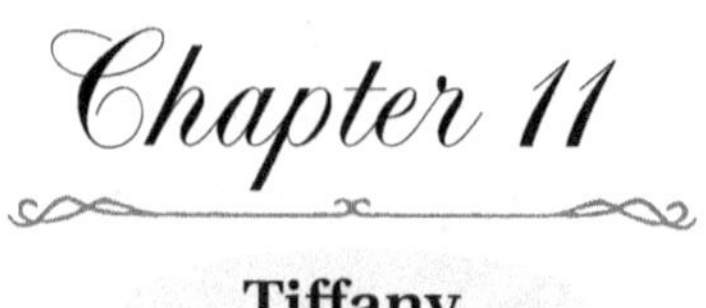

Tiffany

I blindly fled the hospital room and ran toward the public restrooms. Thankfully, no one was in the ladies' facility. I dived into a stall, slammed the door shut, and locked it. I couldn't breathe. Black spots swam in my vision. I perched on the edge of the toilet before I fell into it.

"Tiffany?"

Sam's voice. I couldn't deal with her. Not right now. "Go away."

"Tiffany, I need your help." Steps approached the stall I huddled in.

"I said go away." My lungs ached. My head pounded. How the hell did Ptolemy possess Jake? Was Jake even still inside his body? What the hell had happened to my boyfriend?

A shadow fell across my feet, and something thumped against the door.

"I called Caesar and Bebe," Sam said. "They're on their way here. Tiffany, please. I need your help. Not for me. We can't let Audra and Eddie know what's going on. Not until we know for sure."

I stood and yanked the door open so fast Sam nearly fell on top of me. "How dare you use his parents against me?"

She straightened and glared at me. Silvery-blue light shone from her eyes. Okay, so she was upset, too. It made me feel a little better.

"You're the enforcer, bitch. I'm just the coven master's wife," she growled.

"You're not 'just' anything, motherfucker," I responded in kind.

"Motherfucker? Really? Cunt?" She cocked her head. "You're going to drag Satan Spawn into this?"

I sighed. She was right. I had been the one who invoked the Mother-in-Law from Hell. I couldn't quite bring myself to call her "former." She was my daughter's grandmother, whether I liked it or not. But somehow it seemed appropriate that Elizabeth Howell had given birth to a goddess of Death.

I sucked in another deep breath and released it. "What did Duncan say?"

The silver-blue glow of Sam's eyes dimmed abruptly. "I haven't called him yet."

I tilted my head and regarded her. If she and my uncle were having marital problems again, I really didn't want to know. I could always find out with the rest of the California population when the coast sank into the ocean during their next spat.

Unfortunately, concern for my daughter's mental health forced me to take the high road. She loved her "Uncle" Jake. "As you pointed out, you're the coven's master wife," I said. "He needs to know if one of his enforcers has been possessed. How do you think he's going to react hearing it from me or Alex instead of you, especially since you were here?"

Sam frowned. "Speaking of which, Alex isn't here. He called and said Jake's accident may not have been so accidental. Thought you should know."

"Who?" I growled.

She hesitated for a fraction of a second. "Marcus Giovanni."

"That rat bastard." I charged for the restroom door. "I gonna fucking kill—"

"No." Sam grabbed my arm.

I reached for my Glock.

"I get it. I get your rage," she said, releasing me. "Max was my brother. I want Giovanni's head, too, but we need to deal with this problem first."

The fact Sam hadn't teleported straight to Alex instead of telling me said a lot. I relaxed, released the grip of my sidearm, and lowered both hands.

She blew out a deep breath. "I'll call Duncan, but you need to keep that ghost occupied, if it really is Ptolemy, until Caesar gets here. You knew him. I didn't. And we definitely can't drag Audra and Eddie into our world. Not right now anyway."

When I didn't say anything, she whispered, "Please, Tiffany. For Jake's sake, if not yours and Ellie's."

I'd never heard Sam beg before. Frankly, she didn't have it in her to beg even when she'd been Normal. Now that she was a goddess, she didn't even have to ask nicely. She could have made me go along with her plan. The fact that she didn't and she still cared about the Wongs, even though she and Jake had been over for nearly a decade, said even more than her staying here with me.

Guilt pried its way through two years of my hate and anger over her failure to save my husband. Her own damn brother.

"Fine," I muttered. "But put it on speaker."

I half-expected her eyes to flash silver at my order, but she remained fairly calm. Good. Maybe she finally understood how much I didn't trust her.

She pulled out her phone and jabbed at the touch screen. The device rang twice before the connection clicked and the clipped British accent of my uncle issued from the speakers.

"Hello, Samantha."

"Honey, Tiffany's with me. We have a problem."

Duncan groaned. "I am very tired of playing referee between you two—"

"Jake was in an accident on-set," I bit out. "We're at Cedar Sinai."

"How bad?" Duncan asked.

I looked at Sam, and my vision blurred. I couldn't cry. Not now. But I couldn't talk without the tears rolling out.

"He . . . the EEG flatlined across the board," Sam started. "The doctors called the family in. The rest is going to sound weird, even for us. He woke up when Tiffany went in to see him."

She swallowed hard. "Something else is inside of Jake's body. The entity claims he's Ptolemy Philadelphus Antonius."

The phone speaker was silent for a long time before Duncan said softly, "That cannot be."

Sam closed her eyes for a moment. "I'm sorry, honey. I panicked and called Caesar first. He and Bebe are on the way here."

"That is perfectly acceptable, darling," he said. "Have you contacted Alex yet?"

I sniffed. "Yeah. We dropped off Ellie at his and Phil's place before we came to the hospital. Alex was supposed to follow us over here, but he got a lead on the accident." Old anger burbled to the surface. "He thinks Marcus is behind it."

Duncan made a faint sound, almost like a grunt. "That would explain the cryptic phone call I received from Miko."

"Miko?" I looked up at Sam. Her frown matched the one I was sure I wore. "Where's she taking Alex?"

"She did not say." Duncan went silent again, and for once, Sam didn't fill the void with her inane chatter like she usually did when she was uncomfortable.

However, the quiet drove me crazier than I already was, so I resorted to formality. "While the chief enforcer chases down his lead, what do you wish me to do, Master?"

Sam's jaw dropped. I never used Duncan's title. Not since I swore my oath as a member of the St. James Coven the day he took over from Caesar.

My words shook my uncle out of his own head space. "Stay at the hospital. Keep an eye on . . . our ghost until Bebe arrives." The whistle of his exhalation warned me I wouldn't like what he said next. "How well do Elizabeth and Audra get along?"

He was totally serious, but the image in my head made me laugh through the threatening tears anyway. "Better than Elizabeth and Sam."

"Enlist Elizabeth's aid if she is willing to lend us such to keep Jake's parents out of the way," Duncan said. "Tell Elizabeth I'm willing to give her some travel privileges if she agrees to assist us. Bebe can give us a course of action once she has examined our . . . guest. Alex will call when he has any information."

Damn. My uncle was seriously worried if he was willing to cut Elizabeth some slack on her house arrest. Caesar should have taken her head for her treason, but the coven needed her blood for the cure to the V-virus. Ellie was too young to donate the amounts Bebe and her team needed, Max and Sam's grandmother was too frail, and Sam's DNA had been fucked up by the nanites that turned her into a goddess.

"Anything else, honey?" Sam asked.

"No, darling," Duncan answered. "Please keep me informed. I love you both."

I rolled my eyes. "Now I am going to puke." It wasn't often my uncle got mushy, but when he did it made me . . . worry. Everyone who cared about me had died. I didn't want him to care about me that much. It would sign his own death sentence.

Sam ended the call and handed me the phone. "I did my share. You get to call my mom."

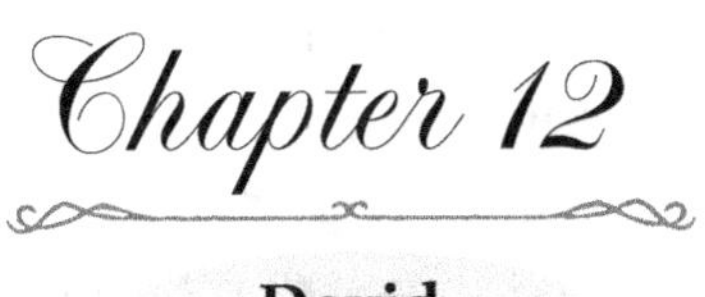

Chapter 12

David

It was fully dark outside when Yvonne raced through the door of David's private room. Their eyes met, and she burst into tears before throwing herself on his chest. The pain was everything he deserved and more. Yet, he still wanted to grab her and never let go, but he could barely move.

A tall, broad-shouldered man followed her into the room. His dreads were tied back, and he sported a short beard and moustache. It took David a moment to recognize Jean-Pierre Rousseau, the master of the Southeastern United States Vampire Coven.

"Oh, Davy." Yvonne straightened and swiped at her tears. Streaks of mascara marred her dark skin. "I was beginning to think—" She sniffed and Rousseau handed her a handkerchief from his suit pocket.

That's when the glint of the plain, gold band on her ring finger caught David's attention. "What? That I couldn't stand up at my own sister's wedding?"

Rousseau chuckled, a deep bass note. "More like you weren't awake for it, mon."

David looked Brandon. "Why didn't you tell me?"

He tilted his head. "'Cause it's something you should hear from Yvonne, not me." He rose and stretched. "I'll leave you guys alone to catch up."

As the door wheezed shut behind Brandon, David couldn't help but notice Rousseau stayed. That he had his arm wrapped around Yvonne's shoulders. That he had a matching wedding band on his own left ring finger.

"What? How?" He tried to Look at Yvonne, but the effort only left him dizzy. "Yvonne, please tell me you didn't let him bite you."

"No, he didn't. A lot of things have changed since you . . ." Yvonne frowned.

"Since I acted like a stupid fuck." David swallowed and wished he could pull out the damn feeding tube still shoved down his nose. It rubbed against his throat, triggering the sensation of choking.

"Among other things," Rousseau said dryly. "C'mon, baby. Take the chair on the other side of bed so you don't get tangled in his tubes." He guided her around the bed and to the seat Brandon had vacated.

Only then did David notice how bad she was trembling.

Another fuck-up. So worried about his own shit, he couldn't comprehend, much less pay attention, to his own flesh-and-blood.

Once she was situated, he said, "I am so sorry for what I did to you. To Brandon. I don't understand how you-you could—"

The huge lump in his throat had nothing to do with the tube. How could she even stand to be in the same room as him?

She grabbed his free hand. "We're blood. How could you even think—"

Guilty tears rolled down his face. "'Cause Ridgeway was right. I'm no better than Jenkins."

Yvonne placed her fingers over his dry, cracked lips. "Listen to me, Davy. Listen to me very carefully. One, you are *nothing* like him."

His sister's expression was one of pure fear. "And two, you *cannot* say her name. Don't even think it. I don't want her coming to Miami. I don't want her knowing you're awake. You hear me, Davy?"

There was more than fear in his sister's eyes. Even Rousseau looked concerned.

"Because of what she is," David said softly.

Yvonne's right eyebrow rose. "You know?"

"I-I saw her. The real her. When she bound me. Beautiful and scary as fuck at the same time."

"Her powers have grown since you tangled with her, David." Rousseau's eyes had shifted from their deep brown to gold. "You need to stay here and do your PT and live your life. You cannot go off half-cocked, especially to St. James territory. You're my brother by marriage, but I'm not foolish enough to think I could stop her from killing you and doing God knows what to your soul. Hell, I don't think her damn husband has any control over her despite the front they put on."

"St. James territory?" David's attention shifted between the two. "She helped Duncan overthrow Augustine?"

The familiar clack of Yvonne's beads filled the room as she shook her head. "Caesar's wife Bebe found the cure for the V-virus. Jean-Pierre and I had a long talk." She looked up at Rousseau and patted his hand resting on her shoulder before turning back to David. "Caesar took the cure after planning an orderly transition. After some bumps, so did a lot of other vampires. I received my vaccination before Jean-Pierre and I were married."

David stared at Rousseau. "You couldn't give up immortality for my sister?"

"I asked him not to, Davy," Yvonne bit out sharply. "I needed to make sure you were protected."

"You whored yourself to him?"

Yvonne gasped. "Davy!"

Rousseau's eyes flamed from gold to neon yellow. "You're damn lucky you're family, boy."

David winced, not at the vampire's threat. Per usual, he'd said things before he thought them through. "I'm sorry, Yvonne. Mama married Jenkins for all the wrong reasons, thinking she was protecting us. I don't want you making the same mistakes she did, even if you're doing it for me."

"It's reality, little brother." Fierceness snapped in her gaze. "I happen to love Jean-Pierre. I've loved him for a long time, and he loves me. But yes, I damn well would have sold myself to Jean-Pierre, to Augustine, whoever I had to in order to keep you safe!"

He couldn't meet those hard eyes anymore. "I don't know what to say."

"You could say thank you to your sister," Jean-Pierre rumbled. "After the first attempt by the Laveau Coven to kill you here, she's the one who forged alliances with the other covens in my territory. Even Laveau split in two over you and St. James's wife. Ironically, it's the quietest the Southeast has been in two centuries."

"Why would anyone in New Orleans care since I was in a coma?" David asked.

Yvonne squeezed his fingers. "They were concerned you were *hers* since you were bound by her, and none of us could break the binding."

He glared at his sister. "I would never do anything for S—"

"They didn't know that," Rousseau interrupted, and David realized how close he came to saying the bitch's name. "Between the new peace treaty between the Queens of Fae and the Vampire Nation brokered by the weres and the deal St. James's Normal niece negotiated with the ghouls, the witches were worried they had been left out. It didn't help when they found out about the cure, and a few witch covens took it upon themselves to administer the cure on their own, whether the vampires they trapped wanted it or not."

"You have to understand something, Davy." Age and experience weighted the lines around Yvonne's eyes. Too much experience. She reminded him of Mama right before Jenkins killed her. "Some witch covens used you as a rallying point. A victim of vampire excess. And it wasn't just the ones here in the United State. These idiots didn't care about the truth. They didn't care about you.

"Jean-Pierre made sure Brandon knew the basics of Normal enforcer training. But neither he nor I could be here all the time. We had to rely on Jean-Pierre's people and the Miami coven to keep you safe. So yes, Davy, I will do anything I must to take care of you."

Silence reigned in his private room as he tried to take in everything his sister and Rousseau told him. So much in the supernatural world had changed, and not all for the better. Even the machines seemed quieter as if they waited for something more to break.

Finally, David said, "Thank you, Yvonne." And for once in his life, he actually meant it.

Chapter 13

Angela

The bus's airbrakes wheezed as the vehicle groaned to a halt at the next stop. Angela leaned back against her seat. Taking a taxi would have been faster, but the bus was cheaper, and this way, she'd arrive at the university's main campus close to the end of Libbie's last class for the day.

More passengers climbed aboard. The other riders twitched and furtively watched the rowdy teen boys as they claimed two benches on the other side of the aisle a few rows ahead. She focused her mind and really Looked at the five of them while the bus lurched into motion again.

Double auras surrounded all the boys. Weres. None of them the same subspecies. Not an unusual occurrence in Seattle. The loose coalition of various tribes and families had kept the peace and kept out the European wolves for centuries. And when a group of rogue weres tried to take over the city nearly thirty years ago, the Augustine vampires had actually backed the were coalition and the witches.

Only the werecougar noticed her scrutiny. His eyes narrowed and his nostrils flared as he matched her stare and tested her scent. Finally, he nudged his neighbor, who looked over his shoulder at her.

"Hey, Ms. Penrose!" The second boy rose and made his way back to her bench. "What's up?"

His large dark eyes and impish smile clicked in her memory. "Kamil? I haven't seen you in ages. How are your parents?" The boy was no longer all scrawny legs and arms. No wonder she hadn't recognized him at first. Now, his broad, heavy chest resembled the mountain ram of his second form.

"Great!" He plopped down next to her. "The new house is okay, but I think Dad misses your tomatoes and fresh herbs."

"I'll call him next year when I have some ripe ones."

"Great!" he repeated, but this time, his smile seemed forced. He glanced at his friends who watched them closely. Kamil checked how near the Normal passengers were. Now, that the boys had quieted, the rest of the riders ignored them and each other.

He lowered his voice anyway. "Can I ask you a question, uh, in your, um, specialty?"

Angela frowned. It wasn't like Kamil to be cagey. He'd never been in the five years he and his family lived next door to her. "What's wrong?"

"Have your cards said anything was wonky?"

His friends rose and took seats in the benches in front and behind her. She took a deep, cleansing breath. No doubt the boys had scented her own unease.

She eyed Kamil. "Before I answer, may I ask what prompted the question?" She twisted in her seat so she could more easily see all the boys.

"Nightmares," the smallest one said, a wereotter from his prominent front teeth. He tilted his chin as if challenging the others to dispute him. "We all are having nightmares about the end of the world."

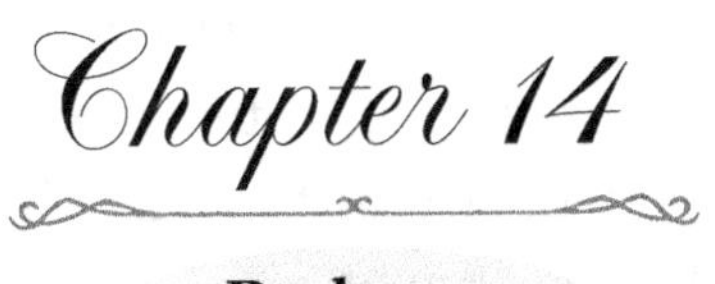

Chapter 14

Ptolemy

Ptolemy wanted to howl in frustration. Or agony. Or both.

Pain barraged his arm and head just as the nurses and doctors continued to barrage him with questions. Questions he couldn't answer other than repeat the name of the man whose body he now inhabited.

"Let me see Tiffany!"

"Mr. Wong, we need you to calm down." The nurse who'd spoken patted his uninjured shoulder.

Jake's shoulder. He needed to remember that. Even though the gods had arranged for extra time in this body, Ptolemy had no illusions he'd be yanked out and sent back to the banks of the Styx as soon as his task was accomplished.

And he was having trouble remembering what that task was.

The only thing stuck in his mind was that Tiffany Stephens sat at his bedside when he awoke. Jake's bedside. An older Tiffany. A Tiffany who had turned into the beautiful woman he'd known she'd become.

What in Hades' name was Jake Wong to her?

He wouldn't find out unless he talked to her. Swallowing his frustration, Ptolemy tried a calmer tone. "Just let me see her. Please."

The medical staff mumbled amongst themselves for a moment. The couple of phrases he could make out involved "he should be dead" and "it's a miracle".

Unfortunately, they were right. Jake was dead, and this was a miracle only because of the divine intervention in a much larger game that had nothing to do with a deceased Normal.

"All right," the doctor said to Ptolemy finally. "A brief visit while we see about getting you scanned."

"Thank you, sir," Ptolemy said.

The medical staff filed out of the room. All except the last nurse, a middle-aged, no-nonsense type. She held up her hand to someone in the hallway he couldn't see.

"I'm sorry," the nurse said. "Only one visitor at a time right now."

The door swung open and banged into the doorjamb. Tiffany shoved her way past the nurse, but the woman inserted herself firmly in front of the tall blonde who followed. The blonde who'd tried to choke him before Tiffany raced out of his hospital room.

"I'm a member of the family," the blonde said, waving her hand in front of the nurse's face.

"You're a member of the family," the nurse said. Her voice sounded normal, but the smile spreading across her face was peculiar.

"These are not the robots you're searching for," the blonde said.

"These are not the robots I'm searching for," the nurse repeated.

"Sam, stop it," Tiffany hissed. "Before someone sees you."

The blonde ignored her. "You're going to take a very long shit in the bathroom, and if anyone asks, you tell them you have irritable bowel syndrome. Then you sue them for violating your rights under the Americans with Disabilities Act."

"I'm going to take a very long shit in the bathroom," the nurse said. "And if anyone asks, I tell them I have irritable bowel syndrome. Then I sue them for violating my rights under the Americans with Disabilities Act."

"Go." The blonde shooed at the nurse.

"Go." The nurse shooed right back.

Now that he was in a Normal body, Ptolemy couldn't tell if the blonde was simply a young, inexperienced witch or an incredibly incompetent vampire.

Tiffany smirked. "Problems, Master Ridgeway?"

Ptolemy blinked his one good eye. Sam Ridgeway. The infant god, or goddess, he was supposed to find. And she was totally insane.

"Shut up, or I'll do it to you," Sam said.

"Shut up, or you'll do it to me," the nurse said brightly.

Tiffany folded her arms. "Try, and my daughter will turn your brains to sushi."

The blonde snorted. "She can't."

"She can't," the nurse repeated.

Tiffany tapped the toe of her right boot, a sure sign she was losing patience with the goddess. "Wanna bet on it? She's getting pretty good with her Hello, Kitty Glock."

Sam cocked her head. "They make a Hello, Kitty Glock?"

"They make a Hello, Kitty Glock?" the nurse repeated.

"Voice on." Tiffany made a clockwise motion with the palm of her right hand. "Voice off." She did the same motion counter-clockwise with her left hand.

Sam scowled. "That's not even the same franchise!"

"That's not even the same franchise," the nurse chirped.

The goddess's eyes glowed a brilliant silver, and she turned to the nurse. "Go take that shit now."

The nurse pivoted and marched out the door.

Tiffany rolled her eyes again. "Malfunctioning your powers are."

"Don't, Tiffany." Sam jabbed her finger in Tiffany's direction. "Just don't."

"Why? Are you going to mindfuck me, too?"

Tiffany was deadly calm. So very different from the girl Ptolemy had known. The Normal who felt the need to prove herself capable in comparison to the supernaturals who raised her. Nor did he miss her slowly reaching for the gun underneath her jacket.

"I didn't—I just—"

"Mindfucked an innocent woman for no reason other than she was trying to do her job?" Tiffany shook her head. "Yeah, you did. And after all the crap you've given the vamps and the fae."

"But I—" Sam's attention dropped to the floor. "Okay. Point taken."

"Go fix it." Tiffany pointed at the door.

"Fine." The goddess stomped out of the hospital room like a recalcitrant toddler.

Tiffany closed the door before she turned to him. "Sorry about that. Sam doesn't always have a firm grip on her powers." A wry smile tilted her lips. "Or her sanity."

"I gathered that," Ptolemy responded. He wasn't sure what else to say.

She slowly approached his bed, pulled the visitor's chair closer, and gingerly sat down. "I heard what you said to the staff. For the record, who are you?"

"You know who I am."

"Please."

The Tiffany Stephens he remembered rarely said please. "I am Ptolemy Philadelphus Antonius, the third son of Cleopatra VII of Egypt. I currently reside in the body of a man named Jacob Jin Wong."

She gasped and excess moisture filmed her brown eyes. "Is—is Jake in there with you?"

Agony unrelated to the injuries tore at him. She obviously cared about the Normal very much. "I'm sorry, but no. He's . . . gone. His body was a convenient empty shell for them."

Tiffany gulped, obviously working hard to keep her composure. "For who?"

"Gods, I think." He struggled to remember what happened between leaving the banks of the Styx and waking up here. "There were four of them. Two of death and two of life. I told them I wouldn't last long in this body . . ."

The events wisped away even as he desperately tried to cling to them.

"Why are you here?"

"I'm supposed to do something for them. But I-I—" The harder he tried to pull the memory, the worse his head ached. "Hades! I'm sorry. Everything is so mixed up."

Her hand covered his left fist gripping his blanket. He hadn't realized he had done so. He sucked in a deep breath that turned his ribcage into fire, but it was nothing compared to the heat of her touch.

"Listen to me then." Tiffany leaned closer. "Jake's parents want to see you. You're going to have to play Jake for a little while until we get things sorted out."

"No, I need to call Caesar." He jerked his hand from hers and pushed aside the blankets. Rapid-fire beeps came from the machines surrounding the bed. "I remember. That was the first thing I was supposed to do." Agony ripped through his injured arm.

"Ptolemy, stop." Tiffany jumped to her feet and grabbed his left arm, the uninjured one. "This body is suffering from major injuries. You're going to make things worse."

"Then call him! He's your master, too." Or was he? There was something about Caesar they'd told him.

She pressed gently against his intact shoulder. "Sam already called him. He's on his way here. And until we can make a plan, you need to be Jake."

"For you?"

"Not for me. For his parents."

The implications sank through his aching head. "They're not Family, are they?"

She breathed a sigh of obvious relief. "No."

"What do I need to know?"

Tiffany exhaled again, and her expression relaxed as she took his hand once more. "They are Eddie and Audra Wong. Baba and Mom. Audra's from the U.S., but Eddie's originally from Hong Kong. He immigrated in his twenties."

He nodded, then thought better of the gesture. "Mandarin, then." Good, because he didn't know a damn word of Cantonese.

"Yes." Tiffany smiled. "Audra's family have been naturalized citizens for four generations, so her Mandarin is about as good as mine. Jake—" Her voice faltered, and her hand tightened around his.

Jake's hand, Ptolemy reminded himself sternly.

"Jake knows Spanish as well as English and Mandarin," she said more firmly.

"I think I can stumble my way through." He tried to smile, but with the pain on the right side of his face, he was sure it looked horrific. "I can always plead exhaustion."

"That's a good idea," Tiffany murmured. "You came out of surgery not long ago. It's also a good excuse if you slip up, too."

She rose. "Make sure you ask Eddie about the rig."

"Rig?"

"Jake was doing a stunt this morning at the movie set where Eddie's the coordinator." A noise like a choked sob came from her. "Something went wrong, and he fell. If he—" She swallowed hard. "If he were still here, that's the first thing he'd ask his dad."

"All right." He squeezed her fingers. "Send them in while I can still blame my behavior on the head injury."

"One more thing, Ptolemy."

"What's that?"

"Your accent is showing."

Hades. St. James and Stanton's accents were far more pronounced than his. But then, Mother had been proud he spoke Greek with an Egyptian accent, no matter how much his older siblings had teased him or Father disapproved of it. "I'll blame it on Caesar."

A ghost of a smile flitted across her lips. "That would work. Eddie and Audra have met him, and they know Jake worked for him part-time." She pulled free of his grasp before he was ready.

"Wait. What did Jake do for Caesar?" He was supposed to know this, but everything was muddled by the ache in his, or Jake's, head.

Tiffany turned around, the grief evident in the lines around her eyes. Lines that hadn't been there the last time he saw her. "When he's not jumping off buildings for his dad, he's a daytime enforcer."

"And you are, too."

She nodded.

That explained a lot, including the firearm tucked in her waistband, but not why she would be holding Jake's hand. "What is he to you, Tiffany?" he asked softly.

"Jake—" She looked out at the darkening sky for a moment. "Jake and I live, lived, together."

Ptolemy closed his one good eye while curses poured through his mind. Of course. Tiffany would have gone on with her life. Only the gods' perverse sense of humor would place him in the body of the man she loved.

When he opened his eye, she still stood a couple of feet from his bed. "I'm so sorry, Tiffany. I didn't know he was yours."

She shrugged. "If you're right and he's dead, there's not much I can do about it. I just don't know what I'm going to tell my daughter."

"Daughter?" Hades, this was worse than he thought.

With a smirk, the old Tiffany was back. "Don't worry. She's not yours. Or Jake's."

He bit off the sharp retort he was about to launch at her. Of course, there was no possible way he could be the girl's father, even if he were insane enough to seduce the seventeen-year-old girl Tiffany had been when he died. The V-virus left vampires sterile. And the disease was transmitted through bodily fluids, including semen.

"But I assume your daughter lives with you and Jake, and not her father."

Tiffany's mien hardened into something unrecognizable and she stood. "Marcus Giovanni ordered my husband murdered two years ago. Given the circumstances, I'd do some fast talking when Caesar gets here. Otherwise, the rest of the coven will make sure you stay dead the second time after the shit you and Selene pulled." She whirled on the heel of her left boot and marched out the hospital room door.

As if he needed the reminder of his own sins. And he had no doubt that Tiffany would personally gut him for his betrayal since it resulted in the deaths of the men she loved.

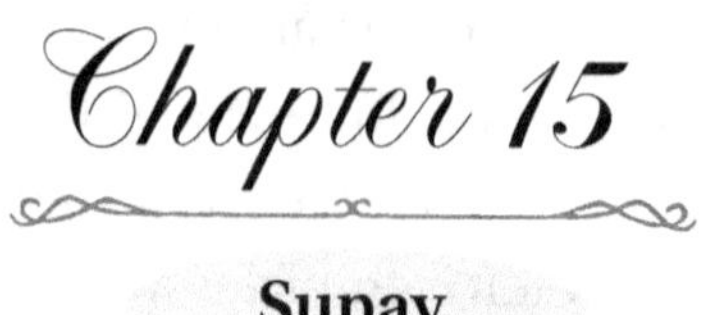

Chapter 15

Supay

The small jet rolled to a stop before one of the large buildings used to house flying craft. It was already well past sundown in this part of the world. White lights illuminated the larger passenger planes that disgorged the mortals at the bigger terminals.

When Miko exited the cockpit into the main part of the cabin, I held up a hand. "Stay here. Refuel the plane and have it ready to go at a moment's notice."

The pilot's eyes narrowed. "Why?"

"I'm sorry. Need to know." I detested the fact Alexander Socrates Stanton apologized to his inferiors far too often, but I needed to play his part for the time being.

Her expression turned incredulous. "Rousseau doesn't know we're here, do they?"

"No, and I have to keep it that way as long as possible, Ms. Osaka."

"Aye, aye, Mr. Stanton," she said, sarcasm dripping from her voice. "Shall I sharpen the stakes that will be used to execute us while I wait for you?"

I suppressed my own irritation. I should have teleported to the necromancer before I possessed Alexander Socrates Stanton. While tougher than most mortals, the vampire's body was too fragile to withstand my full power if I accessed that talent.

Sending Francisco to Miami was out of the question though. The necromancer could control or destroy my favorite demon before Francisco could accomplish his mission if Samedi didn't inform the necromancer ahead of time.

Baron Samedi had been less than receptive to either plan concerning his adherent. I was sure his attitude was sheer spite over me siding with the infant during the last convocation. If his delays upset our planned intervention, Samedi had no one to blame but himself.

And I would laugh while the One Old disemboweled and consumed us both.

"Miko, I need you to have plausible deniability if my plan goes wrong," I said. "That way I'm the only one Rousseau will torture before he beheads me."

"Shit, Alex." She rested her face in her palms for a moment before she looked at me, or rather Alexander, again. "Just please tell me this wasn't Sam's cockamamie idea."

I laughed. "I can honestly say this is not her idea."

"Fine." The enforcer didn't look happy, but she quenched her protest.

"I'll be back in two shakes of a lamb's tail."

Alexander's rural colloquialism seemed to mollify Miko further. I disembarked the small aircraft and raced through the private terminal as fast as I could without drawing the mortals' attention. At the taxi stand, I peeled off several bills from the wad in a pocket of Alexander's leggings and slid into a waiting vehicle.

"St. Elmo's Long-Term Care Facility. There's more if you can get me there quickly and wait while I escort my friend to your cab before we return to the airport."

The driver's eyes widened at the substantial sum I had handed him. "No problem, sir." He tucked the money in his shirt pocket and peeled away from the curb, dodging cars as he wove through the Miami airport's traffic.

I switched from English to Spanish. "However, I would like to get there in one piece, my friend."

The cab driver chuckled. "Now that's an accent I don't hear often. How long did you spend in Peru?"

I started at the mortal's observation, but decided the truth would be easiest. "All my life."

At that statement, the driver shut up. Worried eyes glanced at me in the mirror. In the back of my mind, Alex snickered. *He thinks you're a drug dealer.*

While the idea amused him, I couldn't take the chance the local peace keepers would lock me in a sunlit cell. Alexander's body contained some of my power, but it still had all the weaknesses of any vampire.

"My family were archeologists," I offered.

The driver noticeably relaxed. "Not stealing artifacts, I hope."

"No." I smiled. "Retrieving them for the Peruvian people." Which wasn't exactly a lie. Time to change the subject. "You, however, are not of Cuban or Mexican descent."

The driver chuckled. "Honduran."

As much as the pathetic act of small talk annoyed me, the mortal expected it. "And how did you end up in Miami?"

The mortal blew out a gust of air. "Things have not been so good after the last hurricane."

"Or with the civil violence."

"No, definitely not," the driver said.

I managed to keep the inane conversation going until the driver pulled into a space at the facility indicated for pick-ups.

The driver switched back to English. "I will wait here for you, *señor*." He waved toward the brightly lit main doors. "Unless your friend is in need of a wheelchair?"

"I don't know yet." I glanced at the main doors. It wasn't a wheelchair I worried about. Removing the necromancer without the mortals interfering would be a real challenge with my current limitations.

"Then I will watch for you, and pull up if you need me," he said.

I exited the taxi and strode toward the entrance. What I really needed was a faster way to accomplish this task. If the need for help didn't gall me so, I'd call for Francisco. But my demon would alarm the mortals and make this situation even worse.

In the recesses of his mind, Alexander chuckled. *Suck it up, Your Highness. You're going to have to do things the mortal way.*

I held up a hand. All I need to do was wave it and the necromancer would come straight to me.

More laughter came from Alexander. *We both know you won't. You can't afford to have the Olympians and Sam crawling up your ass right now. Which is exactly what will happen if you do anything godly.*

Rather than admit the vampire was right, I dropped my hand. The doors slid apart, and the air of the facility caressed my skin. I had to admit air conditioning was a rather clever invention for the mortals. I approached the front desk and charmed the location of the necromancer out of the girl.

Once I entered the elevator, Alexander said, *You'd better hope none of Rousseau's people are up there.*

I punched the glowing circle with the floor number I needed. *And why is that?*

Because right now, you're limited by my skills, Alexander shot back. *And I'm not dumb enough to think I can take on Jean-Pierre's best by myself.*

I'm not you, and I can fight quite effectively, thank you.

I know you don't give a shit about getting me killed, Alexander admitted. *But can you do it without breaking that vial of Mamapacha's blood in my pocket?*

I ignored Alex's taunts for the rest of the elevator trip because I'd been asking myself the same questions the entire flight to Miami. If I failed here, thanks to Baron Samedi's pride, I'd make damn sure to kill the loa before the Old Ones got to either of us first.

Chapter 16

David

Long after Yvonne and Rousseau had left, David stared at the television screen. The on-duty nurse had admonished him about getting some sleep, but he refused to let her turn off the set.

Talking more than he had in seven years hurt like hell. Thankfully, Brandon was content to sit next to him and hold his hand while a cable news channel chattered on about the day's headlines. Eventually, soft snores came from his ex.

Or was that current boyfriend? They hadn't really talked about what they were to each other now. But the knowledge Brandon had stayed by his side all these years after what had happened in Los Angeles filled him with a warmth he hadn't felt since his father died in that damn car accident.

Completeness.

When the door swung open, David half-expected the nurse. The rush of cold air and the odor of decay said something else. The tall white man with shaggy blond hair who stepped into the room wasn't dressed in scrubs or a lab coat. Instead, he wore jeans, boots, and a casual jacket over a button-down shirt.

Maybe David couldn't See the stranger, but the rest of his senses worked just fine. Whatever this person was, he wasn't human. Even worse, David couldn't do a damn thing to protect himself or his boyfriend.

"Brandon," he whispered. "Wake up."

"There's no need to wake the mortal, David Jebediah Head." The white dude waved a hand. "And no sense in alarming him either. Let him sleep."

David considered the stranger's words and behavior. As long as he didn't threaten Brandon, David would play along. "Who are you?"

The white dude grinned, a wide spreading of his lips to display the extra-sharp canines. "The flesh suit or the entity inside?"

"Both." David hoped to hell it was Baron Samedi riding one of Rousseau's people. The loa he understood.

"The body belongs to a vampire named Alexander Socrates Stanton. He does not owe fealty to your brother by marriage." While the white dude spoke, he walked toward the bed. "He was foolish enough to swear an oath to me, one he has not yet fulfilled."

"That still doesn't tell me who I'm dealing with." David examined the stranger, trying to get a hint of who or what was inside.

"I am Supay, the Lord of Uku Pacha."

David breathed a slight sigh as Baron Samedi's words rolled through his mind. "I was told you were coming, but I hate to tell you, man, I'm not exactly up to any task at the moment, much less imprisoning a goddess."

The god's gaze swept the length of David's body, and he frowned. "No, you are not, which is why I brought a remedy." He pulled a small object out of his shirt pocket and seized David's face.

Before he could object, or shout for help, Supay forced his mouth open and poured the contents down his throat, then the god slammed his jaw shut and held it. The coppery taste of blood flooded across David's tongue. It immediately twisted into Mama's fresh-baked cornbread and soup beans. Greens and ham. The warm spice cake with caramel frosting she made every year for his birthday until Jenkins killed her.

Fuck! David tried to move, tried to flail away from his attacker. He could barely twitch a finger, much less pry the hands of a god wearing a vampire from his face.

"Swallow it, David Jebediah Head," Supay whispered while stroking his throat. "It's the only way you'll walk out of this place tonight."

Sunshine coursed through his veins when he did. Clouds floated through his head. Grass tickled his feet. Warm, rich loam filled him and crumbled from his fingers. The last time he felt this good was the night the Sabretooths won their first national championship. The same night he met Brandon at the afterparty.

David didn't realize Supay had released him until he reached up and touched his own face. Stubble. The feeding tube. Plastic patches stuck to his forehead and the wires trailing from them. His muscles and joints were stiff, but he could move again. He turned his head to look at the machines.

"Alarms will go off at the nurses' station the minute I'm disconnected from the monitors." David met Supay's gaze. "I can't magick them to send a fake feed. Can you?"

The god frowned. "I could, but not without leaving evidence that I'm here."

They both turned to look at the sleeping Brandon.

"Don't hurt him," David pleaded. "Please. I beg you."

"I have no intention of harming your lover." Supay circled the bed to stand beside the snoring Brandon. "I will move him to your bed once you get up, and we'll place the devices on his body."

David slowly pushed himself to a sitting position. He shouldn't be able to do this according to his doctors. What the hell had been in the blood Supay had forced down his throat? "Will he buy us enough time for you to get me out of Florida?"

Supay smiled, a damn scary one that made David shiver. "I believe he will provide more than enough time."

Chapter 17

Tiffany

The visit with Audra and Eddie went better than I thought it would. Ptolemy followed my instructions and asked the right questions. Jake's parents were so relieved their son was supposedly alive they didn't question his slight accent, though I doubt they would have recognized Ancient Egyptian if Ptolemy had started spouting that instead of English. They were just too ecstatic.

When they left the hospital room, Audra pulled me out with her. "I need her just for a moment, Jake. She'll be right back."

Once the door closed, she released me. "Where's Ellie?"

"She's at my foster mom's right now."

Audra wrapped her arm around my shoulder. "I'll call Phillippa. We'll work out a schedule for getting Ellie to school and picking her up until Jake is released. He needs you here."

Her concern and support surprised me. I'd almost expected her and Eddie to cut me out of the situation. If the man lying in that bed had been the real Jake, that is. It wasn't like we were married.

A wave of grief coupled with her generosity almost made me confess the truth, but I squelched the urge. If there was a way to get Jake back, I'd have to figure out how before I told Audra the person in the hospital room wasn't her son.

Thankfully, Sam was approaching with Caesar and Bebe in tow before I did anything really stupid.

I forced a smile and hugged Audra back. "Thanks, I appreciate your help."

Eddie shook Caesar's hand. Audra released me and hugged Bebe. The numbness from before settled over me as they discussed the accident and treatment options. What if we couldn't get Jake back? What if he really was dead, and his body was a convenient vessel for somebody's sick game? What if someone was playing with Ptolemy's soul?

"Tiffany?" Audra laid both hands on my shoulders and peered at my face.

"Um, I'm sorry." I blinked and swallowed to buy time, but I couldn't remember a damn thing anyone had just said to me. "What was the question?"

"What's your opinion of moving Jake to Good Samaritan Hospital?" Eddie said.

"When Max—" I nearly choked on the old grief that rose up to mix with the new. I cleared my throat and tried again. "They did an excellent job when Max broke his arm, and when the home invasion . . ." I couldn't finish.

Home invasion. The careful euphemism we'd put together for the dino demons and rogue vampires who beat my husband to death and kidnapped my daughter.

The Wongs looked at each other for such a long time I wondered if they were telepathic. Finally, they turned back to Caesar and nodded.

"We'll make the arrangements," Caesar said. "Why don't you two get something to eat? Bebe and I can stay here with Tiffany until you return."

This time, the look the Wongs gave each other was nervous.

"Hey, he's awake and responsive." I tried to give them a confident smile. "If anything changes before you get back, I'll call you."

My statement seemed to relieve them. They nodded and headed down the corridor. When they reached the waiting area, Sam stepped out and spoke with them. After she joined me, Johnny Chin came out and talked to them as well. However, the actor glared in our direction.

Not all of us. Sam. Who responded with a very prominent flipping of the bird.

I slapped her hand down. "Now's not the time."

"What's going on?" Caesar asked.

"Johnny accused me of arranging to have Jake moved to embarrass him," Sam said.

"If he wants to pay some of the overhead at Good Sam, I'll take it," Bebe said in an amused tone.

Eddie and Audra dragged their friend toward the bank of elevators. The last car on the right dinged, the doors slid open, and they pushed him aboard, but not before he responded to Sam in kind.

Caesar looked at her, and the corners of his lips twitched. "I take it he has the same objections to your previous line of work my nephew Brent does."

Sam scowled at him. "I haven't worked at the *Scoop* for nearly five years. Why can't people let things go?"

"If you'd taken embarrassing photos of me and plastered them all over the city, I'd still be cursing you, too," Bebe said as she reached for the door handle to the hospital room. She paused and looked over her shoulder at Sam. "And that would be quite literally." She yanked the door open.

I followed Bebe in, Caesar and Sam on our heels.

Bebe gasped and clapped her hands over her mouth.

The wry smile on Jake's face was definitely not his. "Hello, Doctor Zachary. It's been a few years."

"Ptolemy?" Caesar whispered.

Ptolemy switched to Ancient Egyptian, which I only knew because he and Caesar had taught me so they could both keep in practice. "Greetings, my brother."

Caesar turned to Bebe. "Is that really . . ." he said in English.

Bebe dropped her hands from her mouth and nodded.

Ptolemy pointed at the gold band on her left ring finger. "Did you finally make an honest witch of her, brother?"

"This is impossible," Bebe whispered. "Sam?"

The tall blonde shrugged. "Yeah, it looks like someone did a soul transplant to me, too. That's why I wanted you down here to take a look. I didn't think it was possible, but whoever did this knew what they were doing."

My heart shattered along with the numbness. "What are you two saying? That we can't get Jake back?" My fury and my sidearm focused on the most logical target. "This is your fault, bitch."

Dimly, I was aware Bebe yanked Caesar behind her. The words she said didn't make sense, but gold light flashed in my peripheral vision.

Sam looked at my shaking hands before she met my eyes. "Think about what you're doing, Tiffany. Caesar isn't a vampire anymore. Do you really want to hurt him?"

"Put Jake back." My finger wanted to squeeze the trigger. Connie Torres's mistake two years ago had been taking only one shot at the bitch's brain. Maybe if I pumped an entire clip, if I shredded the brain into pudding and added a little ammonia before setting the whole damn thing on fire—

"I didn't do this, Tiffany." Sam tried to look sad, but I wasn't buying it.

"You're just like your mother," I spat.

Ire flared on her face, and she raised her hands. "Now, wait just a fucking minute here—"

"You couldn't handle Max having a real life, and now you—"

"Picked up Ellie from school this afternoon. I was focused on her. Like you wanted me to be. I didn't know about Jake's accident. I swear."

"So, you had one of your friends do it?" I shrieked. Some part of me pointed out I wasn't a shrieker and I was being stupid.

My Glock wasn't in my hands any more. It simply vanished.

There was a *snap* as Sam hit the release. The clip dropped in her other hand, and she shoved it into her pocket. The Glock itself she simply squeezed like it was putty.

"Not even Ellie throws tantrums like this," she said. "If Ptolemy's right, and Jake's dead, he's already in his afterlife, and there's not much I can do—"

"Won't do, you mean." I sounded like my best friend Siobhan Lannigan-Sifuentes when she was pissed off, except I couldn't sprout teeth and claws to rip out Sam's throat.

Sam tossed my smashed Glock over her shoulder. The metal clattered as it bounced across the tile. She took a deep breath and blew out the air before she answered. "There are rules, Tiffany. Ones not even I'm willing to break. Max wasn't mine to take. Neither was Jake. If you can't handle that—"

She stared at the ceiling for a moment before she looked at me again. "I can't help you." She glanced at Bebe. "Make sure she gets home, okay?"

The doctor nodded, and Sam flashed out of the room.

"Coward!" I screamed.

Bebe pulled me into her arms when my tears started in earnest.

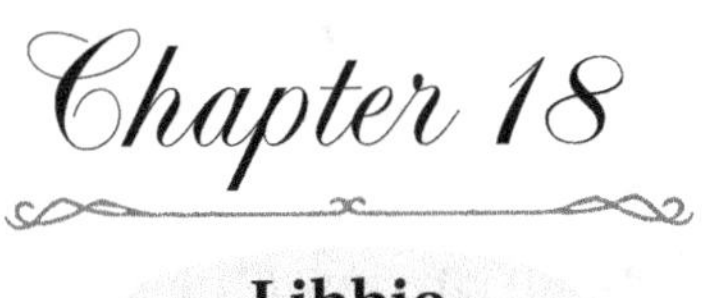

Chapter 18

Libbie

There was a flare of light from the hallway as the classroom door opened. I got a glimpse of purple and silver hair before the door swung shut, and a tall figure leaned against the back wall. Angela. She wouldn't have bothered to come all the way down to the university in person unless something was wrong.

Seriously wrong.

I faltered for a moment before I pointed to the slide. "What was significant about Zenobia's building accomplishments in Palmyra?"

"That the Islamic State blew them to rubble?" one of the boys in the back row said. Everyone in the room giggled, everyone except for my newest student sitting in front of me and my friend leaning against the back wall.

I glared at the undergraduates. "Since the rest of you find the destruction of human history so amusing, I want essays concerning the significance of Palmyra to the Roman Empire on my desk Monday. Two thousand words minimum. Mr. Sayed, see me after class." The bell punctuated the class's groans of dismay.

I flipped on the overhead lights. The boy who hadn't laughed collected his books and papers and approached my podium as the rest of the students filed out. A few of them looked quizzically at the six-foot-tall witch patiently holding up the back wall, but they were smart enough not to say anything.

"Yes, Professor?" Azir Sayed hunched as if to make himself smaller. His behavior only made me angrier. Not at him, but the callousness of the other students.

I checked to make sure the rest of the class was gone before I addressed him. "Your test score was the highest in the class, Mr. Sayed. You're exempted from the essay assignment."

He nodded, but still didn't meet my eyes. "Is that all, Professor?"

Whatever had happened to him during the Syrian civil war had nearly broken him. It only made my determination to show him another side of humanity that much stronger. "I'm looking for a new research assistant. Would you be interested?"

A sharp intake of his breath gave away his excitement before he shook his head. "If this concerns your dig in the Seattle Underground, I'm sure there are American graduate students more qualified."

"I don't have anyone who looks at facts and situations more objectively than you do."

"And no one else on your team is a were." He raised his head, but his expression was one of curiosity, not challenge.

"Is that a problem?" I said.

He hesitated for a moment. "Favoritism can be a double-edged sword."

A different concern hit me. "Are you worried about retaliation by your classmates?"

"No, ma'am." Again, the hesitation. "But I do not wish to be singled out because I am different." Another pause before he added, "Any more than I already am."

"But you are different." I smiled at his startled expression. "You actually listen to me when I teach. You care about the past and what we can learn from it. The rest of these students—" I waved at the door. "They're just trying to fulfill their social studies credits."

My passionate outburst drew a more thoughtful expression from Azir. "May I consider your offer and give you an answer in the morning?"

"Of course." The human part of me wanted to hug the boy, comfort him, but cats and birds hugging came under the heading of a really bad idea. "Have a good evening."

His head bobbed in acknowledgement, and he headed for the exit. The boy eyed Angela warily as he approached the door. She was the only woman I knew who was taller than me, and only by an inch.

"May I ask you a question before you leave, Mr. Sayed?" she said.

He turned to me, his eyes wide.

"Angela wouldn't ask you a question unless it was important." I injected as much reassurance into my voice as I could.

"Actually, it's for both of you," she said. "Have either of you been having nightmares lately?"

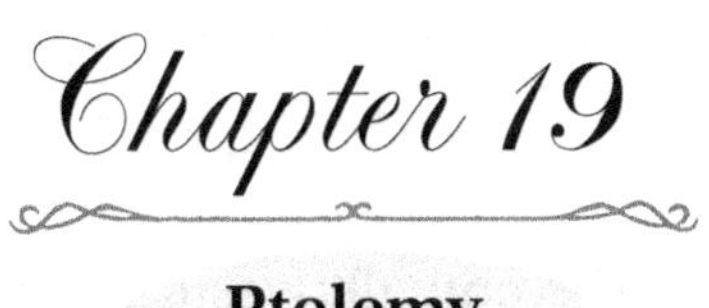

Chapter 19

Ptolemy

Confused, Ptolemy stared at the three people in his hospital room. Tiffany's tiny body shuddered with her sobs. Bebe murmured soft words in her ear, but he couldn't make them out. His brother looked helpless at the feminine tears.

And tired. Very, very tired.

With a glance at Caesar, Bebe guided the weeping Tiffany out of the hospital room.

He sagged into the chair next to Ptolemy. "Hades. She was finally getting through Max's death, moving on with her life. Now . . ." He wiped both hands down his face.

Ptolemy continued examining his brother through his one good eye. He finally figured out what was wrong. Crow's feet. Caesar had crow's feet. And laugh lines around his mouth. His skin didn't have the paleness of a vampire anymore.

"What—" Ptolemy cleared his throat. "What exactly happened?"

"Rogues led by Marcus broke into Tiffany and Max's home—"

"No, I mean what happened to you. You look . . . Normal."

Caesar chuckled. "I am Normal. Bebe found the cure."

So, it was true. Ptolemy couldn't draw a breath. The monitors made alarming noises again. Hermes hadn't lied to him after all.

Caesar reached over and laid his hand on an unbruised spot of Ptolemy's unbroken arm. "Calm down, brother. The body you're in has been severely damaged." He spoke quietly in Ancient Egyptian. The same reassuring tone during those long, frigid nights at Octavia's villa. "I'm sure much of what I tell you about the years since your—"

His death at Selene's hand. Of course, things had changed. As Virgil had written, *fugit inreparabile tempus*. Or the shortened, English version, "time flies." Ptolemy breathed slowly and carefully. The beeping slowed.

Once he was sure he wouldn't hyperventilate again, he said. "So that's what Sam meant about you no longer being the master of the coven. Tiffany said it has been nearly nine years. I guess it's a good thing I didn't let Selene kill your witch." Their sister paid for her crimes with her post-death madness. She would eventually waste away into nothingness. And that was the fate awaiting him if he didn't do the gods' wishes. Whatever they were.

He wasn't sure if it were Jake's injuries or the trauma of being shoved into another man's body that made his memories fuzzy.

However, there was one thing he was sure of, a member of the coven who would rejoice in becoming Normal again. "How is St. James enjoying his humanity?"

Caesar chuckled. "He hasn't taken the cure."

"Really? I would have thought he'd push you out of the way for the first treatment." Too many old regrets swam to the surface. "Selene should not have Turned him."

"She was infatuated."

It was an old conversation between them. Nothing more could be said to make any difference in their lives. But the idea of St. James remaining a vampire . . .

"So, what changed his mind?"

Caesar laughed outright. "You've already met her."

"He rejected the chance because he was concerned for Tiffany—"

His brother grinned. "Wrong woman."

"Sam, then." That revelation was rather . . . disconcerting. He couldn't picture the dour Briton with the fiery blonde who threatened to choke the life out of him. She was a little too independent for Duncan's tastes. "I don't understand. She's not a vampire."

"No, she's not."

"Why would he reject the cure because of a goddess?"

Caesar pulled away from him. "How did you know Duncan's wife is a deity?"

Ptolemy considered lying, but Hermes had said he might need his brother's assistance. "Would you believe me if I said I was on a mission from God?"

"A mission from god? Which one?"

Of course, paraphrasing a popular movie quote flew right over Caesar's head. He had derided film as totally inferior to a stage play when motion pictures had come into vogue.

"You really need to pay attention to current popular culture." Ptolemy's attempt at humor faded. "Actually, more than one deity sent me. And they told me I would need to confide in you."

Caesar groaned. "I should've brought more coffee for this."

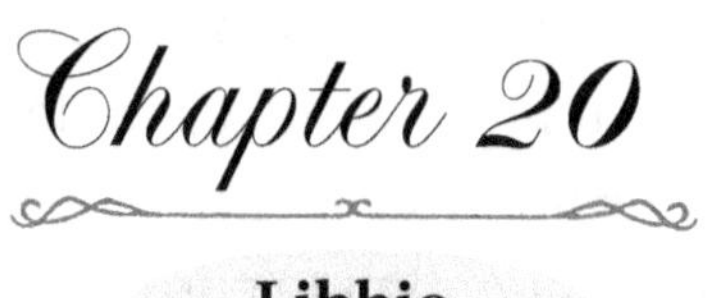

Chapter 20

Libbie

The off-campus coffee shop was fairly quiet. Only a few tables were occupied. After getting our beverages, I led Angela to a secluded corner. I took a sip of my iced Americano before I asked, "What's really going on? You don't randomly ask about my nightmares."

Azir had clammed up when the witch had asked us about our dreams back in the classroom and taken off like the Goddess herself nipped at his heels. When I admitted to my own nightmares, Angela suggested we find someplace less conspicuous to talk.

"How's things with Waldo?" Angela hadn't touched her herbal tea.

I sighed. My relationship had been an issue with the Seattle Were Alliance since Waldo had vowed his allegiance to the new vampire master. I understood my boyfriend's loyalty to Caesar Augustine. The previous master had saved Waldo's brothers when no one else gave a rat's naked tail. The recent change in vampire coven leadership had given Waldo an out. One that the other weres expected him to take, and he hadn't.

Were bullshit didn't explain Angela's question. "Since when are you worried about my love life?"

"Not your love life." The ashy scent of fear overwhelmed the witch's natural ginger odor. "Has he said anything about . . . the new master's wife?"

Waldo had said plenty, but his secrets weren't mine to share. On the other hand, the way everyone tiptoed around the issue annoyed me. When even Angela was afraid to say the woman's name, things had gone too far. I took another sip of my Americano before I said, "Everybody west of the Mississippi has an opinion about Ridgeway."

Angela glanced around us. She murmured something under her breath and tapped the stone floor three times with her staff disguised as a cane. Ozone filled my head.

"There." Angela nodded in satisfaction. "No one will overhear us. Has

St. James Coven learned where and when the battle between her and the Old One will occur?"

I jerked. The lid of my cup popped off, and sticky, cold coffee sloshed over my hand. I yanked a couple of napkins from the dispenser on the table and wiped off the liquid. The damp paper was tightly wadded in my fist before I could look at Angela again.

"How'd you find out?"

"Do they know?" Angela repeated. The worry and fear in her eyes reflected her scent.

I slowly shook her head. "Not for sure, but they think they have it narrowed down to three places. Now, tell me how you found out."

Angela's expression was somber. "The cards say it will be here."

Air caught in my chest. In my friend's hands, tarot cards were more reliable than anybody else's facts. "In-in the middle of the city?"

Angela shrugged. "Close enough I don't think it will matter. Seattle was one of their possibilities, wasn't it?"

Well, she had figured out enough on her own, she might as well know the rest.

I nodded. "They think a weak spot between dimensions is reflected by a weak spot in the earth's crust. The conception of a new pantheon weakens the bonds further close to the first deity's birthplace, which is why they think it'll be on the West Coast. Remember the murdered women my students found in my dig a few years ago?"

"Yes." From the grim set of Angela's mouth, she still had nightmares about the corpses and their dead demon spawn, too. "That shop in the Underground sits pretty damn close to the minor fault line that runs through the middle of the city." She tapped her index finger on the side of the cup she held.

Same information the St. James enforcers had put together. The coffee did a slow, nauseating swirl in my stomach. "The Old Ones' minions tried to breed on a mountain near Yellowstone and again down in Los Angeles. Except both times they used weres instead of Normals."

Angela nodded. "Both places are ancient volcano calderas. Any others?"

"There were babies in Death Valley, but the vampires ruled it out because the demon-human hybrids were interbreeding at that point and laying eggs. The other two places were live births, same as they attempted here."

Angela leaned back. "Why would that make a difference?"

I chuckled. "For the same reason, I would give birth to a baby instead of laying an egg."

"So, if the current paleontology theories are right about the relationship between dinosaurs and modern birds, wouldn't St. James's people be worried about the avian weres' loyalty?" Angela tilted her head.

I laughed, but it was forced. "If my nightmares are any indication, the Old Ones have already decided we're part of their problem."

Angela blew out a deep breath and stared out the window for a moment before her attention returned to me. "Tell Waldo what I've said, and make sure he passes the information to his master. According to the cards, it'll happen within the next seven days. If we can do a better job of pinpointing the spot, we'll know in advance where *not* to send evacuees." Angela tapped her staff once on the floor. The rich smell of freshly roasted coffee beans filled the air once more. She rose. "I'll be in touch." She stalked out of the café.

And she never did touch her drink.

I stared out the window as a new round of rain splattered against the glass. Well, this just sucked. Waldo and I had tendered the down payment for our farm and signed the paperwork two weeks ago. If Angela was right, everything along Puget Sound could be destroyed any minute by a battle between gods, and I'd be in the exact same position as Azir Sayed.

A refugee with nothing to my name.

And that was assuming anyone survived the coming conflict.

I slurped the last of my Americano. Angela was doing what she could to help. Waldo said he wouldn't have bought the farm if he wasn't sure things would be okay.

I sighed and gathered my things. Maybe I needed to find a little faith, too.

I just wasn't sure where to look at the moment.

Chapter 21

David

Recognition jerked through David at the person waiting for them by the private jet. No, the lithe Asian woman wasn't the Normal enforcer who had accompanied Ridgeway in her assault on his Malibu home. But from the classic nose, high cheek bones, and full lips, she was definitely related.

However, this woman took one look at him as Supay lifted him out of the cab and said, "You have to be fucking kidding me! What the hell are you thinking, Alex? You can't possibly make me fly that bastard—"

"Lower the loading elevator, Miko," Supay ordered. The god placed David in the wheel chair their driver had pulled from the trunk. Supay retrieved the cane from the passenger seat of the taxi. David didn't need to ask who'd left the white-lacquered walking stick with the onyx handle carved as a skull in his private room's closet. It was a mirror-image of the one Baron Samedi carried.

"But—" Miko started.

Supay paused. "Are you disobeying a direct order, Ms. Osaka?"

Her jaw snapped shut, but the look in her eyes was pure murder. The god turned the chair and guided it toward the plane.

Over his shoulder, David watched the taxi roll away until it merged with the shadows and red lights of the airport. If he retained a lick of common sense, he should have left a message for Brandon or Yvonne. Especially since his mobility was still limited, but he didn't want to drag the people he loved into the mess he created. If he hadn't gone after St. James, he wouldn't be in the middle of this clusterfuck.

David's fingers could barely hold on to the cane Baron Samedi had left for him. Supay had said it would take the blood a couple of hours to restore his atrophied muscles and locked joints to their full range of motion, but he wouldn't be the peak specimen he'd been as a pro ath-lete. Maybe the gods needed him, but the woman inside the private jet wouldn't hesitate to kill—

Another memory flashed. He'd seen the same nose and cheekbones on someone else the night he fought Ridgeway. The man who'd pushed Brandon out of the way when David—

Bile rose in the back of his throat, and he bent over the arm of the wheel chair. Dry heaves shook him since there was nothing in his stomach to bring up. Not even the blood Supay had forced down his throat.

Supay handed him a handkerchief from the back pocket of his jeans. When David's stomach paused out of sheer exhaustion, he wiped his mouth.

The woman's attention flicked from David to Supay and back. "What's really going on, Alex?"

"I'm sorry, but I can't tell you right now, Miko," the god said. "I need you to keep quiet about this."

"He killed Grandfather and Jamal! He nearly killed me!"

"I know," Supay said quietly. "I'm not asking you to forgive him or forget what he did. But it's imperative I get him to Seattle as soon as possible."

"Seattle?" Her eyes narrowed. "We're not going back to L.A.?"

"You will. After you take us to Seattle."

She frowned, but she didn't have quite the murderous rage in her eyes she had a moment ago. "It's a good thing you're not taking him home. It's bad enough Duncan and Sam will go nuclear when they find out you brought him into our territory."

"Which is why I need you to be quiet until I can explain to our master's wife what's going on." Now why wouldn't Supay say her name? "Are you going to cooperate, or do I need to find another pilot?"

Miko pressed her lips together and glared at David before she finally said, "Fine, but if you don't tell me the full story—"

"You'll tattle on me to my maker. I got it."

She pivoted and jogged up the short stairs to the interior of the jet.

"She's gonna fucking stake you when she finds out what's going on," David said softly to the god.

Supay chuckled as he pushed the chair toward the descending elevator. "No, she won't. She has every faith in her boss."

"And which goddess has she sworn herself to? Because if it's the one who hates me—"

"If we didn't need a necromancer to complete this task, I would smite you for your impertinence, David Jebediah Head." Supay strapped the wheel chair to the lowered platform.

"That's what I thought." David shook his head. "If Blondie finds out before we trap her, she'll kill us both."

Supay's laugh was bitter. "Then it's fortunate that I am already dead."

The wheel chair lurched beneath David when the cargo elevator whined and began its ascent. He wondered if he'd be joining Supay in death before this episode was over.

✳✳✳

When his entire body jerked, David realized he'd fallen asleep. He looked around the cabin of the jet. Supay sat across from him, eyes closed and hands dangling loosely over the armrests.

Thirst tore at him, and damn, if his bladder wasn't nagging as well.

"Go relieve yourself." Supay didn't bother opening his eyes.

"How am I supposed to do that? You yanked out my catheter, and I can't walk."

A slight smile curved the lips of the god's borrowed body. "Yes, you can."

David made fists with both hands. It was more movement than he had been capable of when he boarded, and a ton more than when he first woke from the coma this afternoon. He wiggled his toes. Even with his shoes on, the sensation of skin against the nylon interior was reassuring.

He relaxed his fingers and pushed on the armrests. Dizziness swept through him as his body dealt with standing for the first time in six and a half years. He grabbed the cane and leaned on it to steady himself. While the stylized wood was a symbol of the Baron and he could feel power coursing through it, the cane's physical support was a necessity for him to remain upright.

David slowly slid his left foot forward, then his right. He made his slow, fumbling way back to the john. If it weren't for the goddess's blood, it would have taken him weeks or months of physical therapy to attain this level of mobility.

He did his business and carefully washed his hands before returning to his seat. Those simple tasks left him physically exhausted, but his mind raced.

"So why Seattle?"

Supay opened his eyes. "Why do you think, David Jebediah Head? It will be her battlefield. Or don't you know what the woman who put you in a coma is?"

Yvonne's warning flashed in his head. "Yeah, I know what she is. Figured it out a little too late is all." Something with Supay didn't feel quite right, then he remembered the thing he noticed before he fell asleep. "I get why I can't say Blondie's name, but why can't you?"

"The same reason, but while your voice is a whisper, mine is a shout."

David frowned. "So why are you and I involved in this mess?"

Supay's smile faded. "She has been eating the Old Ones' demons to quench her hunger, but she does not realize it is a stopgap. Our problem is she's running out of demon to eat. When her hunger returns, and it will return, it will overwhelm her. She does not realize why her opponents have delayed tearing open the fabric between our universe and the Old Ones' prison for the last two years."

"Shit," David muttered. "That's their plan. Get her to turn against us."

"Not consciously." Supay shrugged. "The hunger will drive her insane."

"Dude, she ain't all there to begin with."

The god howled with laughter. He swiped at the pink-tinted tears rolling down his face. "There is more truth in your statement than you know, David Jebediah Head."

He cocked his head as he regarded the god. "And you can't warn her why?"

"We cannot interfere directly. To do so risks ripping apart the very fabric of the universe."

"Well, I sure as hell can't tell her. She'd never believe me."

"And even if someone she'd listen to were to relay the information, we have another problem." A sad expression came over the face Supay wore. "She still wants to believe she's human. If that doesn't change, her stubbornness may doom us all."

Chapter 22

Tiffany

Both the Wongs and Caesar insisted I ride in the ambulance with Ptolemy. I would have argued harder that Caesar should accompany his brother, but as Bebe telepathically pointed out, it made no sense for Caesar to accompany Jake. Not when his girlfriend was there. Caesar was merely Jake's alleged boss at a part-time security job.

The ride across the city took forever. When Max had died, I had the chance to say good-bye even if I'd thoroughly fucked it up. But with Jake, I never even had the chance. From what Bebe told me, he'd died on impact.

Hell, I never had the chance to say good-bye to Ptolemy either when he'd died.

There were so many questions I wanted to ask him. About life. Death. The universe. I was pretty sure the real answer wasn't forty-two.

Regardless of our frequent arguments when I was a kid, I trusted him to be honest with me. He'd been brutally so when I was a kid much to Duncan's anger and embarrassment at times.

Unfortunately, it wasn't a Family ambulance that took us to Good Samaritan. With the paramedic sitting beside me, Ptolemy and I couldn't really talk. Not without telepathy anyway, and him being in a Normal body made that impossible. I didn't know what to talk about without giving him away, so I kept my mouth shut.

"I do not believe you've ever been this silent for this length of time," Ptolemy said. It was Jake's face with Ptolemy's wry grin. Seeing it was weird as hell.

I bit my tongue to stop my initial response that he hadn't been around for the last nine years. In that time, I'd graduated from high school, got married, and popped out a kid. I closed my eyes for a moment. My daughter would know the minute she saw Ptolemy that he wasn't Jake. How the hell did I explain this to a first-grader?

"I'm worried about how Ellie will take you being in the hospital for a while."

Questions danced in his eyes. He glanced at the paramedic.

But bless him, the paramedic picked up the conversation. "Is Ellie your daughter?"

I smiled at this small grace. It allowed me to pass information without Ptolemy and me looking like raging maniacs. "Ellie's mine. Jake was a good friend of my husband. When he passed a couple of years ago, Jake helped out around the house." I shrugged and patted Jake's, ur, Ptolemy's shoulder. I was definitely going to need the straightjacket before this was over. "One thing led to another."

"I'm sorry for your loss," the paramedic automatically replied. "My grandmama always says when one door closes, another one opens."

I tried to suppress my wince, but from the concerned expression on Ptolemy's face, I didn't succeed.

"Who's watching her right now?" Ptolemy asked.

I smiled at his effort to change the subject. "She's staying with Phil. When I left, they were eating chocolate chip cookie dough, but you and I won't have to deal with the stomach ache she'll wake up with at three in the morning."

"You know she probably spoils the girl rotten to get back at all the stunts you pulled as a child."

Ptolemy's insight hit me in the gut. Jake had said something similar a few months ago.

The paramedic chuckled. "Is Phil your stepmom?"

"No, she's—" My heart threatened to choke me. I had always prided myself on not letting any weakness show. Max had torn down my walls in more ways than one. Jake convinced me it was okay to leave them down. Now, I was one raw, open wound.

"Phil is—" Ptolemy hesitated for a moment. "—was Tiffany's co-guardian after her parents' deaths. She's a family friend. Tiffany's uncle who ended up with custody needed all the help he could get."

Dammit! I could see it in the way Ptolemy avoided my gaze. He knew his big sister had been behind my parents' deaths. I wanted to know when he'd found out, but I couldn't ask in front of the paramedic. I was pretty sure Ptolemy hadn't been involved. He wasn't that good of an actor to have hidden it from me for the first seventeen years of my life.

Was my teenage crush the real reason Selene had killed him? Or had she planned to murder him anyway once she had Caesar out of the way? Had Caesar lied to me, to all of us, to protect his baby brother's memory? Or had Caesar lied to himself because he couldn't face the fact Ptolemy had sided with Selene during her rebellion against Caesar's rule over the coven?

I didn't want to believe Ptolemy was the bad guy. Maybe Sam was right. Maybe someone was using him to fuck with us. I wasn't sure which situation was worse, Ptolemy being as evil as his sister or *her* being right.

So, I stayed silent for the rest of the ride before I said something really stupid and exposed the coven to the public.

Chapter 23

Libbie

I flicked my little compact's windshield wipers on high as I drove across San Juan Island. The rain system covered the entire Sound, which was unusual, but if Angela was right, the odd weather could be a precursor to what was coming. It made the ferry ride home a little rough. Maybe I should have simply left my car at the university, shifted, and flown home.

Lights glittered through the raindrops from the cottage at the back of the farm when I pulled into the long driveway. Good. Waldo was already home. Normally, we'd work on refurbishing the main house for a couple of hours every evening, but when I called him on my way to the ferry, he claimed we needed a night off anyway.

The savory scent of salmon and herbs filled the kitchen when I entered. "Why are you making fish? You hate fish." I set my bag on the mud bench and draped my coat over a chair to dry.

Waldo pulled me into his arms and reached up to give me a kiss. He didn't show the premature aging of his brothers for which I was thankful. I didn't think I could bear it if he had a Normal lifespan. And when my brothers teased him about his height, well, they found out just what the burly chest, muscular limbs, and powerful jaws of a werebulldog could do.

We parted, and a rueful smile tilted his mouth. "I was worried when you called and said we needed to have a serious talk. It almost sounded like a Normal relationship problem, and I didn't know what I'd done wrong. I was pretty sure I hadn't left the toilet seat up again."

I chuckled. "That's your brothers. And you know I cut Emerson some slack since he's only been able to walk upright for the last six years."

"So what did I do—"

The timer dinged, and Waldo rushed back to the oven.

I hesitated before I said, "This isn't about you per se. How about I pour some wine to go with dinner?" Because Goddess knew I'd need the alcohol to get through this conversation.

He set the dish on the hot pads in the middle of the table before he scowled at me. "Did something happen at the university? They can't fire you. You have tenure."

"Nothing like that." I fished the corkscrew out of its kitchen drawer and retrieved the chilled bottle of wine from the refrigerator. "You know those nightmares we've both been having lately?"

He made a dismissive sound in his throat as he set two wineglasses next to me. "That was just stress about the closing, especially with all the work we've been putting into this place for the last two years. It's done, and the farm is now officially ours."

I poured for both of us and downed the contents of my glass before refilling it. "Angela came to see me at the university today. It's not just us having nightmares. She said to tell you the battle will be here within a week and to let Master St. James know."

Waldo stared at me, his own wine forgotten. "She's sure?"

"Yes."

"Fuck." Waldo ran both of his hands through his brindled, short hair. "Donna needs to hear this, too. Let me get her and the boss on the phone."

Chapter 24

Sam

My legs stretched up the back of our living room couch and my head hung off the seat when the house phone rang. Emerson O'Malley suggested the position for relaxing the pull of gravity on muscles. Damn, if he wasn't right, even if the advice was from someone who spent the majority of his life on four legs.

Besides, if anyone was calling about Caesar's baby brother in my former fiancé's body, Duncan could deal with that mess. I was still pissed Tiffany blamed me for the fiasco.

I admitted, if only to myself, I had been weirded out when Jake and Tiffany hooked up a year and a half after Max's death. Hell, she had only been twenty-four when my big brother was murdered. Younger than me when I'd met Duncan.

Deep down, I knew I had no right to say a damn thing about her and Jake. In fact, I'd been the one who chewed out Duncan when he got all righteous about acceptable mourning periods. But it took Ellie stating she hoped Jake would be her second daddy that put everything into perspective. And now, my precocious little niece will be disappointed as hell when she learned Jake was gone for good.

Maybe I would have been okay if we weren't around Tiffany and Jake so much. If Duncan and I still lived in Las Vegas. I missed the penthouse. My little agency had actually started picking up more acting clients than just my baby zombies. But Duncan felt it would be best not to move the coven capital with so many other changes in the coven thanks to Bebe's discovery of a cure to the V-virus.

And my husband felt he owed Caesar, so we bought the property next door to Caesar and Bebe. I wasn't sure if Duncan's choice was for their protection, or if he really needed Caesar's help with the giant web of companies and investments that funded the coven.

Samantha, could you please come to the study? Duncan asked.

Crap. Had I been accidentally transmitting my thoughts again? *If it's about our resident Ghost in the Shell, leave me the fuck out of it.*

It is Waldo and Donna on a conference call, and you need to hear this.

Shit. Neither of the co-heads of the coven's Seattle division called without a damn good reason, but if they were conference-calling my husband together, solid waste had hit the proverbial spinning turbine. The last thing we needed was more dino demon drama.

I rolled off the couch and teleported to Duncan's study. Unlike Caesar's OCD-neat office when he ran the coven, my husband had paperwork stacked everywhere. If anyone wanted to ferret out our secrets, it would take them a couple of centuries of shuffling through the piles.

Anne Levy-Fitzgerald, Connie Torres, and Taalish Saravati were already waiting for me along with Duncan. Connie, I could understand. Anne was training the former Army sergeant to replace her as the master's household head of security so Anne could take the recently developed cure for the virus that caused vampirism. But if my husband had Taalish, the Normal who headed daytime security, staying late, this couldn't be good.

My husband appeared worried, even if most people couldn't tell that expression from his happy face. "She is here, Professor Hawker. Go ahead."

I set a stack of papers on the floor and sat on the corner of Duncan's desk. Over the speaker phone, Waldo's girlfriend cleared her throat. If the story pouring out of the lady were had been told to me seven years ago, I would have handed it off to my colleague Agnes at *The National Scoop*. She handled the crazy shit. But now . . .

Now, I was dead, and Professor Hawker's tale wasn't even the first fucking sign today that something horrible was brewing. Everyone stared at me when she finished her recitation.

Well, the ones in the same room as me stared.

This was one instance I regretted telling my husband I could take care of this myself because the professor's info brought me one step closer to my personal *High Noon*. I sucked in a deep breath before I spoke. "Libbie, if your friend can pin down a more specific time and place other than within the next week in the vicinity of Seattle, call me. Waldo has my cell number."

"That's all well and good for you," Donna Whitefeather snapped over the line. "But we've got a million civilians in Seattle and Tacoma alone. That's not counting the towns in every nook and cranny of Puget Sound. If things go south—"

"When things go south, Whitefeather, there won't be any damn place to run." I managed not to say, *Especially, if I fail to stop the dinosaur god who's planning to come through the SeaTac breach.*

But my issues weren't her fault, and I immediately regretted getting pissy with the vampire. "I'm sorry, Donna. I'm—" Admitting my own fear wasn't going to help coven morale a damn bit. I sucked in another deep breath and released it. "—sorry," I finished lamely. "Give us a day to put a plan together. According to Libbie's witch friend, it doesn't sound like I have to suit up in the next twenty-four hours."

"In the meantime—" Duncan smoothly interjected himself into the conversation. "—reach out to your contacts in emergency services. Tell them the truth. A local witch with precognitive talent says a natural disaster will occur in the Puget Sound area within the next six days, and we will deliver additional information as soon as we have it. Our non-essential personnel need to head to safe houses anywhere but Oregon and Washington. Have the Were Alliance and Blue Hawk Coven start issuing evacuation orders as well.

"And, Professor Hawker, we greatly appreciate your assistance."

"You're, uh welcome, Master St. James," she said. "But I'm just passing along a message. Here's Angela's number if you need to talk to her directly." She rattled off the digits.

As soon as he ended the call with the Seattle heads, I muttered, "Tell them the truth, huh?"

His right eyebrow rose. "If we were discussing Tokyo, I may get away with telling the Normal authorities a kaiju will rise from the depths of the earth to wipe out their city. Somehow, I do not believe the Normal authorities in the United States of America will be quite as obliging."

"Wait a minute." I leaned away from him. "Did you just make a Godzilla joke?"

"Is that not what we do in a crisis?" His left eyebrow rose to the same height as the right. "Crack inappropriate jokes?"

I shook my head. "I think I'm wearing off on you."

"What do you want us to do, sir?" Anne asked.

Duncan steepled his fingertips. Did he even realized how much he imitated Caesar since he'd taken over the coven? "Call the Portland and San Francisco enforcers. Tell them to prepare for Family members evacuated from the Seattle division. Remind them to notify the packs and witch covens in their cities to expect refugees over the next few days."

I stared at the glass-covered map of my husband's territory on the wall behind his office chair. "You'll need to clear Spokane, Billings, and Cheyenne as well. Also, put Denver and the Dakotas on alert."

"Your reasoning?" he asked.

I hugged myself as I tried not to let the fear gibbering in the back of my mind take over. "That's how far the ash from Mount St. Helens spread, and she was a normal volcanic eruption." I met his gaze. "You'll need to alert Master Wyclef, too, since some of the damage will extend into Canada."

Duncan leaned back in his chair and smiled at me. "You have been doing your homework."

I stalked over to the map and grabbed a red dry erase marker. "The entire sound is riddled with thrust faults. Seattle and Tacoma each have one. Whidbey Island. Olympia." I drew lines as I named each one. "Then we've got the volcanoes in the Cascade Range, particularly Mount Rainier." I drew a big fat "X" over the dormant volcano closest to Seattle. "It doesn't matter where the bastard breaks through. One event is going to destabilize the entire northwest region. We're talking eruptions, earthquakes, tsunamis, landslides—"

"Dogs and cats living together! Mass hysteria!" Taalish interjected.

"Hey!" I jabbed the marker in his direction. "I'm the only one who gets to make smartass pop culture jokes."

"If Sam's right, Donna's fears concerning evacuating the civilian population are well-founded," Anne said. She rose and joined me in front of the map. "SeaTac and the regional airports will be damaged or destroyed, as will most of the roads into the area. Helicopters won't be able to fly through an ash cloud, and Puget Sound will be choked with debris." She turned back to Duncan. "If there are survivors, food and water will be limited, and we won't be able to get to them in a timely manner. This will make the Katrina disaster look like a fucking walk in the park."

The four of us stared at the diminutive vampire. Hell, she had worn her Amish upbringing like a nerdy badge of honor for nearly eighty years. To hear her swear rocked what little equilibrium I had left.

"What?" she said.

I cocked my head. "Y-you said a bad word."

"You're the one who told me years ago there was a time to curse." Anne reached up and tapped her fingers on my scribbles. "This qualifies as one of those times."

"The problem is we don't have a dome, super or otherwise, to house all those people like Houston did for New Orleans after Hurricane Katrina," Taalish said.

"Anne, Connie, pull anyone on the nightshift who has disaster preparation experience and/or survival skills," Duncan ordered. "Start a list of actions we need to take. Alex deposited the stolen money he recovered from the rogues three years ago into a special slush fund. Use that to garner what supplies and accommodations we'll need."

While Duncan issued orders, I capped the dry erase marker and tossed it on its tray with the rest before I stepped away from the map. If only I could distance myself from my destiny so easily.

"Yes, sir." Connie actually looked more relaxed. She'd done a couple of stints in the Middle East while she was a Normal. This was her wheelhouse.

Duncan turned to Taalish. "You will pick up in the morning where Anne and Connie leave off. Tell everyone to get some sleep now because they may not be able to once . . ." He turned to stare at me, his eyes glowing neon green.

"We'll get started, sir," Anne murmured. She crossed to me and squeezed my hand before she strode from Duncan's office. Connie winked at me before she followed the other vampire out of the room.

Taalish rose to leave but crossed to stand in front of me. "You've got this, Sam. We'll take care of the rest." White teeth gleamed against dark skin, but his confident grin didn't comfort me. He left, closing the door quietly behind him.

Without a word, Duncan stood and pulled me tight against his chest. There simply weren't any more words to say between us. He couldn't save me this time. I had to save myself.

And the world.

Chapter 25

Tiffany

When we reached Good Samaritan, Bebe and another healer from Silver Bear Coven kicked Caesar and me out of Ptolemy's room to evaluate his injuries.

Jake's injuries.

Jake's fatal injuries.

Caesar and I were standing on the same Murphy-damned floor in the same Murphy-damned waiting room while Ptolemy was in the same Murphy-damned room where Max had died. I paced because I didn't know what to do with the buttload of emotions threatening to drown me.

"Tiffany—" Caesar said.

"What?" I whirled so fast my ponytail smacked me in the eyes. With everything going on over the last couple of years, I hadn't bothered going to the salon. And Jake had said he liked my hair longer. My lungs froze, and I gasped, trying to get some air, any air, in them.

Caesar stood in front of me and wrapped his arms around my body. "Just breathe, kiddo," he said as he rubbed my back. "Just breathe. Give yourself a chance—"

"A chance to what?" I muttered into his polo shirt. He was trying to comfort me, and all I wanted to do was kill something. No.

Someone.

I looked up at Caesar. "This is all her fault."

"That's not fair." He didn't even have to ask who I was talking about.

"Isn't it?" I jerked out of his hold and marched away before I whirled to face him again. "She didn't want Jake, but she couldn't take it when we—" More guilt overwhelmed me. Max was gone, and I hadn't even remained faithful to him past Ellie's sixth birthday.

"Sam didn't cause Jake's death any more than she caused Max's," Caesar said.

"You're just like Duncan!" My arms waved around like they'd taken on a life of their own. "You're taking her side because you're afraid of her."

"I'm not taking anyone's side—"

"And you got your baby brother back so what I lost, what my daughter lost, doesn't fucking matter!"

"That will be enough, Tiffany." Caesar's eyes no longer glowed neon, but a very human anger spat from them. "I understand you're upset. I understand you need to grieve about your loss. But I won't tolerate you acting like a spoiled brat."

I got in his face though I had to stand on my toes to do so. "You're not my boss anymore, asswipe."

"I'm still Family whether you like it or not." He leaned forward until our noses nearly touched. "And I won't tolerate being treated like shit by an enforcer whose ass I wiped before she was potty trained."

He was right, but my rage refused to disengage, so I resumed ranting about my original target. "If Alex is right about his lead, then the remaining dino demons killed Jake because of her. She knew what she was becoming. She should have left like the other gods told her to, but noooo . . ." My fury-induced sarcasm dripped in thick blobs. "What she wanted mattered more, even though it put all of us in danger."

"Do you need a tranquilizer, Cherry Blossom?"

I whirled around to find Ares, aka the Olympian god of war aka my foster grandfather, standing behind me.

"Trust me," he said. "Doctor Bebe has some very good ones." A wry smile followed his words. He knew from experience after he got handsy with the witch.

"Do you have any idea of what is happening?" I snapped.

"Yes. Phillippa called me." He cocked his head. "Jake's accident does not explain you berating Caesar."

"Jake's dead!" I marched over and jabbed an index finger into his chest. Not that my nail did anything to the solid wall of muscle beneath his scarlet t-shirt. "If you really wanted to help me, you'd tell me how to kill her."

"I'm sorry, Cherry Blossom. I liked the boy, and he was good to you and Ellie." He rested a huge palm on my shoulder and shook his head. "But you cannot kill what is already dead."

"You know what I mean," I said between gritted teeth.

Flames danced in his eyes. "You would condemn Ellie to the Old Ones to salve your grief? That, I will not agree to, Tiffany."

"Has it occurred to any of you that maybe the Old One won't show up if she's wiped out of existence?" My hand swiped left through the air. "It's her presence that's fucking up the quantum vibration of the universe!"

"The damage to our planes has been done." Ares folded his arms over his chest. "It cannot be undone, only healed. Unfortunately, the healing rests on Samantha's shoulders. And if you destroy her, your daughter and everything else on this plane will be wiped out of existence."

"Of course you'd take her side," I hissed.

"Um, Tiffany?"

I whirled to find Bebe behind me. "What!"

Instead of bitching me out for my rudeness, she raised one dark eyebrow. The skin beneath her eyes sagged and was nearly as dark as her hair. "Ptolemy's asking to see you."

My rage didn't exactly deflate, but I couldn't inflict it on someone who—well, I wouldn't exactly call Ptolemy innocent, but obviously, someone, somewhere, thought he deserved a second chance, even if it was in the body of someone I loved. I charged down the hall to his room.

Inside, Doctor Goldstein, one of the Silver Bear healers, jotted something on his electronic tablet with a stylus. He looked up and smiled at me. The lines and dark circles around his eyes were as pronounced as Bebe's. I would have sworn he had more gray in his hair than he did when he walked into this room. "Don't push it too far, you two. Ptolemy's going to need some sleep while the body recovers from the healing. I'll be back to check on you in an hour."

I gingerly sat on the chair next to the hospital bed. A shiny white scar lined Ptolemy's right forearm. The swelling on the right side of his face was gone, but he still sported ugly bruises around his eye and on his forehead. The witches wouldn't waste energy on the minor wounds. His smile was an odd mix of Ptolemy's and Jake's.

"You hurt Caesar's feelings by not asking for him first," I said.

His smile faltered. "I know, but—" He drew a deep breath. "He has his humanity back and he's with the woman he loves. I can't jeopardize his happiness."

That didn't make any sense, so I stuck with the more obvious question. "Why me?"

"I thought I was supposed to act like Jake," he murmured.

"You don't have to here." I waved my hand. "The Maura Lannigan Wing of Good Samaritan Hospital specializes in supernatural and Family care. That was the whole point of bringing you here. So Bebe and her staff could heal you without too many questions asked." I started to rise. "I'll get Caesar."

"No." The grip of his left hand on mine was tight. "I need your help."

"My help?"

"Yes. The reason the gods sent me back was to trap your sister-in-law Samantha."

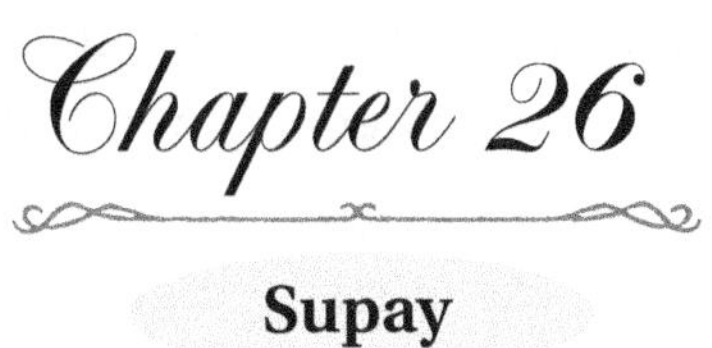

Chapter 26

Supay

Using Alexander's knowledge, I drove south to a coven safehouse in Tacoma. Miko had tried to talk me, or rather Alexander, into calling the vampires in Seattle since I refused her offer to act as my bodyguard. I finally convinced her to fly back to Los Angeles by telling her the truth—that she would be bringing someone else up here soon.

Silently, Alexander called me every obscene name he could think of for putting his stepdaughter in danger. Of course, he knew our plan since our minds were intertwined with my possession of him. However, I knew he would not believe me that the girl's involvement was consequential to the overall strategy. No, he believed I was retaliating against him and his wife for venturing into my domain.

So, I let Alexander continue his stream of invectives and did my best to ignore him.

David Jebediah Head cleared his throat. "So once the dead guy joins us, what exactly are we supposed to do?"

"As I said, we will imprison her," I said. The vegetation in this section of the mountains was different than the highlands where I was raised by Mother and Uncle. Maybe I should have explored more, instead of becoming set in my ways, only leaving Uku Pacha to collect those souls due me.

"Man, you are putting way too much faith in my abilities." David whistled. "I couldn't hold her when she was only a couple of months old."

"Baron Samedi and I will be your—" I searched Alexander's mind for the correct concept. "—batteries. The most difficult item to acquire will be her icon of power."

I glanced at David, but the mortal stared at the cane he held, the one that was the mirror image of Samedi's.

"What's her icon?" the necromancer asked. Of course, he would ask such a logical question. I hated not having all the answers myself. She hadn't carried anything to the convocation I was aware of, not like the rest of us. I had my tumi, Samedi his cane, Kali her belt of skulls. If the infant hadn't selected an icon, whether consciously or unconsciously, the spell we planned would not work.

When I remained silent, David snorted derisively. "You don't know, do you?"

I ground my teeth, or rather Alexander's.

"Goddamn, we are fucked," David spat.

The mortal wasn't wrong in that regard. If we didn't discover her icon soon, or if she didn't have one, we wouldn't be able to control Samantha when her hunger struck. She would devour the planet before the Old Ones' minions broke the seal. Without worshippers to strengthen them, all the pantheons would die regardless of who won the battle between Samantha and the Old One.

It had been so long ago since my own battle with one of the ancient deities, the details blurred. All I remembered was the hunger. I had depended too much on Uncle to remind me of mortal things. Of my life before my death. Now, Uncle was gone. Destroyed by the Old Ones' demons in their efforts to widen the crack between dimensions.

Maybe that was what endeared me to Francisco, though I would never admit such a thing to him. He had Uncle's pragmatism coupled with his enjoyment of his existence.

I exhaled when I realized David expected some kind of an answer. "For those of us with dominion over death, our icons, our emblems of power, are often tools we used while living. You knew her when she was alive. Surely, Samedi questioned you about such things."

A bitter laugh erupted from David. "Man, if it were me, it would definitely be a basketball. But her . . ." His fingers rasped across his stubble as he rubbed his chin. "She was a tabloid reporter. Paparazzi. Her camera? Maybe *The National Scoop*?"

"*The National Scoop*?"

"Yeah. The rag she used to work for. Roll up a magazine and smack someone with it." David snorted. "It's what Jenkins would do to me and my sister. Hurts like a motherfucker on your bare ass."

"Jenkins? Your father?" I glanced at the necromancer before returning my attention to the road. I could understand why Alexander preferred his pickup to the vehicle I currently drove. It could handle the mountainous terrain better and faster than this rented sedan. Even the recalcitrant llama Uncle owned when I was a child would be faster.

"My mother's second husband," David snapped.

Obviously, this Jenkins didn't try to be a father like Uncle had. Grief over his loss still clung to me like a shroud. Mother's betrayal, her alliance with the Old Ones' demons added a layer of suffocating weight to the shroud.

The silent wave of sympathy from Alexander made me grit his teeth again. The vampire had been fond of Uncle, but the last thing I needed was pity from any mortal.

However, I couldn't kill the vampire for his impertinence. Not while I was using Alexander's flesh. It didn't mean I couldn't torture the vampire for the rest of eternity for daring to feel sorry for me after Lady Samantha's task was complete. I was the Lord of Uku Pacha.

Really think either Sam or Phil are going to let you do that to me, Alexander taunted.

You made the bargain with me to find and kill the thieves who took my tumi. The women cannot interfere with such a deal, no matter how powerful they may be.

A horn blasted in front of our vehicle. David jerked on the steering wheel, forcing our car out of the path of the much bigger truck and its load of logs.

"Christ, man! Pay attention to the road!" The ashy scent of the necromancer's fear filled the cabin of the vehicle.

"I'm driving." I smacked David's hand from the steering wheel when I really wanted to disembowel him for daring to correct me.

"No, you were drifting into the path of oncoming traffic." The necromancer leaned back in his seat. A quick glance showed a sheen of perspiration on his forehead. "Is something wrong? You were like a million miles away instead of paying attention to the now."

"It was nothing." I ground my teeth some more while Alexander resumed his mockery.

"Dude . . ." David exhaled. "Look, I know you can't kill the damn vampire. At least, not yet. But you need to shut him down before he gets me and him killed. Otherwise, y'all ain't saving shit on this planet. Ya feel me?"

As much as I hated to admit it, the necromancer was correct. I took a deep breath and released it. "Do you have a suggestion? If I try to channel additional power, I will burn out this vessel before our task is complete."

"Yeah, I think I can help," David replied. "But I need some quiet. Can you hang on until we get to this safehouse of yours?"

"Do you doubt me?" I snapped.

David snorted. "This ain't about belief or doubt. If you lose control of his body long enough for him to call out to her, you and I are both fucked. And that's before the Old Ones get here."

For all his crassness, the necromancer's practicality reminded me of Uncle, too. "I promise he will not slip from my control before we reach his haven."

But in the back of my mind, Alexander Socrates Stanton assured me he would endeavor to do just that.

Chapter 27

Tiffany

"Trap her?" While part of me rejoiced at the thought, worry prickled along my skin. "Why on earth would the other gods want to trap her?"

Ptolemy winced, but the uncomfortableness obviously didn't seem to stem from the subject from the way he reached for his head with his right hand. "They-they said the Old Ones' demons . . ." His grip on my hand became painful.

"Take a deep breath and relax," I murmured as I brushed a remaining lock of hair from his forehead. Jake's forehead. Not Ptolemy's. The grief brought a lump to my throat, and I swallowed hard. "Your memories are probably still integrating with Jake's brain. Take your time. It'll come back."

"No, this is important." Frustration twisted his features. "The demons know she's running out of food. Now, they're deliberately delaying their master's entrance into this plane, hoping she will lose control."

My own stomach twisted at the thought. I'd seen Sam on a few of her hunger rampages, and that had been back when she was first created by Selene's mad scientists. At the beginning, a case of Twinkies would take the edge off, but nothing truly satiated her hunger until the night she ate a charred dino demon. In all fairness, she blasted the thing to crispy bits because it shoved a tentacle down her throat.

The daughter of the last full-blooded demon hid for the last two years in what the witches and fae called Otherwhere. A space between the dimensions. Her children had been breeding among themselves on our plane, and they were too human now for Sam to eat.

But if Sam lost control, she wouldn't care who was human and who was dino demon . . .

"Shit," I muttered. "How the hell do they expect you to trap her? Jake's—" My chest ached. "Jake's Normal, which means you're Normal. Even if you were still in your original body, a vampire can't possibly take her on."

"I was supposed to have help." His expression was so forlorn. I'd never seen Jake look like that.

But I had seen that emotion on Ptolemy's face once before.

The night of my junior prom.

Duncan had been off doing Murphy-knew-what for the coven, so I was staying at Caesar's mansion. Miko had been helping me with my make-up and hair. When we came downstairs, Ptolemy had that damn forlorn look. I asked him what was wrong, but he made some snide comment about how American society wasted too much money on their kids playing dress-up. At the time, I launched into an obscene tirade, and he flipped me off. All of which I took as our normal bickering. Now, I wondered what had gone through his mind that night, but this wasn't the time to broach the subject. Not if the dino demons planned to make Sam lose control of her appetite.

I squeezed Ptolemy's hand right back. "Who is supposed to help you and what are they supposed to do?"

He closed his eyes. "I am the dead man who is alive. A living man who is dead will identify himself to me. And there is a bridge . . ."

"A bridge?" I prompted.

"Someone with the skills and tools to help you both." Ptolemy sounded like he was reciting something.

"Who told you this?" I asked softly.

"They didn't tell me. They sang. K-k-k . . ." He shook his head and opened his eyes. "I'm sorry. It's gone."

This was weird even by my estimation, and I was raised by vampires and an Amazon, my best friend was werewolf, and my sister-in-law was a god. Ptolemy's words almost sounded like a poem.

Or a spell.

And the only bridge between life and death was a deity. A psychopomp.

Or a necromancer.

My heart tried to climb out of my throat. A necromancer obsessed with Uncle Duncan had kidnapped him and tried multiple times to kill Sam. Hell, he sent zombies to my own damn wedding. Grandpa Jamal had died in that attack. Grandpa Kensai died trying to rescue Duncan.

I'd been two months pregnant and severely injured in the zombie battle in my in-laws' back yard. Max and I almost lost Ellie. It was a miracle we didn't.

"Let me make a quick phone call." I stood, but Ptolemy wouldn't let go of my hand.

"To whom?" he demanded. Damn, if he didn't sound like his old, haughty self. The problem was I was starting to get used to him talking out of Jake's mouth.

"My boss." I shot him a vicious smile. "Now, let go of me, or I'll break your left arm."

Ptolemy sighed. "Of course, you will." But he did let go of my right hand.

I tried to surreptitiously shake some feeling back into my fingers while I pulled my phone from my left pocket with my other hand. With a swipe and a thumb, the phone automatically dialed Alex's number.

"What's up, darlin'? I'm sorta in the middle of something."

"Have you heard if there's been any change of status regarding David Head and his coma?"

The silence on the line lasted so long I wondered if I'd lost the connection.

"Who are you with, Tiffany?" Alex sounded far more serious than normal. Was there a connection between his lead on Marcus Giovanni and the fucking necromancer?

"Just Jake." I knew I should have explained the situation to Alex. He was the coven's chief enforcer after all. But something about his tone bothered the hell out of me.

"Who are you really with, Tiffany?"

My mouth went dry. I don't know why, but the urge to protect Ptolemy swept over me. "Uh, that's a little hard to explain." I glanced at the man in the bed. "Give me a sec, and I'll get us some privacy."

"No," Alex said. "Put me on speaker."

Why did I have the feeling my curiosity over Alex's weirdness was going to kill me? I tapped the icon for the speaker function.

"To the person inside Jacob Jin Wong's body, please identify yourself."

A shiver ran through me. It was Alex's voice, and yet, not. I watched Ptolemy, but from his expression he was as confused as I was.

Ptolemy hesitated for a moment before he said with his snotty attitude, "You first."

The chuckle that came through the receiver chilled me to the bone. "I am Supay, Lord of Uku Pacha. Alexander Socrates Stanton owes me a favor, and I am collecting on it."

A living man who is dead will identify himself to me.

I wanted to toss my phone across the floor. I wanted to scream for Grandpa Ares to save me. I wanted to find this bastard and force him out of my stepfather's body.

Ptolemy met my horrified gaze as he said, "I am Ptolemy Philadelphus Antonius, the youngest son of Cleopatra VII, the last pharaoh of Egypt."

"Have you told Tiffany Jane Stephens your purpose for being here?"

"Yes."

My jaw dropped. He hadn't told me everything yet, but the fact I was the person he trusted most next to Caesar shocked and pleased me.

Then the guilt rushed in. I'd finally beaten most of the emotion back when it came to falling in love with Jake so soon after Max's death. Now, I found myself in the same damn position I was in six months ago—grieving for one man while attempting to deal with my feelings for another.

Murphy damn it! Jake hadn't even been dead for twenty-four hours.

I was definitely due for a nervous breakdown.

But until then, someone needed to take charge of this little impossible missions team from Hell. "According to Ptolemy, you guys are going to need a necromancer."

"I've acquired one." Supay sounded like it was the most obvious thing in the world, which only irritated me more.

"Is Head going to release . . . *her* at the proper time, or is he going to be stupid like he was at my bachelorette party, my rehearsal dinner, and my wedding?" I snapped.

"I'll release her."

My blood froze in my veins. Head was already awake and with Supay. "Do Yvonne and Master Rousseau know you're walking around?"

Head's laugh was self-deprecating. "They definitely know I'm out of the coma. They probably know I've left Miami by now."

I'd bet my trust fund Supay used Alex's body to get Head out of Rousseau territory. Our entire coven was so fucked. I closed my eyes in an effort to calm myself.

"Who knows Head is with Alex?" I asked as mildly as I could.

"What difference does that make?" Supay snapped.

"Because we don't want two vampire covens getting in our way," I said like I was explaining something to my daughter. "If Head's missing and Alex was the last one seen with him, you will be hunted by both St. James and Rousseau. And I'll bet a case of my sister-in-law's Twinkies you can't channel your full power through Alex. Therefore, you'd better fucking tell me so I can cover for you."

There was a very long pause, and I began to wonder if Supay would pop into Ptolemy's hospital room and smite me.

Finally, he said, "Miko Osaka is the only one who is consciously aware David Jebediah Head is with me."

I swallowed hard, not liking his implication. "Can you be more specific about what you mean by 'consciously'?"

"I have not killed anyone or taken their souls. I blurred the memories of the people I encountered at the long-term care facility and our taxi driver. I also ensured David Jebediah Head's lover remained asleep in his private room. For the purpose of bringing Ptolemy Philadelphus Antonius to me, I kept the pretense I was Alexander Socrates Stanton with Miko Osaka and told her she would need to bring someone else to me soon, though I was not specific about who," Supay recited with the bored air of a teenager, but his tone abruptly changed with his next words. "Have you acquired her talisman of power?"

"No." Ptolemy looked at me nervously. "I never knew her in either my life or hers. I was about to ask Tiffany for suggestions."

"What has she kept from her days as a reporter?" Head sounded terribly calm. Nothing like the arrogant pro basketball MVP or the crazed witch he had been seven years ago. "Any of her cameras? A favorite recorder she might have used for interviews?"

The only things Sam had when her goddess garb manifested were her two ghost rabbits and . . .

"Her phone," I said softly. "That has to be it. It's the only thing she still uses on a regular basis. Its tech is similar to the nanites Selene's scientists administered to rewrite her DNA."

Ptolemy slowly nodded. "Of course. Modern phones allow her to perform all the tasks she would have done as a journalist. Notes. Vocal recordings. Photographs and video." He cocked his head as he regarded me. "And if she was born of information technology, then a computer, even a miniature one such as a smart phone, would be her talisman."

"Are you two sure?" Supay sounded skeptical.

"They're on the right track," Head said. "The question is how are you two going to nab it and get it to me before she catches you. I can't get any closer to Los Angeles without her knowing I'm awake."

"Lord Supay, please call Miko." I voiced my request as graciously as I could. Last thing I needed was the god killing Alex out of spite. "Have her prep the jet for take-off. Ptolemy and I will be at the airport in two hours."

"Very well." Supay relayed the address of the Tacoma safehouse. "Do you know where this place is?"

"Yes, sir," I said through gritted teeth. Nothing I hated worse than someone treating me like I was stupid. I was finally earning the respect of the rest of the coven, only to have some South American god question my competence.

"Be cautious with your ghost," Supay warned. "Your rebel vampire Giovanni was seen heading in this direction. No doubt any surviving minions of the Old Ones will be on their way to this area as well."

"With all respect, my lord, *she* is going to be more of an impediment to our task than that asshole will." Even though I wanted to chop off Giovanni's head and dance on his entrails for what he and his friends did to Max, I needed to keep my focus on the real mission. Besides, *she* will be perfect bait for Giovanni and his buds.

"What happens if she catches them?" Head asked.

I sucked in a deep breath and released it. "The more important task is for you to have everything for your spell prepped by the time we get there. Once she realizes we took her phone, she'll be on your doorstep as fast as she can think it."

"Very well," Supay said. "Notify me when you have additional information." My phone beeped at the abrupt ending of the call.

"Wow." I shook my head as I shoved my phone back in my pocket. "Talk about a lack of manners."

But a rude god was the least of our problems. I didn't trust Head to release Sam when he was supposed to. The dino demons had done a number on his mind long before she put him in a coma. We needed to get our asses up to Tacoma to make sure Head behaved himself.

On the other hand, putting Little Miss Holier-than-thou in her place was an opportunity I couldn't pass up. I just hoped I didn't get Ptolemy killed a second time to assuage my pride.

Chapter 28

Ptolemy

A thread of worry wormed its way up Ptolemy's spine. The glint in Tiffany's eyes had boded trouble when she was a teenager.

"You're going to get yourself killed if you retaliate against Lord Supay for the same rudeness you used to display on a regular basis," Ptolemy said.

"It's not him I'm concerned about," she muttered as she tapped on the screen of her phone. When she raised the device to her ear, she held up her right index finger.

"Duncan, Alex just told me Head's awake." She dropped her hand when Ptolemy remained silent. "He thinks it's linked to Ptolemy's situation."

Ptolemy cocked his head and stared at her. She was literally revealing everything to the Briton. He opened his mouth to object, and she admonished him by waving her index finger.

"Crap," she muttered. "That doesn't give us much time. How much dino demon meat does Sam have left?" After a pause, she murmured, "That's not good. Here's the plan. Alex will cut Head off before he reaches Washington state. I'll use Ptolemy as bait to wrangle a dino demon for her."

Ptolemy didn't need his vampiric skills to hear St. James's obscene protest.

"Did you kiss Grandma Margaret with that mouth, or is my sister-in-law rubbing off on you?" Tiffany winked at Ptolemy as she lectured her uncle. "We'll call you once we have news. Love you." She ended the call. Her index finger tapped against the side of the device, and a frown formed a "V" between her dark eyebrows.

"What in Hades' name do you think you are doing? Telling St. James—" Ptolemy started.

"The truth makes a much better lie." She shrugged and shoved her phone back into her pocket. "We need to go home and pack a few things before we steal her phone."

"You cannot possibly be planning to break into their home?" Ptolemy didn't want to question Tiffany, but she'd done more than her fair share of foolish things as a young woman.

She shot him a disbelieving look. "Breaking into the home of the master of the Western United States Coven? Did you leave part of your brain on the shores of the River Styx? I'm a lot of things, but I'm not suicidal."

"The enforcers wouldn't kill you—"

"Yes, they would." She spit out the words like bullets. "You haven't faced a dino demon. They can become anyone. They can fool everyone, including the fae. Alex's orders are to shoot first and ask questions later when it comes to both Duncan and Caesar's safety. When we go there, we're walking in the front door."

Tiffany started pacing at the foot of Ptolemy's hospital bed. "The question is how to distract both her and Duncan so neither of them read our minds."

"What if we cloned her phone?" Ptolemy asked.

Tiffany paused in midstride. "Even if Head's spell relies on sympathetic magick, a cloned phone might not work."

"No." Ptolemy started to shake his head, but a wave of dizziness made him stop. "Substitute the cloned phone for hers to buy us a little more time. I was supposed to deliver a message to her. That will distract both her and your uncle." He chuckled. For all of Officer Nguyen's helpful advice, he'd forgotten all of it when he awoke in Jake's body. The body *she* tried to throttle. Now was the time to put it to use.

Chapter 29

Angela

The roar of voices in the confined space of the Blue Hawk temple made Angela want to clamp her hands over her ears. The only problem was most of them were the mental variety. She couldn't tune them out in a formal circle.

"Silence!" Silvia Wood, the high priestess of the coven, slammed her staff against the floor, but it was her tweak of magick through the circle that quieted everyone. She turned to Angela. "Are you sure?"

Angela nodded. After her talks with Libbie and Kamil, she called her husband. Jim ran her idea past the staff at the aquarium, describing Priscilla's behavior. Jim's friends discounted the cat's conduct, but they confirmed a Japanese team was researching the idea that cetaceans could predict earthquakes. Something to do with the creatures picking up the subsonics prior to the actual shaking. When Angela relayed her information to her greater earth elder, he immediately ordered the coven meeting. Angela called Jim again and told him she'd be home late.

Goddess help her, she would have preferred snuggling under a blanket with Jim and watching a movie this late at night, rather than being the focus of her own coven's attention. But the signs were overwhelming, and she couldn't ignore them. Especially not when Libbie confirmed the St. James Vampire Coven suspected Seattle would be the place for the battle.

"You expect us to take the word of a child?" Emma Warren, the Greater Elder of Air, flicked her attention between the high priestess and Angela. Warren made no secret of her opinion that no witch under the age of one hundred should be on the council.

Angela bristled at the insult, but Howard Johnson squeezed her left hand.

"I would not have nominated Angela as my Lesser Elder of Earth if I believed she was incapable of handling the task," he said.

"Do the St. James Coven and the were alliance know about your prognostication?" Sylvia asked. Her question was more to cover her ass if Emma stirred up too much trouble. Howard had already relayed all the information to her.

Angela nodded. "I informed my friends Libbie Hawker and Waldo O'Malley after I spoke with Elder Johnson on the phone this afternoon. I recommended they pass the information to their respective leaders."

"What do they say?" Sylvia asked.

Angela tried to lick her dry lips. She hated telling anyone bad news, but this . . . this was beyond her paygrade. "St. James has ordered all their non-essential personnel out of the SeaTac area. Also, they are notifying Normal Family members within Washington's emergency services. The Were Alliance is meeting now, at the same time we are."

"The vampires were expecting this." Warren sneered. "They don't care . . ."

"Of course, they were expecting this," Sylvia snapped. "They needed Angela's reading to pin down the time and place."

Their high priestess's attention swept the circle, meeting the gaze of each member of the coven in turn. "We all know what St. James's wife is. We should be thankful the Old Ones' minions have not targeted any supernatural located in the vicinity of the Sound since their last attempt at nesting here. And we should be doubly grateful, our Lesser Earth Elder is able to give us as much warning as she has."

Sylvia shook her head. "That being said, this means the area will be flooded with dinosaur demons over the next few days. Emma, contact the Oregon and California covens. Find out how many of our people they can shelter. Have your Lesser contact the covens east of us and warn them of potential fallout. Evan—"

The Greater Elder of Fire nodded. "Transportation and supplies. On it."

Sylvia turned to Maureen Whitcomb, but before the high priestess could issue any instructions, the Greater Water Elder quietly said, "My element will be staying."

Maureen turned to Howard. "I'm assuming you and Angela have a plan because there's no way we can get everyone in the Sound evacuated in time."

Howard looked at Angela and grinned. "I'm sure Angela does."

Nausea swept through her, but everyone's lives depended on her knowledge. "Well, it really depends on how the Old One manifests, but we're looking at earthquakes, tidal waves, and the eruption of Mount Rainier."

Worried murmurs swept around the circle.

"The safest place is the northern half of downtown," she said firmly. "Anyone who can't get south of Portland before the volcano blows, they need to come to the north side of downtown. If we have enough earth and water specialists, and some of the coven willing to back us with additional power, we can ride the mini-plate like a raft."

"That's insane!" The high priestess's second Valerie Cox stared at her. "Hell, it's impossible."

"Anything's possible with enough power," Sylvia said. "Or do you believe we should leave the Normals to their deaths?"

Valerie's cheeks glowed bright red under the light of the candles illuminating the temple. "No, High Priestess."

"Very well, then." Sylvia nodded sharply. "The Air and Fire Elders will make arrangements to get every witch under eighteen south of Seattle along with our Family members. I'll contact the Were Alliance about combining our forces to escort our members south." Once again, her gaze swept the circle, meeting each member's eyes. "Emphasize with your Normal Family members the danger. An eruption of Mount Rainier would be catastrophic under plain old plate tectonics. For all our combined powers, we're going to have two gods duking it out literally on top of us. This will be much, much worse."

Angela could already hear what Jim would say when she got home.

"Are you out of your mind, Angie?" He glared at her. "You have to come to Vegas with me. If things are as bad as you say, I can't tell your mom and brother I left you behind!"

She searched her mind for something to reassure him, but she had enough trouble with her hindbrain gibbering in fear. "Honey, I don't want to end this discussion on a knock-down drag-out fight, but you *are* getting on the damn plane tomorrow, even if I have to lay a spell on you to do it."

Jim folded his arms over his chest. "What about Libbie? Is she staying?"

Angela sighed. Of course, he'd throw her best friend's choices in her face. "Yes, but—"

"See? I'm staying."

Angela matched Jim's stance. "That's different. Waldo is one of the St. James Coven's leaders here—"

"And you're staying to protect the citizens." Jim's hand slashed through the air.

"Dammit, Jim!" She wanted to throttle her husband and kiss him senseless at the same time. "I need to know your safe!"

"Angie." He stepped closer and pulled her into his arms. "Don't you realize I have the same damn need?" She opened her mouth, but he laid his index finger over her lips. "Besides, you are going to need help herding civilians to downtown. The aquarium has a couple of buses—"

She smirked and grasped his hand on her mouth. "You can't drive, honey."

"Doesn't mean I can't tell people where to go." He grinned back.

Angela sighed and shook her head. "All right. You win, but I'd better not hear you bitching in the afterlife."

"I won't." He leaned forward and kissed her forehead.

She hugged him tightly and prayed to the Goddess she hadn't just made a horrible mistake.

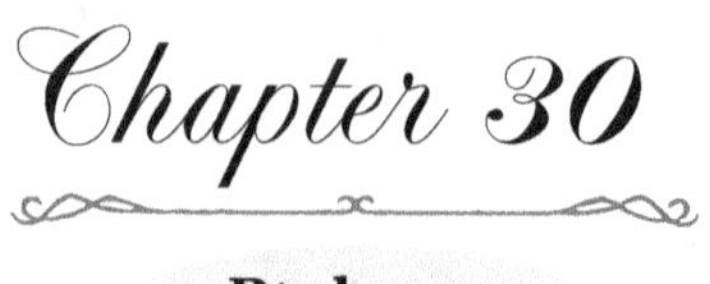

Chapter 30

Ptolemy

Ptolemy examined the ranch-style house connected to the driveway Tiffany pulled into. He'd finally nagged Doctor Zachary into releasing him. He claimed he wouldn't be able to sleep if the nurses were checking him every couple of hours and waking him up. Maybe she read enough of his surface thoughts to know he was highly uncomfortable with the number of weres working at the hospital.

"How do you handle it?" he murmured.

"Handle what?" Tiffany said as she shifted the transmission into "Park" and turned off the vehicle's engine.

"Feeling helpless around beings who could kill you in an instant."

She stared at him for a long moment before she turned her attention to the front of the vehicle and exhaled. "I never thought about them that way." She shrugged. "But then, I've known about the existence of supernaturals from the moment I was born. And I've always been the underdog. Is that what set you off about leaving the hospital?"

Of course, she didn't understand.

"Never mind." He yanked on the door handle, and a twinge went through his arm as he shoved the door open.

Not his arm. Jake's arm. The bitterness of this damn situation made everything worse.

Tiffany remained silent as she followed him up the walk to her front door. He stepped aside so she could unlock it. That's when he noticed the white SUV parked two houses down the street. The feeling of being watched crawled beneath his skin.

"Tiffany," Ptolemy whispered. "Don't look, but we need to turn around and get back in your vehicle."

Of course, she turned around and looked anyway. She waved, and the headlights flashed once. She returned her attention to the door and twisted the key. The deadbolt snapped back, and she pushed the door open. He followed her inside.

The theme from *Cops* started playing from her pocket. She pulled the device from her jeans as she dropped her knapsack on a chair.

"Hey, Saif!" A pause before she forced a laugh. "No, Jake was just confirming who was on duty tonight." Another pause. "Yeah, he got his clock rung pretty good this afternoon." A third pause. "Stepdaddy is heading up the investigation personally, so of course, he suspects Giovanni and the dino demons. According to him, they are the root of all evil. Speaking of which, we're packing and heading back out in a few minutes."

She grinned at Ptolomy. "Exactly. Have a good night."

"Why is Saif Al-Issa watching your house?" Ptolemy cocked his head. "What kind of danger are you in?"

"The protection detail is more because of Ellie." Her grin disappeared. "She's immune to the V-virus."

Ptolemy felt his jaw drop. It took a couple of tries before he managed to say, "She's the source of the cure?"

"One of the possible sources." Tiffany beckoned him to follow. "She's too young to donate the amounts Bebe needed. Max's mom and his maternal grandmother share the same immunity, so we've had double guards around all three of them for the last couple of years."

"What about . . . your sister-in-law?" The reluctance to say Sam's name surprised him, but if she really was a goddess, it made sense not to draw her attention by saying her name until it was necessary.

"Selene and Mallory's nanites corrupted her DNA too much for Bebe to use it."

"Tyrone Mallory?" Ptolemy asked. "The bio-tech tycoon?"

"Yep." Tiffany flipped on lights as they walked through her house. "The crazy bastard thought he could use Natasha Petrov's research to become immortal and still walk in the sun. He tested the nanites on *her* before he injected his daughter."

"So, there's more like your sister-in-law running around?"

"Nope. Tyrone's daughter killed him before he took a dose. Then she accidentally killed herself by biting my sister-in-law."

It sounded like Selene had found allies just as psychotic as she was.

Instead of thinking about his own crazy sibling, Ptolemy focused on his surroundings. The home was decorated in an eclectic mix of Eastern and Western styles, but they didn't clash. It was cozy. Domestic. Or as domestic as he ever imagined Tiffany Stephens becoming.

And purple. A lot of purple in various shades. Her favorite color. Except for one bedroom that appeared pink from the hallway light.

They reached the room at the end of the hallway, and she flipped the switch. Two black standing lamps glowed in opposite corners of the room. The walls were, of course, painted a dusky purple.

But his eyes were drawn to the dark cherry bed frame. The bed itself was neatly made with a white comforter covering it. No frilly decorative pillows. For some reason, that reassured him Tiffany was still the same girl he used to know.

"That dresser is Jake's." She pointed at the five-drawer monstrosity to their right before she headed into the walk-in closet on the opposite wall next to a cherry vanity that matched the bedframe and dresser. She pulled out two small carry-on suitcases with wheels.

"What's wrong?"

Ptolemy held up his hands in a helpless manner. "I feel like I'm snooping through someone else's belongings." Which he would be.

Tiffany grimaced. "If I didn't know better, I'd think you're trying to get out of doing actual work."

"Fine," he snapped. He marched over to the dresser and yanked open the top drawer. Sure enough, it contained undergarments. However, Jake Wong favored cotton briefs in a multitude of colors, not plain white ones.

Ptolemy grabbed the first two pairs and tossed them on the bed. He reached for a couple pairs of socks when his fingers brushed something hard. From the armaments Tiffany was pulling from the closet, it couldn't be a weapon.

He brushed aside the socks covering the item. A velvet-covered box. Part of him knew he shouldn't look, that what was in the box would shatter his heart. He picked it up and opened it. Inside sat two gold rings. One a plain wedding band. The other a matching band with a solitaire, round-cut diamond. It was perfect in its simplicity.

And it totally matched the woman it was meant for. The woman Jacob Jin Wong would never have a chance to give it to.

A sob yanked Ptolemy's attention from the rings. Tiffany stared at his hand as if it held the knife that had plunged into her heart.

Which it had.

Tears rolled down her face as she fled her bedroom. The bedroom she shared with the man whose body Ptolemy now wore.

How did he manage to always screw up when it came to Tiffany Stephens?

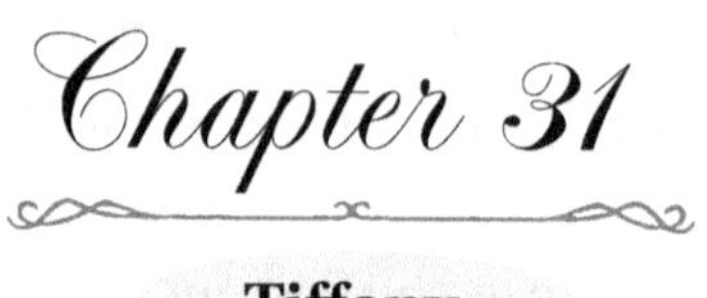

Chapter 31

Tiffany

Jake never made any secret how he felt about me. And Ellie dancing around the house, singing, "I have a secret," had been a pretty big clue. Seeing the evidence though made everything too damn real.

And he would never come home. Never have the chance to ask me.

Deep down, I wanted to be asked.

I didn't blame Max for not really popping the question. Finding out I was pregnant through one of the weres' noses had been bad enough. But he demanded I marry him because of Ellie. He didn't ask.

At the time, I would have kicked any other guy in the nuts and stomped away. Maybe I went along with it because I didn't want my baby to grow up like I had—with no parents.

Nor could I bear to break Duncan's heart by having an abortion, even though I wasn't ready to have a kid. I was the last of his sister's line, thanks to Selene.

Rage flooded through me. Ptolemy had known what his bitch of a sister had done. I'd seen it in his eyes earlier at the hospital.

I swiped at the wetness on my face. The beer I'd opened twelve hours ago still sat on the kitchen table where Sam had left it in our rush to get to the hospital. So were the deck of cards from the Karnak casino. Six goddesses of death had sat around my kitchen table, playing poker with my daughter, while the man I loved died.

Sam claimed she didn't know about Jake's accident, but she had to have known.

Except I couldn't walk into hers and Duncan's home in this mental state. They'd both pick up my scent, even if they didn't read my thoughts.

I picked up the bottle and took a sip of the flat beer. It tasted like Jake's kisses. As much as I wanted to drink all the alcohol in the house and cry myself to sleep, I couldn't. Not if I wanted my daughter to live.

"I'm so sorry, Tiffany. I didn't know."

Jake's voice, but not Jake's voice.

I swiped at the tears with the back of my hand before I turned around. He wore the forlorn expression that was purely Ptolemy's.

"There's no reason you should know." I tried to smile, but it probably looked more like a grimace. "I wasn't supposed to know either."

"But you did." A statement, not a question.

"I didn't snoop if that's what you're accusing me of." I took another sip of the beer. Citrus and hops rolled over my tongue. A little bit of normalcy in my crazy world. "Ellie could keep the secret, but Jake talks— talked in his sleep. He was going to give it to me at Christmas."

"I'm so sorry." He shook his head. "I shouldn't have asked you to help me. I'll call Caesar. Have him come—"

"No," I said firmly and set down the bottle on the kitchen table. "You need someone who knows Head and how he works. Necromancers are rare, but I don't know why the Incan god would choose that asshat unless he's pissed off *she* turned down his proposal."

"He proposed to her?"

I shrugged. "So did Grandpa Ares." I rolled my eyes. "There's no accounting for taste."

He smirked. "You realize you're referring to your own uncle, don't you?"

"It adds a whole nuther layer of gross incest." I charged past him. "C'mon, we need to get those bags packed and hit the road."

I turned onto the street to Duncan's place. "The enforcers on duty will stick us both with an Olympian bronze pin. Act like you do this all the time."

"Why are they poking us?"

"The dino demons are shapeshifters. To the point, weres can't smell the difference, witches can't see the difference, and vamps read their minds as Normal."

"What about the fae?"

"They'll never admit it, but they can't tell the difference either."

He snorted in amusement. "So what does the pin do?"

"Not a damn thing to us, but it hurts the dino demons so they can't keep their shape."

"You sure it's not going to do anything to me?"

I glanced at his worried expression. Shit. I hadn't thought that one through. "Let's hope not," I muttered.

I turned the SUV into the driveway and braked before the gates to Duncan and Sam's place. Neither of them were the Brentwood types, but he thought it was important to be close to Caesar during the transfer of power without actually kicking the man out of his own house. So, Duncan made an offer to the previous owners of the place next door, the proverbial one they couldn't refuse.

Connie Torres sauntered up to my window. The former Army sniper owed her life to Sam. I owed Connie my daughter's life. She'd turned on Giovanni once she learned the truth about him and the dino demons. If it weren't for her, I wouldn't have found Ellie before those asshats sacrificed my baby to bring forth their gods.

"Damn, Jake!" Connie shook her head. "You don't look as close to death's door as I was told."

Ptolemy leaned toward the vampire. "'The reports of my death are greatly exaggerated.' But I don't think Mark Twain had witches in his back pocket."

"Then present those fingers, folks." She retrieved her pin from the lapel of her black jacket and brandished it in our direction. The Olympian bronze glowed softly in the darkness.

I breathed a slight sigh of relief. Ptolemy had passed the first test. Unless Duncan and Sam warned Connie.

She poked my finger, then Ptolemy's, before she passed us both anti-septic wipes. Connie stepped back and waved at the enforcers on the side of the gates before she disappeared into the shadows of the foliage by the left wall.

I rolled up my window before I looked at Ptolemy. "Feeling okay from the pinprick?"

"Yes." He shrugged as I pressed the accelerator. "It's odder not being able to Hear the enforcers on duty."

For the first time, it really hit me how helpless he must feel in Jake's body. No telepathy. No superstrength. No superspeed. He had those abilities over two thousand years. To wake up as an invalid in the hospital had to be the worst experience in his life. Or death.

I tried to laugh, but it came out pretty pathetic. "Welcome to my world."

"Now I understand why you felt the need to prove yourself to Caesar and Duncan," he said softly.

And you. I choked down the lump in my throat. "We need to focus on our mission. How exactly are you planning to distract her?"

"It would be best if I don't tell you."

"Why?"

He chuckled. "Plausible deniability."

I braked more sharply than I intended in the closest space to the side door of their mansion. "Please tell me you're not going to piss her off enough that she'll kill you again."

"No," he said. "I am merely relaying a message from someone claiming to be her friend."

I turned off the engine and summoned my rage at both Sam and Giovanni. She and Duncan would have a tough time reading my mind through the swirl of fury inside me.

Ptolemy and I both exited my SUV and headed for the side door. Leona Alvarez, another enforcer, opened it, a friendly smile on her face.

"Look what the enforcer dragged in. How you feeling, Jake?"

"Like I fell off a five-story building with a broken rig," Ptolemy shot back with a grin.

Leona laughed. "Maybe it's time to hang up your stuntman's hat and go full-time with us."

"Maybe," he said agreeably.

I released the breath I didn't know I was holding. Leona had known Ptolemy, but so far, she wasn't batting an eye. And Ptolemy's responses were in line with what Jake would have said in the same circumstances.

"Look, I don't want to be rude—" I started.

Ptolemy snorted. Somehow, I resisted the urge to stomp on his foot.

"—Leona, but this is business."

"I figured that's why Bebe hadn't tied down your boytoy." She pivoted to lead the way through the house.

"Where's Anne?" Ptolemy asked as we followed.

"Planning the evacuation of our people out of Washington."

"Wait!" I grabbed her arm. "We have a place and a time?"

"Puget Sound Area, but Sam's leaning toward Mount Rainier," Leona answered. She continued walking in the direction of Duncan's office in the center of the house. "One of the Blue Hawk witches says it'll be in six days. The clock's ticking."

I envisioned a picture of the October calendar. "Shit! She's wrong."

Ignoring protocol, I raced for my uncle's office and burst through the door. "The Seattle witch is wrong! We only have two days!"

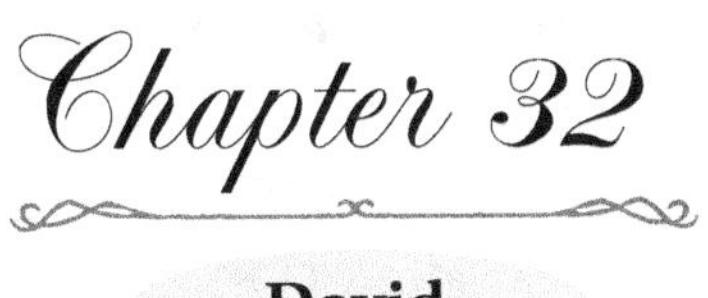

Chapter 32

David

Silvery moonlight dappled the walls, carpet, and furniture while David walked through the St. James safehouse. Actually, only the ground level looked like a house. The rest was more like a bunker, buried in the side of one of the smaller mountains near Rainier.

This year was one of the rare occurrences of a full moon on Samhain. With all the shutters wide open, it was nearly as bright as day inside even though it was three days before the High Sabbat.

"You should be sleeping, David Jebediah Head."

The eerie voice came from an armchair. For the briefest instant, it wasn't the vampire's body sitting there. Red eyes surrounded by skin blacker than anything stared at him.

David blinked. The vampire's hair gleamed silvery gold under the moonlight. Blue eyes glowed softly in the shadow of the support beam. His brief Sight was gone.

A reminder of who he really dealt with.

"I've slept enough for the last seven years," David said. He flopped down on the couch across from Supay and dragged both hands down his face before he faced the god again. "Plus, I think I'm still high from that blood you forced me to drink."

"Would you prefer dying helpless in your invalid facility bed?"

David raised his hands in surrender. "It wasn't a complaint, man. I just can't relax right now."

Something howled outside. A sound that rose and fell before other voices howled in harmony to the first. Then just as abruptly, silence fell. Not even insects and birds whispered under the glow of the moon.

"What was that?"

"The creatures of this land feel the tremors between this world and the Old Ones' prison," Supay said. "They are relaying the alarm and fleeing."

David rose and crossed to one of the massive windows. To the east,

Mount Rainier towered in all its majesty. The snowcapped summit reflected the light from the moon.

"What happens if we can't hold her?" he asked.

"We will be the first to die, but it will be at her hands, not the Old One."

A shiver rippled through David's body. He didn't have a damn choice. If he wanted to save Brandon and Yvonne, he'd have to keep Ridgeway trapped here until the last moment.

Even if it killed him.

Chapter 33

Ptolemy

When Ptolemy and Leona entered the room, Duncan's office was nothing like he expected. A huge map of North America hung behind his desk, but slashes and a circle with an "X" marked up the state of Washington. Piles of paperwork were stacked haphazardly on most level surfaces. Photos of each of the major cities in the coven's territory graced the other three walls. The art choices and apparent disorganization was nothing like the Briton he remembered. Of course, Ptolemy's last memory of Duncan was when he had his brother and Doctor Zachary at gunpoint on the tarmac of the San Francisco International Airport, and Duncan literally wanted to rip him apart.

Duncan and Samantha rose from their chairs. Or maybe they were in the process of standing when Tiffany burst into the room ahead of Leona and Ptolemy, yelling.

"What are you talking about?" Duncan didn't seem the least bit perturbed by the interruption. His gaze shifted to Ptolemy. "It's been a few years, Your Highness."

"Yes, Master St. James." Ptolemy inclined his head, which seemed to startle Duncan.

"You two can continue your prick-waving contest later," Tiffany blurted. "Sam, what's the status on your Twinkies?"

Samantha and Duncan exchanged uncomfortable looks before Duncan turned to Leona.

"That will be all Enforcer Alvarez."

From her lack of expression, she was used to the oddities of the diet of the new master's wife. Leona closed the door behind her.

Tiffany crossed her arms, stared at the hardwood floor, and tapped the toe of her right boot.

After several long seconds, Samantha said, "She's clear. What's really going on?"

"What's the status of your demon stash?" Tiffany said, slightly less out of breath than her previous outburst.

After a very long pause, Samantha said, "I ran out yesterday."

"Fuck, that's what I was afraid of." Tiffany dropped her arms. "Alex is in Tacoma. Giovanni was spotted heading toward Washington. That as-shat knows the shit's about to hit the fan."

"Tiffany . . ." Samantha shook her head. "You guys aren't going to be able to stop this."

"We can keep Asshat and the rest of his minions off your back," Tiffany bit out.

Samantha's entire body sagged. "I appreciate this—"

"I'm doing this for Ellie, not you."

Ptolemy didn't need his vampiric abilities to recognize the anger Tiffany carried through most of her childhood.

She visibly pulled herself together before she added, "Speaking of which I need to see both of your phones. I've got some security updates to push. Last thing we need in the middle of this mess is another communications fiasco like the fae bringing down our phone system a few years ago."

Both Duncan and Samantha produced their phones without question and handed them to Tiffany. She crossed to a side table to begin her alleged work.

Ptolemy cleared his throat. "While Tiffany attends to her task, there are some things I need to say."

Duncan resumed his seat and steepled his fingers. "Go on."

His gesture was so reminiscent of Caesar's mannerisms Ptolemy almost forgot what he wanted to say. He swallowed hard before he began.

"Master St. James, I apologize for my actions toward you and for betraying the coven. I knew right from wrong. I have no excuse. The only potential recompense I can give you is my horrible second death."

Ptolemy turned to the blonde who was still standing. "Lady Samantha, a mutual acquaintance of ours, an LAPD officer I only know as F. Nguyen, asked me to relay a message to you. Please return his vintage Winnie-the-Pooh watch to his sister Tranh. He said you would know what that means. However, if you have any question as to his veracity, he said he saved your ass during the South Central riots."

The color drained from her already pale face. "Where is he?"

"Purgatory," Ptolemy said. "Or he was there the last time I saw him."

Duncan turned to his wife. "You still have not returned that watch?"

Perturbation swept across her face. "Between the cracked glass, the séance, and the sudden move to Las Vegas, it got lost in the shuffle."

"All of which happened six years ago." Despite Duncan's sour expression, there was an undertone of teasing affection in his voice. He returned his attention to Ptolemy. "How did you end up in Purgatory?"

"I didn't. I've been drifting along the shore of the River Styx since my death. No coin for the boatman."

"I am sorry," Duncan murmured.

Ptolemy shrugged. "It was a far gentler fate than I deserved."

"The Furies didn't come after you?" Samantha asked.

Ptolemy shook his head. Her question was one he'd pondered at length as he sat on his favorite rock on the shores of the Styx.

"That's weird." She rubbed the back of her neck. "After what went down in Las Vegas between the three siblings, they still should be kicking your ass."

He shivered. "I can offer no explanation other than I shielded Doctor Zachary when my sister tried to shoot her."

Duncan looked at his wife again.

She held up her hands in a defeated gesture. "If Persephone were topside, I could ask. I'm not getting my ass chewed by Cerberus to satisfy your curiosity."

"That doesn't explain why Ptolemy is here. Now." Duncan's eyes shone with an emerald light.

"Supay's using Ptolemy to sneak something to Alex." Tiffany strode past Ptolemy and handed the phones back to Samantha and Duncan.

"And you believe Ptolemy?" Samantha gestured with her phone in his direction.

"He didn't say a damn word." Tiffany propped her fists on her hips. "Supay is how we know Giovanni is on the move. The Lord of Uku Pacha has had a price on Asshat's head for the last seven years for his role in stealing Supay's tumi."

"What is he carrying?" Duncan scowled at Ptolemy, but he was fairly certain it had more to do with the Incan god than him.

"Ptolemy can't remember, and Alex and I figure the knowledge is keyed to Alex somehow." Tiffany was no longer the snotty teenager or the grieving girlfriend. This was a confident woman who could easily be chief enforcer. However, she spoke of Stanton as if they were the closest of friends.

Which threatened to drive Ptolemy into a rage until Samantha looked at him.

"I could dig it out of Ptolemy's brain," she muttered.

"No." Tiffany stepped between him and the goddess. "You're like a bull in a fucking china shop. You'll end up destroying whatever Supay's trying to send to us."

"You can't trust him—" Samantha started.

"Which him?" Tiffany cocked her head.

"Both of them." The goddess scowled at Ptolemy. Of course. Duncan hadn't painted him in the best light to his bride, but it was his own damn fault.

"Excuse me?" Tiffany marched the few feet to confront Samantha and poked the goddess's upper sternum with her right index finger. "Who's the one who keeps throwing the so-called rules in my face?"

Samantha's eyes glowed like a vampire's, but the color shifted from neon blue to a silvery white. "That doesn't mean—"

"He or any of the other gods can't help you directly against the Old One. We know." Tiffany poked Samantha again for emphasis. "They know. However, we all have a vested interest in you winning this fight, so if we have to do a sideways cheat to make sure you win, then by Murphy, we're going to fucking do it."

Tiffany took a step back. "We gotta a plane to catch. Two days, Sam. My daughter's birthday. The day after my husband died. Remember that." She whirled on her left boot heel and stomped to the door, making sure to bang it against the doorstop.

Ptolemy looked at Duncan. "It's good to know there are still some constants in the universe." He followed Tiffany out of the house. None of the enforcers tried to stop them, though they had to have heard the two women shouting at each other.

He waited until Tiffany drove out of the Brentwood neighborhood before he spoke. "Do you think telling her the truth was the wisest course of action?"

"You of all people should know the best lies are constructed out of truth."

Any wishful thinking he held about her evaporated. Caesar may have forgiven him for his past transgressions, but Tiffany never would.

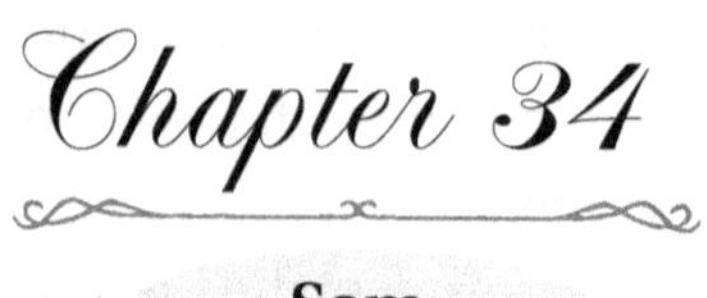

Sam

I stared at the open doorway a moment before I pivoted to face Duncan. "Now, what the hell was that all about?"

"It sounded like the same resentment Tiffany has carried for the past two years to me." He raked his right hand through his hair. "I had hoped we were getting past that, but Jake's death . . ." He shook his head, his disappointment plain.

"I'm not talking about the Max crap."

Duncan frowned as he scrolled through something on his own phone before he looked at me again. "What do you mean?"

"Why did Tiffany switch my phone for one of the same model?" I held up the device.

His frown deepened. "How can you tell?"

"Because I modified mine." I turned in the direction of the office doorway again, trying to puzzle out Tiffany's weirder than usual behavior, before I looked back at him.

His right eyebrow rose in question.

"Mine has more memory capacity than it should, and I have my deity contacts on it." I stared at the phone in my hand. "This has the regular stuff cloned from mine, but it's missing my mods."

"You are concerned Tiffany has access to your friends?" It was his polite way of tiptoeing around my relationships with the other death goddesses.

I shrugged. "Goth Girl probably could hack the lock I have on that section, but I still don't get why she didn't just tell me she was switching phones."

Leona. Connie.

Both enforcers appeared in the office doorway.

"Yes, sir?" Leona said while Connie jumped to "What's wrong?"

"Has Alex or Anne authorized a new security update for coven personnel phones?"

The two vampires looked at each other before they turned back to Duncan and shook their heads. The plastic casing squealed in my husband's grip.

"Don't!" I held up my right hand.

"Why not?" he growled. Brimstone filled the air of his office.

I searched for the right words to get through his rage at whatever scheme Ptolemy had pulled Tiffany into. Or vice versa. It wasn't often Duncan was this pissed, but when he was, his male ego usually got in the way.

"Connie, please have someone look at both mine and Master St. James's phones." I crossed to Duncan's desk, and he reluctantly handed his cell phone to me. "We have reason to believe they're infected with spyware."

I strode over to our head security trainee and gave her the phones.

"It'll be a few minutes to program the new ones from a clean backup," Connie said.

"That's fine. If Anne needs you though, that's still your top priority." I smiled before I turned to her fellow enforcer. "Leona, call Miko and tell her Tiffany and Jake are on their way to the airport per Alex's orders."

The vampire cocked her head. "What am I fishing for?"

I knew I loved these two ladies for a reason.

"Find out where our pilot has been ferrying our chief enforcer for the last day if you can."

Leona frowned. "I could simply go down to LAX and read her mind." Her expression shifted to real concern. "Unless one of our three Normal enforcers in Los Angeles is a dino demon?"

"It is not like Alex to withhold information from me," Duncan said. "I am more worried he has been compromised. Miko, Tiffany, and Jake would follow his orders without question."

My heart did a little jump. It was reassuring Duncan was taking my hunch seriously, but I didn't like his additional concern. Not one bit.

Leona's cheeks puffed out before she said. "All right. Anything else before I make the phone call, Master?"

Duncan shook his head.

Leona strode out of his office to carry out her task, but Connie hesitated.

"I was at the gate, and I pricked both Tiffany and Jake personally when they came in—"

"We know you did." I held up my hands. "This isn't about you."

A muscle in her jaw twitched. "I should be your top suspect."

"Constanza, you forget that both Sam and Yvonne Rousseau thoroughly examined you," Duncan said. "Or are you saying my wife and Master Rousseau's lied about you?"

Tears shimmered in her glowing yellow neon eyes. "I want to say no, but . . ."

"Connie, do you need to see Duke Millanthropas?" I didn't like the relationship between my protégé and the power behind the Seelie throne, but for some reason, their dark desires kept them both in check.

She shook her head. "I can play when this is done." She sucked in a deep breath to calm herself, and her irises faded to their normal brown.

I kept forgetting she was a baby when it came to being a vampire.

"Thank you for your trust, Master St. James." Her smile was tremulous, but her stride was more confident as she left the office, closing the door behind her.

I crossed back to Duncan, pushed back his chair, and sat in his lap. "Thanks for trusting me, too, Master St. James."

"Do not say that," he murmured.

"Address you by your title?" I ran my fingers through his hair. I hated his new style, but I understood why he did it. Image was everything in the Vampire Nation. He could no longer look like Caesar's hulking black knight. No, he had to appear as a modern leader.

"Yes." He took my hand and kissed the inside of my wrist. "It sounds like you are mocking me."

"Never." I kissed him lightly on the lips. "Should I pop in and check on Alex?"

"Not just yet." He frowned again. "I want to hear what story Miko gives Leona before we decide our next action."

I didn't like his decision, but I understood the strategic necessity. We needed to evaluate everything over the next few days carefully because this was a war I couldn't afford to lose.

Tiffany

I pulled up to the St. James private hangar at LAX and parked my SUV. The one small grace was not needing to haul blood with me on this trip. With that random thought, I realized Ptolemy had nothing to eat except IVs the whole night. And I hadn't eaten since lunch at the campus coffee shop. It was too late to get anything now, other than the snacks on the plane. I'd have to do drive-thru food on our way to Tacoma.

Miko was waiting for us beside the steps up to the jet, but her expression was far from her usual easy-going grin. Crap, had Supay told her who she was transporting while he was pretending to be Alex?

Someone else sat in the cockpit, but I couldn't make out who it was in the dark.

I slid out of my seat and rounded the vehicle to the rear hatch. Ptolemy joined me to get his bag, too.

"Osaka is staring at me," he whispered. "Does she have an issue with Jake?"

"Nope." I slung my bag strap over my shoulder and slammed the hatch shut. "She has an issue with you."

"I told you that you shouldn't be so honest," he hissed under his breath.

"Remember that the next time you beat up her and Mai because your big bully of a sister told you to," I shot back.

His mouth worked before he finally said, "You're right."

"It took you two thousand years to figure out you shouldn't hit people?" I rolled my eyes and charged toward Miko.

"Hey, cuz!" I smiled. "Ready to head for SeaTac?"

Her eyes narrowed as she glared at Ptolemy. "If both the coven's master and chief enforcer hadn't ordered me to fly you to Washington, I'd shove your body out of my plane somewhere over the Cascades for what you did to my sister."

"And I'm still paying for it," he murmured.

"By stealing Jake's body?" The fingers of her right hand twitched. I recognized the sign, felt it too often myself. Miko really wanted to shoot Ptolemy.

I stepped between them. "That was nearly nine years ago. I need him here and now. If you can't fly us, say so. I'll find another way to get him where Alex needs him."

The way Miko's cheeks worked, I thought she would hock a loogie over my head and into Ptolemy's face. Finally, she snapped, "I know my duty, and I'll do my job." She whirled around and boarded the plane.

I turned to face Ptolemy. "Get in there before she changes her mind."

"I'm not sure climbing into a pressurized tube while she has a loaded weapon is such a good idea," he said, staring at the open door of the jet.

"It could be worse." I shrugged. "A very pissed off goddess could show up in that pressurized tube while we're in midair if we don't get our asses out of California *now*."

"Are you this imperious with all of your significant others?" he asked.

"I don't have to be." I smirked despite the jab to my heart. "Max and Jake obeyed me because they knew what was good for them."

I turned and jogged up the steps of the plane. I needed to focus on the mission and grieve for Jake later. My lie to Sam about the timing would hopefully distract her long enough for us to get to Washington and set the trap. A week without dino demon meat sounded about right for her to lose control, but my estimate was based on her appetite two years ago. How much had she been eating lately?

While Phil and Ares would do anything to protect Ellie, they couldn't handle an Old One. Not by themselves anyway. Which meant we had to help Supay.

Ptolemy followed me on board the jet and immediately flopped down in one of the seats. Some things simply didn't change. I shook my head, pulled up the door, and sealed it. Why the hell did I ever have a crush on that asshat? I tossed my bag in the storage closet and headed for the cockpit.

"Where are you going?"

I turned around to find Ptolemy peering around the edge of the chair.

"I'm relieving Miko. Alex probably has her at the federally mandated time limit for pilots."

He frowned. "You have a pilot's license?"

"It's been nine fucking years." I cocked my head, but I managed to keep any other insults from blasting through my mental filter. "Things change."

I pivoted and marched into the cockpit. To my surprise, Colin Fitzgerald sat in the pilot's seat.

"What the hell are you doing here?"

"Like you told Ptolemy, Miko needs a statutory break." A wry smile tilted his mouth. "And from what Sam said, you've been awake nearly twenty-four hours." He shrugged. "Anne and Connie are in full disaster prep, so my wife very politely suggested I get out of her fucking face by helping Miko ferry evacuees from the SeaTac area."

"Anne didn't actually use the f-word."

"Believe it or not, she did."

I chuckled. Anne had to be stressed to the max right now. But I sobered when I realized he knew that wasn't Jake in the passenger compartment.

"You know."

"Yep." He turned back to his pre-flight checklist.

I tapped Miko on the shoulder. "Go get some sleep."

She stood and scooched past me, a scowl still plastered to her face.

"Without killing our passenger," I added.

"Can I hurt him a little?"

"No."

"Killjoy." She stomped toward the back of the plane. I watched to make sure she didn't do something I'd regret, but she settled for merely giving Ptolemy a dirty look as she passed him.

When she entered the sleeping compartment, I sighed and closed the cockpit door.

"So Duncan told you," I said as I slipped into the co-pilot's chair.

"About Ptolemy?" Colin chuckled again. "That's the real reason I'm here. I don't have a personal beef with him since he died before I joined the coven." He grinned, his fangs prominent in the slight yellow glow from his eyes. "But I understand why everyone would hate his guts. Alex seems to be the only one keeping his head straight in this mess, but Duncan and Sam aren't happy he lied to them about Head's participation. Miko's relieved everything's out in the open."

I paused in putting on my headset. "Wait. Alex finally talked to Duncan?"

Colin's grin faded. "That's what Miko got from Leona."

Why all the need for secrecy if Supay was going to blab everything else to Duncan and Sam anyway? I put on the headset.

"What's wrong?" Colin asked.

"I don't know what game my stepfather is playing," I said. "But I'm going to kick his ass when I see him."

I helped Colin with the rest of the preflight checklist. A half hour later, our little jet circled northward, climbing toward the dawn.

And I tried very hard to think about the football season, Ellie's upcoming ballet recital, and my winter holiday gift list. Anything to keep Colin from poking further into my mind and finding the truth of why Ptolemy and I were heading to Tacoma.

Chapter 36

Sam

"Thanks, Colin. I owe you a dinner at Anthony's once you can eat solid food again." I hung up on the call, wolfed down my third breakfast, and headed for Duncan's office.

Bebe, Caesar, and Duncan had kept my dinner situation from the coven enforcers. Until now, only Ares had suspected how close I was to running out of the one thing keeping my hunger and my sanity in check. The god offered to accompany me hunting for the dino demon who'd escaped in Otherwhere. Of course, Duncan threw a fit about that idea. Or as much of a fit his stiff British lip would allow.

I should have known a certified genius like Goth Girl would have figured out the truth.

Maybe I was lying to myself about why I allowed my new girlfriends over to Tiffany's house. Yeah, I was a little squicked by Jake and Tiffany's relationship, but maybe I was really worried about Ellie's safety. I'd saved the last bit of demon meat for breakfast yesterday, but I didn't know if it would be enough to squelch my appetite until Tiffany or Jake got home. If I lost it, I trusted Morrigan to teleport Ellie to safety while the other gals would hold me down and call for help. It was kind of nice the deities of death had a bond that went beyond their respective pantheons.

When I slipped inside Duncan's office, Anne was giving Taalish and Duncan the rundown of her and Connie's preparations so far.

"Donna refuses to leave Seattle when Waldo's staying." Anne sighed. "But he's staying because Libbie is. The witch friend she told us about is actually Blue Hawk's lessor earth elder. Sylvia's evacuating everyone except the adult earth and water talents and a handful of the air talents. She says they have a plan to save the Normals who can't get out of the Sound if the people can make it to downtown Seattle. Roughly half of the Were Alliance adults are staying along with our enforcers to protect the witches and Normals from Giovanni and his allies."

Taalish shook his head. "Why would Giovanni waste his time with people who aren't a threat to his master?"

"What if you downed a case of Red Bull?" I grimaced. "That's what all that soul energy would do for the Old One. Even worse, the psychopomps will be trying to collect the souls, and they're a better source of power. If the people aren't dying, the psychopomps won't show up. No deaths and no psychopomps means no additional juice for the Old One. All of which comes to Asshat and his minions will need to stop the witches."

I glanced at Duncan's map. My lines and circles still covered the State of Washington. "But how the hell are the earth witches going to protect the Normals? The whole region is going to turn to Jell-O when the Old One breaks into our dimension."

"Essentially surfing." Anne rose from her chair and crossed to the map. She stood on her toes and tapped the line I'd drawn through downtown Seattle. "They believe if they can collect everyone on the north section, they can ride that bit of crust through the worst shocks. With the current winds projected for the next few days, they will have some ash fall, but it will be manageable with the assistance of the wind talents staying behind."

"That's not going to stop the lahars," I murmured.

"The lahars of the largest know eruption of Rainier went as far as Lake Washington and Tacoma." Anne traced both paths with her index finger. "Through Family, the United States Geological Survey has issued a mandatory evacuation of Tacoma and the towns surrounding the mountain, but that's going to clog the roads for everyone north of Tacoma."

"What about the tsunami?" Duncan asked.

"The height of the tsunami depends of the depth of the water, and Puget Sound is relatively shallow." Anne dragged her index finger down the length of the body in question. "The plan is the water witches will siphon off the energy of the wave and transfer it to the earth witches. In turn, some of the earth witches will drop the bottom of the Sound itself, deepening it while the rest raise the northern section of Seattle and keep that sliver of land relatively stable. Most of the islands in the Sound will probably end up underwater, and they'll sacrifice southern Seattle."

"They are bat-shit crazy." Taalish stared at the map with wide eyes.

But Duncan slowly nodded. "It might work. We do not want a repeat of Hurricane Rita where there were more Normal fatalities from heat and stress during Houston's evacuation. Anne, tell Donna she can stay if she wishes. However—" He gestured at the map. "Any coven member who does stay remains in Seattle at their own risk. Ash and debris will cut off contact for days. Possibly weeks. Tell her to make sure she's stocked with water, blood, and food. If even one vampire drinks from any Normal during this crisis because they refused to evacuate, I will, to quote my wife, get medieval on their ass."

"That's actually a Quentin Tarantino quote," I whispered.

Taalish chuckled while Anne rolled her eyes.

Duncan simply ignored me. "Taalish, start recruiting independent pilots and planes. We'll send supplies up to Donna during our ferrying trips."

"Yes, sir." He stood and left the office.

"Colin called you?" Anne's expression was hopeful despite the dark circles ringing her big brown eyes. She probably hadn't consumed any blood at all during the night.

I nodded before I met Duncan's gaze. "We were right. Tiffany knew about Head being out of the coma, but Colin thinks she knows more about whatever Alex is planning."

Duncan leaned forward in his executive office chair. "He read her mind?"

"No." I shrugged. "This was good, old-fashioned body language reading by an experienced attorney. Unlike Miko, Tiffany wasn't relieved that Alex allegedly spoke with you. It seemed to make her more tense."

Duncan leaned his right elbow on a bare spot of his desk, his chin resting on his thumb and third finger of his hand while his index finger tapped his lips. Whatever he was thinking, he wasn't sharing it with me, telepathically or otherwise.

"Look, I can teleport up there—"

"No," he snapped as he straightened. At both mine and Anne's scowls, his own expression softened. "I apologize for my tone, darling. You will be in the middle of a battle soon enough. I do not want to endanger you earlier than necessary."

"I hate to say this, Master." Soft pink spots highlighted Anne's pale cheeks. "But we don't know what's really going on in Seattle with our chief enforcer. I don't like to even think this—"

"Alex wouldn't betray Duncan," I bit out.

"Do we know this person is our Alex?" she said softly.

Duncan's nostrils flared. He released his breath and nodded. "Your point is taken, Anne. Tiffany's own questions on the matter may be what Colin detected."

I flung my hand in the direction of Seattle on Duncan's map. "Which makes it imperative one of us finds out what the hell is going on up there."

Duncan looked at the map. His right index finger lay across his lips again, his favorite thinking pose since he became coven master. "Let's wait and see what Tiffany uncovers."

I aimed for a different tactic. "Do you really want Tiffany in danger if that isn't Alex?"

"Are you not the one who told me multiple times I needed to let her grow up and make her own decisions?" he said.

"I wasn't referring to dumb, suicidal ones! Anne—" I looked around the office, but the diminutive vampire was gone. "When did she leave?"

"Around the point you started shouting at me," he said dryly.

"I wasn't shouting!"

At his raised eyebrow, I lowered my voice. "I wasn't shouting then."

Duncan pushed to his feet and enveloped me in his arms. "Let us get some sleep. If we don't hear from Tiffany soon, I won't stop you from teleporting to Seattle."

"First smart thing I've heard you say," I mumbled into his suit jacket. Leaning my head back, I looked into his eyes. "You know, I could just go anyway."

"Yes." His expression turned somber. "But when you come back, it will be after your battle with the Old One. I don't know what you will be, and it . . . scares me."

"It does me, too." I pulled his head down for a long, deep kiss. Maybe that was the real reason I hadn't gone to Seattle anyway. I was as frightened as my husband was about what I would become once this war was over.

Chapter 37

Tiffany

The caffeine I'd been chugging on the drive started to wear off about the time we hit the road up to the safehouse. I had caught a nap on the flight to SeaTac. Colin needed the solo hours towards his license anyway. But the couple of hours of sleep hadn't been quite enough.

On the other hand, Ptolemy was far from sleepy. It had been an unusually sunny day at the airport for October. Once we'd hit the freeway, he rolled down the window on his side of the SUV the Seattle daytime enforcers had brought to the hangar for us. Donna had also sent blood with the vehicle. I hadn't said a damn word, so Colin must have called ahead. In a way, I was glad someone was actually thinking of Alex's body, even if they didn't know about the god riding him.

Ptolemy seemed hypnotized by the play of sunlight on his arm as I drove. Hell, I had to remind him to put on his sunglasses. The dumbass was trying to stare at the sun without any protection. Luckily, the St. James members at the airport chalked it up to Jake's head injury. For once, I was happy the coven grapevine worked so fast.

"Why does St. James have so few pilots?" Ptolemy said.

I'd gotten so used to the wind whistling through the passenger compartment being the only sound during the drive that his voice startled me. I glanced at him before I answered. "There's been a number of deaths over the years."

"Who rules Las Vegas now?"

"Why the questions all of the sudden?" I said.

"A morbid sense of curiosity." But he sounded like that curiosity was genuine.

I sighed. "As far as pilots go, Jamal died during the zombie invasion at mine and Max's first wedding."

"First wedding?"

"The attack happened before the minister could finish. Then some dumbass decided wiping his memory was a good idea before he signed the paperwork. At that point, it was easier to go down to the courthouse and have a judge do it."

"That makes slightly more sense."

I ignored Ptolemy's color commentary. "Kensai was killed during Duncan's rescue. Both deaths were courtesy of David Head, the necromancer currently with Supay."

"Duncan's rescue?"

"Head had a crush on Duncan. After Selene was killed—"

"You mean after your uncle murdered my sister," he said.

I shot Ptolemy a dirty look. "I hate to tell you this, but I was there. And she was doing her damnedest to strangle me at the time, so excuse me for not being sympathetic."

After a moment of silence, he said, "I'm sorry. After Selene died, Head thought he was free to pursue Duncan?"

"Yeah, but by then, Duncan and Sam were an item." I shook my head at the memory. "Somewhere along the way, the dino demons got their hooks into Head. Turned his crush into a full-blown stalking obsession. Head sent zombies to my bachelorette party, my rehearsal dinner, and my wedding with the plan to kill Sam and kidnap Duncan. He succeeded in the abduction on the third try. By then, he'd cut a deal with the Seelie queen."

"Trying to start a war?" Ptolemy asked.

"That's what the dino demons hoped for. However, Sam bound Head's powers so tight he ended up in a coma. Duke Millanthropas realized what Sam was and staged a coup to prevent his queen from starting said war. Finally, Siobhan Lannigan-Sifuentes, the duke, and I managed to hammer out a treaty between the Vampire Nation and the Fae Courts."

"You? Negotiating on behalf of the coven?"

I didn't need to see his incredulous expression. I could feel it. "Nine years," I reminded him.

"And Las Vegas?" he prompted.

I grinned because I knew how much this news would piss off Ptolemy. "Right now, Stan and Mai."

"There's not even a vampire in charge? Is St. James insane?" In my peripheral vision, his hands made jerky motions as he continued. "Caesar's penchant for mutts is bad enough. Why would St. James expand on that idiocy? He's setting himself up for a takeover—"

"Like the one you and your sister tried to pull?"

At my comment, Ptolemy's hands dropped to his lap. He remained silent until I braked in front of the steel traffic bollards that guarded the last half mile of road in addition to the spikes on the rock wall surrounding the estate.

"I tried to stop her," he said softly.

"Really?" I glared at him. "Was that before or after she ordered my parents killed?"

Of course he didn't have the grace to look at me.

"What are you really planning to do here, Ptolemy?" I choked the words out. "Meet up with Marcus and have him bite you?"

"No!" Ptolemy's head whipped around to face me.

It was the answer I wanted. That didn't mean it was the truth. I waited.

Finally, he looked at his hands clasped on his lap and said, "They told me this was my chance to redeem myself. That if I helped them, maybe I can cross the River Styx when, when . . ."

"When this body falls apart," I said softly.

"They did something so I can stay in Jake's body longer than a regular ghost could, but I know my time here is short. I'm not wasting three days of it in a V-virus coma."

This was the first time I felt like I was having a conversation with the real Ptolemy Antonius, even if he was in Jake Wong's body. And for the first time, vulnerability appeared on his expression. How much of his bullshit behavior had been a front for the scared eighteen-year-old kid he'd been when he was accidentally Turned? Was he so afraid of being alone that he'd follow his sister to the gates of Hades because his big brother had fallen in love and left him behind?

I blew out a deep breath. "Did they say how many days?"

He shook his head, still not meeting my gaze.

I snagged my phone from the console and punched the speed dial for Alex's number.

"Yes?"

"We're here. We have it. Drop the bollards."

The steel pillars dropped into their slots. I drove through the opening. The bollards immediately snapped into place behind us. I continued up the drive.

"I don't remember this place being the Tacoma safe house," Ptolemy murmured.

"Alex and I put this refuge together along with a couple of others after you and your sister's last coup attempt. We needed someplace she didn't know about." I glanced at him. Dark pink flushed his cheeks.

Something that had been bothering me for the last nine years blurted out before I could stop it. "Why did you save Bebe if you believed she was going destroy the vampires?"

"I don't know."

"Or you don't want to admit you knew Selene was wrong from the beginning?" When he didn't answer, I shook my head. "I never figured you for the world domination type."

"What's that supposed to mean?" he snapped.

"World War II."

Another glance at him showed his mouth hanging open. "Caesar never found out which supernaturals were aiding the Nazis."

"Well, duh," I drawled. "You and Selene played him pretty good."

"I . . . she . . ."

The second stone wall appeared. Razor wire guarded the top of this one. The steel gate swung open, which meant Supay used the cameras and all of Alex's knowledge to keep an eye out for us.

I drove through, and Ptolemy gasped as he took in the place. On the surface, it looked like some billionaire's weekend retreat, but underneath was a reinforced bunker built into the granite. It may be smaller, but it could give NORAD's base at Cheyenne Mountain a run for its money when the upstairs shutters were closed. The only way to get here besides the road we took was by helicopter.

Or teleportation. Thank Murphy, the dino demons couldn't or didn't know how.

"I didn't know about Selene's involvement with the rogues during World War II," Ptolemy finally said.

I braked the SUV before the second door of the huge garage, turned, and glared at him. "She wasn't just involved. She was their leader."

The garage door slid up, and I drove inside. I almost started laughing when Ptolemy waited until the garage door closed and the space was sealed from daylight.

"Really? After leaving the window open the entire fucking drive?" I bit my tongue, shook my head, and climbed out of the vehicle. I pretended not to notice his embarrassed flush while I retrieved my bag and the cooler of blood.

He stood by the door into the bunker. "You know you're asking me to change two thousand years of keeping myself alive."

I held my palm against the print reader. With a *schnickt*, the lock released, and I yanked open the door. As I passed through the coat room to the kitchen, I muttered, "You're lucky you're still alive now."

"So Alexander's concern over you harming the ghost was warranted."

Air froze in my lungs. Like Ptolemy, the voice was familiar and unfamiliar at the same time.

Alex stood in the entryway to the rest of the bunk, his arms crossed and his stance wide. Except it wasn't my boss/stepfather looking at me.

"It's not me you have to worry about. It's the rest of the coven." I set my bag on one of the kitchen chairs and took the cooler to the refrigerator. "When was the last time you drank?"

He scowled at me. "You will treat me with respect, mortal."

"Dude—" I propped my hands on my hips. "—my sister-in-law is a colleague of yours, and I will treat you with the same respect I treat her."

Something chased the rage off his face, and he burst out laughing. "I would have assumed your cocky attitude was due to your relationship with a certain Olympian, but Alexander says you have always been like this."

"May I please speak with my stepfather, Lord Supay?"

"Alas, you cannot, child." He shook his head. "Alexander swore an oath to me. I am collecting on the remainder of that oath."

Of course, I couldn't. Would Alex be all right once this shit was over? However, there really wasn't a damn thing I could do at this point except to see Armageddon through and hope we came out relatively intact on the other side.

I exhaled and nodded. "All right, but I respectfully request that you care for his body while you are using it." I pulled out a pint of cow blood before I placed the rest of the bottles in the fridge rack.

Supay was still smirking as I poured the cow blood into a mug and stuck it in the microwave. I punched the timer and turned to him.

This whole time, Ptolemy stood there like the proverbial deer in the headlights. However, I could only deal with one possessed person at a time.

"Does Head have everything ready?"

"Do you have the totem?" Supay retorted.

I crossed to my bag, unzipped it, and retrieved Sam's phone. "You don't have long. She's on to us. The reason she's not here yet is because she's still trying to figure out what Alex and I are up to."

"She doesn't know I'm involved?" Supay asked.

"Not yet, so don't touch her phone." The microwave beeped, and I set the phone on the table. "Ptolemy, you'd better not fucking touch it either."

"I don't understand." A perplexed expression twisted his face.

"Because if Supay touches it, *she's* going to know another god has it." I poked the button for the microwave door and pulled out the mug. "And since multiple gods had a hand in bringing you back from the dead, you might trigger the same reaction."

I handed the mug to Supay. He took a sip and made a disgusted face.

"This isn't human blood," he protested.

"You're supposed to be Alex, remember?" I grabbed Sam's phone and my bag. "If I brought human blood, the coven would definitely know something weird was going on."

I headed into the living area. "Head!"

"Yes?" He came out of the right hallway.

David Head no longer looked like the hottest star in professional basketball, and it wasn't just the lack of wild hair color. His curls were gray now, and he walked with the aid of a white cane. His motions were that of an elderly man. He wore gray sweatpants and a black t-shirt, both of which hung off his emaciated frame.

This was the asshole who ordered zombies to attack my wedding guests. I almost lost Ellie and Max in that battle. So many other people died that day, including Jamal. My cousins lost both of their fucking fathers within a couple of days because this jerk's actions.

Next thing I knew, my bag and Sam's phone hit the floor, and my new Glock was aimed at Head.

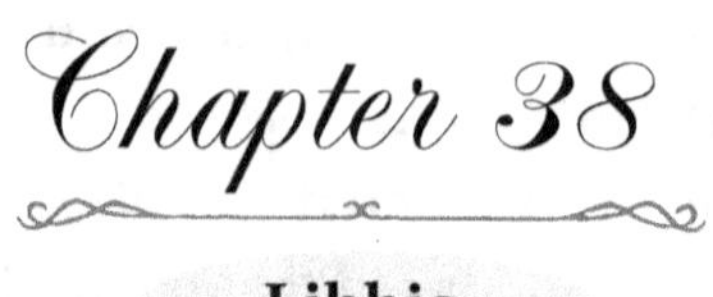

Chapter 38

Libbie

I stared forlornly at my book collection. I wanted to save them all, but I couldn't. If Angela was right, and I didn't doubt one bit that she was, there simply wasn't enough time. The cottage would be underwater in less than six days, assuming the tsunami didn't sweep it and the main house off the island.

"Honey?" Waldo crossed my office and stood beside me.

"I can't decide." I gestured hopelessly at the shelves.

"Then may I make a suggestion?" He reached up and pulled a volume from the shelf with my own titles. "Take the one that was nominated for a Pulitzer. It's my favorite."

His thoughtfulness touched me, and my eyes stung.

I leaned my head on his shoulder. "I can't believe we worked so hard on this place, and it'll be gone next week."

"I know, honey." He wrapped his arm around my waist. "But we have enough forewarning we can save our important documents and the smaller mementoes." He looked around my office. "We don't have much time. The ferry leaves soon."

Waldo swallowed hard before he continued, "Is there anything I can do to change your mind about staying?"

I lifted my head. "No, so stop it. You enforcers are going to need aerial surveillance to pick out stragglers heading for the main shelter and to recon the area once the show's over." A weak laugh burbled from my throat. "Do you think the ancient covens and Families tried to evacuate Naples Bay before the '79 eruption of Vesuvius?"

"I don't know." He chuckled. "Do you want me to call Master St. James and ask?"

"No." I sighed. "If we survive all this, I'll ask Mrs. St. James or Mr. Augustine. They've been working on a comprehensive history of the vampires for the last few years."

"I didn't know that."

"I think somehow Mr. Augustine had his own premonition he wouldn't last much longer after his brother and sister died." I took the book from Waldo and slid it into my laptop case. "Everything else is packed, and I have multiple backups of my work. I just wished I could have finished the excavation of the Seattle Underground." I slung the strap of my case over my shoulder.

"We'll find you another project that excites you, honey." Waldo twined his fingers between mine. Together, we walked through the cottage for what was probably the last time.

Once outside, Waldo paused and locked the front door. The superfluous gesture made me giggle despite the tears threatening to spill.

He grinned at me and shrugged. "Force of habit."

We walked down the steps together and paused to kiss before we each climbed into our respective vehicles. The caravans of weres, witches, and Family would need them for the trip south on I-5 even if Waldo and I were staying.

I glanced in the rearview mirror for one last view of our dream farm as I drove down the lane. Only then did I let the tears roll down my cheeks.

Chapter 39

Tiffany

My hands were steady as I aimed at Head, even though the rest of me shook.

"Tiffany Jane Stephens, put down your weapon."

I ignored Supay. Even with Alex's vampire speed, I'd get one shot off before he could reach me.

Jake's face appeared between me and Head. Not Jake any longer. Ptolemy.

"Tiffany, listen to Supay." He held up his hands. "I know you're upset about Jamal and Kensai's deaths. Killing Head isn't going to bring them back."

"You didn't see the slaughter at my wedding." My finger was on the trigger. Part of me knew this was a stupid stunt on my part. I didn't expect the visceral hate when I saw the asshat's face again.

"Then you need to kill me, too," Ptolemy said softly. He lowered his hands.

I didn't know what to say.

"Tiffany, I've done far worse than Head. The Old Ones twisted his love. He didn't know what he was doing. I did." He thumped his right fist against his chest. "I knew she had her men kill your parents. It doesn't matter I thought she merely used the chaos from the other attacks that night to cover her tracks. I could have said something to Caesar, and I didn't."

My throat tightened, and I blinked at the wetness blurring my vision.

"I'm the reason she kept coming after you." He closed his eyes. "She knew I'd fallen in love with you. She couldn't handle that any more than she could handle Caesar falling for Bebe. I knew what she was doing, and I still didn't say anything!"

His eyes opened. "I'm a coward. You have every right under all the gods to shoot me, but I'm begging you not to hurt the witch. He was manipulated by your dinosaur demons, and Lord Supay still needs him. I wasn't tricked or used like Head was. The task the gods gave me is complete. Take your revenge on me."

The barrel of my Glock quivered. He was right and wrong at the same time. I wanted to hate him, but I just couldn't.

"Tiffany Jane Stevens, may I give you one truth before you decide to use your weapon?" Supay asked. His voice seemed very far away and very close.

I tried to answer, but my vocal refused to work. I settled for a slight nod.

"Your husband's sister didn't tell you the truth about the night of your wedding because she did not wish to cause more pain, but there is something you should know. Both Maxwell Theodore Howell and the daughter you carried were supposed to die during Head's attack on the night of your wedding. In her efforts to save her own mate, she saved their lives."

"Wh-what are you saying?" I choked out. I couldn't look at him. I knew I'd go insane if I did.

"She had already interfered with your husband's death once. She could not do it a second time. Not without . . . repercussions."

"D-does this mean Ellie—"

"Has it occurred to you that her relationships with us are her way of protecting your daughter?"

My arms dropped at the overload of truth in my brain.

"I'm assuming y'all brought her totem?" Head asked softly.

"Yes," Ptolemy answered, but his attention remained on me.

"We need to get this set up now," Head said. "The authorities are already putting out disaster alerts."

My hands were still shaking as I holstered my weapon. Why didn't Sam just tell me what the hell was going on?

Because you didn't give her a chance to, my conscience whispered.

Silently, I gathered the phone and my bag before I followed Head down the steps to the basement room we'd set up with a silver pentacle for Bebe. Only when we entered Bebe's emergency workshop did I realize Ptolemy had one arm wrapped around me for the entire walk.

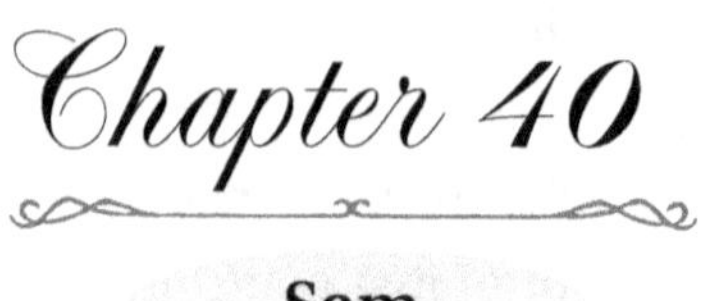

Chapter 40

Sam

Despite Duncan's best efforts, I couldn't sleep. It didn't help that sex felt like one last desperate act between us. But being a guy, my husband was fast asleep minutes afterward. So I grabbed a change of clothes and the phone Tiffany had switched for mine and headed into our bathroom.

There was a time when cleaning up and dressing after sex with nothing but a thought had been pretty awesome. Now, though?

Now, I took a shower the slow, manual way. The way every other human on the planet took a shower. Maybe this would remind me of what I was fighting for when I went totally off my rocker. Because what else would I have to be to go head-to-head with a god millions of years older than me.

The cramps in my gut hit me, and I had to lean against the shower wall. This wasn't a quick few seconds of pain like it had been before I realized I could eat the dino demons. I slowly sat, water sluicing off my head and into my eyes. I hugged my knees to my chest at the knives that seemed to carve through my intestines. More to keep myself from smashing up our bathroom. The cramps hadn't been this bad when I first woke up in the basement of Mallory Labs.

Slowly, the agony receded, and I could uncurl from my fetal position. I carefully stood, finished rinsing off the soap, and turned off the spigot. Did I tell Duncan about what just happened?

I snatched my towel off the rack and stared at the black terrycloth. I'd ruined most of his towels the night he took me to his townhouse. The night I died. I'd bled all over them from a pointblank gunshot wound to my chest. I literally had a hole in me.

Then I woke up, and my entire death changed everything I thought I knew.

No, I wouldn't tell him. Duncan had put up with my shit for the last seven years. He had more than enough to worry about for the next few days. Not to mention, we were both troubled about the outcome of this battle with the Old One.

Hell, I had my own doubts about defeating this thing. As my buddy Fred pointed out years ago, I was one dumbass kid thinking I could waltz into the middle of a riot, take some pictures, and not get hurt. This time, I was going to wade into trouble with no illusions.

I towel-dried and braided my damp hair, before I pulled on my jeans and favorite P!nk t-shirt. I chose it to remind myself I needed to be one badass bitch when the shit started. The new phone rang as I finished tying my athletic shoes. I checked the call ID. As I suspected, it was Tiffany.

I pressed the button and steeled myself. "Hey, anything new?"

"Don't fuck with me." Her snort came through loud and clear. "I know that you know Head's awake and here in Tacoma."

"Oh, so now you decided to come clean," I spat back.

"I'm no fan of his either." She lowered her voice. "I don't have much time. Head's not the problem. The guy here is not Alex. I need you to get your ass up here and 'port Ptolemy and Head out of the safehouse."

Tension ran along my neck and shoulders. "What about you?"

"I've got a clip of special recipe bullets with his name on them. I need to find out where Giovanni is keeping Alex."

"I can help with that." The sudden urge to eat the bastard disguised as Alex took me by surprise. I shoved down the feeling, but it was difficult.

"Figured you might want to."

I could envision the maniacal gleam in Tiffany's eyes.

"You got my location?" she asked.

"Yes."

"Give me five seconds to get away from my phone," she whispered. "I don't want him to see you 'port in until the guys are clear."

I sucked in a deep breath. I didn't relish having to deal with David Head again, but I knew I'd have to eventually. Bindings simply didn't last long on a necromancer. Something about their ability degrades the spell. I was lucky Head had stayed bound for the last seven years.

"No problem." I ended the call and counted out the seconds.

At five-Mississippi, I twisted space-time from my bathroom to the point where Tiffany's phone signal had terminated. Green and black diamonds flared in my eyesight, blinding me, and I fell flat on my ass.

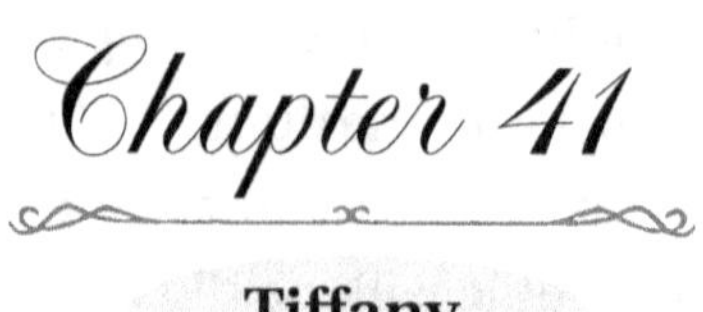

Chapter 41

Tiffany

I raised my hands to shield my eyes from the flare of green and sparkly black light. Ozone stung my nose. If Head's superpowered circle couldn't hold Sam, we were all in deep shit.

"What the fuck!" she screeched.

I blinked, but a few spots of white and orange still danced in my vision.

"Tiffany! What the ever-loving fuck!" Sam climbed to her feet. "David Head, when I get my hands on you—" Her tirade stopped momentarily. "Supay? You're in on this, too?"

"It was necessary," he said.

She cocked her right arm and punched the shield. Green and black sparks flared and died at the point of impact. Another wave of ozone filled the windowless room. When the light show stopped, I could see the bones in her fist knit themselves back together. The sight made me want to hurl.

"A blood circle?" Sam stared at the floor. "With human and vampire blood? Are you all insane? Please tell me you didn't sacrifice someone."

"The donations were voluntary," Ptolemy said.

"Dammit, people! You need to let me out!" Sam's stomach rumbled.

"You've got two cases of Twinkies in there to take the edge off," I said.

"You don't understand!"

I crossed my arms and glared at her. "I understand perfectly. Both my former coven master and my current one covered for you when it came to how close you are to completely losing control because you're out of demon meat. You lied to me about why you wouldn't save Max. And you're lying to yourself, Sam. You're a danger to every human on the planet, both Normal and supernatural."

"Not if I eat enough." She held out her hands in a pleading gesture.

Ptolemy stepped up beside me. "Did you return the watch to Tranh?"

Sam drew back at the sudden shift of topics. "What?"

"Officer Nguyen asked you to return his watch to his sister," Ptolemy prompted.

Her gaze dropped. "Not yet."

"Wait a minute." I glanced at Ptolemy before I looked at her again. I should have paid closer attention to Ptolemy and Sam's conversation back in Los Angeles while I was stealing her phone. "Is this the same watch Fred Nguyen asked you to return during the séance with Bebe?"

"Yes," Sam snapped. A blue glow emanated from her eyes. "I haven't returned it yet. I've been a little busy."

"For the last seven years? How fucking self-centered are you?" I could only stare at the bitch in disbelief.

"Samantha—" Supay shook his head. "Those in our position must keep our promises, even if the promise is to those souls we have not collected."

"How do I know he isn't lying about talking to Fred?" Sam jabbed a finger in Ptolemy's direction.

"I'm not." Ptolemy's tone was both hurt and offended. I could kind of understand why. He'd been trying to make amends to the people he harmed since he returned. Sam didn't have a real reason to hate him, not like the rest of us. This was just her pissy attitude. He turned on his heel and strode out of the room.

Sam shook her head. "I can get why Head would stab me in the back. Or Supay. Or hell, even Ptolemy. What I don't get, Tiffany, is why you would put Ellie's very existence at risk! Do you understand what will happen if you keep me in here?"

"Yeah, I do." I just couldn't deal with all the shit thrust upon me over the last twenty-four hours. I pivoted and followed Ptolemy out of the room.

⬥❈⬥

I didn't expect to find Ptolemy in the kitchen. I figured he'd go hide in the bedroom he'd claimed. It's what he would have done when he was still alive—hid and pouted.

I used to think he was ancient, tortured and romantic. Murphy, I was an idiot as a teenager. I hoped Ellie didn't do anything remotely close to the stupid shit Max and I had done as kids.

Of course, if the Old One killed Sam, none of us would live long enough to find out.

I crossed the kitchen and fished a cola out of the first refrigerator. I wasn't sure how Alex kept this place stocked and cleaned. He had to have told someone else about it. The most logical explanation would be Grandpa Ares. Neither Alex nor I could be out of touch with the rest of the coven long enough to accomplish the task.

"Why are you making faces?" Ptolemy watched me from the table where he nursed a bottle of guava juice.

"I just realized my foster grandfather has been using this bunker as his booty call getaway."

"Is that so bad?" he asked.

"He's been doing booty calls for millennia." I shrugged and unscrewed the cap off my soda and took a swig. "I don't see how I'd be able to change him now."

I gestured at Ptolemy's juice. "Aren't you hungry?"

"Yes." He played with his bottle cap. "I wasn't sure what to try next."

I laughed. "Not a fan of my peanut butter and jelly sandwiches."

A wry smile crossed his face. "They tasted more like a dessert than a meal."

"Well, let's start with the next basic comfort food—mac and cheese." I pulled open the pantry door. Most of the stock was canned goods, dry goods, and MREs, but there were a few doubled-sized boxes of my favorite brand of macaroni and cheese. I grabbed a box and the package of powdered milk.

A quick check of the second refrigerator verified that Ares had indeed brought lady friends up here. There was real butter and a package of feta cheese. I was so giving him shit the next time I saw him. Not in front of Phil of course, but still.

I pulled out a jug to mix the milk and a pan to boil the macaroni.

"Man, I haven't had that shit in so long." Head plopped down at the table next to Ptolemy. "May I please have some, too, Ms. Stephens?"

"Well, since you said please." It felt damn weird cooking for my dead crush and the necromancer who killed, tortured, or maimed a good chunk of my family, but then, my entire life had been one weirdfest after another.

I measured out the water and powdered milk into the jug before I carried it and a large spoon over to Head. "Make yourself useful and stir this."

"Yes, ma'am."

"I take it you got tired of Sam's whining, too," I said as I filled the pan with water.

"No, Lord Supay told me to get something to eat and some sleep. He said he'd watch her while I did," Head said. "FYI, he's planning to leave at sundown."

"Leave?" I flipped on the burner before I turned to look at him. "Did he say why?"

"To fulfill his mission." Head smashed a large clump of powder against the side of the jug with the spoon. "Don't ask me what it is. I don't question gods."

"They don't tell you the whole story anyway if you do ask," Ptolemy said.

The sad part was both men were right. A long time ago, I could have counted on the gods in my life, but now I was an accessory in kidnapping one. Sort of like how Grandpa Ares had been abducted by the dino demons years ago.

I found the salt, roughly measured it in my cupped palm, and dumped about two teaspoons into the heating water. Gods weren't the only ones who didn't tell the whole truth. I grabbed the box of mac and cheese, ripped off the top, and tossed the powdered cheese packet on the counter. I'd lost count of the number of times—

Shit! Alex mentioned Francisco Chavez, the Lima Coven's chief enforcer, had struck a deal with Supay. What if Alex had done the same damn stupid thing?

I turned to the men sitting at the kitchen table. "Ptolemy, dump the macaroni into the pan when the water boils. Turn the heat down to medium and stir occasionally. I'll be right back." I charged out of the kitchen.

I was halfway down the basement corridor to our makeshift jail when the concrete rocked and cracked beneath my shoes.

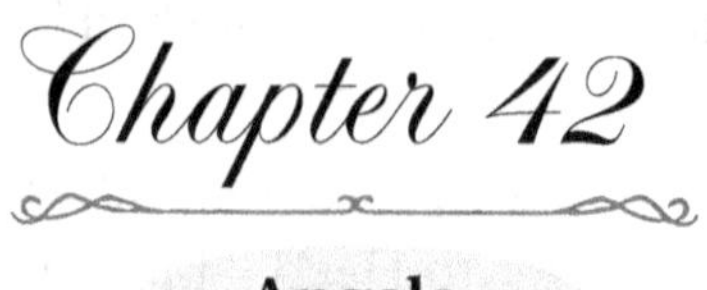

Chapter 42

Angela

Angela had just turned over the last card of her reading when the wood strips of their living room floor rippled beneath her bare feet, and keepsakes rattled and chimed on their shelves. Everything settled by the time she counted to four though she heard more than one car alarm blaring in the neighborhood.

"Is this it?" Jim said breathlessly. He leaned over the staircase railing. "Do we need to head downtown?"

Angela looked up from her tarot cards and flashed him a reassuring smile despite her own nerves dancing under her skin. "Not quite yet, honey. That wasn't even Rainier clearing his throat."

"You sure?" The sour taste of worry and concern emanated from him.

"Yes, but something's happened to change the timetable." She tapped the Two of Swords. "I need to make some phone calls. Is Priscilla in her carry crate?"

Jim held up his forearms, showing some nasty looking scratches from the cat. "What do you think I was trying to do when the tremor hit?"

Angela bit the side of her cheek to keep from laughing at his misfortunate timing. When she was sure she wouldn't so much as chuckle, she said, "Let me make my calls, and I'll come help."

"No." He came down the last few steps. "Make your calls. I'll open a can of tuna."

The high priestess had given Angela permission to contact the vampire master and his wife directly about any further prognostication, as long as she dialed Sylvia next.

Angela pressed the first contact icon. After four rings, a bright, young woman's voice said, "You've reached Sam Ridgeway-St. James of Golden Stars Agency. I'm currently with a client. Please leave your name and number, and I'll return your call during normal business hours."

She tried the goddess's number again with the same result. Anxiety buzzed along her nerves. She thumbed the contact icon for the vampire master. This time, the phone only rang once.

"St. James," he said in a crisp British accent.

"Master St. James, this is Angela Penrose," she blurted. "I can't find your wife."

"Slow down, Elder Penrose—"

Damn, she hated that title. She should never have given in when Howard nominated her. Her ability to predict events weighed on her too much as it was.

She drew in a deep breath and released it. "The cards say the timing of the breakthrough has changed. It'll happen the day after tomorrow. I tried to phone your wife twice, but I only got her voicemail."

Fabric rustled over the receiver. "She is not in our bathroom, though it appears she has recently showered. Let me find her and have her return your call—"

"Sir, I think she may already be up here." Angela wasn't sure she should be tattling on the vampire's wife, but everyone involved needed to be sharing any and all information. Mrs. St. James being missing and the tremor couldn't be just a coincidence. Not with all the other signs. "We had an earthquake here less than five minutes ago."

Silence was the only thing coming through the phone.

"Master St. James?"

"I am still here. I fear you may be right, Elder Penrose. None of my enforcers saw her leave the estate."

"I need to inform my high priestess of these events."

"Of course. Please relay my regards to Sylvia and my thanks."

"Yes, sir."

The signal went dead, and her phone beeped to say the call ended. A warm hand gripped her right shoulder about the same time she got a whiff of tuna.

"You're doing the right thing," Jim said softly. "And the next time your mom bugs us about moving to Las Vegas, I won't say no."

His statement drew a chuckle from her. She took his hand, kissed the back of it, and patted it with her left.

"Let me call Sylvia and I'll help you get Priscilla out from under the bed. Jafar and Kamil will be here soon to pick her up on their way out of town."

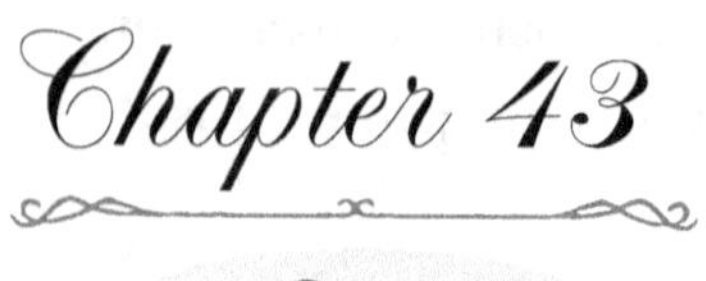

Chapter 43

Sam

The concrete and silver shook beneath my feet. While cracks appeared in the floor outside of the circle, the silver inlay was too malleable for the earthquake to break. At least not at its current force. It felt around a four-point-five at the most.

A girl didn't grow up in the Greater Los Angeles Metroplex without knowing how to guesstimate earthquake magnitudes. However, a worried look appeared on Alex's, or rather Supay's, face.

"It's a minor tremor," I said. "We get them all the time."

His expression turned downright annoyed. "I have experienced a quake before. Unfortunately, this is not Mama Pacha rolling over in her bed."

"Where the fuck are you taking Alex tonight?" Tiffany roared as she charged into the room. Her fury wasn't aimed at me for once.

"What business is that of yours?" he said coolly.

It was a little weird seeing Alex's warm cordiality disappear under Supay's haughty facade.

"I know you're violating the deal he made with you." Tiffany stopped before the god and poked him in the chest.

"You have no knowledge of our deal, child." He sneered.

"So, a deal does exist," I said. Maybe if I could get these two to do something stupid and break the circle, I could deal with my real problems, like my hunger and the Old One.

After I kicked everyone's ass in the bunker.

Supay shot me a dirty look before he turned his attention back to Tiffany. "Alexander Socrates Stanton still owed me from the oath he made to me in Uku Pacha. I am merely collecting."

"Funny how you chose now," I commented.

But it was Tiffany who turned to me and yelled, "Shut the fuck up, Sam!"

"Mine and Alexander's goals mesh in this matter." Supay almost appeared bored by the conversation. "He owes me the deaths of all who stole my tumi. Fortunately, he wants the death of Marcus Benito Giovanni as much as I do."

"Shit," Tiffany muttered. "Marcus is here in Washington?"

"Yes," Supay said. "He was seen with two apparent humans, who Alex suspects were half-breed demons of the Old Ones."

"There's going to be more than just a vampire and two dino demons," I said.

"No doubt." Supay's expression was anticipatory, if not downright bloodthirsty. "But someone needs to keep the lowly gnats off your lovely backside."

I had the impression he was being lewd on purpose to distract me. "I didn't ask for any favor from you, Supay."

"Like mine and Alexander's goals align, so do some of yours and mine, Lady Samantha." His smile was something you'd see on a cartoon villain after he tied the heroine to the railroad tracks. "Once Marcus Benito Giovanni is dead, you will be on your own in this battle." His smile widened. "Unless you accept my proposal, of course."

"I'm not that desperate," I muttered.

"I'll let you out," he taunted.

"You can't!" Tiffany thrust her petite frame between him and the magick circle.

"Don't sweat it, Goth Girl." I sat down and ripped open a box of Twinkies. "All I have to do is wait until the four of you are dead." Cellophane crackled as I tore it. "My guess? Since all four of you were necessary for the trap spell, I only need one of you to die."

"Alex is still alive!" she shrieked. "What did he do to you?"

"The cowboy vampire made a really stupid deal with an Indian god." Yeah, I was being crass and politically incorrect on purpose. I bit into the spongey vanilla goodness. "You could be smart and save all your lives by letting me out now," I said around the mouthful of crème and cake.

Tiffany stepped away from the circle, a horrified expression on her face. Maybe she was worried I really would kill her. But I pictured the annoyed look Duncan would get if I did, especially since he and I worked so hard to keep her alive.

"We can't," she said.

I shrugged. "Then I don't want to hear it if Supay gets your stepdaddy killed. To quote Doctor Cooper, 'I informed you thusly.'"

She shot a look of sheer hatred at him before she wheeled around and stomped out of the room.

Supay inclined his head. "You're getting better at manipulating mortals, Lady Samantha."

"Why, thank you, Lord Supay." I waved another wrapped Twinkie in front of him. "Want one?"

He smirked. "I'll pass for now."

"Your loss."

I popped the rest of the first one in my mouth and tore open the cellophane of the one I'd offered to Supay. My impression was Supay told Tiffany the truth. If Giovanni had been siring more vampires and the red-headed daughter of the last full-blooded dino demons had been birthing more children, they could shift the balance of power in my upcoming battle.

Even worse, Tiffany's con of the Old One breaking through the day after tomorrow may be coming true if the tremor was any indication. I hoped Duncan and the other supernatural leaders stepped up their game for evacuating the Puget Sound vicinity. If they didn't, those civilians would be appetizers for the Old One and his demons.

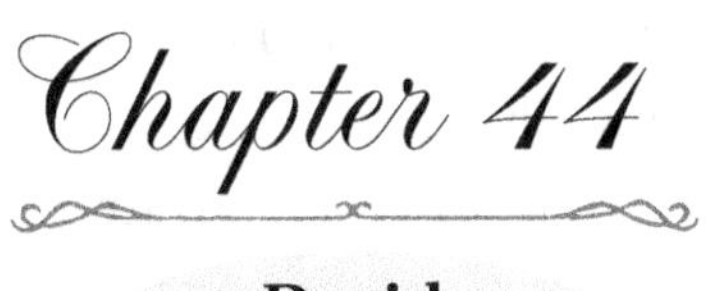

Chapter 44

David

Inside the bunker's armory, David held out his hands. "Listen to me, please, Lord Supay." He'd beg. Hell, he'd drop to his knees and suck the deity's borrowed dick if he had to. "We need you here to keep the circle powered."

"No, you don't David Jebediah Head." The god smiled as he filled his knapsack with two extra clips and a couple of boxes of bullets. "You've already used Alexander's blood infused with my essence. You have Mama Pacha's blood coursing through your veins and Baron Samedi's power in the walking stick. You are fully prepared."

"You can't leave me alone with these people." David jabbed his right hand in the general direction of the house's shared space upstairs. "Stephens will blow my brains out the first chance she gets."

"That is a distinct possibility." Supay zipped the knapsack. "But you did ruin her pre-wedding celebrations as well as her nuptials."

"I'm not saying I'm innocent," David bit out. "But if she kills me, and Sam Ridgeway escapes before we're ready, we are all fucked."

"Ms. Stephens is more concerned you are still being influenced by the Old Ones, and you won't release Samantha at all." Supay slung the knapsack over his shoulder and headed for the doorway.

"Either way, I'm still dead!" Why the fuck wasn't the god listening to him?

Supay paused at the doorway and looked over his shoulder. "Give the child a reason not to kill you. If I were you, I'd start by saving her dead prince." Two steps and he disappeared around the corner.

David frowned. He'd noticed the secret, moony looks the ghost and the girl shot in each other's direction when they thought no one was looking. It reminded him a little bit of how Brandon and he acted at that post-championship party. Before David got tired of the game and slipped Brandon the spare key to his house.

David ran his hand over his curls. What surprised him was that Supay had noticed the attraction between the two Augustine, er, St. James people. Maybe the Incan god was right. Maybe finding a way to keep the kids together would give everyone what they wanted.

And make sure they all stayed alive in the process.

Chapter 45

Tiffany

I yanked off the elastic band and ran my free hand through my hair while I held my phone to my ear with my left. Alex and Phil's home phone rang once. Twice.

After the third ring, Phil picked up. "Alex?"

"No, it's me." Tears stung my eyes. "I'm calling to talk to Ellie."

All I could hear for a moment was harsh breathing before Phil said, "Where's my husband?"

"Here. Sort of." My mouth grew terribly dry.

"I'm not in the mood for playing games, little girl."

Little girl. Her signal for letting me know just how pissed she was. But if I said a damn thing about Supay possessing Alex, she'd tell Grandpa Ares, and there was a fucking good chance of my stepfather getting killed.

"Phil—" I licked my lips. "I can't tell you what's really going on. We can't take the risk of someone finding us. Giovanni's in Washington, and you and I both know damn well we can't afford a leak. Not now."

"Is Alex really with you?" This was the first time I'd ever heard Phil . . . frightened.

I couldn't answer that question. Not when Supay had just driven through the last gate according to the security monitors.

"Phil, I need you to promise me you'll raise Ellie. I changed the guardianship papers after Max died. Call Ronnie Monroe. She'll help you with the legal shit. May I please talk to my daughter now?"

Silence reigned for a few seconds before I heard Phil's muffled voice call for Ellie. My foster mom wasn't a fool. She wasn't about to blather on about me being morbid.

I wasn't a fool either. I practically sat on ground zero, and I couldn't leave. I had to make sure Head released Sam when the Old One came. It was my only chance at saving my daughter.

"Hi, Mommy!" Ellie's cheerful voice caused the tears to spill from my eyes.

"Hey, baby. How was school today?"

"We made paper jack lanterns." She hesitated for a second before she blurted, "Can we have my birthday party at the hospital so Uncle Jake can be there?"

"W-we'll have to see," I choked out. Murphy help me, I didn't want to lie to Ellie. I swore I would never do that to her. "I'm sorry, baby, but I may not be there for your birthday either."

"Don't cry, Mommy. It's okay if Uncle Jake needs you more."

My heart wanted to explode. "That's a very grownup decision. I'm very proud of you, sweetie."

"Besides, we can always have a un-birthday party when he comes home." Her exuberance rang through the connection.

"That sounds like a good idea." I laughed through my tears.

"Grandma Phil says I have to brush my teeth now, but that you better not hang up. G'night, Mommy. I love you. Give Uncle Jake a kiss from me."

I considered hanging up anyway, but another part of me wanted to hang on the connection for as long as I could. "I love you, too, baby."

After some rustling, a whoosh, and the sounds of city street traffic, Phil said, "I've already spoken with Duncan." A second whoosh came through the receiver. She must have gone out on the balcony, so Ellie wouldn't hear us. "I know about Jake and Ptolemy, and I know about the prediction of the Seattle witch. He's suggesting I head to Las Vegas or Phoenix. Father has already said he's coming with me and Ellie."

She sucked in a deep breath and blurted, "What I don't get is why you or Alex didn't tell me what's going on." Hurt trilled on top of the fear in her voice.

"B-because we both needed you to protect Ellie." The tears fell faster, and I sniffed back the snot. "Not getting yourself killed by being with us."

"Hades take you," she spat. "You're with Sam."

"Yes."

"So help me, I'll wring that bitch's neck if she gets you and Alex killed." It was obvious Phil wanted to scream at me, but she kept her voice low so Ellie couldn't hear.

"Don't worry." I chuckled despite my own fear. "I plan on haunting her for the rest of her life."

Phil snorted back her own laughter and tears. "Evil child. I love you. Don't make me raise your military princess."

"It's combat ballerina."

"Not with that multi-million-dollar tiara she brought with her."

I could envision Phil shaking her head in amusement as she said that. I really needed to get off the phone before I dissolved into a sobbing heap of damp clothes and tears.

"I love you, too, Phil. You are the best mom ever." I thumbed the screen to disconnect the call and scrolled through to the picture of the three of us at Disneyland for Ellie's birthday last year. I would have to hold on to their love to get me through my last two days on earth.

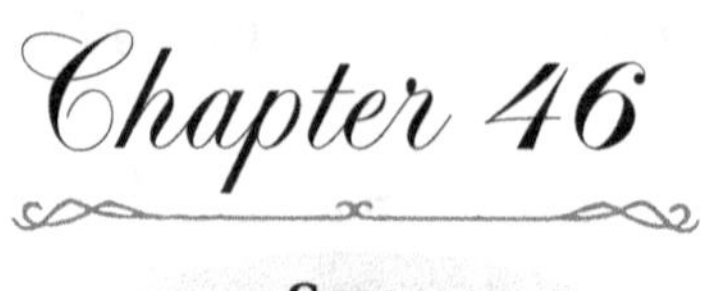

Chapter 46

Sam

I lay on the concrete floor amid cardboard boxes and cellophane wrappers, clutching my knees to my chest from the pain. I wasn't sure how long it'd been since I devoured the last of the Twinkies. Normally, I could tell the time, even when I couldn't see the sky. However, the hunger was getting worse, the beast within me demanding to be released. That seriously fucked with my perceptions. The necromancer's magick didn't help either.

"H-how do you say, 'Where's the bathroom'?" I asked between panting breaths. I'd spent the time getting Ptolemy to teach me Ancient Egyptian. Anything to distract me from the gnawing misery in my stomach.

"This is ridiculous," Ptolemy muttered in Mandarin. "You need food." He rose to his feet. "I'll wake David."

"No, you can't." I gasped as another wave of agony ripped through my gut. "It's too late."

Ptolemy switched to English. "What do you mean?" He took a step back from the circle. "Why is your skin turning silver?"

I held up one shaking hand. Sure enough, a metallic sheen covered me. "It's steel. Head can't drop the circle now. I'll kill all of you."

"No." Ptolemy shook his head. "There's got to be another way."

His gesture and concerned expression reminded me too much of Jake. How the hell was Tiffany dealing with another man inside Jake's body? Had Jake even had a chance to pop the question yet? He'd come to Duncan to ask permission for Tiffany's hand.

The prince in my ex's body though? Everything I knew was through Duncan or Caesar's eyes, and they had radically different views of the dead man standing outside of my prison.

"You need to be careful, Ptolemy." I chuckled. "I might start to think you had a heart."

"You don't know me at all," he snapped.

"There's the snotty asshole who rebelled against his brother," I spat back. "Just like every other Ptolemy. You'll do anything for the throne."

That wasn't fair of me, but I couldn't seem to stop myself. The irritation at my guard was a good distraction from the pain.

"St. James chose you over Selene?" He sneered. "I didn't realize he was into batcrap crazy."

"Bite me."

"I wish I still had the fangs to do it." Ptolemy started laughing, not mocking me, but realizing the situation. "Guess we should have put some milk of magnesia in the circle before Tiffany summoned you."

I giggled, too. "I don't think it or Pepto-Bismal would make any difference."

Another cramp hit. It felt like someone was poking my intestines with knitting needles. When it passed, I lay in a pool of my own sweat, gasping like a beached fish. Why did magick circles have to put off so much fucking heat?

Tiffany strolled into the room, carrying a large peanut butter and jelly sandwich on a plate and a bottle of cola. I wished I could say the drool spilling from my mouth was due to the sandwich. But unlike Ptolemy's peculiar odor, she smelled like the best medium rare steak I could get at Anthony's, the ritzy, popular restaurant owned by one of Caesar's nephews.

"Why don't you take a break, Ptolemy, and get some sleep? I'll watch her for a while," she said.

"Do you think torturing her with your snack is wise?" The scent of roses poured from him.

Shit! That shouldn't be happening. Not when Jake was . . . oh, my! Was Goth Girl even aware that Ptolemy had a thing for her?

Tiffany shrugged as she glared at me. "Payback's a bitch."

"Go on, Ptolemy," I said. "This is nothing compared to her literally stabbing me in the back at my brother's wake."

"You're lucky I didn't still have Grandpa Ares' dagger," Tiffany said.

"I'm well aware of that," I said sourly. "Go on, Your Highness. She can't do anything to me without breaking the circle. And if the girl with the genius IQ does that, well, she'll get what she deserves."

Ptolemy looked at Tiffany for a long time before he said, "Very well," and left the room.

Tiffany sat down on the concrete floor, her back propped against the wall. She had washed her face, but that didn't hide the red rimming her eyelids or her bloodshot eyes. She'd been crying.

"Tiffany, go home to Ellie," I said softly.

She looked up at me. "I can't. Someone needs to make sure Head releases you."

Her admission caught me by surprise. I had figured helping Head trap me was a revenge move. But it also said she didn't trust the necromancer any more than I did. "That's not worth your life."

"No, it's worth Ellie's."

"Is it worth Ptolemy's? He won't leave unless you do," I said.

Once again, the concrete jiggled and bounced beneath my cheek, harder than the last time. I managed to push myself upright. Cracking my skull open during a tremor would only speed my descent into madness thanks to the nanites using more of my resources to heal the injury. The weird part was I felt better during each little earthquake we experienced.

Tiffany shielded her PB&J with her jacket, but she stared at the ceiling as if she expected it to fall and crush her at any moment. When the tremor subsided, she muttered, "I fucking hate being right."

"Right about?" The cramping started again, and I lay back down on the concrete and silver.

"It's the morning of the thirtieth," she said.

An awful anniversary in both our lives. But tomorrow?

Tomorrow was Halloween. Mine and Ellie's birthdays. She would turn six, and I would be . . .

Shit. Thirty-three. What the hell was the significance of that number? I'd have to ask Bebe if I survived this insanity. And if she did.

But Halloween, Samhain, All Soul's Eve? Whatever you wanted to call it, tomorrow was the day the dimensional walls were the thinnest. Maybe the Fates decreed the battle between me and the Old One had to happen on the thirty-first. I should have asked Supay more questions before he left.

"Listen to me, Tiff—" Another wrenching spasm twisted not only my intestines, but all my muscles and ligaments as well. I couldn't stop the scream that spilled out. But with the pain, a certain clarity crystalized in my brain.

When I could breathe again, I said, "Tiffany, Ptolemy's staying because he's in love with you. That's why they needed Jake's body. The other gods needed a dead man who loved you as much as Jake does to come back to earth."

"What are you insinuating?" she hissed. "That Max didn't love me?"

"No, dammit," I snapped. "Think about it. Max went to Heaven because he earned a place there. He couldn't come back if he wanted to. Ptolemy was condemned to roam the shores of the River Styx. As a vampire, he didn't have enough of his corpse for Caesar to put a coin under his tongue to pay Charon."

I squeezed my eyes shut as another flare of agony rippled through my body. When I opened them, Head stood over Tiffany. He leaned so heavily on his cane it looked like the man could barely stand.

"Ridgeway's right," he said. "I tried to talk Ptolemy into grabbing you and getting the hell out, but it's too late."

"What do you mean?" I growled. A white glow filled the room. A glow beyond the LED lights. A glow that came from me.

"They just announced on the news the bridge over the Carbon River at Route 165 has collapsed thanks to the last two tremors." Head slowly slid down the wall to sit next to Tiffany. "Y'all are stuck up here."

"So are you," Tiffany protested.

"Oh, chére." He chuckled. "I know my bill's come due for all the shit I did in my life. My only regret is that I did Brandon wrong a second time."

I couldn't care anymore about what the stupid fucking moron had done to his boyfriend this time. "Tiffany, call Ares!" I yelled. Part of me knew the god couldn't hear me past Head's circle, but I had to try.

Her eyes watered, and she shook her head. "Phil promised me they would stay with Ellie and keep her safe no matter what."

I wanted to scream obscenities at her. There was no fucking reason for her to be here. So I turned on Head with the only weapon I had left. Words.

"You are a fucking selfish prick, David Jebediah Head. So afraid to die by yourself you'd drag a couple of innocent people along with you. I should have destroyed you, body and soul, when I had the chance."

"Yeah," he said wearily. "You should have."

This time, I screamed in sheer rage, not pain. And I kept screaming until I couldn't breathe any more.

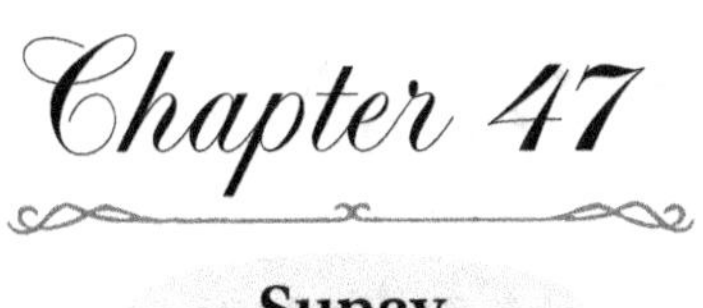

Chapter 47

Supay

Perched on the branch of a Douglas fir, I spotted the small army of vampires and dinosaur demons through the dense underbrush ahead. They were young and terribly loud, so I heard them long before they came into view. I didn't need the night sky to hide my presence. The children simply didn't bother to look up. They believed they were the ultimate predators in this forest. Animals fled the area because the children's stench overwhelmed everything in the vicinity.

I smiled to myself. They were the perfect camouflage for my own scent. Or rather, Alexander's. I had tracked them and listened for leagues. Unfortunately, the thief Giovanni wasn't with them. However, they planned to meet with him in the forest outside of the human city of Seattle.

Finding Giovanni was my priority. But I didn't need all of his little army to lead me to the thief.

Using the gun's going to tell 'em you're following them, Alexander murmured in the back of my mind.

That's what the sword is for, I replied silently. I would have preferred my tumi or even the stone-tipped spear I made under Uncle's guidance when we were both still human. However, the weapons Alexander and the Olympian of war provided would suffice.

Blood thrumming with excitement, I leapt lightly to the forest floor and began my hunt.

Chapter 48

Constanza

"Sir, heading to the Portland headquarters is not a good idea. Not with the eruption of Rainier imminent." Constanza matched Master St. James' stride from his bedroom in his Brentwood mansion and down the hallway toward the stairs. Anne Levy-Fitzgerald had to jog to keep with them.

"You are out of order, Enforcer Torres," he snapped.

"With all due respect—" She reached out and grabbed his arm at the top step and jerked him to a halt. "—it's the job Enforcer Levy-Fitzgerald is training me for."

Green sparked in his eyes. "It is not your decision any more than it is Anne's." He yanked free from her grip and charged down the stairs.

"I'm worried about Sam, too!" She jogged down the steps after him. "But you going off half-cocked isn't going to help her, and I don't want to explain to her how you got yourself killed!"

He stopped by the front door of his home and whirled to face her. His eyes brightened to full neon green. He was definitely used to using his size to intimidate people, but she'd experienced men in the Army who were bigger. He didn't scare her.

Constanza glared right back at him.

Finally, his shoulders sagged. "I cannot stay here and do nothing."

"Wasn't Caesar saying exactly that your biggest pet peeve when you were chief enforcer?" Anne said softly.

"You are not helping," he scolded. "And what about Caesar's safety?"

"Leona and Taalish will stay here to protect him," Constanza said. "You should be staying here, too."

His eyes narrowed. "If you are so worried about my care, why are you not remaining here?"

Before Constanza could formulate a response, Bebe choose the moment to burst through the front door. "Whoever's going with me better move it! The clock's ticking!"

The scent of brimstone filled the foyer. Master St. James slowly turned his piercing gaze on Constanza. "Yet, Doctor Zachary is going to Portland?"

"Quit barking at your enforcers, Duncan." The physician glared up at him. "I'm a surgeon. You're not."

"You are also a member of this coven, and therefore—"

"I am serving this coven at the request of our witch allies, Master." Bebe gave him an innocent look. "Or are you telling me the witches need to die in your people's stead?"

Constanza wasn't sure whether to cheer or wince. Sam had told her about how Bebe's parents were slaughtered in front of her by Selene's rogues. Despite the doctor's love for Caesar, she didn't put up with much bullshit from any other vampire.

Instead of getting angry, Master St. James smiled. "That is exactly why we both need to go, Doctor Zachary. I would not order my people into a situation I would not go myself."

Unsure of what to do, Constanza looked at Anne.

The tiny woman made an exasperated noise. "Thank you, Bebe. We almost had him talked into acting sensibly. I guess we are all going to Portland. Give me two minutes to pack a bag." She dashed up the staircase.

"If you two get yourselves and me killed, you both can explain it to Sam," Constanza grumbled as she bent over to grab her canvas duffle.

"I will not have to explain anything provided you do your job," Master St. James said coolly.

Constanza chewed on the inside of her cheek to keep from saying something she'd regret. Once they were on board the jet, she was mixing the vampire version of a Bloody Mary. And she was leaning toward leaving out the blood.

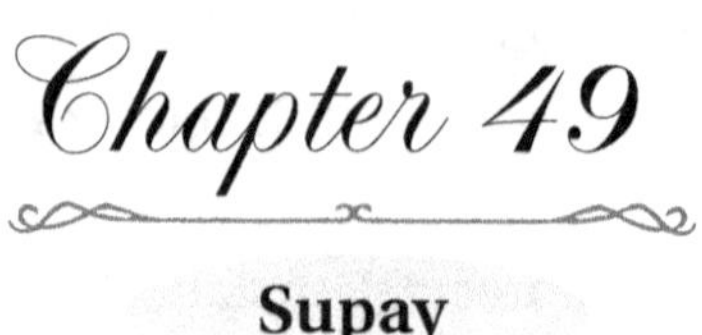

Chapter 49

Supay

I hadn't been hunting in so long I had forgotten the feel of it. The exhilaration of tracking my prey. The sweet smell of their fear. Their wild-eyed, jerky motions, knowing death was coming for them but not which direction.

I had picked off half of the group I followed by the time they reached their rendezvous with the thief and the rest of his forces. While I focused on the demons, I killed an occasional vampire to keep them from becoming suspicious of my real motives.

Dust blocked the sun as it rose behind us for the second morning in a row. I didn't need to worry about Alexander's flesh burning beneath the solar rays. Ash drifted over the land now, a warm snow that didn't melt. While it was easier to track the thief and his compatriots, it made keeping my own presence concealed much more difficult. It also made breathing with Alexander's flesh nearly impossible.

Surprisingly, he made the suggestion of stealing things.

You know how I feel about thieves, Alexander, I chided him.

I'd like to keep my lungs once you're done with me, he whispered in the back of mind. *You've kept my wallet in the back pocket of the jeans we're wearing. Write down the list of things we need and leave the money.*

The slips of green and white paper?

Yes, he whispered with a hint of exasperation.

I don't understand why you mortals don't use something more substantial to signify your wealth.

I sure as hell ain't takin' the time to explain bank accounts and debit cards in the middle of this crisis. Alexander's shout sent a stabbing pain between our eyes. *Now, go into the big store with the orange and white exterior—*

The thief's army went into the building with the unnaturally-colored kayaks—

For the love of Jove—

Excuse me?

You can get better protective gear than they can by going to the place I recommend. Giovanni is a fucking idiot for just using ski masks with this ash.

Well, I could definitely agree with Alexander's assessment regarding the thief. Nor did I sense any deception by Alexander himself. He wanted to survive my possession of his body.

I jogged toward the building he indicated. The ash fell faster and deepened on the grass and artificial stone. I tried to ignore the rumbles of the mountain, but it was difficult with Alex's worry permeating my thoughts.

The building had been abandoned like nearly every other place we'd passed during the past day and a half. Alexander sent me to a side door. I twisted the latch until it snapped and entered the store.

Inside, dim light permeated from the giant windows in the front of the building. Vampire eyes were predator eyes. I could see clearly even with the poor illumination. So many building supplies in one place. The tribe of my childhood could have built a city to rival Cuzco itself with this abundance.

Alexander directed me to an aisle with a certain kind of masks. The triangle in the middle formed the base. Two circles were attached to the bottom corners. A wide rectangle sat on the top point. The rectangle was clear, but it was not formed from glass or crystal.

Grab a couple of extra filters. You'll need them.

It galled me to follow his directions, but he was more informed about the tools we would need. He directed me to another aisle to retrieve another box containing thin, damp cloths. I shook the ash out of our hair and cleaned our face. Finally, I slipped the mask over our face and went back outside. I took a deep breath to test the mask.

Better, isn't it? he asked.

Yes, I had to admit.

Once again, I ran to keep the thief and his army within hearing. They reached the second bridge, the one into the main city, and they began to run even faster, stirring the ankle-deep ash so it blew directly at our face.

You're not going to have any cover on that bridge, Alex pointed out.

Something wasn't quite right. I looked to my left. Another gout of ash and steam belched from the volcano. An old memory tickled me. Only Mother and Uncle had been with me the day I fought the Old One and his minions. Why would Giovanni and these minions run from their master?

Shit! Alexander swore several other obscenities before he said, *Giovanni's going after the civilians trapped in the city.*

Such a large sacrifice to their master could turn the tables of the battle. Grim silence filled our head as we raced across the indecently long bridge.

Chapter 50

Tiffany

The earthquakes were coming harder and faster throughout the day. They almost reminded me of my contractions when Ellie was coming into this world.

Except the Old One breaking through the barrier was going to be a lot worse than my water breaking.

We were able to keep up with the news until KBTC out of Tacoma lost their broadcast antenna. The signal repeaters for satellite internet access died about a half hour later.

We gave up on trying to sleep in the bedrooms because we were getting jounced off the beds with the stronger tremors. Ptolemy helped me drag pillows, mattresses and blankets downstairs and into the room where we kept Sam. Then we fetched food that we didn't have to cook, water, and weapons. On second consideration, I went back for an oxygen tank. It wasn't enough to keep the four of us alive for long, but it could make a difference on defeating the Old One.

"You shouldn't be in here," Sam croaked for the umpteenth time. "Call for Ares."

She looked horrible curled up in the middle of Head's circle. It wasn't the steel coating her skin. Her flesh seemed to be melting before our eyes. To the point where a skeleton looked fucking healthy. The metallic sheen of her blonde hair faded until it fell out in clumps. Her lips stretched into a horrible rictus, showing steel-coated teeth.

"He's with Ellie," I repeated for the umpteenth time. Guilt chewed on my soul for what we were doing to her. I'd blamed her for Max's death for so long I had thought I'd enjoy seeing her suffer.

But no one deserved to be starved to death.

Head toppled over so slowly we were lucky he was sitting on one of the mattresses.

"David!" Ptolemy crawled over to the necromancer, crouched next to him, and laid two fingers against his neck.

"I'm still here." Head patted Ptolemy's arm, his motion awkward and uncoordinated. "It's been three days, so Mama Pacha's blood is wearing off."

"Supay dosed you with the goddess's blood?" I asked.

Head chuckled. "It's the only way I could stay on my feet after being in a coma for the last few years."

Shit. Alex had drank from Mama Pacha after the dino demons staked him and Francisco Chavez, the Lima Coven's chief enforcer, on a mountain terrace to die of exposure by the sun. Alex didn't talk about it much. I chalked it up to guilt that Francisco died, but he was still alive. Seeing Head now made me realized how badly Alex had been burned. How close Phil, we all, came to losing him.

However, as a result of the goddess's blood, Alex had been able to walk under the sun for three days. And I resented that he'd gone surfing without me because I was pregnant. I guess Head and Sam weren't the only selfish bitches in the room.

Head laid his left hand flat on the concrete. "Gases and magma are moving faster. Won't be long now."

I pulled my Glock from its holster and rested it and my forearms on my crossed legs.

"You won't need to use that," Head murmured.

Sam laughed, an awful rasping noise. "It's not you she's worried about anymore, David."

I cocked my head and smiled. "Well, no offense, bitch, but I'd rather die instantly in a pyroclastic cloud, than be eaten by you."

"Think I want to eat you, twat waffle?"

We both laughed. It was the closest either of us would come to saying we were sorry for being buttheads over the years.

Ptolemy crawled over to my mattress. He sat beside me and wrapped his right arm around my shoulders. I sighed and leaned against him.

"Tell her," Sam said. "Tell her before it's too late."

"Tell me what?" I looked up at Ptolemy.

Sorrow filled his face, but he remained silent.

"Tell her, dude, or we will," Head murmured. "Don't make the same fucking mistakes I've made."

I waited for Ptolemy to say something, scared at the same time. Was he going to admit to killing my parents? What awful thing was he afraid to say to me?

His Adam's apple bobbed, and he squeezed my shoulders. "I love you, Tiffany. I always have."

That's when the world turned upside down.

Literally.

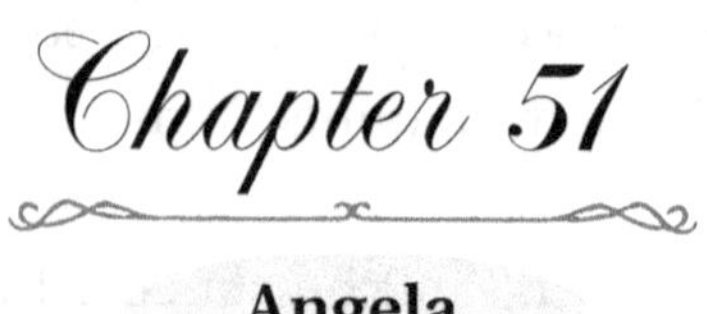

Chapter 51

Angela

Ash drifted through the downtown air like one of Seattle's rare snowstorms. The sky had turned gray over the last two days as the stratovolcano pumped tons of ash and rock into the atmosphere. Despite it being nearly noon on Halloween, the dense clouds of dust over Puget Sound blanketed the area in a cloak of late dusk.

Angela brushed away the layer of the damn stuff that had landed on her goggles in the last few minutes. Pressure beneath her feet thrummed a rapid, deep heartbeat. Mother Earth herself screamed in agony. This wasn't her shifting in her slumber. Something was tearing its way through her flesh.

Everyone from Blue Hawk Coven with earth talent lined South Jackson Street. Volunteers from the covens in Spokane, Portland, and San Francisco poured into the city as civilians flew out. The Vancouver and Los Angeles covens had set up triage centers while the packs from the surrounding states formed search-and-rescue teams.

To everyone's surprise, the ghouls had volunteered their efforts and resources as well.

Mount Rainier growled again, belching another plume of ash and toxic gases thousands of feet into the atmosphere. Despite the prevailing winds, they simply didn't have enough of those with air talent remaining to keep Seattle itself clear of the volcanic debris.

Donna Whitefeather, who co-ruled Seattle's branch of the St. James Coven, and someone in a burqa and goggles joined Angela. "Elder Penrose, this is Ambassador Tanis ibn Yassef of the Ghoul Clans.

"A pleasure, Ambassador." Angela held out her hand, then cocked her head as her Sight really saw the other woman. "You're an earth witch?"

The ambassador inclined her head as she shook Angela's hand. "A great many of our people have magick or shifter talents. We have come to serve. And please call me Tanis."

"Angela."

When she released her grip on the ghoul's hand, lightning flashed in the darkest clouds over the volcano. The low rumbles of thunder followed. Not a true storm, but static from the tons of ash floating overhead.

"I don't remember Tahoma this angry the last time he erupted," Donna commented. "But then an Old One wasn't trying to breach him either." Like everyone else, the vampire wore goggles and a mask to keep the glass-sharp dust out of eyes and throat. Heavy denim jeans, boots, and a coat with a Salish-pattern weave completed her protection.

"The volcano hasn't erupted in two hundred years," Angela said.

There was a twinkle in Donna's glowing yellow eyes. "No, he hasn't. But then, it has been that long since I last walked in daylight."

Tanis shook her head. "I cannot imagine such a lengthy lifespan."

"This will be close to Mount St. Helens when I was teenager," Angela said. "Just bigger and more spectacular."

Tanis laughed behind her veil. "The eruption of Mount St. Helens was a few decades before I was born." Her laughter cut off abruptly, and she dropped to her knees.

The jolt of power that fell the ghoul ambassador ripped through Angela. At the same moment, a roar burst from the mountain. Through the tears of pain, she watched as giant tentacles thrust from the summit and literally rip the mountain top in half.

That's when the screaming started to the east.

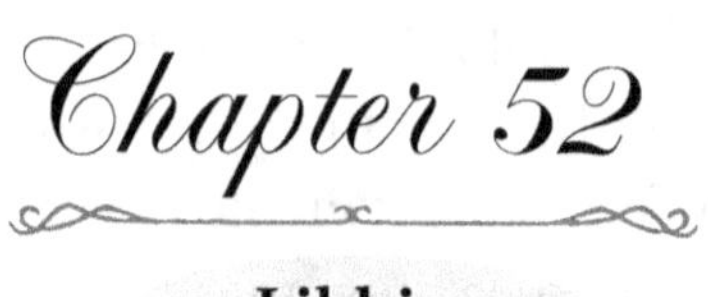

Chapter 52

Libbie

My skin itched in a way that had nothing to do with the scratchy ash falling from the sky or the wooden stakes in my hands. The instinctive desire to shift and flee almost overwhelmed me, but I needed to stay for my own peace of mind more than anything. To know I did everything I could to protect my home.

The damn goggles I wore impeded my view. Even in human form, my peripheral vision was much better than my forward eyesight. I hoped Waldo and his boss were wrong. Last thing we needed was an attack by rogues in the middle of this eruption.

The smell of ash didn't just come from the flakes drifting down and coating everything. Everyone along the shore of Lake Washington, witch and were alike, were a tangle of nerves.

A bundle of clothing dusted with gray approached me through the swirling flakes from the west. "Professor Hawker?"

Despite the scarf across the person's face muffling sound, I recognized the voice. "Azir? What in the Goddess's many names are you doing—"

More shapes came out of the drifting particles, all of them weres from what little scent I could pick up.

Anger sparked under my itchy skin. "What are you kids doing here? You should have been on one of the buses two days ago—"

"It's our home, too," another boy said fiercely. He smelled of mutton and high mountain meadow grass. A mountain sheep. "Ms. Penrose told my parents to leave before the evacuations were ordered, but she's staying. So, we are staying, too."

"But your parents—" I said.

"They took my sisters and ours and Ms. Penrose's pets south."

"That's Kamil," Azir said. He introduced the rest of the boys and girls. "Where do you need us?"

"Back at the shelter," I snapped, straightening to my full height, hoping to intimidate them into obeying me. I couldn't have my own student on my conscience, much less the younger children.

"I've already lost my home once," Azir said fiercely. "It won't happen again. Nor do I wish that fate on you or any of my compatriots."

"Professor Hawker?" Kamil pointed behind me. "There's people running toward us on the Murrow Bridge." Through the swirling ash, I could see forms moving across the floating span toward us. Fast.

A deafening crack made all of us look at Mount Rainier. The summit had split in two, the halves rolling down the sides. Enormous tentacles waved above the broken rock. What looked like a giant silver robot, or maybe a skeleton, ripped and tore at the tentacles.

I squeezed my eyes shut. I was definitely hallucinating if I was seeing a giant robot fighting a monster.

ROGUES! ROGUE VAMPIRES INCOMING!

I don't know who started the alarm, but all the witches and vampires were screaming the same damn thing inside my brain. I looked out at the bridge and realized how fast the group was coming toward us.

Remembering the briefing Waldo gave everyone, I looked over my shoulder at the kids. "Stay back! If one of them engages you, whatever you do, don't bite them. Their blood could be poisonous."

"But, Professor, our teeth and claws—" Azir protested.

"Are our greatest liability in this fight!" I pointed at a pile of sharpened stakes. "Use those!"

In the distance, Mount Rainier continued to crumble. A wave on the south side of Lake Washington seemed to drag rocks and dirt into the water. In horror, I realized it was really office buildings and houses falling into the lake from a landslide.

The rogues spilled off the bridge onto the sliver of land before I-90 dove into the tunnel. They aimed directly for the witches. If we couldn't keep enough of them alive, the tsunami would kill us all.

I added my shriek to the howls, roars, and shouts as members of the Seattle Were Alliance and the St. James enforcers charged the rogues.

Chapter 53

Tiffany

A giant tentacle smashed through the roof and into the hemisphere of the magick circle. Green and diamond black light flared. David cried out and slapped his hands to his temples.

Sam shrieked. Her eyes no longer were glowing white. Both orbs were blacker than midnight. She beat her fists on the magick forming her prison. Hell, I don't think she was even sane now.

"David! Drop the circle!" My heart tried to leap out of my chest as I raised my weapon.

To my relief, he held out his hand and yelled something in a language I didn't understand. Sam fell forward as she tried to hit the energy sphere again.

My fear returned when her attention fixated on us. She was nothing more than a shiny skeleton covered in black rags.

Hu-u-u-un-n-n-g-g-r-r-y," she moaned.

The tentacle rose, distracting her. She leapt and chomped on the alien appendage. Black blood splashed on the concrete, sizzling and hissing as it dissolved the walls and floor of the bunker. The last thing I saw before the generator gave up and we lost the main lights was Sam clutching the tentacle and gnawing on the scaly flesh as it withdrew through the opening it made in the roof.

"Get on the pentacle!" David yelled over the grinding of concrete and rebar above us.

Ptolemy flipped on a flashlight. Together, he and I dragged David to the debris-covered pentacle. I ran back and rolled the oxygen tank toward the circle before I collected a couple gallons of water and a large box of granola bars.

"Tiffany! Now!" Ptolemy roared.

I dived inside the pentacle with the supplies I'd grabbed. Green light snapped to life around us. With a sick feeling in my stomach, we dropped straight down as the ceiling collapsed above us.

Chapter 54

Angela

Word flashed telepathically through the ranks. A contingent of rogue vampires and dino demons had charged over one of the I-90 floating bridges and were attacking our folks on the shore of Lake Washington.

Angela looked at Donna and Tanis. The vampire and ghoul appeared as alarmed as she felt.

Hold your places, witches! Sylvia's voice rang through Angela's mind. *If we fail, everyone here, supernatural and Normal, will die.*

As if to emphasize the high priestess's mental command, Angela could feel the fault in front of her jump.

St. James enforcers, to me! At Donna's mental shout, she and the closest vampires raced east on South Jackson Street toward the battle, leaving clouds of ash in their wake.

"What do we do?" Tanis asked as she climbed back to her feet.

Another deafening roar shook downtown. Glass shattered. Shards tinkled as they hit the sides of parked cars or items inside the buildings. Angela winced against the pressure pain as she and Tanis tried to keep their balance during the tremor. Through slitted eyes, she watched the two halves of the summit exploded apart. Clouds of debris rolled down the side of the volcano.

She closed her eyes and concentrated past Rainier's pain. Pyroclastic flows. The city of Tacoma was about to be buried. When it was, the Puget Sound tsunami would be tearing their way.

Angela opened her eyes and looked at Tanis. "We stay put and do our job."

Her heart wanted to break. Jim was with the rest of the Normals sheltering in and around Seattle University. She had to keep him safe. So, she'd keep the line even if it killed her.

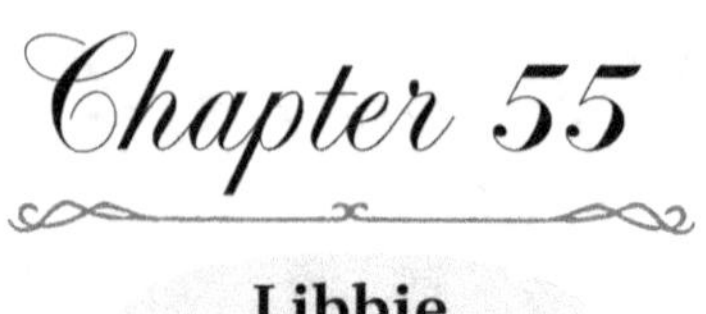

Chapter 55

Libbie

I ducked the demon's slashing talons. The itch to change became worse, but after my foe's acidic black blood burned off the tip of the stake in my right hand, I understood the St. James warning not to bite the dino demons. Especially when the damn thing carried the distinctive sandalwood odor of a vampire despite its resemblance to a velociraptor in clothes.

Gasping, I backpedaled to get some distance between me and the demon. I was a professor, not a fucking enforcer. This creature would wear me down if I didn't make short work of it.

Something grabbed the collar of my jacket and yanked me backward. Another figure leapt between me and the demon. A high-pitch note sounded before the demon's head departed from its shoulder and rolled across the ash-filled street.

I could barely make out the Salish pattern of the coat under the ash dusting the material. A familiar coat. One I'd seen slung over my kitchen chairs on several occasions since Waldo and I became an item.

The figure turned to me. Donna Whitefeather's eyes glowed neon yellow behind the goggles she wore. Black blood dripped from the long blade in her right hand.

I stared at the weapon, totally perplexed. The metal should be dissolving with that amount of acidic blood. It took me a moment to realize the blood dripped a millimeter from the steel. The blade was coated with what looked to be glass.

"Were you bitten, Professor?"

I shook my head, but Donna and the male vampire who had grabbed me from behind double-checked anyway. Donna patted my shoulder.

"Sorry, but the demons have poison-injecting teeth like a rattlesnake. That shit is worse than their blood—"

A shot rang out from the direction of the Murrow Bridge. I dove into the ash on the ground along with the two vampires. More shots were fired.

Bodies fell. On some, the flesh melted from their bones. Others exuded noxious fumes as the acidic blood ate away the corpses' protective clothing.

The battle that had ebbed and surged around me halted as everyone else, both local supernatural and rogue, ducked for cover. Once again, I fought the urge to shift and fly away from the carnage. Instead, I crawled over to an abandoned car. Donna and the other vampire followed me.

I crouched and peered over the ash-covered hood. A lone gunman stood on the edge of the bridge, a small firearm in each gloved grip. The frequency of the shots slowed. It took a few seconds for my human brain to process whoever the person on the bridge was, they were more selective of their targets with everyone hiding. And it was only the rogues they were picking off.

"Who the hell—Alex?" Donna stared at the figure, disbelief in her voice.

"Holy shit," the male vampire said. "That *is* the boss."

Closer to the shoreline, a male voice howled, "Stanton!"

The St. James chief enforcer? What the hell was going on? Why was he on the bridge by himself?

The same male shouted, "Get him! He killed your parents!"

As one, the demons raced for the bridge. The rogue vampires appeared totally nonplussed by their sudden abandonment.

Donna and the rest of the St. James enforcers took advantage of their surprise.

I had seen death before, but this . . .

This was a series of executions.

The man on the bridge took off back toward Mercer Island. Leading the demons away from the witches and the Normals we were trying to protect. Both the St. James chief enforcer and his pursuers disappeared into the falling ash. More gunshots rang out after I lost sight of them.

I huddled behind the car and squeezed my eyes shut. Bile rose in my throat. It was one thing to hunt for dinner. A war was a much more horrible experience, and this was only a minor battle in it.

"Professor?" Someone shook my shoulder.

I opened my eyes. Azir's golden-hazel orbs peered over the top of his scarf.

"Are you injured?" He glanced in the direction of the shoreline. "The witches are saying we need to move inland a bit."

I nodded. Azir and the werepanther boy helped me to feet. The pavement swayed and the car I'd been leaning against jittered of its own accord.

A horrendous *BOOM* shook everything. Vehicle alarms started wailing. The boys and I turned to Rainier in time to see what was left of the summit slide down the sides of the mountain. A billowing plume of ash and smoke obscured the figures I thought I'd seen and what was left of the volcano.

Despite the ashy scent of the volcano and the scared people around me, ozone filled the area as the witches started their spells. The boys and I jogged west with the rest of the weres and St. James vampires. Some of them carried their fallen compatriots over their shoulders.

Now, it was up to the witches, and I prayed to the Goddess they were strong enough for the task. If they weren't . . .

Well, it wouldn't matter because everyone in Seattle would be dead.

Chapter 56

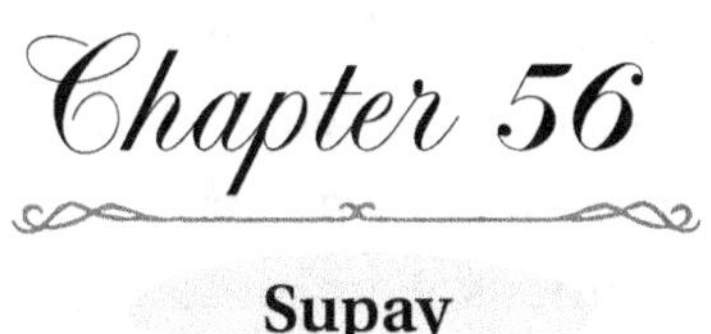

Supay

I didn't bother to look at the explosion, nor did I check to see if my pursuers still followed. Instead, I focused on my steady pace across the island. Even the thief had stopped calling out Alexander's name, insisting he come back and fight.

Turn around and kill the bastard! Alexander roared in the back of my mind.

And where will that leave you with so many of the dinosaur demons in pursuit? I replied. *Besides, I have a plan.*

Oh, goody. Sarcasm dripped from the vampire's silent words.

I reached the twin spans connecting the island with the eastern mainland and halted. The bridges swayed and jerked as both sides yanked them in different directions while the volcano continued to empty itself. As Alexander had promised, the mask from the orange and white store aided my breathing much better than the items our pursuers wore. I checked over my left shoulder. The thief and his collection of dinosaur demons had fallen a bit behind, and now they spotted me. The shrill cries of the pack leaders re-energized my pursuers.

The timing of my plan had to be perfect. I glanced to my right. I couldn't see the water through the ash fall, but I could feel it. Just like I could feel the fifty-three mortals in the city at the south end of the sound, who died instantly by inhaling the blistering gases rolling down the riverbeds and through their homes. I detected the lower roar beneath the mountain's wailing I'd been waiting for. I charged across the closest bridge.

What the fuck! But Alexander could only hang on for the ride.

Both I and my pursuers reached the halfway point when the demons realized their danger. A fierce joy at outwitting my foes filled me as I raced for the other side. Some continued their pursuit. The rest tried to turn back. The roar of the wave deepened, the water being forced higher since the east side of the lake was so much narrower than the west side.

I leapt for the road on the shore an instant before the bridge disappeared beneath me. The ash cushioned my landing on the broken pavement. I turned on my side and looked back.

The bridge and the demons were simply gone. The debris-choked wave continued rolling north, carrying the broken corpses with it.

A figure rose from the ashes a few yards away. "You fucking bastard!" the thief spat in Italian. "You ruin everything!"

"I ruin everything?" We climbed to our feet. "You shouldn't have recruited our aunt to steal our tumi."

"Your tumi? It was . . ." From the dawning horror beneath the ashes coating his face, the thief realized who he truly confronted. "It was the Old Ones' demons who approached her. Not me. If you wanted her loyalty, maybe you shouldn't have turned her into a zombie llama!"

"You are not totally innocent." We raised our right hand, our index finger on the gun's trigger. "You tried to take our tumi from Alexander Socrates Stanton and his beloved on multiple occasions."

"I was merely attempting to return it to you, my lord." The thief spread his hands in a supplicating gesture.

Alexander's rage spilled past mine. "Then there's the matter of you assisting the Old Ones' demons in attempting to sacrifice our wife and her father in order to summon one of those bastards." We squeezed the trigger.

Nothing happened. The clip was spent.

We threw the weapon at the traitor-thief's head. At the same moment, he dipped, scooped ash in his hands, and threw it at me.

While, the ash didn't harm us, it did obscure our vision for a few crucial moments. We shuffled to our right, expecting the traitor-thief to charge for the gun still in our left hand. The anticipated rush never came.

We stepped out of the cloud. Tracks in the ashes led to the east. Our tracks and those of the army when we headed west had been obliterated by the falling ash. We retrieved the gun we threw. It would be difficult to refill the clip in the ash fall without the device malfunctioning. Using our body to shield the weapon, we checked the clip in the second gun. Only three bullets left. They would have to suffice. We couldn't let him escape again.

Lightning created weird shadows through the gray landscape. Thunder crackled overhead. We trudged through the falling ash after the traitor-thief.

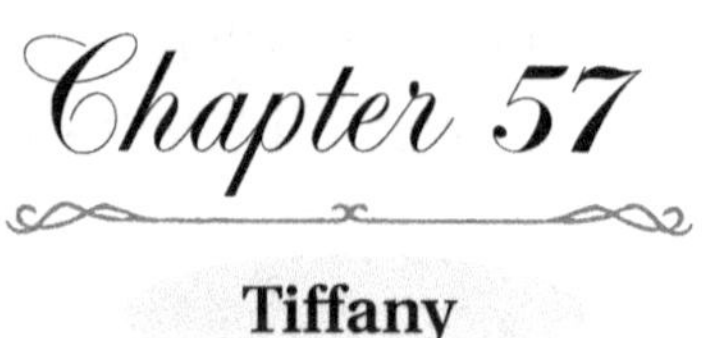

Chapter 57

Tiffany

I was startled enough by the sudden drop I screamed. Someone grabbed me and pulled me close.

"It's okay," Ptolemy murmured in my ear. "We're alive." He pointed his flashlight at the edge of the silver circle. Dirt and rock rushed by as if we were in a fast-moving industrial mine elevator. The concrete circle we sat on slowed and moved to my right. It picked up speed again.

"David?" I murmured.

"Hush, I gotta focus." He may have been a necromancer, but underneath it all, he was still an earth witch. His eyes were screwed shut in a look of concentration. His legs stretched out, his feet twitching. His elbows were tucked to his sides with his palms up and his fingers dancing in a pattern. If I didn't know better, I would have assumed he was playing a virtual reality game without the equipment.

As it was, this reality sucked.

Our little concrete and silver circle, probably all that was left of our bunker, swooped and dived and rose. Heat rose in the half-dome to the point I stripped off the jacket and sweatshirt I'd pulled on over my navy tank. I wasn't sure if it was the temperature or the rollercoaster trip that made me nauseated. About the time I was sure I would puke, David slowed and stopped our perch.

Ptolemy shone the flashlight at the witch. A sheen of sweat covered David's visible skin. He blinked and opened his eyes.

"This should be safe for the time being," he said. He swiped at the moisture on his forehead. "Sorry for the rough ride. There was a lot of cracks in the mountain before the Old One started beating on it. Had to go deep when the fighting collapsed the damn mountain, and then dodge the steam and gas vents as well as the magma tunnels."

"What do you mean the mountain collapsed?" I said.

"As in the glaciers and snow have been chipping away at the mountain for the last couple of centuries. First, the summit blew. Then the rock that was left fell into what had been the huge gas and magma pocket below ground level." David wearily shook his head. "Ridgeway and the Old One just created one hell of a sinkhole."

"Why can't we go to the surface?" I didn't want to stay down here. I needed to find out who won. Was Ellie safe? What was our next move if there was an Old One on the loose?

"Sweetheart, there's boiling mud, oven-hot pumice, and ash on the surface over a hundred miles in every direction." David shook his head. "That doesn't include the poisonous gases. I don't have the juice to get us to a safer place on the surface." He sighed. "At least, not right now."

"How deep are we?" Ptolemy asked.

David chuckled. "Deep enough I'm going to have to make a slow ascent so we don't get the bends. Sorry about the sauna. This was the coolest section of crust I could find."

"Are we too close to the magma?" Ptolemy asked as he stripped off his hoodie.

"Nah, man." David shook his head. "This is heat from friction. The faults in the area were rubbing against each other while Rainier shot its wad. It'll start cooling down in a couple of days. It'll be uncomfortable for us, but we aren't going to cook."

He looked at Ptolemy. "Hate to ask this, man, but I need your help getting my shirt and pants off." He flashed a grin at me. "Don't worry, girlfriend. I'm not coming onto your boy."

"He's—" What the hell was Ptolemy to me? A teen fantasy, if I were honest with myself. Would he stay in Jake's body for what should have been Jake's natural lifetime? And what he said to me before the Old One broke through. How the hell do I deal with that three days after Jake died?

Ptolemy watched me as all the questions rolled through my head. "Since we were interrupted—"

I held up my hands. "Just stop. Please. I—" I sucked in a deep breath in an attempt to calm down, wishing it was claustrophobia causing the ache in my chest. "Don't say anything else until we get out of here."

"So you have the opportunity run away?"

"My live-in boyfriend just died asshat," I growled. "He was going to ask me to marry him. You're in his body. And on top of all that crap, you lay on me you've had a thing for me since I was a kid? It's a little much."

"Quit making me out to be a child-lover!" Ptolemy shouted. "Seventeen is a perfectly marriageable age for a young woman even in your society!"

David's piercing whistle bounced around the half-sphere. Both Ptolemy and I slapped our hands over our ears.

"You two need to chill the fuck out. It's a tight enough space without you verbally smacking each other." David jabbed an index finger at Ptolemy. "Turn off the damn flashlight. You're wasting the battery. Second, both of you need to turn off your phones. We're going to be down here a while, and we're going to need the damn phones to call for a pick-up once we resurface."

He was right though I didn't want to admit it aloud. Ptolemy and I did as David suggested. Instead of absolute darkness when Ptolemy flicked off the flashlight, soft green light filled the space. The flecks of quartz in the surrounding granite reflected the magick, making the space even brighter. It was beautiful.

"Smart move on bringing the extra oxygen tank," David said as Ptolemy helped him strip off his clothes. "Our problem is going to be scrubbing the carbon dioxide. Let's hope I don't accidentally kill us in the process."

I paused in removing my socks. "Kill us?"

David laughed while Ptolemy leaned him against the shield. "I didn't have that much control over my normal—" He made quote signs with his index and middle fingers. "—witch abilities. After the New Orleans coven bound my powers, I couldn't practice. I tried to practice in my coma though."

I frowned. "What do you mean you tried to practice?"

"Your girl made a replica of the farmhouse where my sister and I lived when we were tiny. Mama's copy of the Book of Shadows was there, too." David rubbed his chin. "I was never sure why she did that."

I laughed. "Knowing Sam, it was probably an accident—" Our little safety bubble bounced and shook. The scent of ozone grew stronger.

"That's not me," David murmured. He laid both his hands on the concrete, his face scrunched in concentration. His eyes widened. "Shit! Hang on!"

We tumbled through granite as David fought to keep his circle intact.

Chapter 58

Angela

Power invaded every cell of Angela's body as the water witches syphoned the kinetic energy from the approaching tsunamis on the lake and the sound and shifted it to her and the other earth witches lining South Jackson Street.

Now! Sylvia shouted telepathically.

Angela, along with half the other earth witches, grabbed the tendrils of magick along the north edge of the downtown fault line and pulled up. Sylvia and the other half pushed down.

A roar and a crack nearly as loud as the volcano ripped through the air. The pavement beneath her feet shuddered and rippled and slowly rose.

Despite her grip on her staff, Angela dropped to her knees, the excess energy spent along with a good chuck of her personal reserves. She'd probably sleep for a week after this. Other witches were also having problems staying upright. A few had even passed out. Tanis sat down abruptly next to her.

"I've never tried anything on that scale before," the ghoul ambassador murmured.

"Welcome to the club," Angela replied. They looked at each other, and they both started laughing.

Something moved on Fifth Avenue. Something under the ash, which shifted and bubbled. Water. She forced herself back to her feet as did everyone still conscious along the line. Parked cars shifted and slid. Gray mud ran north on the street.

Angela held her breath. The gray mud spilled into the slight chasm the witches created by pulling the fault apart. A few cars floated along until they bumped into the soil and rock wall. The chasm was too narrow for them to fall. But after a few minutes the water didn't get any higher than a foot.

If she discounted the ash clogging the street.

Inside her head, confirmation rang out that both tsunamis were dissipating with minor flooding on the coastal streets only. A ragged cheer went up, muffled by the still falling ash.

Angela sagged against her staff. Shower, coffee, and a soft bed would be nice, but her husband and her cat were safe. And those things that mattered most would get her through the next few weeks of chaos.

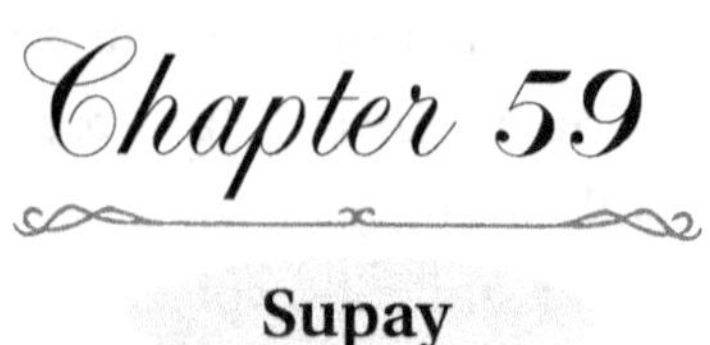

Chapter 59

Supay

We tracked the traitor-thief by his footprints. The ash was falling thicker and faster. From the trembling of the ground beneath our boots, the mountain's final collapse was imminent.

The trees ended at a sharp incline. At the bottom, a creek ran, or would have if the bed wasn't clogged by ash and other debris. It was barely a trickle of gray mud oozing through cracks and past branches. And climbing over the broken and shattered wood was the traitor-thief.

We slid more than climbed down the ravine. Despite the growling of the mountain and thunder overhead, the traitor-thief scrabbled faster over the debris pile. More trash slammed into the makeshift dam and jarred his hold. He lost his footing and fell. A jagged tree limb impaled his side, and he let out a horrendous wail.

We had him.

We leapt from a boulder onto the top of the pile. Lightning flashes gave his blood a black appearance, and we hesitated a moment. If this were a trick by the Old One's minions, we would be hard pressed to defeat a demon in this body.

Our pause gave the traitor-thief time to snap the limb which had impaled him. The scent of his blood triggered our feeding lust and his. He was definitely not a dinosaur demon. Yellow light filled the space beneath the makeshift dam. He snatched up another jagged piece of wood.

We grinned at him and drew our weapon. "You don't bring a stick to a gunfight, boy." We squeezed the trigger.

Instead of freezing as we expected, the traitor-thief tossed his weapon as one would a spear. While its aerodynamics left something to be desired, the wood had the traitor-thief's desired effect. We dodged the missile, and our shot went wild.

The traitor-thief charged us. We tumbled through the gray mud. He slammed our hand against a rock, and the gun slipped from our broken fingers. We kicked the bastard in the family jewels and yanked on the wood protruding through his abdomen at the same time.

He howled and jerked back. The wood slipped free of his body with a delicious sucking sound and a few streamers of his intestines.

The traitor-thief stumbled back and threw rocks at us, a desperate attempt to gain time for the V-virus to heal the gaping hole in his gut. We batted aside the projectiles with the bloody tree limb in our left hand. However, our right hand healed faster.

We caught a fist-sized rock he aimed at our head and whipped it back at his. It caught the traitor-thief in the middle of his forehead and he dropped into the muddy stream. We flipped the tree limb to our right hand before we strode forward, grabbed his collar, and raised the pointed wood.

The traitor-thief's mask slipped from his nose and mouth, and he laughed. We did not expect that reaction in the face of his death.

"Go ahead, Stanton. Supay. Whoever you are." He leered at us. "Kill me. It won't save St. James."

We jerked him closer to our face. "What are you talking about?"

"I made sure your maker died for killing my maker if the Old One lost." His laughter took a maniacal quality. "It was the best way to hurt you and that bitch he threw aside my grandmother for."

We shook our head, but there was no sense arguing facts with a madman. "You can't get near him. The enforcers—"

"Your precious enforcers won't dare to touch his wife."

Anne wouldn't let anyone, including Sam, near Duncan without testing them. Unless—

Unless the dino demons figured out a way to keep Olympian bronze from reacting with their bodies.

We caught a flash of glitter as he tried to stab us in the left arm with something.

Fury hit us and we plunged the wood through the traitorous bastard's heart. His eyes slowly dimmed, and we released his jacket. A moment later, his flesh turned to sludge.

A bright light blinded me.

I was no longer inside Alexander's body, but I was still in the ravine.

I stood in front of Alexander, the thief's body between us. Alexander seemed as surprised as I was. The rest of me tugged on this piece to return to Uku Pacha.

A series of booms and cracks filled the ravine. Trees, dry from the hot ash falling over the last three days, burst into flames above us. Boiling mud spilled through the cracks and over the top of the debris dam.

I turned to him and yelled, "Run!"

Alexander whirled and raced for the rocks and boulders edging the creek bed. The last thing I saw was him leaping on the closest boulder before the tons of boiling mud smashed through the debris dam and I was yanked back to Uku Pacha.

Sam

I stood in nothingness. There was no length, no width. There was no up, no down. Or there wasn't any down until I decided to sit cross-legged. A soft silvery light came from my hands. Curious, I undid the top two buttons of my coat and looked down inside it. The light came from all of my skin. I frowned and rebuttoned my coat. The pain and unrelenting hunger were gone. I felt fractured and whole at the same time.

Something twitched in my left coat pocket. Peter poked his head out and asked a question in rabbit language.

"Yeah, I think it's over." I didn't see the Old One anywhere. I vaguely remembered tentacles and teeth and claws, but there was no evidence on my clothes and body. No remains nearby. Only this emptiness.

Flopsy crawled out of my pocket, sat in my lap, and looked up at me. Her question bothered me more than Peter's.

"I'm not quite sure. I don't think I'm dead. Again." I looked around wishing there was a source of light besides me. I blinked. No, I wasn't imagining it. It was getting brighter, but there wasn't any obvious source projecting the luminescence.

Flopsy peered around, then made a suggestion. I concentrated on the color green. Sure enough, the vague light changed from grayish to lime. To double-check it was me actually doing it, I pictured the walls of my old bedroom at Mom and Dad's house. The light shifted from green to hot pink.

The lack of anything I recognized beneath my ass bothered me. I made it the pink shag carpet from my old bedroom as well. At its appearance, I ran my hands over the fibers. It felt exactly the same except it went on forever in every direction.

Peter crawled out of my coat pocket, sniffed at the carpet, and made a sarcastic remark.

I gave him a dirty look. "This wasn't exactly what I had in mind for your paradise either. Give me a chance to figure this out—"

What sounded like a knock on a wooden door rang through this weird pink carpeted emptiness. Flopsy hopped off my lap and pointed behind me with her left forepaw.

I looked over my shoulder. My old pale pink bedroom door stood upright on the forever carpet in its original frame with its original gold-colored doorknob. The door I broke in half shortly after my death because I didn't know my own strength. I had been arguing with Duncan because he'd kissed me. I had gotten so pissed at him I slammed it, and the wood split down the middle. Mom and Dad had since replaced the door. The new door was white with a brushed nickel latch, but my old bedroom walls were still obnoxiously pink because Ellie loved the color, too. She slept in my old bed whenever she spent the night at their house.

Someone knocked again. I climbed to my feet, walked over to the door with the rabbits trailing behind me, and opened it.

Two familiar people stood on black sand on the other side. I frowned and leaned around to see the back of the doorframe. From that angle, it appeared the door didn't exist.

I straightened and looked at SHE-WHO-BRINGS-LIFE-AND-DEATH and Norman again. The sienna-colored light of Otherwhere shone behind them.

"It's bigger on the inside." Norman grinned. He poked at his tortoise shell glasses with his left index finger. Like he usually was when outside of his own afterlife, he was dressed in a black turtleneck, cream trousers, and a brown corduroy jacket with elbow patches. His curly brown hair reminded me of Bob Ross, the television art teacher turned guru, and his afro.

"Ha, ha," I muttered.

"I brought an afterlife warming gift." He held up a diamond-encrusted platinum bottle.

"Thank you." Accepting it, I half-expected the bottle to contain his beloved brandy when I looked at the label. "Paisón Azteca?" I looked up at him.

Norman shrugged. "I know you prefer tequila."

"Thank you." I smiled at him. Norman handled the souls of those who didn't believe in a particular god or any god, like agnostics and atheists.

The physical laws regarding the conservation of energy applied to souls just like everything else, so someone had to deal with them.

SHE, however, held what looked to be a homemade clay pot with a live—

My jaw fell open. "Are you giving me pot?"

A crease appeared in the middle of her heavy, broad forehead. "There is a living plant in the pot."

Norman snickered. "That's what the mortals call your plant these days. Pot."

"Ah." She smiled, showing wide heavy teeth, and held out the potted plant. "Then yes, I'm giving you a pot of pot."

If Norman looked like a liberal arts college professor, SHE appeared to be a living Neanderthal. Her bone structure was heavier than the average modern human. Her dark brown hair formed dreds. Her huge breasts were bare beneath her bone bead necklaces. Her only clothing besides the necklaces was a skirt made of skins.

I accepted her gift. "Come in." I stepped out of their way and tilted my head.

They stepped through the doorway, and I bumped the pink door shut with my hip.

Norman took a good look around my pink paradise. He propped his left hand on his hip and scratched the back of his head with his right. "Not exactly what I was expecting, kid."

"If you want a Neil Gaiman-Amanda Palmer goth-burlesque afterlife, that's my sister-in-law's department." I focused on creating a shelf for the plant and the tequila. If I thought about Tiffany, I would puke. There was no way she could be alive after what happened on that mountain.

Did Ares pull some strings and get her into the Elysian Fields? Or had Azrael collected her soul, and she was now reunited with Max and Jake in Heaven?

I turned back to my visitors. "So how did I end up here? Did I win the battle with the Old One?"

"It is difficult to explain, Samantha." SHE waved her hands. "This is the space the Old One and her entourage occupied."

"Her entourage?" I cocked my head and wondered if I was dreaming this whole thing.

"Her children. Her minions. Her priests." SHE shrugged. "Anything that curried her favor. When you consumed them, it left a hole in the universe if you will."

"A hole you'll occupy as the guardian of this afterlife," Norman added. He scuffed his Oxford against the pink carpet. "But really? Shag? That went out with Elvis."

"Elvis Presley never goes out of style," I shot back.

"Stop, Norman." SHE laid a hand on my shoulder. "Samantha may design this place how she wishes."

"That's right." I look down at the rabbits at my feet. "But who's going to come here after they die besides Flopsy and Peter?"

"They will." She pointed at a group of people standing in the middle of my pristine pink carpet. People I hadn't noticed before. They were all human. I recognized the dark-haired man in front.

"Marcus Giovanni? What the ever-loving fuck?" I marched toward them. The entire group, all one hundred or so, cowered behind him, but he lifted his chin as I approached.

"I will accept whatever punishment you deem fit for the entire group," he said. "They are not your enemy."

"They are Sunshine Believers!" I gestured at the cowering idiots. "They are as much my enemy as you are."

"You're responsible for my grandmother's death," he spat.

"Your grandmother was fucking psycho." I threw my hands in the air. "All this shit went down because she experimented on me!"

SHE pulled me away from Giovanni. "Settle, child. You are in control here, not him."

"But what are they doing here?" I whispered to her and Norman.

He shrugged. "They pledged themselves to the Old One. They arrived here about the time you . . . defeated him, so they have no place else to go. No other representative of Death would accept them."

On one hand, I was rather glad he avoided the subject of me eating the dinosaur god and its entourage. On the other—

"I refuse to acknowledge you as a goddess," Giovanni hissed from a few feet away.

"That's all right." I bared a vicious grin at him. "Better yet, I won't judge you. I'll let Connie decide your punishment. Remember her? Sergeant Constanza Torres. The woman you let the dino demon rape in Death Valley."

I'd seen in Connie's mind what Giovanni and the red-headed bitch, who was the daughter of the last full-blooded dino demon, had done to her. No one deserved the horrors they'd put the former Army sniper through.

The light turned black in my little kingdom. A murmur went through the crowd of souls. I took a deep breath in an effort to calm myself. The luminescence brightened to a medium gray.

"Can they leave here?" I asked.

"Only if you let them," SHE said.

"All right, here's the plan—" I started.

Instead of a polite knock, someone pounded on my pale pink door. Not angry pounding. Desperate pounding. It matching the muffled begging from the other side. I strode to the door and yanked it open.

Supay stood on the black sand in his red and black regalia. Gold decorated his ears, arms and long black hair. He held his hands out to me. "Lady Samantha, you must come! It's Alexander! I can do nothing in the territory of your believers!"

"What?"

"We separated when he accomplished the task he swore to do for me. A river of boiling mud swept through the creek bed and . . ." His voice faltered. "I'm so sorry. I never meant to have harm come to your friend. Nor did I wish to earn the Olympians' enmity."

"Where is he?" I growled.

Once he gave me the coordinates, I turned back to Giovanni. "I'll deal you and your band of idiots later. Flopsy! Peter!"

They hopped over to me, and I picked them up. Peter grumbled a bit about going back into my coat, but Flopsy pointed out it was better than a bunch of stinky human spirits on the ugly carpet.

Supay leaned over to see who and what was in my queendom. A malicious grin spread across his handsome features. "I would be happy to punish Marcus Benito Giovanni for you," he offered. "On your behalf of course, my lady." He made a sweeping bow.

When he straightened, I jabbed my index finger in his face. "You possessed one of my friends, and you think you get to play with my toys? You can go fuck yourself, Supay."

He scowled at me, but he was smart enough not to say anything else stupid.

SHE and Norman followed me out the door, and I locked it behind me.

"Sorry about this guys, but thank you so much for the presents," I said.

"We'll have your party once you deal with your friend," Norman assured me.

I didn't know if I could handle another god celebration. The last one almost got me divorced before I was married. Instead of saying anything that would offend SHE and Norman, I waved and teleported with my ghost rabbits in my pocket.

Chapter 61

Alex

Burnt, blackened flesh tore from my hands and feet as I climbed another incline. The river of mud had doused the forest fire, but I didn't feel like cooking my junk off again. The more worrisome part was I no longer felt any pain, only a deep, desperate thirst. I was going into shock.

The lahar had swept Giovanni's corpse away. If my death was the price for that traitor to be out of the coven's hair for the rest of eternity, so be it. My only regret was not telling Phil I loved her one last time. My phone was gone along with most of my clothes. The only plus was I managed to rip off the respiratory mask before it melted to my face.

I reached the top and rolled my body onto the ash-covered flat surface of the boulder. Flakes continued to fall from the sky. A pity I couldn't see the sun again, but I'd made the choice to stay a vampire if it meant no more melancholia and I'd live as long as my beloved Phil. That was a decision I definitely didn't regret.

The ash made it harder to breathe. If only I could hunt, find a critter to drink from, but everything with any sense had fled the area. Those with no sense or that had panicked in the cataclysm had been cooked or burned like me. The eruption was a battle between gods really, but no one outside of the supernatural community and Family would ever know the truth.

I started coughing, the spasms so hard the muscles of my chest split apart. My ribs shone white through the membranes and ligaments that held them together. Too bad we succeeded in killing Giovanni. Supay could have taken my soul otherwise. Uka Pacha wasn't that bad the last time I visited.

After all the explosions and roars and bullshit, it was terribly quiet in the charred forest below me. Did that mean Sam won her battle against the Old One? Surely, the ancient god and the dino demons would be flooding the area if Sam had lost. Did she eat the Old One the same way she ate the demons?

And where the hell was the red-headed demon Giovanni ran around with? Had she stayed in Otherwhere? Was she biding her time, waiting for the next pantheon to be created? Waiting thousands of years for her next chance to bring her father's gods back to this plane of existence?

No, wait. Giovanni had admitted she was planning to kill Duncan if her god lost.

Shit! There was no way I could reach Seattle in time to alert our enforcers, even if I were relatively intact.

Ares! I waited a moment and telepathically shouted again, *Ares!*

Nothing.

If things had gone south in Los Angeles, Ares would have escaped with Phil and Ellie.

I coughed again. This time I choked on liquid. I was drowning in my own fluids. My left arm was paralyzed. It took everything I had in my right side to roll over. Blood spilled from my mouth. This was more than the forest fire and boiling volcanic mud.

White light flashed behind me, terribly close. Instead of a peal of thunder, someone rolled me on my back.

"Holy crap, Alex," Sam muttered. The light I'd seen was her eyes. She knelt beside me.

"Hey, darlin," I croaked. "'Bout time you showed up." Night was closing in. Ash still fell, but it seemed to slide around us, not land on us. "Mind toning down the headlights."

"Sorry." Her eyes dimmed to neon blue. "Better."

"Yeah—" I started choking again. She lifted me and turned my head. More blood spurted from my mouth. She rested my head and chest on her thighs.

"Oh, no. No, no, no!" She grabbed my left arm and examined the wrist. "That bastard didn't tell me you'd been poisoned."

"Poisoned?" My tongue felt thick in my mouth. "Giovanni had something in his hand right before I killed him."

"Alex, it's dino demon venom." Tears trickled down her pale cheeks. "Even if I get you to Bebe . . ."

"Not a damn thing she can do," I choked out. The image of Isabella was still fresh and raw in my mind even after seven years. The Huamán Coven enforcer had bitten the first dino demon we encountered. Her death still haunted my nightmares. And the dino demon venom was even more dangerous than their blood.

I laid my right hand over Sam's. "Never mind me. Tell Duncan he doesn't have to worry about Giovanni. But the red-headed daughter of the last demon is after him. You need to get back to Los Angeles—"

"I'm not leaving you here to die alone," she said fiercely.

"Sam, I—" I could feel the blood running down the back of my throat. Just like it had when Giovanni and the demon bitch who'd slaughtered Phil's assistant Jane had staked me and Francisco Chavez on the Incan terrace in Peru to be roasted by the sun.

I could feel Sam's pulse throb, her blood singing beneath her skin. I was so damn thirsty. Thank Jove, I couldn't do a damn thing about it. Except I couldn't drink Sam's blood. It wouldn't heal me like Mama Pacha's had. And Sam would stay here with me out of guilt, instead of protecting her husband.

"You can't help me." I choked again. "Please go."

Her eye shifted from blue to white. "Alex, do you trust me?"

"Course I do." I patted her hand, hoping to placate her into leaving.

"I have an idea on how to fix you." Her throat bobbed. "But it means killing you first. And you won't be human when I'm done."

"So I'll be one of your baby zombies?"

"No," she whispered. "You'll be like me."

I laughed. Well, it started as a laugh before it turned into another choking fit. When I could speak, my voice wasn't much more than a rasp.

"I seem to recall your husband offering me a similar devil's deal once upon a time." I smiled up at her, or tried to. From her grimace, my smile was probably horrifying. "I didn't want to die then. I don't want to die now. But if dying is the only chance I got, then I'll take it."

"Are you sure? Because I can't undo it once it's done."

Like a hundred and fifty years ago, my heart answered. "Do it."

She released my left wrist and laid me gently in the ash. "Close your eyes, Alex."

I did.

Suddenly, I was standing. And between me and Sam was a grotesque, burnt corpse.

My heart would have stopped at the realization I was looking at my own body if Sam hadn't already stopped the infernal organ first.

Chapter 62

Constanza

Constanza poked Sam's index finger with her Olympian bronze pin. "Thank you for your cooperation, Mrs. St. James." Per usual, the other two vampires at the gate to the master's Portland estate exuded waves of ashy odor at the presence of his wife, but this evening, Sam smelled like brimstone and death.

After what Constanza saw on the local newscasts of the events at Mount Rainier, she could understand why.

She escorted Sam toward the main house. "Did you find Alex, Tiffany, and Ptolemy?" Constanza asked softly once they were out of earshot of the other enforcers.

"No," Sam snapped.

No wonder she was in a foul mood. She entered the house and stalked down the hallway toward the room Master St. James had co-opted as his office. Of course, she would know where her husband was.

Except why hadn't Sam teleported straight there?

"Did they leave the bunker?' Constanza asked.

"Why are you pestering me—" Sam stopped herself. Her smile was rueful. "I'm sorry, Constanza. You're only doing your job. But can I report to you and Duncan at the same time so I don't have to repeat myself?"

"Of course, Mrs. St. James." Constanza inclined her head though the hackles on the back of her neck rose. Sam never called her by her full name. The master worried Sam would be different after her battle. Hell, everyone in the coven did, but if Sam hadn't found Alex or Tiffany, Constanza was sure Sam would still be looking for them. Even if it meant bringing their bodies home.

They continued walking toward the office.

Anne? Would you join us in Master St. James' office? He would want his household chief of security present if Alex were still missing.

"Why did you call for help, Constanza?" Sam hissed. Something glittered in her hand.

That's when the pieces clicked inside Constanza's brain. Sam hadn't teleported directly to Master St. James because this wasn't Sam.

"Demon!" Constanza shouted vocally and mentally. There wasn't time to figure out how the bitch had passed the bronze pin test.

The intruder slashed down at her abdomen, no doubt hoping to disembowel her. Constanza jumped back and pivoted to kick, but fire raked across her left thigh. The demon leapt out of the way of Constanza's half-assed kick. She whirled and plunged through the door into the master's office.

Constanza lunged to catch the demon, but her injured leg gave out, and she collapsed on the carpet.

"Duncan, that's not Constanza! That's a demon!" the intruder shrieked.

Master St. James already had a sword in his hand. It may have been decorative, but this one looked like it had a wickedly sharp edge. The intruder ran to his side. He automatically wrapped an arm around her.

"No!" Constanza howled as the demon stabbed him in the chest with the object. The glass knife glittered under the office lighting. The sword dropped from his hand. With a surprised expression on his face, Master St. James crumpled to the floor.

"You should have stayed with us, Constanza," the demon purred. "You would have lived longer." Its form melted and shifted until Marcus Giovanni stood in front of her. "A pity. We had such a lovely time that night."

Raw rage swept through Constanza. This was the bastard who raped her. Who forced her to have a demon child. The daughter she had to kill because the child was too dangerous to live.

Constanza grabbed onto a nearby antique black leather and cherry captain's chair and forced herself upright. "You lost, *puta*. Otherwise, your precious god would be devouring the world right now."

"I'll simply wait until the next time." An ugly grin curved his lips. "I've got the time. You don't."

"You should have bitten me," Constanza said. "The venom would have acted quicker."

"Now, where's the fun in that?" he mocked.

Behind the demon, Master St. James's hand twitched. Constanza felt a little thrill of joy. *Sam, please, I need you to hear me. You have to save your husband. Come now.*

The demon shook his head and chuckled. "You really believe that bitch can answer your prayers when she's dead?"

That was the key. Belief.

Abuelita had raised her as a good Catholic girl, but that had been when Constanza was human. Now . . .

Behind the demon, Master St. James grasped the pommel of his sword.

Constanza threw her heart and soul into her words. "Lady Samantha, guardian of the vampire dead, I beg you to aid me in my direst hour."

"Shut up, bitch!" The demon charged her, shifting as he moved. At the same time, Master St. James slid his sword across the carpet in her direction.

She ducked the swipe of the demon's talons, pivoted on her good leg, and snatched the pommel of the sword with her right hand as she drew her pin with her left.

The demon spun to face her, and she plunged the Olympian bronze into its eye. It screamed in pain, a wail Constanza echoed as acidic black blood and vitreous splashed on her fingers. She swallowed the agony and swung the sword with all the might she had left.

The grotesque reptilian head bounced once on the carpet. Constanza ducked her face, but drops of black blood sprayed over her skin and clothes. Fire filled her inside and out, and she collapsed to the floor once again.

The demon's corpse slowly toppled in the direction of its head. More blood spurted from the sliced arteries. Both the sword blade and carpet sizzled and smoked as the acidic blood ate them.

Anne rushed into the room, her skirt flaring at her sudden stop. She clenched her sai in her tiny fists. "What on earth?" More enforcers peered over the tiny Amish vampire's head.

Constanza crawled painfully over to Master St. James and pulled his torso into her lap. The glass knife stuck out of his chest. At least, the demon had missed his heart. Only her right pinkie finger was unburned. She pressed it against his neck where the carotid artery ran beneath his jaw. He still had a pulse, but it was very, very weak. She looked up at Anne.

The chief of household security turned to one of the enforcers on her right. "Go fetch Doctor Zachary from the clinic! Now!" The vampire scurried out of sight.

One of the enforcers on Anne's left muttered, "We'll get the baking soda." He nudged the woman next to him, and they took off as well.

Master St. James's eyes fluttered open. "You did . . . well, Constanza. Samantha will . . . be proud . . . of you." He exhaled, but there wasn't another intake of breath.

"I'm sorry, Anne." Constanza looked up at her trainer. She could feel the hot tears coursing down her cheeks, but the rest of her felt so damn cold. "I fucked up."

"No, you didn't." Anne knelt next to her. "I don't know how it managed to bypass the Olympian bronze, but it's not your fault. You followed protocol."

"I should have known." It was getting harder to draw a breath. "Sam would have teleported straight to Duncan. She would have brought Tiffany and the rest home. They're family. She wouldn't leave them."

Constanza knew she was babbling, but she couldn't seem to stop herself. "Maybe my daughter can rest in peace now that the demon who impregnated me is dead. I always wanted a daughter, but not like this. No one should be brought into the world in such a horrible . . ."

She couldn't think of the next word. Master St. James's flesh liquefied and slid from his bones. The sludge soaked her uniform pants. Weird how good the coolness felt against her hot skin.

"Connie," Anne murmured. She stroked Constanza's forehead with a washcloth containing a paste of water and baking soda from the smell. "Stay with me, sweetie. Bebe's on her way."

"Don't touch the glass knife!" Constanza wanted to push Anne away from her. "There's demon venom on it!"

"I promise I won't let anyone touch it," Anne said soothingly. "I need you to calm down. Take slow deep breaths. We need to keep the poison from reaching your organs."

"It's too late for that." Constanza smiled or tried to. "Thank you for everything, Anne."

Lady Samantha, I offer my soul into your care.

Constanza fell into the overwhelming blackness, sure of who she'd see on the other side.

Chapter 63

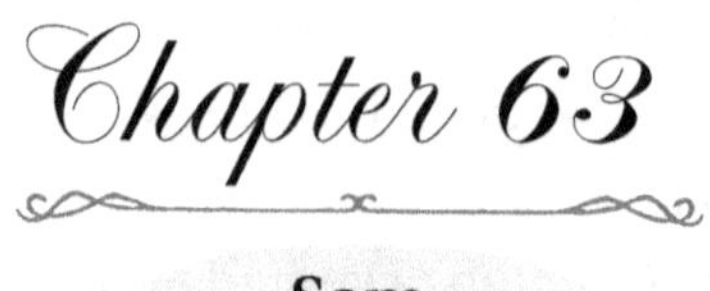

Sam

"Don't leave that spot, Alexander Socrates Stanton," I ordered. "Do you hear me?"

"Fine. I won't." He folded his amorphous arms. "What are you planning to do to my body?"

"I'm going to rebuild it. Now, hush." Between observing Ptolemy's soul transplanted into Jake's body and Supay's possession of Alex, I realized something. The human body was too fragile to hold more than its own single soul. That's the other part of why ghost possessions went wrong. The other gods had actually modified Jake's DNA sufficiently to bond with Ptolemy's soul without changing the body's outward appearance. And since Jake's soul was gone, there wasn't two souls to overload the body.

Alex's issue was a little more complicated. Part of it was his bargain with Supay. However, Supay modified his piece of soul to be compatible with Alex's DNA. He would have retained possession of Alex's body until the contract was completed. So basically, I had to modify Alex's old DNA to where it was strong enough to hold and bond with his soul as well as deal with the demon poison. And there was only one way to accomplish all of that.

I was about to add a second god to my new pantheon.

Sucking in a deep breath, I willed myself to relax. Alex's DNA spread out before me, and I started to weave it into a new pattern.

And I finally had my answer to when I really died. The nanites had stopped my heart on that operating gurney before they started rebuilding me.

⊰❉⊱

It could have been minutes. Hours. Days. All I knew was that it was dark when I finished. Ghost Alex still stood patiently next to his corpse. Now for the next step.

I looked up at him. "Ready to get back inside?"

"You're kidding me right?" He waved at the crispy, black exterior of his body. "Even if you put me back and restart my heart, that's not going to stop the poison."

"Cowboy, I've got to stick you back inside to activate all the crap that will take care of the poison. I won't shit you." I waved a hand at the corpse. "It's gonna hurt like a mother-fucker, but you will be alive."

His vague transparent face still didn't look certain. "How are you keeping my body together? It should have liquefied by now."

"If I take the time to explain it, it will liquefy," I snapped. "Either you trust me or you don't. Do you want to stay dead?"

His arms dropped to his sides. "What do I have to do?"

"Not a damn thing." I grabbed his soul before he could bitch anymore and shoved him back into his body. Reconnecting the bits was easier now I'd seen how Ptolemy was stitched into Jake's body. The final step was jumpstarting Alex's heart.

Reflexively, he took his first breath and howled from the pain.

And continued howling.

It made me grateful for the sedative Selene and Mallory's mad scientists had given me. Or maybe my screaming had simply been annoying to them.

Flesh grew over the naked bones of his hands and feet. The dead, black skin started to flake off his body. Hair grew back in all the correct places.

Alex's howling quieted to occasional grunts of discomfort. He abruptly rolled over on his side and vomited. The weird bloody mass was similar to what I puked up while I was trying to escape from Mallory Labs.

Finally, he stopped heaving and rolled onto his back again. I kind of wished he hadn't. It's just not appropriate seeing the private bits of the husband of one of my closest friends. I closed my eyes and concentrated.

When I opened them, Alex wore the clothes he had on the day Tiffany and I dropped Ellie off at his and Phil's condo, plus some socks and his favorite pair of boots.

"You know, I could have dressed myself," he drawled.

"I know, but it would take longer to teach you how than either of our spouses would appreciate." I climbed to my feet and gave him a hand to gain his own. "You're going to feel a little weird over the next few days."

"No shit." He looked at the blackened forest around us. "Wow! How are these trees still alive?"

"The change in perspective is disorienting." I smiled at him. "At least, you'll have some peace and quiet to adjust—"

I heard something that wasn't a sound. Someone was crying, begging for my help. I stiffened. It wasn't telepathic communication or anything else I recognized, but it was definitely Connie Torres I felt.

"Shit," I muttered. "We need to go." I grabbed Alex's hand. "Let me handle this trip. I promise I'll teach you how to teleport later."

"All righty." He grinned at me and squeezed my hand in return. "Lead the way."

⊰❖⊱

Connie wasn't in Los Angeles, so I followed the feel of her anguish.

Alex and I popped into a back hallway of the main coven house in Portland. A vampire enforcer I'd only met once aimed at me and pulled the trigger.

Alex held up his hand, and the bullet paused in midair. "Dammit, Edwards! You been taking lessons from Cara Lannigan? Dino demons don't teleport."

He could deal with his people. I darted inside the room where I felt Connie and skidded to a halt. One bloody skeleton sat with its back against the front of a desk. The upper body of another skeleton laid across its lap. The liquefied sludge of dead vampire puddled around them. A wedding band that matched mine hung from the fourth finger of the prone skeleton's left hand.

Worse, the translucent shape of Connie Torres stood next to the corpses and stared at me. Sparkling, pearlescent ectoplasm dripped from her eyes.

"Sam?" Anne stepped toward me and laid a hand on my right arm. Behind her, black blood spilled from the headless corpse of a dino demon and ate the carpet. Fumes wafted from the ruined material, but another vampire spread an industrial-sized box of baking soda over the acid. More boxes sat next to the corpse, a couple of them empty. A pile of white powder covered a round object nearby. They had been neutralizing the mess when Alex and I arrived.

I swallowed hard. I knew the truth, but my heart couldn't accept it. Alex had warned me.

"Wh-what happened?"

"She disguised herself as you," Anne murmured. "Witnesses swear Connie pin-checked her."

"She's the last child of the original trio," Alex said behind me. "She may have been able to resist the effects of the Olympian bronze longer than the others. You did good, Anne."

"I didn't kill it," Anne said. "Connie did. The demon—" She gulped, obviously trying not to cry herself. "It poisoned them with demon venom. There wasn't even time to get Bebe at the clinic."

I didn't realize I'd moved until my knees sank into the ooze that had been my husband and my protégé. I looked up at Connie. "Why are you still here?"

"I couldn't leave until I apologized to you." Her nostrils flared as she tried to inhale, but it was only the memory of breathing. "I'm so sorry, Sam. You trusted me to protect him, and I failed both of you."

My gut clenched as I realized what it was I'd felt from her a few minutes ago. She had prayed to me as she was dying. She was my responsibility.

"Where is he, Connie?"

"I don't know." Her form blurred in response to her guilt and anguish. "He died a few minutes before I did. It stabbed him in the chest with a glass knife coated with demon venom. It only scratched me on my thigh. When I found myself next to our bodies, he was gone."

I forced myself to my feet "Stay here, Connie," I ordered just like I had Alex when he was a ghost. "Don't move. I'll be right back." I turned to face the three living enforcers. "Do not touch their bodies until I get back. You got me, Anne? They need to stay exactly where they are."

The enforcer who had been helping Anne didn't move a muscle. He smelled like he was about to pass out from his fear.

"What about the dinosaur demon's corpse?" Anne asked.

"Leave it here, too. I'm going to need it." If that little bitch thought she was going to escape me by dying, she was very, very wrong.

"Sam?" Alex laid a hand on my right shoulder as I passed him. "Where are you going?"

I shrugged off his hold. "To get my husband's soul back."

Chapter 64

Tiffany

I would never complain about my tiny bathroom in my Tarzana house again. It stunk to high heaven within David's magick sphere, but that was mainly from body odor. Three very sweaty humans in a hot, tight space? I had no idea how the astronauts in the fucking space station managed.

David created a hole in the concrete and fashioned a lid from the same material between two of the silver star's arms. Since there was an air pocket below what had been the concrete floor of the bunker, we had a space for our waste. That was one small grace as far as the stink went.

If I concentrated on the stink, I could forget about the pain in my leg. When the witches in Seattle did whatever it was that sent David's sphere tumbling through the earth, the oxygen tank slammed into my lower right leg. We were lucky that was our only problem. Once David stabilized his sphere and found us another safe spot. Ptolemy had to set the bones and splint them with David's cane and tie strings from sweats and shoes. I should have grabbed the medkit. Vicodin would be very tasty and welcome right now.

And if I focused on the pain in my leg, it distracted me from the burning sensation when I peed.

Ptolemy reached over and touched my toes of my right foot. "They are still warm."

I was starting to get some sensation back. Instead of being numb, my toes tingled. Otherwise, I would have been shrieking with laughter since any touch on my lower extremities tickled like hell.

His touch shifted to the pulse point along the top of my foot. He looked at David who nodded.

I matched David's silent count while Ptolemy kept track of my pulse.

"Time," David said.

"A strong sixty-three," Ptolemy announced.

"So I'm not going to lose the leg, doc?" I grinned at them.

"That's not funny, Tiffany," Ptolemy said. "When I was a child, a double break like that *could* result in the loss of a leg."

"Yeah, have y'all seen the clip online where Washington quarterback Joe Theismann broke his leg on a play?" David waved his hands excitedly. "That video is totally sick. The stadium mikes picked up the sound of his bones snapping—"

"You're not helping," I said through gritted teeth. I wasn't sure what was worse—the pain in my leg or the nausea from David's description. I'd kill for even those disgusting orange-flavored baby aspirins right now.

"I kind of miss not being able to tell what time it is," Ptolemy murmured.

"Is that like an instinctive vampire thing?" David asked.

"Yeah, it is." I grinned. "You don't want to accidentally fry yourself by coming out of your coffin too soon."

Ptolemy shot me a dirty look. "No one sleeps in a coffin unless it's a transport type for commercial intercontinental flights."

David settled down along the diameter of the circle. He was the tallest so it only made sense for him to lay there. I kind of liked him separating me from Ptolemy. Not that I'd do anything really stupid in front of someone else, especially with my leg killing me. But I still wasn't sure if I should be happy he's back or if I should hit him for what he said earlier.

"So," David said after he stretched out. "This cure and vaccination for the V-virus, how long has it been around?"

"The vaccination for about eighteen months," I answered. "The cure came almost a year ago. Why?"

He chuckled. "Just trying to figure out when Yvonne got married to Rousseau."

"Jean-Pierre got married?" Ptolemy shot David a quizzical look before his attention turned to me.

"It'll be a year this Christmas." I smiled at the memory. "They were sweet enough to ask Ellie to be their flower girl."

David sighed and rested his clasped hands behind his head. "I should have been there to give her away."

"Your cousin Theo did," I said softly. "I hope you don't give him too hard of a time over it."

"Theo?" David frowned. "They all disowned me and Yvonne."

"Brigette pushed things too far over you and Sam." I shrugged. "Her actions ended up splitting the New Orleans coven in two."

"A city can't survive with two witch covens," David said.

"They can when Brigette and her followers were forced to move to Slidell." I grinned. "She managed not only to piss Sam off, but Baron Samedi as well. If she or any of the Slidell idiots step out of line, they're not going to know what hit them."

"So, you were at Yvonne's wedding?" he asked.

"Yes." I reached over and patted his knee. "She really wanted you to be there."

"Ridgeway coulda released me," he grumbled.

I sighed and leaned against the magick shield. Though it was warm, it felt good against my back, which was weird because I'd been sweating this whole time. "She was afraid of accidentally killing you."

David snorted derisively. "Yeah, right."

I hated the fact he was making me defend her.

"Let's talk about something else," Ptolemy said. "Did Marvel ever put out the Avengers movie they planned to make?"

Both men looked expectantly at me. I shook my head.

"I hate to tell you guys this, but Disney took over Marvel Studios, Lucasfilm, and the movie division of 20th Century Fox while you both were . . . out of the loop." I grinned at the surprised looks on their faces. "Yep, that's right, boys. Princess Leia and the xenomorphs are now officially Disney Princesses."

My shiver took me by surprise though the urge to urinate didn't. Great. That's what I needed on top of every thing else. A full-blown urinary tract infection while I was trapped in a tiny space with two men.

The next two days were going to be sheer torture.

"Let's see," I started. "When you died, Ptolemy, they hadn't released any of the Captain America or Thor movies yet, had they? Oh, wait!" I snapped my fingers. "Disney rebooted the Star Wars franchise, too!"

Thank Murphy, I had the plots of most of the recent pop culture movies memorized thanks to Ellie watching them ad nauseum. I just hoped I didn't run out of material before we could resurface. Otherwise, I just might kill someone after all.

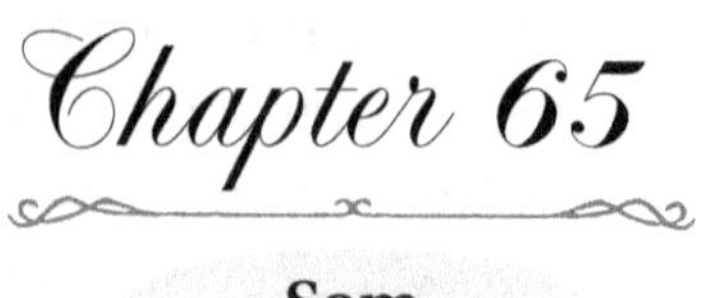

Chapter 65

Sam

I strode through the clouds straight for Heaven. Azrael taking Duncan was the only possible explanation why my husband's soul was gone. Like many other nobles, Duncan's father had renounced the Catholic Church when Henry VIII cut ties with the Vatican.

But at Christmas, he went to midnight mass at the local Catholic services in Los Angeles or Las Vegas.

What would I cling to from my previous life a few centuries down the road if I didn't have him?

The massive blindingly white walls and the pearlescent gates appeared ahead. The white-robed gatekeeper stood in front of his polished maple podium, his bald head shining under the indistinct sunlight.

I approached him, and he frowned at me since I didn't have an angelic escort.

"Tell Azrael I want my husband back," I demanded.

His frown deepened. "Your husband?"

"Duncan Henry Evander St. James," I hissed. "I want him back."

The gatekeeper held up his right index finger. "Let me check." He ran his finger down his long scroll. "I don't see . . ."

My rage welled up inside me, pushing aside any grief. "You've got exactly thirty seconds to produce my husband—"

"Ah, here he is. That's odd." The gatekeeper looked up at me. "Azrael should have brought him with the group from the Mount Rainier volcanic eruption earlier today."

"Duncan wasn't at Rainier!" I slammed my right fist on the top of his podium. It splintered and collapsed. The top of the scroll with its gold roller literally rolled off the cloud and out of sight. "I was! Where the hell did Azrael take him?"

At the gatekeeper's appalled look, I grabbed him by the top of his white robe. "You'd better not tell me Azrael took my husband to Hell."

"That's not my department," he stammered.

One of the huge gates swung open, and a dark-haired archangel exited with a flaming sword. "Release Peter, and begone Heathen!"

Of course, it would be Michael, the one fucking archangel I didn't get along with who answered the door.

I released Peter and crossed my arms. "Not without my husband Duncan."

"He's not here." Michael glowered at me.

"Then I want to speak to Azrael," I growled.

"He's not here either," Michael said.

"Don't make me come in there—"

There was a rustle of thousands of wings. I looked around. I was surrounded. The cherubs didn't appear that dangerous with their tiny bows, but I'd heard through the god grapevine they were especially vicious.

"You and what army?" Michael wasn't mocking me. He was deadly serious. I couldn't enter Heaven without a fight. And the Heavenly Host weren't even the big guns.

I'd already had one god smackdown today. I wasn't ready for a second one.

I returned my attention back to Michael. "I'd better not find out you lied to me."

"I didn't."

There wasn't anything more to say so I pivoted and walked away. The angels parted to let me pass.

Time didn't have any meaning. First, I went to Uku Pacha on the slim chance Supay sent me to help Alex in order to steal Duncan's soul because I'd turned down the deity's proposal. He actually appeared embarrassed he'd unintentionally set our friend up to die, then delighted at what I had to do to save Alex.

Delighted in a very bizarre bromance way. I'd have to warn Alex when I got back to Portland.

I checked with my goddess girlfriends. None of them knew who might have claimed him, much less had taken him themselves. Kali promised to teach me some awesome torture techniques if I found out who stole my husband's soul.

Out of desperation, I went to Norman's afterlife. He assured me he hadn't taken Duncan because my husband was a devoutly spiritual man.

SHE just looked at me, rolled her eyes, and let the mammoth skin that covered the entrance to her afterlife drop back into place.

I even paid Charon to carry me across the River Styx, which he only did because I was already dead. The tongue thing was creepy, and his fingers tasted funky, but hey, I'd done weirder things to get a story when I was a reporter and still alive. As he pushed off from the dock, a howling, ephemeral ghost raced up to the edge.

"Who's that?" I asked.

"One of the people who killed you." He chuckled.

There was only one person who could possibly end up in the Greek afterlife. "Selene Antonius?"

Charon nodded.

For the first time since I died, I actually felt sorry for Caesar and Ptolemy's sister. I looked over my shoulder at her. She screamed imprecations at me for stealing her boyfriend.

When I reached the main gates, Cerberus wasn't an issue despite the dog's reputation. In fact, I got drenched thanks to getting licked by three huge tongues. A ghost escorted me to the throne room. I was a little surprised to find it empty except for two people.

"Sam!" Persephone raced down the steps from her ebony throne, her arms wide. She enveloped me in a huge hug. She was dressed in a black chiton that reached her bare feet, and her hair was dark brown, like it always was around my birthday, but swept in an updo with topaz jeweled pins.

"Thank you for seeing me, Your Majesties." I nodded to Hades on his jeweled throne. It was slightly more ostentatious than his wife's. Like her, he also wore a black chiton, but his was cut to his knees. Gold sandals adorned his feet.

"Don't be silly." Persephone looped her left arm around my right and tugged me forward. "You're family."

"Only because of Ares and Phil," I protested.

"My nephew is an asshole," Hades muttered.

"Husband!" she chided.

"I'm sorry to say, but this is business." I considered my words carefully. Hades had refused to speak to me in the past. I couldn't blow this now. "One of the Old Ones' demons murdered my husband. His soul should have gone to Heaven, but they claim they do not have it. I was hoping you might have some knowledge of what may have happened to him, Lord Hades."

While he was just as handsome as Ares, Hades exuded an elderly "get off my lawn" air. He scowled at me.

"You know the rules, child. Has your husband pledged his soul to you?"

My mouth opened. Shit. I shut it abruptly. Two years ago on Virginia Dare's lawn, Duncan had tried to make me promise to let him go when he died. I told him I couldn't because if I did and he changed his mind, we were screwed.

I bowed to Hades. "Thank you so much for your wisdom, Your Majesty. I hope you will attend my celebration soon."

"Yes!" Persephone pumped her right fist. "Party time!"

Hades rolled his eyes at me. "You just had to say that in front of her, didn't you?"

I hugged Persephone. "See you soon." I released her and nodded to Hades. "Thank you again, Your Majesty." I practically skipped out of their throne room.

Ghosts crowded in the massive hallway. They parted as I passed. I patted Cerberus on all three heads and got another tongue-washing for the effort. I reached the dock and climbed into Charon's boat.

"I don't usually take anyone back," he said, stroking his long gray beard.

"Do you think your king will be happy if I throw a hissy fit?" I smiled brightly at him.

"Why don't any of you folks ever try to ask nicely?" the boatman said.

"Mister Charon, would you please take me back across the River Styx?"

"See? That wasn't so hard, was it?" He pushed away from the dock with his pole. He was silent for the rest of the trip.

When I stepped onto the dock on the other side, I noticed Selene floating among the other shades on the shore. I turned to Charon. "What happens to the souls who can't cross?"

He shrugged. "If they can't pay the toll through no fault of their own, the king allows leniency once a year."

"On Halloween," I murmured.

Charon nodded. "Took one load across the night before last." He shrugged again. "Otherwise, they go mad and melt away."

"Can I drop a hint that you could pass on to your queen?"

He nodded once more.

I smiled. "Cleopatra Selene Antonius's soul would make a lovely celebration gift."

Chapter 66

Angela

The tangy scent of oil of bergamot woke Angela to another gray day. Or that was the only light filtering through the high, grimy windows of the gymnasium. She stretched, or tried to. Every freaking muscle in her body ached.

"Morning, beautiful." Jim grinned at her. He sat in a chair beside her cot. In his hands was a steaming paper cup with a lid from one of the local coffee shops.

She pushed back the blanket and sat up. "What time is it?" She scrubbed her eyes before she accepted the cup from him.

"Four in the afternoon."

"I only slept two hours?" She sipped the tea. "No wonder I feel like shit."

"Try twenty-six hours. It's November 1st."

Well, crap. On one hand, it was good to sleep through the post-disaster shenanigans that she was sure went on for the last day after everyone realized they survived the initial eruption, earthquakes, and tsunamis. On the other hand, everyone would be stuck here for a few days, waiting for the ash to dissipate enough for helicopters to reach the survivors.

"How's everyone else doing?" she asked before she sipped more tea.

"If you mean the other members of Blue Hawk, everyone's in a similar condition to you," Jim said. "Just plain exhausted. Over the last day, some have woken up long enough to eat and drink something and immediately passed out again. Everyone else has been waking up over the last couple of hours. That's the reason I got you the tea."

"The coffee shop is open?" She looked at Jim, a little puzzled.

"Nope, donations."

Her bladder suddenly reminded her she hadn't emptied it in over a day. She handed her cup to Jim. Her balance was a little shaky when she stood. Jim reached under the cot and pulled out her staff.

Angela smiled at him and patted his cheek. After nearly thirty years of marriage, some things didn't need to be said.

As she walked past the other cots, some people smiled and nodded to her. Others stared with expressions of fear. She wasn't sure what was going on, but her entire body throbbed too much to find out, and her bladder didn't give a rat's ass.

She found the porta potties that had been trucked in or confiscated by the local authorities for disaster relief. They were tucked under an outdoor portico so the fumes didn't make everyone sick. Someone had arrange plastic sheeting and tarps to block most of the ash. When she finished her business, she followed her nose inside to find some food to settle her stomach.

Inside the makeshift dining area, Libbie waved at her from across the room. Once again, some people smiled and acknowledged her while others looked at her with fear and revulsion as she crossed the room to sit with her friend. Libbie shoved a disposable bowl filled with grilled zucchini, green peppers and mushrooms in Angela's direction as she took the seat across from Libbie.

"Eat these," she said around bites of the salmon on her plate. "The authorities are serving the most perishable stuff first to extend the generators' fuel supply.

"What in the Goddess's many names is going on?" Angela whispered. "People are staring at me like I've turned purple and grown a second head."

"Well, you do have purple stripes in your hair." Libbie grinned.

"Cut the bullshit," Angela growled. "You know what I mean."

Libbie looked distinctly uncomfortable as she chewed and swallowed. "We've been outed."

Shock ran through Angela. "The weres have been outed? By who?"

"Not just us." Libbie made a face. "All of the supernaturals. Apparently, some Normal kids caught our battle with the rogues on the northeast waterfront with their phones' video. Same with the witches' efforts to lessen the tsunamis and keep this section of the city steady."

Angela leaned back in her chair and groaned. "Please tell me you're shitting me."

"Oh, it gets worse." Libbie grimaced. "The little brats uploaded the video by satellite phone. Apparently, it's all over the internet now."

Angela let her face fall into her palms. This was terrible. The supernatural leaders outside of Seattle had to be going completely apeshit over those videos. And the internet was forever.

When she scrubbed her hands down her face, she was surprised to find a little girl of about eight standing beside her. She wore tan cotton twill pants and a smudged white polo shirt, probably a school uniform. Her loose dark brown hair looked like it hadn't been combed in a couple of days. Even wilder, the little girl threw her scrawny arms around Angela's neck.

"*Gracias, bruja! Gracias!*" She smiled shyly before she tore off toward the exit.

Angela shook her head and looked at Libbie. "If the proverbial cat's out of the bag, what do we do now?"

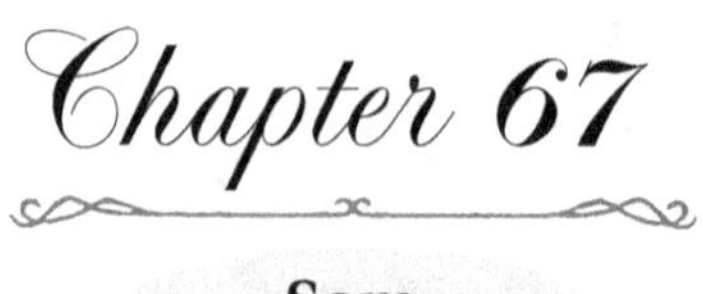

Chapter 67

Sam

I returned through Otherwhere to my own domain. Creatures watched me from a distance, but none of them cared to get closer. Maybe I carried the stench of the dead Old One with me. Or maybe I gave off a bitch goddess on the warpath vibe. The monsters didn't even growl in my direction.

As I approached my pale pink doorway, two figures stood in front of it. I broke into a run and leapt into Duncan's arms.

"I've been looking all over for you," I said in between peppering his face with kisses.

"Darling," he said in a low voice. "Not in front of company."

He was dead, and he was still worried about propriety?

I unlocked my legs from around his waist and deliberately slid down his body. Thankfully, ectoplasm was pretty solid in Otherwhere. I turned to Azrael, who for once wore only a kilt around his lower half instead of jeans and a white t-shirt or his black Grim Reaper robes.

"What the fuck, dude!" I poked his naked, hairless, well-muscled chest. "Is this revenge for accidentally resurrecting the baby zombies?"

"No." The angel gave my husband an exasperated look. "He changed his mind right at the point of death."

I looked up at Duncan and grinned. "Told ya you would."

"I needed to know whether you defeated your foe," he said archly.

"Your wife was quite incredible. She was tenacious and brilliant," Azrael said.

"What?" I glared at him. "Did you guys set up stands and sell popcorn?"

"I'm actually a Junior Mints angel myself." Azrael grinned at me. "When Duncan changed his mind, I brought him straight to your domain. However—" He waved at the pink door. "—you were not here."

"I had to run out to answer a couple of prayers."

"You answered prayers?" Duncan stared at me aghast. It wasn't worth getting into this now.

"Are we kosher?" I asked Azrael.

"Yes, my lady." With a flap of his giant white wings, he was gone.

"What happens next?" Duncan asked. "Do we go inside?"

"Nope." I clasped his hand in mine. "We're going back to Portland."

"Samantha." He shifted to stand in front of me. "I know what has happened to me. I have no body to go back to. If you think you can do to me what the other gods did to Ptolemy, that is wrong. As you and Tiffany would say, that is wrong on so many levels."

"I promise I'm not body snatching anyone." I grinned up at him. "I'm going to do what I did to Alex."

Worry flickered in his emerald eyes. "What did you do to Alex?"

"I got to see him naked," I teased.

❈

Duncan was still yelling at me when we popped into his office in Portland. Thankfully, almost everybody couldn't hear him. Unfortunately, thanks to me, Alex was one of the few people who could.

". . . how would you feel if I looked at Phillippa while she was naked!" Duncan paused. He wasn't finished, not by a longshot, but he hadn't figured out he didn't need to take breath as a ghost.

"Why the hell would you be looking at mah wife naked?" Alex yelled.

"Because you exposed yourself to my wife!" Duncan tried to punch Alex, but his fist passed through the cowboy's head.

Bless, Anne. She escorted everyone else out of the room except Bebe. The Amish enforcer couldn't throw Connie out because she couldn't see either of the ghosts in the room.

Connie perched on the edge of the desk. Bebe sat next to her in an antique captain's chair. I hoped the doctor was keeping Connie calm until I arrived.

"I didn't expose mahself!" Alex shouted. "My clothes burned off along with most of mah skin and my man parts when I was caught in a lahar!"

"And why were you sneaking around Washington instead of doing your job?" The picture frames on the walls shivered and a couple pieces of glass cracked at Duncan's yelling.

"Because ah got possessed by the Incan god of death!" Alex was so mad he looked to be on the verge of a stroke. Unfortunately, his anger manifested in a different way. The entire house shook.

Out in the hallway, enforcers and other St. James personnel were hollering about aftershocks and taking cover. I pinched the bridge of my nose, preparing to do some yelling myself, but Duncan abruptly calmed down.

"He what?" My husband spun around to look at me, streamers of ectoplasm trailing in his wake. "Did you know about this?"

"I found out when your precious niece tricked me into Supay's trap."

Of course, Duncan ignored Tiffany's part in this mess. "What are you going to do about it?" he snapped.

"Not a damn thing." I crossed my arms. "Alex is the numbskull who bargained with Supay to deliver the heads of everyone involved in stealing his tumi on a silver platter. Giovanni was the last. It was just bad timing. Alex and Supay had killed Giovanni seconds before the lahar swept through. Since their contract was complete, Supay couldn't help Alex directly, so he came to get me."

Duncan's eyes narrowed. "You said you were out answering prayers."

"I didn't pray to her," Alex protested.

I looked at him. "That's because you come under the family exception."

He blinked. "How?"

"My brother married your step-foster-daughter." I turned back to Duncan. "Which, by the way, is your fault since you made Phil Tiffany's co-guardian. And for the record, I slapped some clothes on him as soon as his injuries healed."

"Then where have you been for the last twenty-four hours?" Anne threw her hands in the air. "Do you have any idea what's been going on here?"

I leaned back against the force of the diminutive woman's fury. "Looking for Duncan. Psychopomps of certain afterlifes can be worse at losing things than National Direct Shipping."

"I was not lost," he snapped. "I was on your doorstep. You were not there for delivery."

I ignored him. "What happened?"

"A few things," Alex murmured. "Tiffany, Ptolemy, and Head are missing."

My blood chilled. They had been in the bunker with me when the Old One tore into it. At least, I thought they were. My extreme hunger made things from that time a little fuzzy. I wasn't sure how any mortal could have survived what happened on top of Mount Rainier.

"Missing?" Duncan roared.

"Bebe kept Connie company while I searched the wreckage," Alex said to me. "I couldn't even find any bodies."

"The Old One cracked the bunker like a nut, coming after me. The heat—" I started.

"No bone fragments." Alex shook his head. "No ash. Nothing. The odd thing was no silver either."

"The pentacle you created for Bebe?" Duncan asked.

Alex nodded. "It should have been slagged by the eruption, but the metal would still exist. There's a good chance Head got them out."

Or I could have eaten them in my feeding frenzy. I wanted to pray to someone that wasn't the case, but I couldn't. Not anymore. No sense saying the words aloud and starting another fight with everyone until I knew for sure.

"Wait a minute," Bebe said. "What pentacle?"

"After Selene's attempted coup nine years ago, we created a series of special safe houses across our territory," Duncan said. "Ones she could not possibly know about. Bunkers really. Some place we could stash you and Caesar if things went badly for us."

"Why didn't I know about this?" Bebe asked.

"Not even Caesar and I knew where exactly they were," Duncan said. "Only Alex and Tiffany did."

I shook my head. "That explains a lot."

This time, Duncan ignored me. "What else has happened?"

"We've been outed," Bebe said.

"The witches?" I asked.

"All of us!" Anne shouted. "All of the supernaturals! It's all over the fucking internet!"

All of us stared at the Amish woman. Her anger was understandable, but the fact she said a bad word?

"Also, word has already gotten out about you, Duncan," Bebe said. "The Vampire Nation Congress is meeting in two days. Alex and I talked about him attending in your stead with Caesar in an advisory capacity."

I looked at Alex. "They're going to know the instant you walk in you're no longer a vampire."

"Is that why he's glowing white like you do?" Duncan said. "You put nanites in him?"

"No." I shuffled my boots on the carpet, readying myself for the explosion about to go off. "No nanites. I killed him and resurrected him."

"You what?" Duncan said quietly.

I looked up at him, my own rage coming out. "Before the lahar hit Alex, Giovanni poisoned him with dino demon venom. I wasn't going to let him suffer. You know how ugly and painful of a death that is."

"Why didn't you come to me?" Pain filled his eyes.

Oh, how I wanted to hold him, reassure him. "Supay told me about Alex. Alex warned me Giovanni and the dino demons were targeting you. I made the decision to help Alex instead of coming straight here." I swiped at the wetness on my cheek. "You can be pissed at me for not coming sooner, but if I had, you would have been pissed that I left Alex alone to die.

"The only person here I'm truly responsible for is Connie." I pointed at the silent ghost watching this insane charade. "I can rebuild both of your bodies, but I have to make you like me in order to keep the demon poison from killing you again."

"You mean gods," Connie whispered.

"No!" Anne held her hands out to Duncan. "This is wrong. To even think to raise yourself above the Lord of Heaven . . ."

I looked at Bebe as Anne continued. *Really? She's been able to See Duncan and Connie this whole time?*

The witch's shrug was barely perceptible. *She and Connie needed to talk while we were waiting for you.*

And you didn't think to warn me?

I wasn't paying any attention to Anne's tirade, so her slap across my face caught me by surprise. It stung, but it would have broken a Normal's neck.

"I'm already so beneath you that you can't even bother to listen to me?" Anne turned to face Bebe. "Have your clinic in Los Angeles prepare cures for myself and my husband." She whirled back to Duncan. "I hereby tinder my resignation, Master St. James." She pivoted and stalked out of the room.

After a long moment of silence, Connie started to laugh. She laughed until tears of ectoplasm rolled down her transparent face. When her laughter died to the occasional chortle, I asked, "What's so funny?"

She grinned. "You all are a true family. Totally dysfunctional. Now, why are you really keeping the demon corpse?"

"Do you want to go on to the afterlife, or do you want to be resurrected as a god?" I smirked. "I have a special project for you no matter what you choose."

"Resurrected," she said. "I still have some things on my bucket list."

I looked at Duncan. "I have one condition for you before you decide."

"But . . . I am your husband," he protested.

"Which is exactly why there's a condition for you."

He scowled at me. "What is it?"

I folded my arms over my chest. "If you choose resurrection, you are not going to beat up Alex."

"I would not . . ." A sheepish expression appeared on his translucent mug, and he turned to Alex. "I apologize for attempting to strike you. The circumstances were extraordinary, and you were not at fault."

"Thank you, Duncan." Alex smiled. It was a little weird to see his cocky grin without fangs.

It took me a little longer to rebuild Duncan and Connie's bodies than to simply rewrite Alex's DNA. But in the end, I got the job done.

The guys needed to deal with the rumors of Duncan's demise and the outing of the supernaturals. That shit was now all over the mainstream news outlets. The now-defunct Vampire Liberation Front had wanted to expose us in order to instill fear in the populace. Now that the secret was out, the supernatural leaders had to find a way to spin this so Normals didn't panic.

Connie and I made a girls' roadtrip to my afterlife with our resurrected dino demon prisoner.

I sectioned off a part of my domain and dragged Giovanni and the dino demon into the private area and chained them to the concrete floor. I also rewrote the DNA of the dino demon I'd known as Maddy into the form I'd first met her in—that of a red-headed teenage human with freckles.

"I'm not afraid of you," she spat. "My master—"

"Is gone, my dear. I ate him." I manifested a chair and straddled it so I could rest my arms on the back. Connie stood at my right shoulder. "I didn't even need a Tums afterward."

"You are not the judge of the dead." Giovanni lifted his chin. "I do not recognize your authority."

"That's fine." I shrugged. "It doesn't make a difference, you know. I inherited both your souls when I defeated the Old One."

For the first time ever, fear flickered in Maddy's eyes. "So you will make us non-existent?"

"Nah." I grinned. "Worse." I gestured at Connie. "I believe you two remember Sergeant Torres."

"Constanza, you don't have to do anything she—" Giovanni started.

"Shut the fuck up, you asshole." Connie manifested a ball gag to keep him from talking. I had to bite my lip to keep from laughing at the bright yellow ball with the smiley face on it.

"See," I started. "You two raped her, bred her with a demon baby, and Turned the sergeant into a vampire. All without her permission I might add." I made a pouty face at them. "Oh, did I forget to tell you I removed the memory block you stuck in her head?"

I waited and let their own imaginations churn for a bit. From their expressions, my stunt was much more effective than slapping them around.

"Since Sergeant Torres is now a goddess like me, I'm gifting you two douchebags to her as a coming out present." I grinned at them before I

looked up at Connie. "What's your pleasure? Waterboarding? Thumb-
screws?"

"I was thinking of what you did when you captured me." She smirked.

"Hey!" I protested. "Tiffany's the one who shot and stabbed you."

"I was thinking after that." Her eyes glowed red. I wasn't sure if she did
it on purpose or if it was the manifestation of her warrior side. "When
you chained me in the basement. If you don't mind me borrowing your
demons who tortured me, that is."

I grinned at her, then turned my smile on our prisoners. White surrounded both Giovanni and Maddy's irises. Their chains rattled because
of their quaking. However, only Maddy gave off the ashy stench of terror.
Giovanni peed himself.

"Why, that's an excellent idea, Sergeant." I stood and flick the chair
out of existence. "Let's go find them."

I manifested a doorway. Once Connie and I walked though it, I elimi-
nated it. One look at each other, and we both cracked up.

"Rabbit tickle torture, huh?" I said while wiping my eyes.

"Yep." She looked around my domain. "Why does your afterlife look
like a preteen girl's bedroom?"

"My old bedroom at my parents' house was the first thing I could
think of." As I spoke, Flopsy and Peter raced up to me, perched on their
hind legs, and started squeaking in Rabbit.

I held up my hands. "Whoa! Slow down, you guys. I can't understand
you when you're both talking at once."

Peter started to speak, but Flopsy shoved him aside and imperiously
demanded they could no longer share space with the stinky humans,
and she wanted her heaven now.

Connie knelt down in front of them. "How about you two help me torture some bad people while Sam creates a space for you?"

Her compromise calmed Flopsy down, and Peter vigorously nodded
his head in agreement. While they re-entered the prison, I got to work.
They weren't the only ones tired of the strawberry ice cream paradise of
an eleven-year-old kid.

I smiled to myself. However, no matter how much anyone bitched, I
was definitely leaving the sky pink.

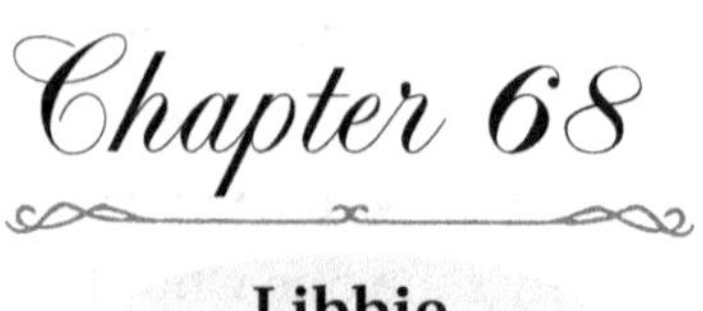

Libbie

Finer bits of volcanic ash still drifted eastward in the air currents. I'd be coughing up black crap for the next week, but the atmosphere was breathable compared to the last five days. Catching a thermal coming off the cooling pumice and mud, I shot higher into the sky. The less flapping I did, the less ash I'd breathe in.

Green light flashed to my right in the middle of the Lake Washington lahar. The sunlight was dim thanks to the dust cloud over the entire state. Was the spark I saw merely debris or something else? I couldn't take chances and banked in that direction.

Nope, something was definitely moving across the mud. Three people. They seemed to be skating across the mucky surface on a piece of concrete. I dived for a closer look, and the acrid scent of ozone filled my beak. Green and black sparks flashed around the two men and woman in a circular pattern. I flew past them and caught a hint of ginger. One of them was definitely an earth witch.

Angela, I found three people. Is anybody with earth talent from your coven missing?

A hint of other people whispered in her mind before Angela answered, *Whoever you found isn't one of ours.*

If all of Blue Hawk was accounted for, who the hell was in the middle of the disaster zone? Someone from another coven camping in the back-country? The initial tremors started a couple of days before the eruption. Surely, an earth witch would have realized the danger.

I turned ahead of the trio and circled to land on a log jutting from the mud. My back flapping to slow down stirred up more ash. My coughing fit ended as the sphere decelerated close to my perch.

I shifted into human form and stood on the muddy bark. "You folks need some help?"

"Tiffany Stephens," the black-haired woman with the splinted right leg said. The vaguest scent of apples came from her and the man with Asian features. "I'm an enforcer with St. James."

"Libbie Hawker, Seattle Were Alliance."

"Hawker, huh?" The Normal woman grinned.

If she made so much as a crack about my second form being a red-tailed hawk, I'd peck the woman's eyes out.

Instead, Stephens said, "You're Waldo's girlfriend, right? The professor?"

"Yes." I cocked my head. From the mix of ginger and ozone, the African-American man had to be the witch, and he sure didn't look well. Hell, none of them did. But Waldo never mentioned his master having an eclectic. "What in the Goddess's many names are you folks doing out here?"

Stephens laughed. "That's a long story. You wouldn't happen to have a phone nearby, would you?" She held up her device. "David accidentally shorted ours when he threw up a shield to protect us from a pyroclastic flow. I just need to check in with Master St. James."

Libbie would have given anything not to be the bearer of bad news. If she remembered Waldo's coven gossip correctly, this woman was a Normal relative of St. James. "You have my condolences, Ms. Stephens."

The woman's face paled, and she looked like she was about to pass out. "Wh-what happened?"

"Your master was assassinated by the last dino demon in Portland yesterday."

Chapter 69

David

Two weeks later . . .

David tried really hard not to groan as Jack, his seatmate in first class, continued to ramble. Maybe he should have taken St. James up on the offer of a private flight, but he wanted, no, he needed to feel like a regular human being again so he took a commercial flight.

". . . I still can't believe the Sabretooths traded Head to New Orleans. He was the greatest rebounder of all time." The elderly actor sitting next to David waved his hand in excitement. Or maybe it was outrage. He couldn't tell with the aviator glasses covering Jack's face. "I've had season tickets for center court floor seats forever. Damn, I miss watching that man play."

"Head was a free agent, and he had family in New Orleans," David murmured.

Jack lowered his sunglasses and peered over the top rims. The devilish smile, the one that graced many a theater poster and magazine cover over the decades, curved his mouth. "I knew it. Don't worry kid. I don't blab. Anybody Sam Ridgeway screwed over is a friend of mine."

David couldn't help chuckling at the man's venom. "I appreciate that, man."

The two of them shook hands as the PA system crackled to life.

"Attendants, prepare for final approach to Miami," the captain announced.

⚜

Brandon and Yvonne, along with a couple of Rousseau enforcers, waited for David outside the security area of the Miami International Airport. David smiled and tipped the airport lady who had driven him in her little electric cart from the gate.

David leaned heavily on his white cane as he walked past the metal detectors and scanners. He'd half-expected the cane to disappear after he released Ridgeway from his circle back in Washington. And he was touched when Doctor Zachary returned it to him once Tiffany had a temporary cast on her leg. Maybe the cane was Baron Samedi's way of claiming his soul.

However, his heart belonged to another man. David reached for Brandon, pulled him close, and kissed him. A thorough kiss that poured all his love and longing into that simple touch.

When they parted, Brandon looked up at him in amazement. "It's been a long time since you've kissed me like that."

"I owe you a hell of a lot more than a kiss." David asked the question he feared the answer to the most. "Can we start over?"

"As long as you don't run off and leave me hooked to the damn monitors again." Brandon's admonishment carried a teasing tone though, so maybe, just maybe, they could make their second time work.

"Before you two devour each other, may I have a hug?" Yvonne asked. David pulled her into a tight embrace.

"Let's get you home," Brandon murmured.

David hesitated. "I can't just yet." At their worried expressions, he smiled. "Nothing bad. I just need to talk to Jean-Pierre first. St. James has a deal in mind my brother-in-law might find interesting."

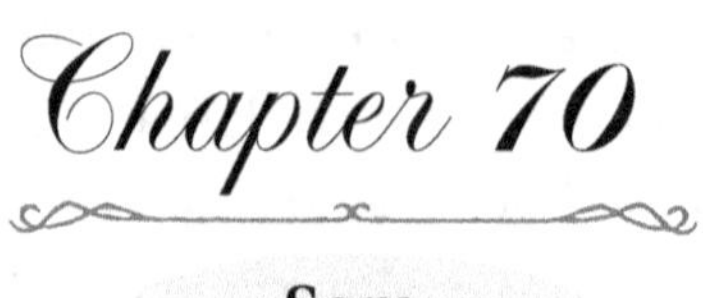

Chapter 70

Sam

"So what do you think?" I asked. Anticipation trilled along my nerves. I'd worked hard on this little section of my afterlife. A place that was just mine and my husband's.

Duncan circled as he took in the garden. "It looks magnificent, darling!"

"I did a lot of research on Elizabethan styles—"

"It is perfect." He kissed me. It seemed like it had been forever since the last time I kissed him. We didn't have to worry about him accidentally biting me and dying anymore.

Flower blooms exploded around us as we kissed, filling the air with the scents of lilac, jasmine, and rose. Flopsy and Peter giggled with delight as they raced around our feet. Even though I'd built a western mountain prairie for the rabbits, they decided they liked the English garden better.

When we parted, he smiled. "There's one last thing we need."

The sun dress I'd created rippled and changed into a black Tudor gown, cut a little too revealing for even my taste. Silver trimmed the bodice, sleeves, and skirt. Instead of the slacks and dress shirt, Duncan now wore matching black doublet, hose, and shoes.

"You just wanted to show off your legs," I teased.

He huffed. "All the ladies at court said they were my best feature." He took my hand in his, and we walked along one of the paths.

I looked up at him. "You know Goth Girl screaming at you on the phone this morning about you being dead was her way of dealing with her grief over Jake's death, right?"

"I do, and please stop calling Tiffany Goth Girl." He frowned at me. "That is disrespectful to your sister-in-law."

"And your niece," I teased.

"That, too," he said. We continued our stroll.

"Is Virginia still throwing a hissy fit about you and Jean-Pierre merging your territories?"

Duncan chuckled. "Yes, but Jean-Pierre said any supernatural who wishes to live peacefully within the new territory is welcome to do so as long as they obey the laws and pay their taxes."

"Everyone knows you're the power behind Jean-Pierre's throne."

"True," Duncan admitted. "But I never wanted to be master of my own coven. Caesar simply had no one else old enough and strong enough to turn to when Bebe found the cure."

"So what happens next?" I asked.

"Well, the masters of Canada and Northern Mexico have sent delegations to open talks about creating a North American union—"

"No, silly." I slapped him lightly on the chest. "I meant us."

"I have no idea." He stopped and turned to look at me. "I'd like to watch Ellie grow up. After that—" He shrugged. "I never thought I'd be free of the disease and still spend eternity with you."

"Do you have any regrets?" The last thing I wanted was to force him into something he didn't want. Selene had royally screwed with his head for centuries after she infected him. As much as I wanted to keep us both alive, I feared he would change his mind again.

"No." He wrapped his arms around me. "I made my choice."

"Then I need to show you how glad I am you decided to stay with me." I stepped back and tugged on his hands.

"How exactly are you planning to do that?" However, lust glimmered in his green eyes.

I dragged him into the small grove that was just ours. Not even the rabbits were allowed in. It had the softest grass and the sweetest flowers. The hedges gave us perfect privacy.

Frustration set in as I tried to figure out how to undo his doublet. Finally, I got fed up and willed the damn garments away.

"That was not fair," he protested, standing there naked as the day he was born. His erection sent more than the usual shiver of desire through me. I'd worried I might have screwed up when I rebuilt his body.

"It's totally fair," I said. "You already removed my bra and panties."

"I know." The look he gave me was totally lascivious.

I shoved him, and he deliberately flopped on the ground. We were both laughing as I hauled up the voluminous skirts in order to straddle him.

But everything felt so damn right as his cock slid into me. Duncan got frustrated with the lack of access to the rest of my body and zapped my gown away. His hands touched and tweaked until he grabbed my hips, urging me to ride him harder. Faster. Until we both exploded into a nova.

✦❖✦

"That was a first," I murmured an hour later. My head lay in the crook of his right shoulder and my fingers traced patterns in his chest hair as we sprawled on the grass.

"First what?" Duncan asked.

"First time I deflowered a virgin."

"Excuse me?" His offended tone rose just like I knew it would. "We've been married for six years!"

"This is the first time I've done it with this body," I said.

He opened his mouth to argue but stopped and stared at the tree limbs above us. "Logically, that's true."

I rolled to my side and propped my head on my palm. "So, you going to tell me why you never learned to drive?"

Duncan made a disgusted face. "Do I have to?"

"Yep." I grinned at him. "Telling me a story is the price of this paradise."

He rolled his eyes, a gesture so reminiscent of Tiffany I cracked up laughing. "What did Alex and Constanza tell you?"

"Before they died, they each told me the story of their Turn."

Duncan scowled at me. "Is that the story you really want from me?"

"Nope." I toyed with his right nipple. "I want to know why you can't drive."

"I can drive," he bit out.

"Then why don't you?"

"You're not going to let this go, are you?"

"As you said, we've been married for six years." I reached up and tapped the tip of his nose. "What do you think?"

"Very well." He sighed in exasperation. "I don't because I'm afraid."

"Afraid?" I almost felt bad. It wasn't like him to admit to any weakness. "Of what?"

"Sophia, she would have been Tiffany's fourth great-grandmother." He swallowed hard. "Sophia was a lot like you and Tiffany. Very forward thinking. Always up on the latest technology. She bought one of the first automobiles. One powered by steam. She's the one who taught me to drive."

For once in my life, I stayed silent. Like the tale of every other family member descended from his sister Margaret, I got the feeling this story wasn't going to have a happy ending.

"We were out one night. I was practicing. The boiler exploded. I took the brunt of it, but in the process, I lost control of the vehicle. We overturned. Sophia—"

I pretended not to see him swipe at his eyes.

"Sophia was tossed from the seat. We didn't have the safety measures that exist today. She broke her neck instantly."

"It was an accident, sweetie." I stroked his cheek.

"I've been cursed my entire life," he said softly. "Sometimes I think the curse has effected everyone I care for." He turned to look at me. "Even you."

"You didn't curse me." I rolled on top of him. "You've been the best thing that ever happened to me."

And I kissed him until he agreed.

Chapter 71

Tiffany

Alex, Ptolemy and I stared at each other over untouched cups of coffee at my kitchen table. Our meeting with Jake's parents this morning had been tough enough. Ptolemy insisted on telling them the truth now that the supernaturals had been outed. That bringing them into the Family was the right thing to do.

Audra and Eddie had been shocked of course. But Ptolemy's request that they be his surrogate parents after he told them his biological parents had committed suicide when he was five broke whatever resistance they had left. They welcomed him into their family and agreed for all intents and purposes Jake was still alive to the rest of the world.

But he was definitely retiring from the stuntman business.

Explaining everything to the Wongs had been good practice for the next conversation I had to have. This one was going to be much harder than the last one had been.

My doorbell rang, and I stood and went to answer the front door. Part of me was glad Ares didn't 'port Phil and Ellie straight here. It gave me some time to figure out what to say to a six-year-old.

I opened the door, and Ellie leapt into my arms. "You missed my totally awesome birthday, Mommy!"

"I know, baby." I hugged her tight and kissed her soft cheek. "I'm so sorry I did. I promise not to miss another one."

"That's okay." She held up a Disney princess doll. "See what Grandma Phil bought for me!"

I glared over the top of her head at Phil. Last thing Ellie needed was yet another toy. But my foster mom's attention was totally locked on her husband.

"Alex?"

"It's me." His smile was tentative.

"What on Olympus?" Ares' jaw fell open, and he stared at Alex.

"Shit." I smacked my head in mock annoyance. "I knew there was something I forgot to tell you on the phone."

"Mommy! Language!" Ellie struggled to get down, so I set her back on the floor. She raced over to Alex and hugged him. He knelt and returned the hug.

She leaned away from him and wrinkled her nose. "You smell different, Grandpa Alex."

He cocked his head. "Is it bad different?"

"No, you smell like horses." Her eyes widened. "Did you go riding without me?"

"No, sweetie." He placed his right hand over his heart in mock dismay. "I would never go riding without my partner."

She peered closer at his mouth. "Where's your fangs?"

"I got hurt really bad, Ellie." He glanced up at Phil, gauging her reaction. "When I got fixed, some changes had to be made. I'm not a vampire anymore."

Ellie jiggled with excitement. "Can you go out in the sun now? Does that mean we can go to the beach and you teach me how to surf?"

"That's up to your mom," Alex said. She looked at me with those big beseeching blue eyes.

"Baby, there's something we need to tell you—"

"I have to give Uncle Jake a hug first," Ellie said, like it was the most obvious thing in the world.

"That's what I need to talk to you about." My heart ached. No one told me this would be the hardest part of being a parent. And I've had to make this confession once already today.

Ellie looked at Ptolemy and back at me. She started shaking her head. "No. No! Jake said—" She gulped, and huge tears ran down her face. "He's standing right there!" Her tiny index finger pointed at him.

My knees were shaking so bad I knew I was going to fall over, so I made a beeline to our couch. "Baby, when Jake fell, he died."

"And Aunt Sam brought him back, like she did Lily and Bill and Morty?" The hopefulness in her voice was killing me inside all over again.

"No, baby." I swallowed hard to get the lump in my throat out of the way of my words. "Jake's in Heaven with Daddy now." I pointed at the man standing the doorway to our kitchen. That's Ptolemy. He's Uncle Caesar's baby brother."

Ellie's face scrunched up as she tried to understand. "But he died years and years before I was born."

I couldn't help smiling at her description. "Yes, he did. But he kind of got stuck between here and where he was supposed to go."

"Ellie . . ." Ptolemy crossed the living room and sat beside me. "Your mother is trying to be kind to me, but the truth is I did some bad things. I hurt people I said I loved, including my brother. Some of your Aunt Samantha's friends said if I could do some good things, then I could come back here. But—" He glanced at me.

"But they didn't have a body to put you inside because you were a vampire, did they?"

"No, they didn't," Ptolemy said. "An angel named Gabriel asked Jake if it was okay for me to use his body, and he said yes."

"B-but why couldn't they put Jake back?" Her lower lip quivered.

"Because, baby, there are special ties that hold our souls to our bodies," I said. "We can't see them, but Aunt Sam can. So can Grandpa Ares. When those are broken, it's very, very hard to put them back together. And there are rules about when the people like Aunt Sam and her friends are allowed to do that."

Here I was feeding the same bullshit to my daughter Sam had fed me. Murphy help me. I was the biggest hypocrite in the universe.

"Is he going to live with us?" Ellie asked shyly.

"No, I'm going to live with Caesar and Bebe for a while." Ptolemy smiled at her. "I would like to know more about Jake if your mother will allow me to visit once in a while." He looked at me. "If that's all right."

I nodded. "Yes. It is."

Ellie turned to whisper to Alex, except she wasn't as quiet as she thought. "What do we do about Mommy's surprise?"

Alex shot me a very alarmed look.

"It's okay." I smiled, even though my heart was in a million pieces. "We accidentally found the rings when we were getting Ptolemy some socks."

"Damn," Alex muttered. "I am so sorry, Tiffany."

Ellie walked over to me, climbed into my lap, and wrapped her arms around my neck. She still clutched her new doll. "I'm sorry, too, Mommy."

"About what, baby?" I smoothed back a lock of hair stuck to her damp cheek.

"That all the boys you like keep going away."

"Well . . ." I looked over her head at Ptolemy. "One of them did come back."

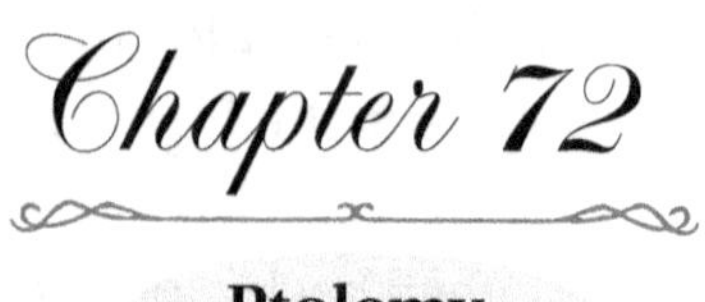

Chapter 72

Ptolemy

After supper, Ptolemy sat at the redwood picnic table on Tiffany's concrete patio with Phillippa and her father, watching the sunset. The ash still in the high atmosphere made it the most colorful sunset he could ever remember. It was a very peculiar feeling. He hadn't sat outside with the sun still above the horizon in over two thousand years. But it was far better than sitting on a rock along the shores of the Styx.

Alex slid back the patio door. He stepped out with four bottles of beer. At least he wasn't trying to levitate them this time. He nudged the door closed with his elbow and passed the bottles to all of us before he sat down next to Phillippa.

"The battle over bath time is continuing," he said as he unscrewed the cap.

"Ellie's right." Phil grinned and took a deep breath. "You do smell like horses. And prairie grass."

"Are you saying I need a bath?" Alex grinned at her.

"I'll make sure I scrub your withers and all the way down." She wrapped her right arm around his neck and leaned her head against his shoulder.

Ptolemy tried not to fidget. Their flirting was unnerving merely because he did not witness their romance blossom. Phillippa treated Alex quite poorly after she became the victim of his practical joke aimed at Selene over a century ago.

"You're making Ptolemy uncomfortable," Ares said before he gulped down the contents of his bottle.

The couple looked at Ptolemy.

"No, you're not," he protested.

"Okay, you two are making me uncomfortable and Ptolemy sad." Ares punctuated his statement with a belch.

"Ptolemy, you need to give her some time." Phillippa pushed her unopened beer over to her father. He promptly twisted off the cap and swigged half the liquid.

"Ellie needs to get used to what happened," Ptolemy said, deliberately misunderstanding her words. He sipped his beer. He rather enjoyed the orange undertones of flavor. It reminded him of a little brewery in Alexandria during the first or was it the second century of the Common Era.

Ares leaned over and said, "Son, you reek."

"Pardon me?" Not even Ptolemy was foolish enough to challenge the god of war over an insult, but did Ares really need to kick him after the god's granddaughter rejected him?

"He's right." Alex tilted the top of his bottle in Ptolemy's direction. "Everybody's known how you felt about Tiffany for a while."

"I-I-I . . ." He couldn't stop stammering, unsure if it were fear, embarrassment, or disappointment.

"Don't worry, Ptolemy." Phillippa smiled at him. "Caesar lied to Duncan about who your crush was so he wouldn't stake you."

"Well, now that Ptolemy's Normal again, Duncan might resort to throttling," Alex said.

"Throttling?" Alarm shook off any effects the beer might have had on him.

Phillippa laughed, banging the table in her fit.

Ares frowned at Ptolemy before he turned to Alex. "Who did Duncan throttle? He is so . . ."

"Straightlaced?" Alex offered.

"Uptight?" Phillippa said.

The patio door slid open. "So rigid he couldn't break a stack of Pringles shoved up his ass?"

Not even Ptolemy could resist chortling over Tiffany's description of her uncle.

She squeezed in between Ptolemy and Ares on the bench. "For the record, it was Max Duncan choked. The morning after we'd slept together the first time. It took Caesar, Alex, and Sam to pull my uncle off my future husband." She chuckled. "But then Sam tried to wring Max's neck because she thought he was feeding me a line to get me in bed."

"You said Ellie could come out and say good night to us," Ares accused.

"Dude, she fell asleep halfway through putting on her nightgown." Tiffany shook her head.

"Would you care for a beer?" Ptolemy asked.

"No, thanks." She covered a yawn. "I've got to get the first draft of my dissertation turned in. I'm already three days late. Thank Murphy, my advisor is cutting me some slack over being trapped in Seattle."

"Dissertation?" Ptolemy asked. She had been adamant she was not going to college no matter how much Duncan pressured her.

"Yeah. Hopefully, I'll have my doctorate in physics next spring." She held up her left hand with her index and middle fingers crossed.

Ptolemy didn't know what to say, which was probably a good thing since most of what he said came out wrong and infuriated Tiffany.

"On that note, we'll cut out of here so you can get some sleep." Phillippa stood and swung one long leg over the bench.

"May I request a ride back to Caesar and Bebe's?" Ptolemy asked as he stood as well. It didn't seem appropriate to stay when Tiffany was still grieving for Jake. "My brother sold my entire car collection, so I need to do some shopping."

"The red Jeep in the garage is Jake's." Tiffany looked up at him. "If you're going to be Jake . . ."

"Maybe we can discuss that at a future date." He didn't want to hurt her feelings, and yet, he also didn't want to take any memories from her either. "For now, I need to figure out how to live again before I make any commitment."

She nodded.

"Do you need me to take Ellie to school in the morning?" Alex asked.

"You are not teleporting my daughter," Tiffany snapped.

"I meant the conventional way," he drawled. "But thanks for the vote of confidence."

"Sorry," she muttered. "No, I told Audra she could do drop-offs and pick-ups for the rest of this week. I think she was looking forward to Ellie being her granddaughter. But at least, she won't be inviting her friends over to play poker when I'm not here."

"Father?" Phillippa's right eyebrow rose. "You coming?"

"I promised Duncan I would stay here and guard them both for the next few weeks." Ares shrugged. "Just in case."

Ptolemy reluctantly followed Alex and Phillippa into the house. Behind him, Tiffany said, "By the way, Grandpa Ares, I have a bone to pick with you about your personal use of our bunkers . . ."

He waited until they were inside the coven-owned SUV and at the end of the street before he asked, "Do you think Tiffany heard—"

"Yep," Alex and Phillippa heard at the same time.

"The bathroom and kitchen windows were open," Phillippa added.

"Phil's right," Alex said. "She had a crush on you back then, too, you know. But right now, she's still struggling with Max's death, much less Jake's. You're going to have to take this one slow."

Ptolemy leaned back in the leather seat. If his time on the shore of the River Styx had taught him anything, it was definitely patience. He'd wait for Tiffany for an eternity if he had to.

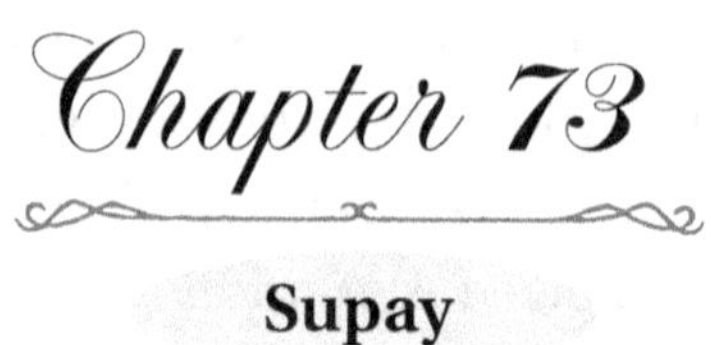

Chapter 73

Supay

Standing in the middle of the bone bridge leading to his palace. Supay leaned against the railing and stared at the bubbles on the dark lake that surrounded the island. A white tentacle playfully slapped the surface, and he threw another chunk of raw meat into the water. His pet quickly gobbled the treat and retreated to the depths. No one wanted to be around him when he was in a bad mood.

Vibrations rattled the finger bone railings, and the skulls forming the foot path moaned. Francisco bounded toward him.

"Master, you have a visitor at the entrance!"

Supay straightened. "They can't enter."

The monkey demon cocked his head. "Not even Alex Stanton?"

"What is he doing here?" Supay frowned. The infant god couldn't enter his domain without his permission, and he didn't think for one drop of a water clock Alexander Socrates Stanton had come for a social visit.

"He is inquiring why you have not responded to Lady Samantha's invitation to her ascension celebration."

Bitter laughter poured from Supay's throat. "Oh, I'm sure."

"He's waiting for you in the church that stands over the entrance your uncle brought us through years ago. He claims an oath of peace for this conversation," Francisco said. When Supay remained silent, the demon added, "Has he ever broken his word to you, Master?"

Supay exhaled. "Fine. I will speak to him."

He flashed to the alcove of one of the Christian saints in the Cuzco chapel that had been built overtop the site of one of his temples. Alexander sat alone in one of the pews.

The new god turned around and grinned at Supay. "Hey there! How's it going?"

Supay warily entered the sanctuary. "Why are you here?"

"You haven't answered Sam's invite." Alexander tilted his head. "I was a little worried about you when you didn't respond."

"Worried about me?" Supay narrowed his eyes. "And why this sudden concern?"

"Giovanni poisoned us with dino demon venom right before we killed him." Alexander shrugged. "I didn't know if it had affected you since you were still inside me at the time."

"I didn't realize he had done so," Supay murmured. There was no way Alexander could survive that, even as a vampire. Yet, another reason for Lady Samantha to despise him. "Is that why she transformed you?"

"Yeah, but she gave me the choice." Another shrug. "Kind of nice to walk in daylight again, so in a way, I owe you my thanks."

"I expected you to be furious with me." Supay edged closer.

"At the end, we both lost our tempers." Alexander chuckled. "Allowing Giovanni to poison us served us both right."

"Poison you, you mean." Supay still wasn't sure about Alexander's sincerity. He certainly wouldn't be so forgiving under the same circumstances.

"You forget we were in each other's heads." Alexander grimaced. "It's not a matter of forgiving you or wanting an apology from you. I'm just saying I understand why you did what you did."

If Uncle were still here, he'd encourage Supay to take the peace Alexander offered. However, it didn't mean Alexander's good will extended to someone else.

"And what about your mistress?"

"Dude," Alexander drawled. He wiped his hands down his face. "Do not call Sam my mistress. I'm still dealing with Duncan and Phil over Sam seeing me naked as a jaybird."

That admission made Supay howl with laughter.

When his humor died down, Alexander asked, "So, are we good, and can I tell Sam you're attending her party?"

"Yes." Supay smiled. "Yes to both."

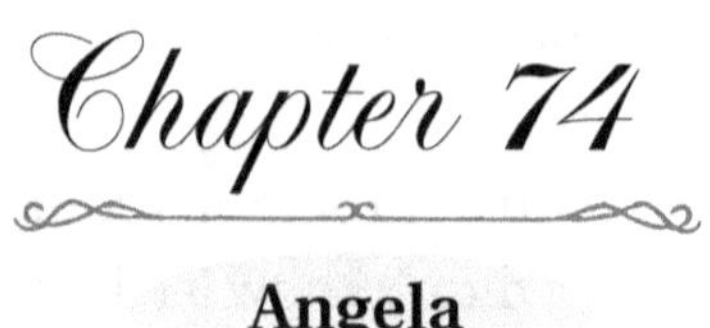

Chapter 74

Angela

Two months later . . .

The cab drove past the cute little mail box shaped like an old-fashioned red barn and turned onto the lane. Azir walked out of the main farmhouse as they drove past, and he waved.

A thread of relief filled Angela when the cab pulled to a stop in front of a quaint little cottage. The driver helped Jim with their luggage while she climbed out and stretched the kinks in her frame.

"Hey, Angela!" Libbie stepped out of the cottage, Waldo behind her. "Need any help?"

"Nah, just need to get Priscilla inside." She ducked and grabbed the pet carrier and her staff out of the backseat. She turned to Libbie. "You two sure it's okay having a cat here?"

"We wouldn't have agreed if it wasn't. Besides—" Libbie grinned. "We already got a cat in Azir."

Angela shook her head. "A dog, a cat, and a bird living together sounds like the start of a bad joke."

Azir ran up to them. "Need any help?" Before she could answer, Azir bent over and looked into the carrier. "Did you know your cat's pregnant?"

"Tell me about it," Angela grumbled. "I asked Jafar to do one simple thing—don't let Priscilla near any male cats. What does he do? He lets his sister-in-law's male cat play with Priscilla because they're both lonely. I don't know what I'm going to do with the kittens when they're born."

Libbie looked at Waldo. "We could keep one." She turned back to Angela and mock whispered, "He needs the incentive for his morning run."

As Jim and the cab driver hauled the luggage inside the cottage, Angela looked around the yards. "I can't believe how good this place looks."

"Hell, we can't believe it's all still here," Waldo said. "The ash took down a couple of trees in the orchard, but overall, we came out okay. If it weren't for you and your friends, there wouldn't be any building standing on San Juan."

Jim and their cab driver stepped out of the cottage. Jim paid the man. He hopped back in his cab and zipped down the lane. Jim joined their little group and wrapped his arm around Angela's shoulders. "Thanks again for letting us stay here while our townhouse is being renovated."

"Again, no problem," Libbie said. "Once you two are settled in, come up to the main house for dinner. We've got fresh steaks and vegetables."

Angela sighed. "The proper thing is to refuse since you're really helping us here, but I'm too tired and hungry to argue."

Everyone laughed, including Libbie's research assistant.

✦❈✦

A couple of hours later, Angela sat at the kitchen table. The three men were outside in a rare sunny evening, debating the finer points of grilling while steaks sizzled on the barbecue.

Libbie set a cup of chamomile tea in front of Angela before she sat down with her own glass of wine. "Why'd you really come home early? And don't give me any crap about you and your mother butting heads."

Angela sipped her tea before she answered. "Howard's resigning as greater earth elder. He claims after the scare with the eruption, he wants to be closer to his grandchildren in Phoenix."

"But?" Libbie prompted.

"No one knows he's a witch down there." Angela shook her head. "Sylvia's insisting I replace him."

"Well, you are the public face of the magickal community." Libbie took a drink of her wine.

"You haven't been dubbed the female Gandolf on TV." Angela leaned her head on her fist. "Would you believe Ian McKellen contacted me about doing a PSA for supernatural rights?"

"That's wonderful!"

Angela straightened. "I don't want this kind of attention! I want my patio garden. I want to read my tarot cards. I want to help people with their little problems like colic and acne and dandruff. I don't want to be on television!"

"Things are changing for all of us." Libbie reached over and covered Angela's left hand with her right one. "My people adapted when the extinction event hit sixty-five million years ago. Our cousins didn't. That's the choice you have."

"It's not much of a choice," Angela grumbled. "But it beats burning at the stake."

Chapter 75

Sam

One year later . . .

Banner and tacks in hand, I levitated to the ceiling in our family room. I was glad I won the battle with Duncan over the color of paint in this room. The federal blue paint and white trim looked pretty damn good with the baby shower decorations. It turned out living next door to the mom-to-be got me sucked into hostess duty, but I didn't really mind. The little, human things kept me grounded.

So to speak.

I stuck one thumbtack through the banner and into the drywall on the left side of the fireplace before I floated over and did the same with the right.

"It's crooked," Tiffany said as she blew up a powder blue balloon with the helium tank.

"No, it isn't," I protested.

"Yes, it is." She tied off the balloon before she wrapped and knotted a matching ribbon around the end. "Float back to the middle of the room and look again."

Her engagement ring flashed in the morning sunlight streaming through the windows. From what Duncan and everyone else said, Ptolemy had changed a lot during his stint as a shade on the shores of the River Styx. He was more patient and humble. All I cared was that he was kind to Audra and Eddie and he doted on Ellie, but I still wasn't sure why Tiffany said yes to his proposal. I just counted my blessings that she'd dropped her grudge against me over Max and Jake.

I levitated backward. Tiffany was right. The two ends were roughly a half inch off.

"Shit." I floated back to the left end and raised it. "Better?"

"Definitely." She nodded.

"You sure Anne's coming to the shower?" I shoved the thumbtack back into the banner and drywall. She hadn't spoken to me since the day she quit the coven and went home to take the cure. I still talked with Colin on a regular basis. He told me the same thing Duncan did—I needed to give her time since I'd literally upended her world.

Truth be told, I hated not having her in my life. Her practicality kept me on the straight and narrow when things had gotten hairy. I didn't realize how much I depended on her strength until she was gone.

"She promised, and she wouldn't disappoint Bebe." Tiffany blew up another balloon, then tilted her head. "You feeling okay?"

"Yeah, why?" I lied. I hadn't felt quite right all morning, but with Bebe's baby shower at two this afternoon, the last thing I wanted to do was spoil the occasion.

"You're sweating." Tiffany frowned at me.

"No, I'm—" A drop of liquid rolled from my forehead and landed in my right eye. I swiped at the stinging orb and looked at my fingers. "What the fuck?"

"Get down here." Tiffany jabbed her own index finger at the white plush carpet.

I landed and immediately stumbled over my own feet. Luckily, I grabbed a matching federal blue wingback armchair to catch my balance. Tiffany stomped over and held the back of her hand against my forehead.

"No fever, but you're awfully clammy." Her frown deepened. "When was the last time you ate?"

I didn't need to eat food anymore, but I always had breakfast with Duncan. He enjoyed making up for not being able to consume solid food for the last four and a half centuries. However, he, Caesar, Ptolemy, and Alex had flown up to Seattle on Thursday for the dedication of the new social sciences building at the University of Washington since they'd donated quite a bit of their personal money to the project. My husband claimed the men were spending the weekend up there to stay out of the way of the shower. I knew better. All four of them enjoyed walking around in daylight again. But since he wasn't here . . .

"I think the last time was Wednesday morning before the guys left." My stomach rumbled and another wave of nausea hit me.

"Let's get you something." Tiffany grabbed my arm. I let her drag me toward my kitchen. "The nanites may be gone, but that doesn't mean your blood sugar can't crash with your revised DNA."

Connie looked up from where she was slicing raw vegetables as we entered the kitchen. "What's wrong?"

"She made herself sick by forgetting to eat," Tiffany grumbled. She pushed me in the direction of the closest kitchen chair.

I squinted and stumbled over to the white-painted seat. Why the hell had I insisted on white cabinets, white appliances, and white tile? I knew I was trying to create the anti-Mom décor, but the brightness hurt my eyes. Was I getting a migraine? Was that even still possible?

"Here." Tiffany set a glass in front of me. "Drink the orange juice while I make you a peanut butter sandwich."

I took a sip. The juice burned when it hit my stomach. I loved orange juice. What the hell was wrong with me? I grabbed a banana from the fruit bowel in the middle of the glass table, peeled it, and took a bite. It had to be gentler on my stomach than the juice.

Tiffany retrieved a plate and bread. "Connie, where's the peanut butter?"

"Pantry. I'll get you a knife." The new goddess wiped her hands on a dish towel before she retrieved the necessary utensil.

My stomach did feel a little better with the fruit in it. I took another bite. Yeah, this was much better than the acidic juice.

Tiffany set the jar on the counter and proceeded to pull a couple of slices of bread out of the plastic bag. I took a third bite of banana, chewed, and swallowed. Tiffany unscrewed the lid and scooped out the peanut butter with a knife.

The scent of the spread hit me. My stomach rebelled at the horrible stench. I slapped my hand over my mouth and teleported to the closest bathroom, the extra full bath off the main hallway. I barely got my mouth over the toilet before everything came up.

"Sam!" Tiffany ran in, Connie behind her. Peanut butter odor clung to her like dog poo on a shoe.

"Please, for the love of Ellie, get rid of the—" My stomach heaved again. What miniscule molecules of juice and banana was left in my stomach departed my body along with a large amount of stomach acid. I swiped at my mouth. "—peanut butter."

She stripped off her t-shirt and jeans and tossed them at Connie. "Those in the laundry now. And dump the jar, the bread, the knife. Everything into the trash."

The goddess took off with the bundle while Tiffany pulled extra clothes and a washcloth out of the linen cupboard. The enforcers had a tradition of keeping spare changes at various houses. Actually, it was a matter of practicality. The enforcers generally had their clothes ruined by claws, teeth, and blood, not puke—

Just that thought had me leaning over the porcelain god with dry heaves while Tiffany scrubbed her hands and arms with anti-bacterial soap like she was heading into surgery.

I leaned back against the pale peach semi-gloss latex painted on the bathroom walls. Its cool surface felt good against my neck and through my own t-shirt.

Once Tiffany was sure she was cleansed of any peanut butter residue and soap, she rinsed and wrung the excess water from the washcloth before she knelt beside me. The cold terrycloth she held felt even better against my forehead.

"I haven't seen you look this bad since the night we pulled you out of Mallory Labs," she murmured.

A weak laugh worked its way out of me. "Yeah, your first time getting shot doesn't sit so well."

"No trouble breathing? Itchiness?" she asked as she wiped the rest of my face.

"No." I inhaled as deeply as I could. The nausea was still there, the same vague uncomfortable feeling I'd woken up with, but nothing like the extreme sensation caused by the odor of the peanut butter. "This doesn't make sense. I've been eating that stuff since the night I was injected with the nanites. Why would it make me sick now?"

"When was the last time you got sick to your stomach?" Tiffany rose and rinsed the washcloth under cold water again.

"The night I woke up in the labs after they experimented on me." Another wave of nausea swept over me, but this one was caused by guilt.

"Right after I killed two people while I was trying to escape." But that had been nearly eight years ago. I hadn't been sick a day since then. How could I be ill when I was now a goddess?

Tiffany chuckled as she knelt and held the cool washcloth against my forehead again. "The last time I moved that fast toward a bathroom was McDonald's when I was pregnant—"

Our eyes met.

I shook my head. "It couldn't be. I can't get . . ."

"You sure?" Tiffany cocked her head. "Duncan's alive and a god now thanks to you. You're a deity, too. So, why not . . ."

I swallowed hard against the rumbling in my digestive track as her voice trailed off. "That's ridiculous."

"There's one way to find out." She jumped to her feet and yanked on the knit shorts and t-shirt.

"We don't know if a pee stick will work with me," I protested.

"Are you saying you haven't been shagging my uncle?" She grinned, a mischievous one that actually looked like the old Tiffany. The smart-mouthed bitch who'd let the air out of my tires and poured sugar in my gas tank the night we met.

"I hate you," I muttered.

"I hate you, too. I'll be right back."

"Don't tell Connie," I called out as she charged out of the bathroom.

Tiffany leaned back around the doorframe and rolled her eyes at me. "You made her a goddess. She can read minds."

"I'm not ruining Bebe's baby shower," I hissed.

"No, you'd better not," Tiffany said, but the mischievous grin was back. She closed the door behind her.

Oh, crap. I couldn't be. Bebe swore the nanites had made me sterile because they used vampire DNA as their primary template. But that was back when they flooded my blood stream. Since I became a goddess of death, it made sense I'd never have children.

I blew out a deep breath and closed my eyes. With my new perceptions, I reached into my body. Sure enough, there was a tiny clump of cells in my uterus, a clump that was part me and part Duncan. It had already attached itself to the lining. I didn't need a fucking test stick.

Holy shit! We were going to be parents.

I reached in my shorts pocket and pulled out my new phone. Primal fear went through me, and I hesitated. My husband should have been the first to know I was pregnant. Not his niece. Last thing I wanted was for him to think I was hiding shit from him again.

Sucking in and releasing my breath, I thumbed the speed dial button. His phone rang twice.

"Hey, sweetie, before you hear this through the coven grapevine . . ."

Thank you for reading the Bloodlines series! If you are
enjoyed the adventures of Sam and the crew, drop me a
line through my website, or Facebook. Recommending the
Bloodlines series to your friends or writing a review would be
even better!

And if you loved the sassy ladies and hot men of Bloodlines,
you might want to check out the awesome attorneys who
specialize in superhero law of 888-555-HERO! Turn the page
for a preview!

CHAPTER 1

Harri Winters skimmed over the letter in her hand. "Give me a break. Professor Venom? Seriously?" She sighed and tossed the letter into her inbox. "Dammit, I thought he'd gone straight." And a half-assed attempt at a threat was the last thing she needed today.

"He's not dangerous?" Patty Ames, Harri's assistant, plopped into the chair in front of Harri's desk. "Is he a wannabe?"

"He's a wannabe wannabe." Harri shook her head. "He's not dangerous. He's just annoying."

"What's he want?" Patty settled back into her chair with a groan. "Sorry. My feet are killing me."

"If you need to go on maternity leave early—"

Patty shook her head. "Nah. It's just been a busy day." She rubbed her belly and smiled. "Not long now."

Harri smiled back. Patty was a good kid and a great assistant, but Harri dreaded six weeks with a temp. Too many cases, too little time, and by the point she got the temp trained, Patty would be back.

"So, what's the deal with this Professor Venom?" Patty said. Her blond curls bobbed in the direction of the inbox. "He says he's going to melt City Hall, and everybody will die—"

"Unless we give him a couple million dollars. Yeah, yeah. Don't start running yet." Harri spun her desk chair and dug into the file cabinet behind her. "Hang on a sec. I have a picture. You gotta see this guy. He's a total loser." She pulled out the "Professor Venom" folder and spun around to face Patty again.

"You usually show at least some grudging respect for supervillains." Patty leaned forward with a frown. "Is it because he addressed the letter to Harriet Winters?"

"Uh-uh," Harri said. "He doesn't have the ability to carry out his threats. And I don't respect the villains. I respect their assets. The forfeiture on Doctor Malevolent's evil lair gave us enough money to rebuild the Commerce Avenue light rail station and replace twenty smashed police cars. Try getting that kind of bank from a superhero. Cheap bastards." She opened the folder and handed it to Patty. "Professor Venom."

Patty looked at the mug shot and giggled. "Arthur . . . Doohickey? No wonder he calls himself Professor Venom. He's so skinny. And that nose is . . . unfortunate."

"Drallhickey." Harri rolled her eyes. "Lots of desire for elaborate mayhem, but more of a minor annoyance. Biggest thing he's managed to do is melt the paint off a couple of benches in Founder's Green. Which were scheduled for repainting anyway. He saved Dale's guys in public works from an afternoon of sanding and scraping. Dale wants the city to give him a vendor contract so he can buy Venom's acid formula."

Patty flipped through the pages. "I don't see his superhero nemesis in the file."

"He doesn't have one. That's how lame he is."

Patty laughed and handed back the folder. "Oh, that's sad."

"It's all kinds of sad." Harri spun on her chair and put the file back in its place. "Nobody takes him seriously. Poor shmuck. He doesn't have the skills to be a regular criminal, let alone the personality to be a supervillain. I'd hate to see this stupid stunt to screw up his probation." She mentally counted the months. "Or has he finished it?"

"You want me to call Judge Inunza's court and find out?"

"No, I've got his P.O.'s number." She stretched her arms over her head and yawned. "But first, I need some coffee, or I'll be useless this afternoon. I'm buying. You want some hot chocolate?"

"Ooh, yes. Thank you. With extra whipped cream." Patty pulled herself to her feet. "God, my O.B. says I've got another month to go, but I already feel like I'm carrying a toddler around in here."

"Hey, you wanted to experience motherhood," Harri said, and immediately regretted it. She wasn't sure Patty had wanted to experience motherhood. At least not yet. She was twenty-three and all alone. She had no family Harri knew of. When Harri had tried to convince Patty the sperm donor needed to step up—at least financially, Patty shook her head, her eyes shiny with tears, and said that he was gone, he wasn't coming back, and she didn't want to talk about it.

Harri yawned again and realized she needed more than coffee to stay awake. She decided to take a walk around the park first. She didn't have anything on her calendar for the afternoon. She'd planned to be in a deposition all day with Seismic Shift, beloved local hero and—in Harri's mind at least—menace to society. But his attorney called at the last minute, claiming Shift had an emergency and they'd have to reschedule.

Seismic Shift had the ability to create pinpoint earthquakes, but not pinpoint enough to keep from making a mess, Harri often grumbled to anyone willing to listen. The last one had taken out the Lake County Retirement Home in his effort to stop a couple of kids who'd ripped off a corner convenience store.

The guns they had turned out to be plastic replicas. And worse, one of the residents of the home had died. Shift was damn lucky the dead guy didn't have any relatives to file a civil suit.

Harri kicked off her pumps and fished her sneakers out from under her desk.

But her job was to give the displaced residents a new home. Sure, Shift stopped the bad guys, but he also made a ton of money off endorsements and licensing deals and those ridiculous comic books. If he was so damn civic-minded, why did she have to fight him all the time to get him to pick up some of the tab for everything he broke?

She'd spent a solid week reviewing the thousands of pages of financial and tax documents Shift's attorney had dumped on her in response to her discovery request. With the deposition now put off for another week, she wondered if she should go back through the pile to see if she'd missed something.

She slipped her feet in her sneakers and yanked on the laces. Going through the boxes of documents again would be a waste of time. Federal law gave registered supers broad latitude to protect their secret identities. Without knowing who he really was, she couldn't get near most of his assets. He had to be making more money than he claimed, but she had no way to prove it. She liked the supervillains more because it was a lot easier to pry money out of them. The feds didn't care about maintaining villains' secret identities.

Harri couldn't figure out why people thought Seismic Shift was so damn wonderful. It's not like he was the Ghost Owl. Canyon Pointe's street criminals might not fear the police or the other superheroes, but they were terrified of the Ghost Owl.

Over the last twenty years, he bordered on urban legend. Lots of sightings, lots of stories, but like Bigfoot, only a few blurry photos. In fact, the first thing she'd done when her job granted her access to the federal registry was check if he was in the database. But if he really existed, he was pure vigilante.

Shift was registered, but he was not only a complete phony, he was a media whore. Yeah, he technically had a super power, but the rest was all marketing. From his financial records, she learned the shock of thick blond hair that stuck out above his cowl was fake. Not to mention, he was starting to get a gut. Not quite the sleek, chiseled demigod his publicist made him out to be. He looked about fifteen years younger and twenty pounds lighter in his publicity photos.

Harri pulled her dark shoulder-length hair into a ponytail, checked her teeth for lettuce in the small mirror she kept in her handbag, and frowned at the gray hairs along her hairline—there was a new one every day it seemed.

Both her best friends Aisha and Jeremy had tried to set Harri up with the colorist Aisha used at Jeremy's salon. But she couldn't afford that kind of money, not on a city salary, and she wasn't about to take charity from either of them.

There were a few times when she envied Aisha's position at one of the top firms in the state, but Grandma Harri had drummed public service and standing up for the little guy into her head from the moment she could walk. Besides, she would have ended up like Aisha with all her money going to her ex in the divorce settlement.

With a sigh, Harri dropped the mirror into her bag and slung the strap across her body. The city's superhero infestation hadn't done a thing to deter the city's purse snatcher community. Hell, one of the assholes had nearly strangled her when he grabbed her bag in the grocery store parking lot last month.

"I'm going to do a lap or two around the Green before I go to Java Joe's," she called to Patty as she walked out of her office.

"Forward your phone," Patty called over her shoulder.

"Forwarding my phone." Harri pivoted, marched back into her office, and punched in Patty's extension on her desk set.

Once outside of City Hall, the bright spring sunshine lifted her mood a bit. The park contained its usual assortment of transients, drug addicts, and the mentally ill, but they generally left her alone. Harri was petite, but managed to convey a sense of height. Eddie used to describe her as five feet of rage topped by two inches of woman.

It wasn't rage. It was . . . Harri didn't know what it was. Righteous anger, maybe? She hated bullies. She hated injustice. And in her experience, superheroes were bullies with commercial endorsements. People needed something to believe in. Instead, they got merchandise to buy.

She passed the playground. Two women held their babies while their older children played in the sandbox. It was exactly the domestic scene Eddie had described during their last fight. The one before he moved out and served her with the divorce papers.

Harri snorted and walked faster, annoyed at the thought of her ex. Stupid Eddie, with his new perky young wife and squalling baby and another kid on the way. He'd wanted a domestic family scene Harri had ultimately been unwilling to give him. She had nothing against babies in general, but did they have to be so stinky? And so loud?

Harri told herself that she simply wasn't cut out for motherhood. An essential mommy-ness had been left out of her character and she was being sensible by acknowledging it. But with Patty's baby on the way, part of her wondered if she'd missed out.

"Stupid hormones," she grumbled out loud.

Crazy Jim approached with a hopeful smile. "Miz Winters, how are you this fine day?"

Harri sighed. Crazy Jim was as sad as they came. When he stayed on his meds, he could function. Barely. That he had to do so living on a park bench, while schmucks like Seismic Shift lived like kings, broke her heart. Breathing through her mouth to reduce the smell, Harri said, "I'm fine, Jim. How are you?" She dug in her purse for some money. "When did you eat last?"

"Yesterday, Miz Winters. Yesterday."

"You could eat every day if you went to the shelter." At least until they closed it. The stated plan was to relocate it, but Harri knew better. The mayor had plans for the shelter site in East Downtown, and somehow, a new shelter would never appear.

Everybody would be so bamboozled by the super show, they'd never notice the bait and switch. The mechanics of local government were dull enough without having to compete with a grandiose parade of idiots in their tight, colorful Lycra costumes, creating crisis after crisis. But no help for folks like Jim because he wasn't super enough.

"Can't," he muttered. "Too many crazy people there."

She couldn't argue that point and handed him a couple of bills. Enough for a fast-food burger and a cup of coffee. From experience, she knew if she gave any of the homeless more, they'd forego the food and buy a six-pack instead. She wished she could do more, but what Jim really needed, she couldn't give him.

He thanked her and went on his way.

She stomped across the street into Java Joe's and bought drinks for Patty and herself. She stuck with plain black coffee because she couldn't walk past Crazy Jim and his lost companions with a concoction that cost her as much as the meal she'd bought him.

Back at City Hall, she gave Patty the hot chocolate with the extra whip cream her assistant requested and headed into her own office. Harri took a sip of her coffee and set the cup on her desk.

Before she had time to sit down or even take her bag off her shoulder, somebody out in the hallway screamed. She took two steps toward the door before an enormous wall of hot air pushed her backwards against her desk. Stunned, she saw a masked figure in black step into the doorway.

"I warned you," the person said in a gruff male voice. "Now, I'll take my revenge for you ignoring me." Something green dripped from a tube connected to his outfit. The substance hit the restored wood of the door-sill and sizzled.

"Excuse me?"

"You cannot escape the wrath of Professor Venom!" the figure said.

That's not Arthur Drallhickey. The man was much wider and several inches taller than the real Professor Venom. Not to mention, Arthur could barely meet the eye of his public defender, much less Judge Inunza, after he'd been picked up on the vandalism charge for the park benches.

She should be afraid. This was a wannabe who meant business.

More people screamed in the hallway and Harri became aware of an acrid smell. Smoke, but with a metallic, chemical undertone.

The man in black lifted his arm.

Harri threw herself over the top of her desk and crawled into the leg well. The kick plate and drawers weren't going to provide much protection, but the reconstituted fiberboard was better than nothing. Liquid splashed with a sizzle against her filing cabinet and the wall.

"You're done, bitch." More splashing. Noxious fumes and smoke rose.

Whoever that was, he meant business. But why the hell would any self-respecting supervillain want to claim he was the nerdy, harmless Professor Venom?

More hissing and the kickplate grew hot against her back.

Harri peered around the edge of her desk. Her attacker was gone, but from her vantage point near the floor, Harri could see the carpet in front of her bubbling before it burst into flames. A lake of chemical fire, too wide to jump, simmered between her and the office door. She heard something liquid drop onto the carpet with a hiss and turned to look. The wall beside her was foaming and steaming. Whatever her attacker had sprayed, it appeared to be eating the plaster.

The steaming foam spread to the ceiling and a moment later something dripped onto her shoulder. It crackled on the fabric of her blouse. Pain seared her skin, forcing back under her miniscule cover. The glass top, protecting the wood surface of the desk, would buy her a little time, but she had to get out of her office, and she wasn't getting out through the door.

That left the windows.

The Canyon Pointe City Hall had been carefully restored, in meticulous historic detail five years earlier, after the friction from Blue Racer's super speed had started a fire that gutted the interior of the building. Harri developed a national reputation among municipal attorneys as an expert in winning superhero compensation lawsuits thanks to that case.

As part of the restoration, the building's seventies-era sealed windows were replaced with historically-accurate oak double-hung sashes. Harri's office was on the fifth floor. High enough to be terrifying, but low enough she might survive a fall with horrible life-ruining injuries. She could crawl out on the narrow ledge. From there, maybe she could find an open window. She felt her stomach knot at the thought.

A drop of the stuff falling from the ceiling splashed against the edge of the desk and hit her hand with a sizzle. She yelped in pain and made her decision. Better a fall than being burnt to death. She scrambled out from under the desk, sprinted to the nearest window, and threw open the sash. Taking a deep breath, she pulled herself through the window as more drops of acid splashed on her legs and melted her pantyhose.

Of all the days to wear the damn things. At least, she still had her athletic shoes on.

A wave of vertigo hit, and Harri glanced back. More acid dripped on her desk, setting her paperwork on fire. Including the Professor Venom extortion letter in her inbox. She couldn't go back.

She clung to the frame a moment, fighting off the dizziness. "Don't look down, Harri," she said out loud. "Don't you dare look down."

Instead Harri looked up. A helicopter hovered overhead, a cameraman hanging out the door. He saw her and waved.

She let go of the window frame long enough to flash her middle finger at him, then resumed her grip. "Gotta move, girl," she told herself as a gust of hot air blew outward from her burning, dissolving office. "Can't stay here."

Harri took a few more deep breaths, forced herself to let go of the window frame, and eased along the narrow ledge toward the next window, which opened into Patty's cubicle. Before she reached it, glass shattered, and hungry flames billowed through the opening at the extra oxygen.

Nauseated with fumes and fear, Harri scuttled backward. She was trying to turn around when the ledge broke away from the building. Harri didn't have time to scream before she was falling through the air.

Eyes shut, she felt something hard hit her.

This is it. Funny, I thought it would hurt more.

Except she was still moving, but now she was going sideways. She felt arms around her, and she opened her eyes.

A man was holding her. A man who was flying.

A super.

God, I hope I haven't sued him.

A bright neon yellow and green spandex mask covered most of his face under a dark gray sweatshirt hood. She had time to register a rock-hard chest and arms before he landed and set her gently on her feet on the grass of Founder's Green.

"Who else is in there?" he asked.

"My assistant," Harri said. "Blond, really pregnant."

He nodded and took off again. He flew, sleek as an arrow, into her open office window. A moment later, he soared out a window on the opposite side of the building with Patty in his arms. He dropped her off on the roof of police headquarters, across the street, and headed back into City Hall. Harri watched him rescue five more people.

"There you are, bitch," she heard a familiar voice behind her. "Not getting away this time."

A cord dropped around her throat, but she got her fingers underneath it before her attacker could tighten the garrote. But she didn't have the strength to push him off her.

Garish lemon and lime flew toward her in a blur. The garrote loosened, and she heard a cry behind her. She turned and saw—

No, it couldn't be. Crazy Jim sprawled on his back on top of the crushed roof and smashed windshield of a parked car. Blood was gushing from his nose, and he moaned. In the distance, sirens whined.

"We need to go," she heard the masked man say. Before she could answer, he'd scooped her up with one muscular arm and soared upwards.

When they flew over police headquarters, she heard the people on the roof clapping and cheering.

I never got to drink my coffee. It was her last thought before she passed out.

Acknowledgements

Wow. We've come to the end of the road for Sam. It's hard to believe she and all the characters of the Bloodlines world started as a crazy idea I had in 2004.

First of all, a big thank you goes to all of you who started reading this series when *Blood Magick* was published back in 2011. Another thank you goes to everyone who has picked up the series along the way. Your notes and e-mails have touched me.

Second, I want to thank Jaye Manus, and Elaina Lee of For the Muse Design for their brilliance and patience in dealing with my schedule and demands. These ladies are as essential to this series as I am.

I also want to thank my friends and fellow writers Angela Penrose and Libbie Hawker for allowing me to put Tuckerized versions of them in this novel since they both live in the Seattle area.

Angela writes fantasy, and her short stories have appeared in numerous anthologies. I highly recommend *The Uncanny Valley* and *Fiction River: Alchemy & Steam* as starting places for her work.

Libbie writes historical fiction under both Libbie Hawker and Olivia Hawker. I first fell in love with her writing when I read *The Sekhmet Bed* (Book One of *The She-King* series) which details the birth of the Egyptian pharaoh Hatshepsut. Her latest as Olivia Hawker is *One for the Blackbird, One for the Crow*.

And I really do believe Libbie will win a Pulitzer and Angela will win a Hugo and/or Nebula someday.

Another thank you to Angela's husband Jim Penrose who agreed to his Tuckerized character appearing in this novel after the character snuck in through a side door.

A special bro nod goes to friend and fellow superhero writer Joseph Bradshire who was my sprinting buddy while I struggled to finish this manuscript.

Finally, all my love to my husband and son. Without their encouragement and belief, you wouldn't be reading this book today.

About the Author

Suzan Harden transitioned from writing information technology manuals for companies and legal articles for a law enforcement magazine to her first love, fantasy and science fiction in all their forms. She's the author of the Millersburg Magick Mysteries, the Soccer Moms of the Apocalypse series, and the Books of Apep series.

Contact Suzan Harden
Facebook: Suzan Harden
Email: suzan@suzanharden.com
Website: www.suzanharden.com

Sign up for Suzan's mailing list